THE KEY

BENITA KANE JARO

THE KEY

DODD, MEAD & COMPANY
NEW YORK

Copyright © 1988 by Benita Kane Jaro
All rights reserved.
No part of this book may be reproduced in any form
without permission in writing from the publisher.
Published by Dodd, Mead & Company, Inc.
71 Fifth Avenue, New York, N.Y. 10003
Manufactured in the United States of America
Text design by Hal Siegel
Maps drawn by Kurt Reichenbach
First Edition
1   2   3   4   5   6   7   8   9   10

Library of Congress Cataloging-in-Publication Data
Jaro, Benita Kane.
    The key / by Benita Kane Jaro.
    p.   cm.
    1. Catullus, Gaius Valerius, in fiction, drama, poetry, etc.
2. Rome—History—Republic, 265–30 B.C.—Fiction.   I. Title.
PS3560.A5368K4 1988
813'.54—dc19   88–3677
ISBN 0-396-09317-5

To MAJ, JCM, PB, and the others

Viuamus, mea Lesbia, atque amemus,
rumoresque senum seueriorum
omnes unius aestimemus assis.
soles occidere et redire possunt:
nobis cum semel occidit breuis lux,
nox est perpetua una dormienda.
da mi basia mille, deinde centum,
dein mille altera, dein secunda centum.
deinde usque altera mille, deinde centum.
dein, cum milia multa fecerimus,
conturbabimus illa, ne sciamus,
aut ne quis malus inuidere possit,
cum tantum sciatesse basiorum.

Come and let us live my Deare,
Let us love and never feare,
What the sowrest Fathers say:
Brightest Sol that dyes to day
Lives againe as blith to morrow
But if we darke sons of sorrow
Set; ô then, how long a Night
Shuts the Eyes of our short light!
Then let amorous kisses dwell
On our lips, begin and tell
A Thousand, and a Hundred, score
An Hundred, and a Thousand more,
Till another Thousand smother
That, and that wipe of another.
Thus at last when we have numbred
Many a Thousand, many a Hundred;
Wee'l confound the reckoning quite
And lose our selves in wild delight:
While our joyes so multiply,
As shall mocke the envious eye.

—Catullus C.V
translated by Richard Crashaw
1612?–1649

All lyric poets are difficult to understand, but
Catullus is almost impossible.
—Gilbert Highet

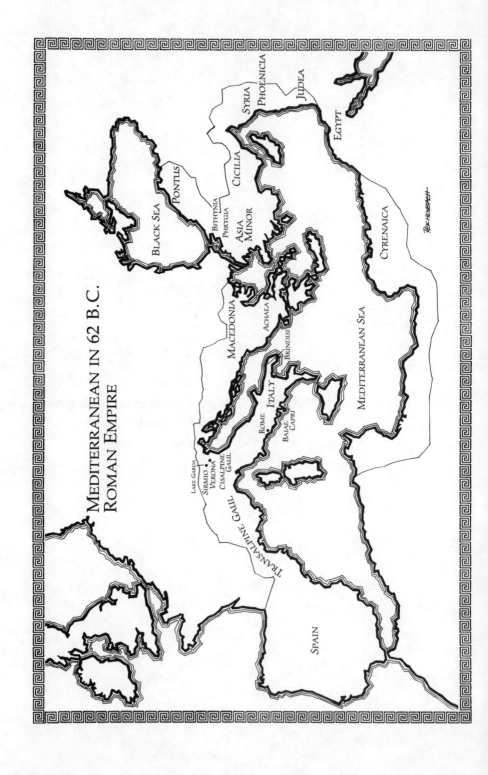

MEDITERRANEAN IN 62 B.C.
ROMAN EMPIRE

PRINCIPAL CHARACTERS

THE NAMES BY WHICH PEOPLE ARE MOST COMMONLY IDENTIFIED IN THE TEXT ARE HERE PRINTED IN BOLDFACE

THE ASTERISK SIGNIFIES A CHARACTER I HAVE INVENTED

Marcus **CAELIUS** Rufus: a Roman knight, preparing for a career in law and politics

Gaius Valerius **CATULLUS**: a poet, friend of Caelius

Valerius Catullus (**THE OLD MAN**): father of Gaius Valerius Catullus

CLODIA (**LESBIA**): daughter of Appius Claudius, wife of Metellus

Marcus Caelius **PHILO**: a former slave, now a freedman of Caelius's

Publius **CLODIUS** Pulcher: brother of Clodia

Gaius Julius **CAESAR**: a Roman patrician, Pontifex Maximus, and City Praetor

Quintus Caecilius **METELLUS** Celer: a Roman patrician, former praetor, and husband of Clodia

Gaius Licinius **CALVUS** Macer: a Roman patrician, friend of Catullus

Gnaeus Pompeius Magnus (**POMPEY THE GREAT**): a Roman general

EGNATIUS: a Spaniard

JUVENTIUS: a Roman youth of patrician family

*XANTHIUS: a Greek actor living in Rome

Marcus Tullius **CICERO**: a Roman political leader

Marcus Porcius **CATO**: a Roman political leader

HELVIUS CINNA, QUINTUS CORNIFICIUS, et al.: friends of Catullus

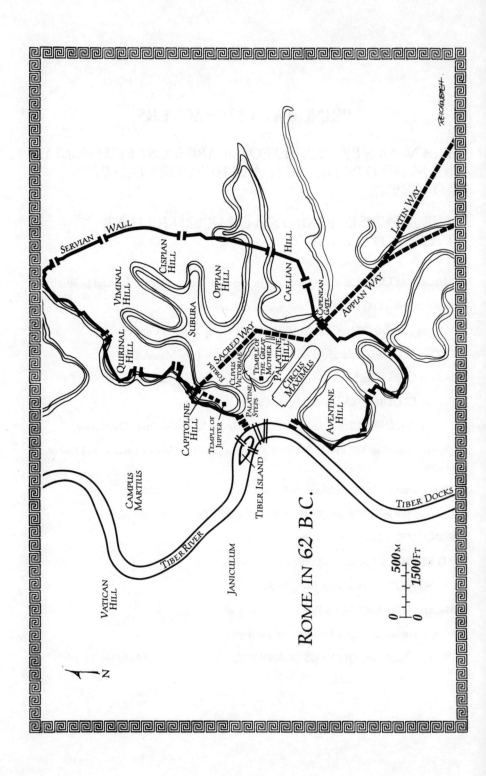

ROME IN 62 B.C.

CHRONOLOGY OF EVENTS IN THIS BOOK

*ALL DATES ARE B.C.; ROMAN DATES WERE
CALCULATED FROM THE (LEGENDARY) FOUNDING OF
THE CITY AND IN THIS BOOK RUN FROM 688 TO 719*

*WHERE DATES ARE UNCERTAIN OR IMAGINARY I HAVE
PLACED AN ASTERISK BEFORE THE EVENT*

83   *Birth of Catullus in Verona.
82   *(May 28)* Birth of Caelius in Interamnia.
62   *(December)* Break-in to festival of the Good Goddess; *Catullus meets
      Clodia. Arrival of news in Rome that Pompey the Great is returning to
      the city from the East, followed by his arrival in Italy at the end of the
      year.
61   Trial of P. Clodius for sacrilege; *Catullus and Clodia begin affair.
      (September) Triumph of Pompey; Caelius leaves for N. Africa.
60   Consulship of Metellus.
      *Catullus meets Egnatius at party in Tiburtina.
      (November) *Caelius returns from N. Africa.
59   First consulship of Julius Caesar.
      (January) Death of Metellus.
      (March) Caelius makes his first speech in the Forum at the trial of C.
      Antonius Hybrida, and becomes a popular success; *Catullus is beaten
      up and left for dead on the street.
      (May) *Catullus goes to Verona to recuperate.
      (July) *Catullus returns to Rome and goes "underground."
58   Tribunate of Clodius.
      (April) *Catullus participates in rites of the Great Goddess.
57   *(Early in the year)* Catullus leaves for Asia with C. Memmius, praetor,
      and Helvius Cinna.
56   *(Early in year)* *Catullus returns from Asia.
      (April 3–4) Cicero successfully defends Caelius against charges
      brought by Atratinus; *Catullus, in Rome, sees part of this trial.
54   *(November)* *Caelius sees Clodia in village market.
53   *(February 24)* *Death of Catullus; Caelius conveys Catullus's body to
      Verona.
      (End of June) *Caelius leaves Verona.

THE KEY

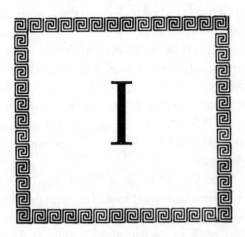

T he old man came to see me today, journeying out from Verona with only one slave, as dignified and ancient as he is, to drive him. He arrived at the gate very upright and stiff—he belongs to the school that regards even a seat with a back, much less a cushion, as a womanish affectation. In the atrium of his son's little house he sat on the marble bench as straight as a javelin, his dark eyes piercing and bright.

"So, Marcus Caelius Rufus, You are ill?" Only his voice resembles his son's, his hoarse, low, pleasant voice. That and something fierce in the set of his head, the sharp glance of his eye.

I could not answer. I am not ill, at least I don't believe I am. I simply could not force myself to go to Verona. When the moment came, I could not move my hand to take the reins, my foot to mount the wagon. . . . But before all that Roman gravity and virtue, how could I say that? How could I lie, or worse still, tell the truth? He would not understand a man whose will has failed. His own so plainly never has.

I could not go to Verona, though it is no more than half a day's journey from this little villa on the lake, where I am sitting now. It was all I could do to come here, and with my arrival my courage ended, suddenly and inexplicably. . . .

I was the one who brought his son from Rome, his dead son, my friend and distant kinsman. Gaius Valerius Catullus, born in Verona, died in Rome, a journey of two hundred miles, and thirty years. It took ten days to bring him the two hundred miles back. For ten days I sat on the wagon with my servants around me, staring into the winter rain that sometimes turned to snow, conscious always of the dead gray face under the cloak in the wagon behind me: the grayness of it took the color from the road, we drove in grayness, past smudged villages, skeletal trees, fields like ash and silver under a dripping sky. A long journey. Long for him, and longer still for me. I could not go any farther. I thought: the old man may call it illness, if that makes it easier to explain.

The old man's sharp eyes rested on me, thinking where to pierce. I felt he had heard what I had not said, and I looked down at the stones. The floor of the atrium was wet, for the wind off the Alps reaches even here; within its granite borders the pool was as full of movement as the lake outside. "A cold winter, sir," I managed at last, hoping he would take this for an answer. "I do not remember one so cold."

"It killed my son," he agreed, merely mentioning the fact. There was neither anger nor bitterness in his tone, though perhaps there was pain. He was too proud to conceal that.

"Yes, sir," I said, feeling the words in my mouth as dry as lies.

"You don't agree?" He was quick, very little escaped him. In that he was like his son, too.

And suddenly I was on my feet, saying, "I don't know, I don't know," and pacing restlessly, moved by a terrible urge to laugh. The wind outside was so loud I could not think.

He sat in his silence and dignity with his eyes on me, but he did not reproach me, nor did he ask me to stop. All the same I sat down again and said, "I beg your pardon, sir."

He paid no attention to this either. His straight body remained unwavering and still, his old white fingers lay in his lap like a handful of little bones. "You loved my son?" he asked. Then he waited. I heard the wind slide over the groaning trees outside, the lake waters lash vainly at the rocks. When his voice began again it was part of these sounds, part of the bitterness of winter, and this place.

"I had two sons," he said softly. His loss was like the wind's, his sorrow like the ancient trees'. "And now both of them are dead. My house is dead, gone forever. Do you see, Marcus Caelius Rufus?" He made a little gesture to blow his house away. "I am seventy years old; my wife, poor girl, has been among her ancestors since the boys were small." His dark eyes turned away for a moment to the past, but his command of himself was as firm as ever, and he did not follow them into his memories, as old men often do. He looked at me again. "Quintus remembered her, but I do not think Gaius did. Yet he was the one who was like her. No doubt that was why I did not understand him very well."

"He was not easy to understand, sir."

"No."

There was a small silence between us for a moment. He was studying me. I looked back at him respectfully, for there was not only his great age between us, but his pain, and the dignity with which he bore it.

"My wife was a Gaul, a Celt from the mountains north of here," he observed in the same low, flat voice. I drew my breath in shock. The next moment I was staring in confusion at the ground, praying to every god I knew that he had not heard.

But he had. "It was legal," he said evenly. "When I married her, it had been legal for a year. My sons were Roman citizens, like you, Marcus Caelius Rufus." He softened for a moment. "And she was beautiful, beautiful and virtuous." Then his softness disappeared. "The Valerii have no need to be ashamed of their birth. There is no family in Rome older or more distinguished than ours."

"Yes, sir," I said, able to look at him again. "I know that." I did not need to be reminded; they are all patricians, the old man's branch of that clan. We Caelii are only knights.

He took pity on my discomfort, or else he noticed it so little he simply went on with his thought. "I did not understand him, and he was so much like her. They were like fire, like air, my wife and my son. You could not hope to hold them, they slipped from your grasp. And if you tried . . ." He made a gesture, putting the tips of his closed fingers to his lips as if they burned. "Do you understand that?"

"Yes, sir."

He looked at me kindly and gently, like a doctor who does not not want to tell the news, but all he said was, "Yes, well, I thought you did.

"Yet you knew him better than anyone," he went on after a pause. "You are the one who brought him from Rome, you knew he loved this place." I nodded.

There was another silence while he studied me again. At last he sighed. "Well, Marcus Caelius Rufus, I have come to ask you a favor." He closed his bluish lips, but he made no other move, only sitting as straight as ever on his marble bench; it was plain he had never asked a favor of a young man before. Suddenly he bent down and pushed a leather case at his feet toward me. "Here."

It was large and heavy, the sort of round case they make for carrying books, but bigger. "Yes, sir," I said when he did not say anything. "What's in it, may I ask?"

He stood up. "What I have of my son. He did not wait for a reply, but called his servant, who when he came drew the heavy traveling cloak around him briskly.

"But what do you want me to do with it?" I asked, standing up myself out of respect.

He gave me one quick glance out of his old, fine-honed eyes. "Explain him to me," he said as he went firmly out the door.

I have been outside for a breath of air, though the wind nearly knocked me over, so violently did it pour itself down off the distant and invisible alps. The low clouds ran before it, the rain drove across the lake in a fury of meaningless energy; out on the point everything dissolved in noise and water. I staggered out and stood in front of the tomb for a while, watching the ribbons on the wreaths thrash and twist like dying men, crucifying themselves wetly on the bars. Back the way I came the road started toward Verona, where it joins the highway south to Rome, but the wind and rain were so heavy it was visible only as far as the end of the property. I stood looking at it a long time, where it faded into the wet emptiness of the day. There was nothing there. After a while I began to wonder if Rome existed anymore at all. Perhaps nothing does, except this little point, with its small, rustic house and its new tomb, the wind, the water, and the dead.

As I watched, I was visited by a wish so strong it was almost an apparition. I thought I saw the woman. She came toward me, picking her way over the stones of the road, between the rows of olive trees near the posts of the gate. She wore light, open sandals, as if she were at home, and the rain did not wet them, though the wind had pulled a strand of her long black hair from under her hood and whipped it across her mouth. Her blank face was a perfect oval, as pale as a pearl. Clodia.

In my mind I spoke to her. "You're late for the funeral. It was ten days ago." She nodded. Even in my mind I could not make her care. She never did when the old man's son was alive, why should she now? Her pity and remorse, if she feels any, would not lead her to this. And he knew it: he knew, by the end, everything about her. He would not have expected her to come all this way for him. Even at the beginning he must have guessed her nature—everyone in Rome knew what kind of woman Clodia Metelli was, and he knew more of what went on in the city, and understood it, better than most men. Yet he loved her. What kind of man could love a woman like that? To me it makes no sense at all. Yet the old man, his father, wants me to explain. . . . It was so absurd I laughed aloud. The wind tore the laughter out of my mouth and blew it toward the distant, invisible south.

It is night, but the wind has not died; even here in this little room it is present. It bustles around, lifting the covers on the bed, jerking the shadows grotesquely across the walls. The brazier shoots out a sudden flare: *Liber Gai Valerii Catulli Veronensis—The Book of Gaius Valerius Catullus of Verona*. His name. It leaps at me from the leather case on the floor where it runs in his swift hand across a page. A hissing draft fingers the papers in the box, going where I have not dared to go myself. I sit and watch it, unwilling to touch it yet. I am remembering.

A memory, late at night before a brazier of coals in the small room they have given me. The round box is open, firelight glints on the leather cover of a book, a roll of poems; it runs along wax tablets' edges, and a heap of paper scraps, scrubbed to take new ink. I see the old man's son, my friend Catullus, young, standing in a doorway, torchlight on his face and hands. He is planted on his legs, solid and square, friendly and alert, just as I have seen him dozens of times on visits to his family in the north; he might be waiting for a friend on a street corner, or a wrestling partner in the palaestra of the public baths. When he sees me, he smiles, widening his mouth in his familiar grin.

He has just arrived from Verona, where he grew up. He is my distant cousin; our fathers are related, I can never remember exactly how. We are closer than that implies, however; all through our childhoods my family used to trundle up the long road to the north to visit the old man his father, spending a few weeks each time at a villa we owned then. My father had business interests in Gaul. In those days Catullus and I took our lessons together, we went to the baths to swim, learned to ride, and to fish, and to sail his little boat back and forth on the deceptively gentle blue waters of the lake. He was two years older than I; I was always in awe of him. Though he never grew tall, he was always very strong; he wrestled—they follow some of those Greek customs up there—far above his weight. Though I am much taller and heavier, I seem to have spent a good deal of time on the ground, looking into his intent and sweating face while he twisted my arm and the trainer shouted in my ear.

At lessons it was different. I was a clever boy, and even in the best school a place like Verona can boast, I had little competition. Certainly I had none from Catullus, who was inattentive and lazy. Often he was so ill-prepared that he could not answer a question in class, though he could always recite whatever he was given to memorize. I think his father believed he was dull-witted, and despaired of him, though he did not say so, only resting his black eyes on his son from time to time in sorrow. At first I thought the old man was right and took a certain satisfaction in this judgment, but as we grew I came to see that my cousin was far from stupid. When Catullus's interest was aroused he was quicker even than I was, and far more original and profound.

In only two ways did I clearly excel. For one, I could run much faster, winning both the short races in the palaestra and the long, cross-country ones that for a time he and I went in for. He was always good-natured about these losses, as he was about my brilliance in school. For the other—well, let us just say that though he was strong, he was short, and very plain. His features were jammed together irregularly under a high and bony forehead; his skin was thin and pale. He did have fine, reddish hair.

And now he had come to Rome. Behind him the buildings of the Capitoline Hill cut black shapes in the sapphire sky, the first stars blossom in the summer night. His hair sparks in the firelight: amber, copper, bronze, gold; his gray eyes look out of a wilderness of shadows. He smiles hopefully at me. At his feet a trunk crouches like a friendly dog.

"Won't you come in?" I say. Already he looks less provincial than I do, and I have been in Rome nearly three years.

"You come out," he says, waving his hand at the city all starlight and shadows under the brilliant sky, as if he owned it. His hand sweeps an arc through the torchlight and out into the darkness beyond it, in a gesture that becomes part of the night. And I am gone after him, following, as I always do, the glimmer of light as he disappears.

Another memory of that same year, crossing the first like thread in a tapestry: a tavern full of smoky lamplight in the city we have both come to love. I am sitting on a bench, thinking that if my father knew he would be angry. He sent me to Rome to make a great career, and now I am wasting my time listening to Catullus argue with Licinius Calvus across a battered table. In the lamplight his face gleams whitely, tense with interest, blunt and bare. Calvus is grinning at him, taken aback, as people always are, by the transfixing gray-eyed stare, the hard white forehead that he uses like a ram to push home what he says. They are arguing about Greek poetry. Why not? They have been arguing about it all night, ever since we left the dinner party where we met. Catullus's hair is dark with sweat; he looks like a man at work digging a ditch or building a wall. He looks, in fact, like any of the hard-handed laborers around us. As I watch, he presses his palms over his head, smoothing it. Nervously I lift my own hands to my hair as he does; the heat in the tavern is making it curl more than ever.

I lift up my wine cup, watching him. The argument is too technical for me, but the wine is sweet, and I have drunk a lot. Rome, I think, seeing the light glisten on his hands, on the rings the cups have left on the scarred table. I am thinking that Licinius Calvus is the same age as I: we have the same birthday—the twenty-eighth of May—yet it is he and Catullus who seem the same age, though Catullus is twenty-one and Calvus and I only nineteen. I cannot work out why this is.

A man is shouting in the background, someone pushes by. Catullus, disturbed, looks up and brushes his hands through his hair again. Why have I never noticed that his smiling mouth is twisted at the corners like the mouth of a man in pain?

A servant has laid a plate before us—oily, smoky little fish that taste like the lamplight itself. They make the wine sweeter in my mouth, and I drink some more.

For some time someone has been playing the lyre. I hear it only now, a thin thread of sound on which the beads of talk are strung. Each bead is separate, arriving at my ear, itself, complete, as if no other talk is part of it. I listen, trying to put together the string.

In my left ear someone is saying, "Egnatius says he's been to bed with her," and I would like to hear more, but the crash of falling crockery intervenes. Shouts. A boy is laughing, and a woman. Who is Egnatius? Whom has he been to bed with? I would like to know. "Pompey will bring his army with him when he comes," someone insinuates softly in my ear. Will he? I have studied enough law to know that it would be a crime: no general may bring his army into Italy. Would Pompey, the great Pompey, do that? Voices rise like the winter sea; the whisper is washed away on their tide. What will happen if he does? I don't know. Yet I want to—I want to know everything about the city; I am consumed with desire to know it, as some are consumed with desire for a woman. An unfaithful one, for everyone in Rome seems to know it better than I do, everyone seems part of it but me. They know all the words, the words like keys that let them into the city. They shout them all around me; they hiss them in my ear. I cannot grasp them, though I try.

Catullus clutches my arm. "Even this child knows," he shouts, leaning over the ring-marked wood. This child—he has called me that. It is only half a joke. "Of course," he cries. "Of course you can use the Phallacian hendecasyllabic meter in Latin poetry." I am tempted to laugh—so much passion for such a subject—but his wild eyes shoot suddenly to mine, the gray stare pierces the thick lamplight, fixing me to my seat. And I do not know, any more than I know what Pompey will do with his army, or who Egnatius has had the good fortune to go to bed with. I am out in the cold again.

But Catullus's hand is on my arm, drawing me in; his eyes refuse to let me go. And I am inspired; I answer with the only name I know that their argument suggests. "Callimachus?" I say, not quite sure who Callimachus is. Catullus tosses his damp hair out of his glowing eyes. "Exactly." He is as satisfied as if I had proved his point for him. Already he has turned back to Calvus; the argument goes on, Catullus flares and sparks into the night, explaining, making up verses to illustrate his points, quoting from poets that no one but he has ever read, swearing violently when Calvus disagrees.

But he has rescued me; I am part of the argument; I lean forward to follow what they say. He is like a torch, a lamp, leading deeper into the maze of the city; by his light I follow, until at last, near daylight, I go home through the sea-gray morning chill in a silent, shuttered town. Lying on my bed I say aloud, "Of course. Callimachus." And holding this key firmly in my grip I fall asleep, certain for one brief moment that the door has opened and the city lies before me in the first full light of dawn.

Another memory, the year before: we are sitting on the steps of the Capitoline Hill. It is night again, another night. Below us a crowd waits under the flaring torches in front of the prison. The light leaps and flows across the buildings around them so that they seem to move, but the crowd is so perfectly still they might be statues instead of men. Their eyes are all turned in one direction, their faces like white flowers in a field.

A figure appears on the steps of the prison: a man in a white toga, banded with red. The edge of it is pulled over his head—he had been in the presence of death. Behind him a group of men file up and range themselves on the steps, their eyes watchful; they have volunteered to guard him if there is trouble. I can see faces among them that I know—an elderly man who does business with my father wipes his forehead, though it is December and the wind that flutters the torchlight overhead is cold; an exceptionally handsome young man I have seen often in the Forum tosses black hair out of his fine eyes. As he does his cloak flies back, revealing the glint of a sword hilt in his belt. The man in the banded toga lifts his head and looks at them, then turns back to studying the crowd.

"Is that the consul?" Catullus asks, whispering beside me on the steps, though we are far from the crowd. Behind us a row of knights has filed up the hill. They have swords, and are watching the crowd below, as if they expected trouble and intend to head it off. Though they eye us, they do not ask us to leave, and we sit watching, undisturbed.

"Yes. It's Cicero."

Something like a breath passes over the crowd, which moves, then is still again, waiting, listening. The man in the white toga waits, too, watching them from hooded eyelids. His shoulders are set: what he has been doing has tired him. Slowly he lifts his head and begins to speak. It is too far to hear his voice, which I know is beautiful, for several years ago my father sent me to study this very technique with him, but the crowd sighs—a long, soft rustling that reaches us even where we sit. The men in the crowd bow toward the voice like heads of barley waiting to be gathered.

"I'd like to be able to do that," I say enviously.

Beside me on the cold stone step Catullus laughs softly. "Do what? Strangle a bunch of political criminals?"

I feel my heart thump in my chest. "Is that what they did? Strangled them?"

"Yes. What did you think?"

I don't know now what I thought—poison, perhaps, like the hemlock the Athenians gave Socrates, or the sword offered in our own traditional way for a man to end his life with dignity.

"They weren't Socrates," Catullus says with distaste. "Just participants in a shabby little conspiracy. They don't deserve better."

"That's not true," I say hotly. "They wanted . . ." In my mind is the image of the charming aristocrat who led them. His name is Lucius Sergius Catalina. He is talking to a group of men in the dining room of someone's packed but hushed house; the meeting of course is secret, and everybody fears that the magistrates might be just outside—Cataline excepted. He does not seem to fear anything. He is smiling as he speaks. Now, in my memory, I can hear his voice, I can see his gestures. His speech is full of words that make my skin tingle—"freedom" is one of them, "youth" is another. I can hear him plainly, but just now I cannot explain what Cataline and his followers actually wanted.

He is looking intently at me.

I say, shamefaced, "I used to go to some of their meetings."

"Oh, gods," he says, pushing his hair back with his palms. "You're not safe out without a guardian."

"But," I protest. "But . . ."

He is not listening. He has jumped to his feet and is pushing through the knights on the steps to the squat red Temple of Jupiter above. Hastily I get up and follow him, saying, "What are you doing?" but he does not answer. When I catch up to him he is already standing in front of the huge statue, his toga over his head, his hand reaching out to drop a thin gold stream of resin onto the smoking altar. The vast vermilion face of the god stares out over our heads, five hundred years old and enigmatic in its archaic immobility; the seated figure looms over us, fearful and remote. Catullus bows and comes toward me, hurrying like a man who hears an approaching storm. "Come on. Let's get out of here."

"What were you doing?" I ask in the cold, unscented night outside.

"Praying for your safety," he answers, as if it were the most natural thing in the world. I am surprised that he would do such a thing—surprised that he cares for me, in the first place, but also that he would take such an old-fashioned way to show it. It is the sort of thing my grandfather, who was, really, no more than a simple farmer, might have done, or my strict, nearly primitive great-grandfather—no one believes in religion like that nowadays. Hasn't he read any philosophy, any science? But I know he has: he has read it all, more than I have, more than anyone.

I grab his arm. "Look," I whisper. All over the city lights are beginning to twinkle—torches and lamps and in doorways; on the roofs of the nearer buildings women are setting out bits of flame that glitter like stars against the sky. "What is it for?" I am awed at the beauty of the sight.

He sighs like a man giving up a difficult point in a debate. "It's for him, for Cicero. For saving the state from the conspiracy. . . ."

"Ahh. That's what I want."

He sighs again and looks out over the now-illuminated city. Far below us in the square in front of the prison the crowd is still listening to Cicero. From here they look small and very clear in the scarlet and golden light around them. I feel that I could count the cobblestones under their feet, the hairs of their hundreds of heads. As we watch they bend, all together, and some of them raise fists, minute in the distance. A faint shout comes up to us.

"Oh," I say. "Just look what he's doing—how he's moving them, making them think what he wants them to. Controlling them. . . ."

If I was surprised by him a moment before, he is astonished by me now. "Why would you want to do that?" he asks, obviously puzzled and upset.

"But that's what a political career is," I protest. He is preparing himself for the same kind of career: I cannot understand why he does not know this. "That's what it's about," I try to explain. "That's leading people."

He is looking at me as if he had never seen me before. "I suppose it is," he says after a long time, very thoughtfully, and on his face is an odd expression of disgust.

"Well, but, after all, you're a patrician. It's expected that you will go into politics. What else can you do?" People like him are forbidden to mix themselves in business or tax-gathering or any of the other careers open to the knights—surely since his earliest childhood he must have known what he was going to do with his life.

"Yes," he mutters. "I suppose so."

"But look," I say again. "Look at the reward." The little lights are fluttering and winking on the roofs, in the streets. . . .

"Come on," he says, still looking at me oddly. "I need a drink."

He will not let me go. All that night he stays with me, walking through the illuminated streets, arguing, listening. Intense, interested, kind. Now and then we stop when a counter open to the street advertises a tavern within, but he does not go in—he is already becoming known in such places and he does not want to talk to anyone but me. We swallow some wine—mixed with hot water, and, in the better places, spiced with pepper—at the counters; then we are striding through the streets again, his low, hoarse voice arguing in my ear. At last, near morning, we climb the Servian Wall and stand looking down over the river to the north. The predawn wind is blowing; it lifts his ghostly hair and the edge of his toga— in the dimness the red stripe that shows his rank looks black—showing the thin, fine linen of the tunic underneath. Behind him the city sleeps at last in the darkness. I lean against the stones to look at it, but he does not turn; his eyes are fixed instead on the starlit country beyond the wall. It occurs to me that he is looking back the way he came, to Verona, in Gaul, away in the north, but what he sees there I do not know.

"What you need to do is go back to Cicero." He has said this over and over tonight, in a vain effort to straighten out the tangle of my life. "Tell him everything. He'll understand. He knows you pretty well, I suppose, and he knows young men often make mistakes. . . ." Again that expression of revulsion crosses his face, but it is not for me, and his voice is gentle and kind, as it has been all night.

And I, exhausted as a shipwrecked sailor in a heavy sea, feel my foot at last touch sand. "He'll be angry," I say, though I have said it a hundred times tonight already. "He'll think I've been a fool." I say this only for the reassurance I know that he will give, for he has given it several times so far. Then, honest at last, I add what is really worrying me. "He'll tell my father," I say very softly into the blowing wind.

"Yes," he says, but he is laughing. "Of course he will. But you don't care.

You're a politician, aren't you? You can make him see it your way. Of course you can."

And I laugh, too, safe and free. "Yes," I say. "I can." For all this long night of cobblestones and torchlight, taverns, lamps, and stars, he has been teaching me what to say. He has made it true.

He taught me, but there were things I did not understand; he led me, yet there were places he went that I could not follow. . . .

A different day: the Palatine Hill, autumn sunshine on the grass near the Temple of the Great Mother. Bright golden oak leaves, long blue shadows, pigeons cooing on the temple roof into a swept blue sky. A girl passes, dove-shy and slender in her cloak. I whisper to Catullus, "What a wonderful girl." We look at one another, one wild glance. "All right," he says, and grins.

"What are you doing?" I cry, but he has already leapt to his feet, as bright in that glowing air as the breeze-brushed sky above. He has his arm around the girl and is cooing to her like the doves; somehow he knows the words that make her tame.

Afternoon among the shadows and the leaves, deeper in the sacred grove: she bares her pointed little breasts to us, her teeth press against our lips. I am aware of his body as much as hers, the hard brown belly with its line of gilded hair going down to his erection in its cloud of darker curls. His hands have slid her dress above her waist, her white legs wrap around him as he enters her. Her head falls back and her small mouth stretches as she moans. I put my tongue inside it, imitating him as he arches over her; I feel their double heave and thrust against me, rubbing, till I want to cry out to them to stop, to go on, to wait for me. Her breasts are in my hands, the nipples give against my palms, her hand has moved along my belly to my groin, but it has rested there as if she has forgotten it. She heaves her body under his; I can see the sweat start out along his back, hear their cries in unison, unconscious of me. His shoulder brushes against my chest, his bare buttocks tense and push, three long, deep thrusts that shudder through me, too, as if I were the girl.

"Quick," he says, rolling off of her. He, at least, remembers me. The girl's legs are sprawled apart, her mouth is open, her lips shine wetly in the slanting light. Then I, too, enter her; she is trembling from his thrusts. She grasps me as I push my hips against her. Just before I close my eyes to blackness and delight I see his face come down over hers, his mouth drinks in the cries that I have forced from her. I see his lashes close over his gray eyes, then see no more; I am coming myself, a long convulsion into darkness and the slow returning of the outside world.

Afterward the breeze is cool on our bodies as we lie in the long grass. The girl is gone. Catullus lies spread out on the bright ground, his eyes are full of sky.

"That was a good girl," I say, laughing with happiness. He murmurs. The blue oak shadows are moving back and forth over his sun-browned skin, like hands.

"Yes." I am sleepy with content. I feel, as I lie beside him in the September sun, somehow more than his friend, more even than the distant cousins we actually are.

"No," he says sharply. "No, she wasn't. Not at all." He is staring up into the leaves, into their flickering translucent gold, as if something were hidden there. His eyes are angry, disappointed, I don't know what.

I laugh again, uneasy and a little chilled. "Oh, surely she was," I protest. "She liked it, didn't she? She did everything we wanted."

He does not answer. Insects hum in the warm air, the birds are calling from the temple roof, the voices of the city, softened by distance, drift up the hillside to us. Somewhere a gong is sounding in a sanctuary, a cart rumbles over stones. Someone far below in the Forum shouts an incomprehensible word. I reach out and touch his hand.

"What is it?" I whisper. "Are you unhappy about something?"

But he has gone away from me, though he lies beside me on the grass, in the cool, pale sunlight of late afternoon. He does not answer, and I do not know.

It puzzled me. All that year of dread while we waited for Pompey to come home, I thought about it. What did he want? Why was he unsatisfied? To me that afternoon was an important memory—something to take out and look at, shining, significant, though mysterious in its meaning, durable. But to him? I did not know.

I did not see him often—having sent me back to Cicero he seemed to feel he ought not to interfere. He wanted me to work. When I met him—at the theater, in the taverns, at the occasional parties he went to—he said little about himself but demanded to know what I had been studying: he felt that studying was the first step to my advancement. He made me tell him what history, poetry, politics I read, what philosophy I had learned, what ancient orators I had learned to imitate and analyze. His head would nod once, his hand would smooth his hair, the twisted mouth would smile. "Good," he would say, but he seldom said more.

In truth I had little time for study. Cicero had taken me back, turned me inside out to find out what I knew about the conspiracy—which was little enough in all conscience—and set me to helping with his correspondence. He was writing to Pompey, still in Asia with his troops—some of the general's supporters in the Senate wanted him brought back to save the state, since Cataline had just been killed in the north and his ragtag army captured. No one knew if there were other conspirators still at large, and the city was worried. No wonder some thought they needed Pompey. Yet to Cicero this seemed as great a danger as the paltry and desperate plot that had prompted it, and he set himself the task of preventing the appearance of those legions on Italian soil. Under the watchful eye of his secretary, Tiro, I drafted letters to Pompey and his lieutenants, to Cicero's backwoods supporters, to the leading men in Rome and the Italian towns—a tedious job, but necessary. I knew more now than I had ever wanted to of Pompey and his men—it seemed a year since I had sat in the tavern wondering what he would do.

Catullus, however, worked very hard, though he gave up the law. Was that what his moment of revulsion that night on the temple steps meant? I can't be sure, but I think so. In any case, he left his own teacher, a former consul called Hortensius Hortalus, and went to study with a literary critic from Cisalpine Gaul, a man he had known at home. Sometimes on the way to the Forum, following the crowd around Cicero, I would pass the entrance to the street where this man, Valerius Cato, lived. Then I would often see the servants waiting for Catullus, for Licinius Calvus, Quintus Cornificius, Helvius Cinna. Sometimes I saw them all, arm in arm in the street, their heads nearly touching as one of them expounded a point they had been discussing. Often it was Catullus they were listening to: he knew more theories of poetry, more forms of verse and prose, more ancient authors, than the rest of them, even all together. Sometimes at night, after one of the long discussions I was now asked to join at Cicero's house, I would go looking for Catullus in the smoky taverns that he loved. There I could sometimes find him drinking by himself, a wax tablet of notes or a book of philosophic commentary on the table in front of him, but most often I went home unsuccessful from this quest. Those nights, once or twice, I walked out to the district where he lived. He had an apartment in the Subura—his father did not give him much money, and he lived very simply in a street in the low-lying and unfashionable part of the city, filled with the noise and heat of plebeian life. Long after the rest of the street had gone to sleep he would sit up over an unrolled book, his gray eyes staring into the flame of the lamp as he traced the complex pathways of a thought into the heart of ancient knowledge. He smiled to see me, he offered me wine or cakes, or a line of a poem he was studying, but behind his friendliness his eyes still followed the thought. Where it took him I do not know. Perhaps he did not know himself. Perhaps, until he found it, its nature was as dark to him as it was to me. But find it he did, his own key to the city, his own word. I saw it—I suppose the whole world sees it now— even the woman who gave it to him must know, though, of course, she doesn't care.

The fire has died, the little room is dark now, and I ache with sitting and with cold. It must be very late—the silence in the house is absolute and the chilly air is stiff with newness, as if no one had used it yet.

I do not want to sleep. Slowly I go through the darkened house, looking for charcoal for the brazier. Near the atrium there is a draft along the floor, freezing cold. The water in the pool is as black as iron, and as still. There are no stars, though the rain has stopped.

In the kitchen at least there is warmth, and the soft scarlet glow of coals banked against the night. Here and there copper twinkles; the room smells of woodsmoke and herbs. When I fill the bucket with charcoal the handle clatters against the side so loudly I fear the house will wake. My freedman, Philo, will not forgive me if he does not have his sleep, still less if the other servants are clumsy in the morning. And like an old soldier with a difficult centurion, he has a thousand subtle ways to show me his displeasure, if he wants. Thinking of this, I pad softly back to my room.

By the light of the rebuilt fire, I see that someone has put out lamps and oil on a table in the shadows by the bed. The lamps are small, a pair of simple shapes, elegant but free of decoration. In some way they remind me of him, there was always something in him, austere, reserved, unornamented. . . .

I fill them both, but when, taking a coal from the fire, I light them, the wicks sputter and smoke. The air is so wet the linen is swollen with damp; I have singed my fingers before I can get them going and carry them to my seat.

Someone has packed the leather box very carefully. Rolls of books are ranked at either end, their plain wooden knobs perfectly aligned. Wax tablets, sheaves of paper, small uncovered notebooks are stacked in the middle, along with a thick bunch of letters wrapped in an embroidered ribbon. A small bronze statue—his little god—lies on the top with a handful of dried violets at its feet. When I lift them they release a faint sweet smell of spring into the winter room. All his disordered life is there, packed with love and care into this small space. It is even smaller than the space he lies in, out in the cold and dark by the lake. At the bottom of the box there is a schoolroom exercise book, and a child's wooden model of a yacht. Why did the old man think I would need that?

For a moment anger grips me, that these pathetic scraps should be forced on me like this. I turn away my stinging eyes and swear, so that the lamplight wavers, and the shadows jerk.

I cannot do this job: the old man asks too much. Let him find someone else for it, some slave-secretary with a Greek education and a heart of stone, some client of the house with literary tastes, who never knew him. Let him take his appalling dignity and grief and go to the woman. Ask her what became of his son.

Yet a book is open on my knees. His book, *Gai Valerii Catulli* in gilt letters on the tag. And from it my own name looks back at me:

Caelius, our Lesbia . . .

I cannot do this job.

All the same, I remember. I cannot keep myself from remembering. I have pulled the thread and the memories unravel along it, drawing me with them into the bright weaving of the past.

Caelius, our Lesbia, that Lesbia
that dear Lesbia whom Catullus loved
more than himself and everything he owned . . .

Lesbia. That was his name for her, the woman, Clodia Metelli, the praetor's wife, the most beautiful woman in Rome. . . .

The notebooks are a strange sight: line after line of small white letters incised in the black wax, tablet after tablet, page after page of notes, conversations, memories, dreams—like the log of a ship or the journal of a military campaign. Like a man on a journey who writes letters describing the country he is traveling in, except that the letters here are written to himself. I have never seen such a thing before. What can have made him do it?

I turn the pages, bewildered, and my eye falls on this:

". . . long wash of winter sky, enamel blue; purple clouds; lawn like green linen. Man in a woman's dress, laughing, laughing . . . Under the cypress he turns, wig over one eye, trips on the yellow dress (sulfur curse against the clear green grass) . . .

"In blue shadow she is standing, watching him . . . pale goddess, blind dark eyes, laugh like perfumed water ringing in a marble bowl. Laughing from her trembling mouth at the sparrow that rides on her wrist. I wish I were that bird. . . ."

Man in a woman's dress, laughing, laughing . . . that was Clodius, of course. And the pale goddess was Clodia, his sister, whom Catullus loved more than himself and everything he owned. . . .

There are other notes: how he met them, for instance. . . .

It was the day of the festival of the Good Goddess, a solemn day early in December of the year Pompey came back. It was her brother that Catullus met first—in a tavern, naturally enough. We had gone there, Catullus and I, after a party; neither of us felt like going home. Catullus had a book—he almost always did. For a while we talked, but as it grew late and I got drunker, he spread the book on the table and began to work.

It was one of those places in Rome that he liked best, this tavern—he liked most of them, I suppose, but this shabby little one more than others.

On a small street by the river, it stayed open all night to accommodate the farmers who came up to the city with their cabbages and onions, their eggs and olives and cheese, to sell in the early-morning market. They were silent men, work-roughened and sun-scarred, in homespun tunics and thick sandals, with hair like faded thatch, but they still lived on their own land, in spite of the great estates and the huge slave-run farms around them, with all the pride and independence of their ancestors. They were preoccupied with their own affairs; they left him alone, and he often went to their bar to work.

That night Clodius was there, too. Among those rough peasants he shone like a pearl amidst turnips; he had a rich man's unselfconscious luxury, a small man's elegance. Like them, he wore the tunic, but his was Egyptian cotton; his sandals were of leather so soft it gleamed. But he drank the harsh, thin wine with a thirst as great as theirs; he talked with them as they talked among themselves. He knew them all, and all about their lives: their mortgages and taxes, their sons in the army or on the dole, their illnesses, their wives, their politics, their slaves. He came from the greatest family in Rome, but he seemed more at home among these simple and uneducated plebeians, the ones the politicians call "the salt of Italy." He seemed to think they really were. That night in the bar he worked hard to make the farmers talk—like the rest of the city at that time, they were silent men, worried, deep in their own thoughts. He talked, they listened glumly, he told jokes, and finally they laughed. Clodius laughed louder, and Catullus looked up from his book to see Clodius's large dark eyes on him.

The small man swayed over to us, his wine slopping over the edge of his cup. "Who are you?" he demanded, looking down at Catullus through narrowed eyes, and ignoring me as completely as if I had not been there at all. He ignored me all through the conversation; plainly I was too young and too drunk to be of interest to him. He was drunk himself—he often was—and it gave his aggression an edge, a glitter of danger.

"Gaius Valerius Catullus," Catullus said and looked pointedly down at his book.

Clodius glanced at him with greater interest. "Where are you from?" he asked.

"Verona."

Clodius grinned. Something excited him, something made him stand out in that tavern more than his elegance and his volatility; alone in the city Clodius was not subdued, silent, worried. I wondered why. "That's in Gaul," he said.

Catullus's eyes grew suddenly light, as if they had turned to silver. I knew that look: he was angry. I imagined now that he suspected a remark about his Celtic blood.

"What of it?" he demanded dangerously. But danger was what Clodius loved. He laughed as he drank off his wine.

"I know Gaul. My brother-in-law's a praetor—he's the governor there."

"Caecilius Metellus Celer?" Catullus was interested now in spite of himself.

"You know him?" He had called for more wine and poured it for them.

"He dines with my father."

"Does he?" This cup, too, he drank quickly, his dark eyes never leaving Catullus's face. "And what do you think of him?"

Catullus said indifferently, "He's a prick."

There was a silence. Even the farmers seemed to have stopped moving to watch. Clodius's black eyes widened, then narrowed. He was very still; his hand had gone to the hilt of the knife in his belt.

Catullus, too, had frozen. His own eyes had not moved from Clodius's face; his hands hung at his sides. He had an air of readiness, alertness, tension. Suddenly the small man put back his head and laughed. He laughed a long time, alone, overcome. "Yes," he said when he could speak, "he is." He laughed again, and the movement in the tavern resumed. "Oh, he is," Clodius cried, and wiped the tears from his eyes. Now he sat carelessly on the bench, and poured them both more wine. "And who else do you know?"

So they talked, and they got drunk together. Somewhere toward morning Clodius decided to visit his mistress, a married woman, the wife of some official.

"You can't," I objected, coming into the conversation for the first time. "It's the festival." The blue light of dawn was already leaking around the doorway. One or two farmers were asleep on the last bench, their heads against the back wall, their open hands cupped loosely around shadow on the tables in front of them. Outside in the market the last carts had rumbled off to wait outside the city until nightfall would let them in again; the first shutters on the shops in the arcade were rolled back; the smell of new bread drifted in to us. "Men aren't allowed at the rites of the Good Goddess. In a house where they're being celebrated all the males have to leave, even the slaves and the animals."

But Clodius, rubbing his hand over his chin, laughed. "What better time to visit her, then? At least I won't meet her husband in the hall." He seemed to have accepted me, he even poured me a cup this time. "Come on," he whispered, leaning over the table to Catullus and me. "I've got an idea."

Somehow a fated meeting ought to announce itself better. The people around it ought to know. Think how the sky must have darkened over Thebes, the air crackled and sparked, when Oedipus, on the road, lifted up his shield and stared across it for the first time into his father's eyes. Think how the Asian plain must have trembled, so that Greek and Trojan alike groaned aloud, when Hector looked from the walls and saw Achilles striding forth. Even the sea birds must have flown in terror, crying to the sun, when the foreign princess Medea stood upon the promontory as Jason first set foot on the shore of her distant home.

Well, it was not like that when Catullus met Clodia; it was an ordinary winter morning, full of yellow sunlight and slanting blue shadows, cold and crisp, and for much of it I was bored.

We were waiting. Catullus leaned against a pillar watching the door of the house where Clodius, disguised as a woman in a borrowed dress, had been admitted some time before; I paced on the cobblestones trying to look as if I had some legitimate reason to be there. It was becoming difficult— the crowds were out and the morning had begun. The Forum was beginning to fill up, the shops were open, the morning worshipers in the temples were drifting out into the deep, transparent shadows of the day.

"He's been in there a long time," I said to Catullus.

"He must have gotten in to see her." He was not bored. His plain, serious face was intent, as it always was, as if he were constantly working out some interesting problem in his mind. I went back to my pacing, wondering if I could stop and get a bit of breakfast at a tavern, or just slip off and go home to bed. I was still a little drunk, and getting very sleepy.

There was a commotion behind me. Women were shouting; Clodius, in a yellow dress and wig, shot violently out into the street. Catullus, trying not to laugh, detached himself from his pillar and went after him, strolling at first, then, out of sight of the women, breaking into a run. I took a moment to walk casually past the women, too, then followed, dodging through the early-morning crowd. Ahead of me, the bright figure ducked between two buildings, then appeared on the Palatine Steps, racing for the hill above. Catullus's hair went fiery, then dark, as he dived through the slanting bars of light after it. Behind me waves of outrage spread; a man's voice joined the shouting, then others, and a dog began to bark.

Up on the hillside the figure disappeared again, only to reappear suddenly in the crowd, yanking at the hem of the dress. I could see his mouth open as he swore, almost hear the tiny rip as the flimsy material gave in his hands.

I bounded up the steps calling, "Hey, wait for me," as beside the woman's figure Catullus appeared, slightly taller, visible by his burning hair. I saw him pause, say something, pause again. On Clodius's cheeks the first blue stubble of his beard had begun to show—the yellow wig was no longer much of a concealment, if it had ever been. Publius Clodius Pulcher: Clodius the Handsome. It was a family name, inherited, but it suited him. Even in the woman's clothes he was a strikingly masculine and good-looking man. He was in a good mood, too. "Come on, honey," he said, mincing a step toward Catullus. "I've got a house near here. Let's go get a drink." He winked from under the wig which he had set, slightly askew, on his head again. "See us home, won't you?"

Catullus blinked once and nodded. "I need a drink," he agreed. Clodius led us up the steps to the landing and into a street of big houses behind the high walls. But down the way two magistrates' bodyguards were standing in front of one of the houses.

"Lictors," I said, coming to a halt. Clodius had ducked behind someone's portico; Catullus's eyes were bright with interest.

"That's my house," Clodius whispered.

The lictors were big men. The sun was glowing on the scarlet wool that bound the sticks they carried; under the shadow of their flat, bronze helmets their eyes glinted liquidly as they scanned the street.

"Two," Catullus said.

"I know them," Clodius answered him. "They belong to the City Praetor."

Catullus drew down his dark brows. "What's he doing at your house?"

Clodius's shrug lifted the pleating on his yellow dress.

"Could they know?" I asked. "Could they have found out it was you? You were disguised."

"I don't see how they could know so soon." Clodius was leaning against Catullus as if he were very drunk. "Come on," he said, "let's go to my sister's. She'll find out what this is all about."

Catching his arm, Catullus beckoned me, and we led him, muttering tipsily, up the street. I was trying to keep from laughing. Even if you believed Clodius was a woman, we must have looked ludicrous.

We were attracting a lot of attention. Passersby stared at us with disapproval; two old women clucked at us in toothless reproach. "Drunk," someone said disgustedly as we caromed into him. Of course we were— why not?—though not as drunk as we were pretending. Catullus laughed and apologized in a thickened voice. Even the guards had begun to stare— I saw one of them shift his weight uneasily on his heavy feet. Catullus's eyebrows rose; he gave me a look over Clodius's bobbing head, and staggered closer to them. "Hello, darlings," Clodius squeaked, looking up at them, as Catullus swore and said in a desperate voice, "Don't be sick again, sweetheart. Please don't be sick again."

The guards backed against the door of Clodius's house, looking out over our heads as if we did not exist. The three of us staggered on to the corner, where Clodius ducked into a narrow alley between garden walls. The slanting sunlight picked out his flying figure as he lifted his skirts and ran. Catullus dashed after; I, slower, or drunker, went stumbling along behind.

Midway down the alley they stopped. In the shadow of a wall Clodius reached under his dress and I saw him hand an object to Catullus. As I came up Catullus was trying it in a low wooden door—an iron key, black and solid. I could even see the faint silver scratches on the wards.

"My sister's house," Clodius explained. "Come on." The door swung open and I had a glimpse of a garden, dark green grass and white marble paths. "Come on," Clodius said again.

But I had had enough. "If there's going to be trouble about this," I said, feeling suddenly sober, "perhaps we'd better separate. The lictors . . ."

Clodius was already through the door. Catullus, ready to follow him, turned back to me. "You think there will be?" He, too, looked less drunk than before.

"If there's trouble, it will be remembered against us."

"He's not worried." He jerked his head in the direction of the open door.

"He was born in Rome," I argued. "And he's a Claudian. But we have careers to make here. It's not the same for us. He's related to half the people in the city—he can go as far as he likes, there'll always be some family connection to pull him out if it gets too dangerous. But we . . ."

From the garden Clodius's voice called, and a woman's mingled with it, low and musical, like a flute at a ceremony underlining the voice of the priest.

"Come on," Clodius called again.

And Catullus threw up his head, his hair flashed in the sunlight, his gray eyes glowed. "Come on," he said softly to me, holding the iron key on his palm.

"No," I said. "Don't do it."

He did not listen; I don't think he even heard. He was gone, in any case, before I even finished speaking, and I was left alone in the alley with the sunlight and the shadows, and the sound of the closing door.

Man in a woman's dress, laughing, laughing . . .

Inside the garden Catullus looked around; he had penetrated to a green heart in the stone city. The grass was as fresh as if it were summertime, the paths clean white, the pool still dark with the reflections of the purple clouds. Somewhere a gardener was burning leaves; the smoke rose, blue in the shadows, silver in the sun, behind a row of cypresses. The peppery scent of the smoke hung on the air like a note of music, plangent and sad.

Clodius was pacing near the pool, an incongruous figure in the harshly colored dress, arguing with someone Catullus could not see. "It was all right, I tell you," he was insisting. "They didn't recognize me—they thought I was a woman come to play for the ceremony. I had a lyre," he added, glancing behind him as if it might be in the garden somewhere. He looked feminine again, lithe and slender as he paced, and though he was arguing, his false yellow head was thrown back, and he was laughing.

An invisible woman answered him from deep shadows under a colonnade. "I thought you might have news. I thought you were serious." It was the voice Catullus had heard from outside, speaking in Greek so the servants would not understand; it was beautiful, and vibrant with reproach.

"Oh, I am," Clodius said in the same language, turning toward the voice with an oddly anxious little gesture of his hands.

A figure detached itself from the darkness under the colonnade and stepped out onto the gravel. A woman, dressed in black and white. For a moment Catullus was confused; he looked from her to Clodius and back again. The yellow dress, the white, the falsely feminine, the real. . . . She had lifted her head and was staring across the lawn at Clodius. She looked like him: she had the same delicacy and beauty of form, the same carved, almost translucent, marble skin. She stood so still the pleats of her white dress were as frozen as the fluting on a column, her cloak cut a black diagonal over her slender shoulders.

"Clodia," the man by the pool said, and Catullus understood why he looked so much like her—this was his sister herself.

Yet for all their resemblance she was far more beautiful, with fine, tilted obsidian eyes under a contemplative brow, and smooth hair so black the lights in it were blue. Her small nose arched proudly from a high, narrow bridge to wide, delicate nostrils; her head was poised on a neck as graceful as a swan's. Only her mouth was ambiguous; it contradicted her reserve and stiffness with a child's secret sadness and desire. She was looking down at a bird she carried, and her lashes cast an arc across the pale oval of her cheek. A curve answered it under the fullness of her lower lip. The bird—a sparrow, with a tiny, appealing cheep—was fluttering on her wrist; smiling faintly, she held out her finger to it. It bobbed and pecked. The curve under her lip grew shallower, the long black eyes slanted upward at the ends. Catullus gasped. She rubbed her finger over the bird's smooth head with a small, repetitive, sensual gesture, and her carved mouth curled in secret pleasure.

"I thought you were going to be serious from now on," she said reproachfully. It might have been to the bird.

"It was all right, I tell you," Clodius muttered again. He was peering at his reflection in the pool. "I look absurd in this thing," he added, pulling off the wig and setting it on the head of a small stone Venus next to the water. It gave a note of disorder to the swept and tended paths, the trim lawns, the banks of winter foliage. The woman put back her head, just as he had, and laughed; the little Venus looked startled and ashamed.

"Well, it was," Clodius insisted. "At least until I spoke." He was suddenly bolder—Catullus thought it was because the woman had been amused. He began to mince around the pool, imitating the women in the house as he talked, though without the wig he no longer looked feminine—he looked stranger and more dangerous, more false than that, with his dark head rising from the frills. The bird on the woman's wrist squawked with protest. "They showed me into a little sitting room and told me they were going to find her. But I waited and they didn't come, so I went looking for her myself. There was music and I was supposed to be a musician. . . . What a barn that place is, I must have wandered around in it for hours. . . . And the furniture; gods, you should have seen it, Clodia. . . ."

"I have seen it," she said, watching him with an impassive face. He nodded hopefully at her, perhaps thinking that she had forgiven him, but she gave no sign if she had, and he continued, lamely.

"Well, anyway, I found them. They were in a room near the back, and they were dancing around." He danced a few steps himself, to show how it had been, tripped on his hem and swore. She laughed again, a freer, warmer sound. Clodius laughed uncertainly back. "They were swirling around, see? I couldn't tell who anyone was. So I just forgot and called out, 'Darling, where are you?' or some such thing. They all started to scream and throw clothes and things over the stuff on the altar—the wine and myrtle leaves and all. . . ."

"Shh." She was shocked. "You're not supposed to know about that, much less talk about it."

He had stopped with one foot in the air and his arms outstretched to stare at her. It was comical, and Catullus, alone and forgotten by the door, smiled to himself.

"You don't care about things like that," Clodius objected.

She flushed as if the blood were shining through her white skin. "Pompeia does," she said.

"What of it?" he demanded. "She's in love with me." His self-satisfaction was evident; he ran his hand over the back of his head and smiled at her.

"She'll tell her husband," she said patiently. "She has to, everyone saw. All those women will tell their husbands, and it will get around. It probably already has. And then he'll have to do something about it—I don't see how he can avoid it. He's the Pontifex Maximus, after all; he's supposed to be in charge of all the rites in the city."

"The Pontifex Maximus?" Catullus cried in Greek, unable to remain quiet. His voice sounded loud in his ears. Perhaps it sounded loud in theirs, too, for they turned to him with the same quick gesture, which even their surprise could not make ungraceful. The bird left her shoulder and flew into a tree, where it scolded him angrily. "Do you mean Gaius Julius Caesar?" he asked, feeling hot and clumsy beside their small perfection, and their calm.

"Yes," Clodia said. "Do you know him?"

From the pool Clodius muttered, "Of course he does. This is no ordinary provincial. Ask him who else he knows."

Her eyebrows rose, and she began to speak, but Catullus, furiously angry, cut in. "I know Julius Caesar. He used to come to dinner with my father."

Clodius said, puzzled, "I told you it was his wife, didn't I?"

"No," said Catullus, light-eyed with anger. "You said she was the wife of the City Praetor, not the Pontifex Maximus."

"He's the City Praetor, too," Clodius said.

"There's no end to that man's ambition," the woman muttered.

Clodius ignored her. "I thought you knew," he said to Catullus.

She turned to Catullus. "Does it matter . . . um?"

Clodius said, shamefaced, "Gaius Valerius Catullus, from Verona. I met him in a tavern and he knows a lot of people. Ask him who else he knows."

"Were you there?" she demanded instead, looking more than ever like a goddess, and one on whom some unwary mortal had intruded. She stood perfectly still, even the pleats of her white dress did not move, but her curved nostril opened slightly, in scorn and anger.

"I waited outside."

"We couldn't find any more dresses," Clodius explained. "He's bigger than the maids."

"Any more dresses?" she inquired. "How many of you were there? A whole tavernful?"

"Just us two," Clodius mumbled. "And another man—he's all right," he added hastily. "He won't say anything."

"Well, that's something at least." She drew her fine dark brows down in annoyance. She turned back to Catullus. "You're a friend of the Pontifex Maximus . . . um?"

"Gaius Valerius Catullus," he repeated, more loudly than he had intended.

For the fourth time Clodius said, "Ask him who else he knows."

This time, hearing something in his tone, she nodded and turned to Catullus for his answer.

"I know Quintus Caecilius Metellus Celer, too," he said, defiant.

She stared at him. "You know my husband?" Her eyes, angry, went to her brother, where he stood idly picking at the stitches of his yellow dress.

"Yes. He's the governor of the province I come from."

"So he is," she said absently, her attention still on her brother. "How could you?" she demanded angrily. "A man you met in a tavern. . . ."

Clodius understood her at once. "He won't say anything. Ask him what he thinks of Metellus."

And Catullus, still hot with anger, so that he forgot the caution and courtesy their position required, said, "I think he's a pompous old fool."

Brother and sister stood watching him, two pairs of glittering black eyes in the same long almond shape, two white faces with the same carved and imposing quietness. The air seemed to thicken, becoming heavy and still; the sunlight fell through silence. For a moment they seemed mysterious in their beauty, like a god and a goddess, full of their own unknown purposes, both more and less than human. Then slowly her mouth curved again, her long eyes filled with laughter, her voice chimed out in the blue morning air. "Oh, he is," she cried.

"I told you," Clodius said.

"Yes," she answered him, still again, her eyes on Catullus. "And you're a friend . . . an acquaintance . . . of Julius Caesar, too?"

"Yes." He was embarrassed now by his candor. "I met him a few times when he was in Verona. He offered to help me if I came to Rome, and I have some letters to him. . . . I thought, my father thought, he might be able to do something for me here, you see. . . ."

"Yes," she said, frowning delicately. "I'm afraid I do see. And now you feel you'll have to go to him about this. . . ."

"Valerius Catullus," he repeated quickly, before she could indicate that she had forgotten it again.

"Yes. Valerius Catullus. You know who we are, don't you? We are descendants of the Sabine War–leader, Attius Clausus, who came to Rome with his army five years after the city was founded, to give his support to Romulus. Ever since then, for seven hundred years, our family has been important in this city. Appius Claudius—perhaps you know about him?—gave the city its first constitution, and another ancestor of ours was a censor, and built the Appian Way, two hundred and fifty years ago. Since then Claudians have been generals, statesmen, senators . . . our aunt was a Vestal Virgin, and our father was a consul. You see? Anything we Claudians do is talked about. You do understand that, don't you? Julius Caesar will be glad of the information that it was my brother who broke into his house. He can make use of it. And since you're ambitious, too—"

"That's ridiculous," her brother cut in. "Caesar won't do anything. What could he do? I didn't commit a crime. And besides, it was a joke. He's not going to try to make something of it."

Behind her the enameled sky had turned to gold, and clouds were long bars of dark blue across it. The sun shone higher into the garden, washing the leaves with light; the color flowed over the lawn. From the tree the sparrow called, and in her ear a pearl shone liquidly as if in answer.

She spoke out of shadow against the goldsmith's sky, and her voice seemed to drop down on him like the sunlight. "Valerius Catullus, my brother doesn't realize it, but this is important to us. A scandal—"

"He won't go to Caesar," her brother said from the other side of the pool, where the water shone like molten gold in the grass.

Around Catullus all the colors and shapes of the garden seemed to rise and flow together. Shadows as blue as seawater lapped the green islands of the grass, the sunlight blurred and ran over the melting forms of the plants. Beneath her haughty calm, she was making an appeal to him. He felt cold and ill, and his hands were sweating; the ground rose and fell in waves, unsteady under his feet.

He was grateful that she had turned away to speak, kindly but firmly, to her brother. "Oh, I quite see how he might have to tell him," she said. Her profile was as cool and sharp as a face on a cameo; he was not sure he had seen her vulnerability after all. "He has his own way to make. . . ."

Catullus said, "I won't go." He had the odd sensation that he had stepped forward into deep water.

"But your letters," she protested. "Your career."

And suddenly he felt buoyant, as if the day were lifting him on its newness. "I don't care," he said. Laughter escaped him; it was true.

They were laughing, too, two voices, light and dark, twined in the morning air. She said, "I'm very grateful, Valerius Catullus. And I know how to be grateful, all Claudians do." He smiled at her, for now he was sure he understood her perfectly.

Somehow he was on the street—he never afterward remembered how it happened. Clodius was standing at the door, grinning at him; three large slaves waited with staffs in their hands to escort him home. He was about to say he didn't want them, for he had nothing of value to steal and he wanted to be alone, when he remembered that if he let them go, she would not know where he lived.

She invited him to a party, sending a slave better dressed than he was with a formal note asking him to dinner a week from then. He borrowed some money from his brother in Verona and bought himself a new linen tunic from the best shop in town, and had his good toga pressed. On the day he presented himself at her huge house in the Clivus Victoriae, this time at the black-and-silver front door.

It was a small party, only the traditional nine people, and it was informal, though the room was garlanded and perfumed like a summer day. He wondered where the flowers came from—he had never seen roses in winter. The food was as exquisite as a banquet: bearded mullet, and pheasant, and something he took to be eggs but discovered when he opened one to be pastry with tiny roasted birds inside, sweets of every description, and half a dozen different wines. Her brother and her elderly, rather uncordial husband shared the head couch with a gray-faced man in his thirties. The other guests were younger—some were no older than he was, and some were not patricians at all, but knights, even one or two well-dressed plebeians, though they were obviously men of education. Clodia sat in an upright ivory chair, dressed in black wild silk and pearls, opposite her husband and the gray-faced man.

During dinner there was talk of the usual political sort, perhaps in deference to Metellus's interests. From time to time a hired rhetor recited from Homer, and the company listened with unusual attention. Catullus began to fear that they had never heard poetry before.

He paid little attention to the recitation himself, keeping his eyes on her instead. Her stillness and silence were so correct, so much those of a dutiful wife in the best Roman tradition, that he began to fear that she had invited him only to ignore him. She scarcely spoke, but watched the men on the couches and the servants passing behind with their trays. In her lap she held the sparrow, absently stroking its smooth head with one oval fingertip as she listened to the talk. Only once did she look at Catullus. He glanced up from his plate to see her eyes resting on him, and knew she had been studying him. His breath caught painfully in his chest and he tried to smile. She looked away indifferently, but her self-command was not perfect; her mouth trembled and her hands had clenched. The little bird screeched violently and flew out of her grasp to flutter angrily from a hanging lamp. Everyone laughed. It was only when she laughed, too, and blushed delicately that he guessed how pale she had been.

It was some time before he realized that it was she who directed the evening. She spoke seldom, and then mainly to the servants, instructing them to fill the plates, to change courses, to bring in the wreaths when the meal was over. It was she, not the nominal host Metellus, who directed the mixing of the wine with the right, rather generous, degree of water when the drinking began. She added little to the discussion of politics and never contradicted her husband or the guests, but when the wine was poured she was the one who, radiant with suppressed laughter, began the game of improvising epigrams in which they all took part, and she was the one who asked the gray-faced man to read.

Of that evening Catullus remembered two things all his life. One was her beauty, and the door it opened into other beauties—the elegance of the painted and garlanded room, the delicately spiced and scented meal, the seriousness of the talk at dinner and the wit of the poetic games they played afterward. He felt like an exile, traveling in a far country, who suddenly and for the first time in many weary miles hears his native language. That it was spoken in freedom, and by a beautiful woman who might have been the queen of that country, only made his happiness more intense.

The other thing he remembered was the poetry of the gray-faced man. His name was Titus Lucretius Carus, and his poem was called "On the Nature of Things." He came from an undistinguished branch of a distinguished family; he looked nearly fifty with his hollow cheeks and shaking hands, though someone whispered to Catullus he was much younger than that. When he rose to read, his voice scratched and sputtered like an ill-burning wick, but his thoughts lit up the room. Even Metellus turned from talking politics and listened openmouthed like the rest. Clodia had turned her face toward him blindly as if he were the sun. As for Catullus, the words fell into the incandescent space in his mind where his own ideas took shape, and his spirit caught fire. When he got home he remembered enough to copy some of the poem into his notebook—the magnificent invocation to Venus in the beginning, and the gentle meditation on the triviality of death. He got them nearly word perfect.

He had rented rooms at that time high up on the top floor of a crumbling tenement in the Subura district. He was a poor man as things are counted in Rome, but he did not need much: a few sticks of furniture, a little bronze statue of his family god in a niche, and he had made a home. His balcony looked out over a courtyard hung with washing and bright with flowers in pots. In the daytime children's voices bounced off the walls, women clattered up and down the stairs with jars of water from the public fountain in the street, older children carried infants in their arms, while their grandfathers played dice in the sunny corners. But at night it was cold and empty, for in the Subura people go to bed early, especially in winter; moonlight lay on the courtyard like a fall of snow, softening the outlines of the beaten earth. He sat by the open door of his balcony with a brazier of coals at his feet and a book open on his knees. He did not read. He watched the moon slide over the opposite roof and shadows below reach out across the cobblestones. He was thinking of the woman, of the elegance of her gestures, the odd, arrogant beauty of her face. He thought of her slim, straight body, too; he was twenty-two years old, and he knew he had never seen a woman who moved him so violently. He saw that he had interested her, her small convulsive clutching at the sparrow had told him that. Besides, he had won the contest for the epigrams, and she had smiled at him with special approval. But she was regal and remote. He felt like an ambassador at an unfamiliar court—he knew he had to see her again, but he did not know how to arrange it. He was sure he could not simply go to her and ask.

He waited. In that time his dreams grew vivid, so that they invaded the daytime as well, and she was often present in his room. He thought of making love to her—he thought of it so often it began to seem real. He saw her sitting on his couch, laughing and talking; he imagined her in his bed, her hair unbound, her eyes closed; he felt her ribs arch under him, her thighs open at his insistence; he heard her call his name. He answered, entering her, again and again, never wanting to continue beyond that. The wild beauty of the moment when he felt himself within her, the fierce effort not to release himself, sufficed him. He rehearsed them so often he could no longer tell if he was dreaming or awake. Sometimes he could bear the tension no more, the time when he could call himself back slipped away in his passion. Then he came, awake or asleep, wishing he had not, for the dreams deserted him, and he was left alone in his shabby room.

In those intervals he ate if he remembered to, going out into the winter streets at any hour of the day or night, buying sausage and bread on the street corners, drinking in taverns. Sometimes it was late, and the streets were dark—he never noticed, though he knew better than to go out alone. His servants followed him at a distance, fearing for him—and fearing more his father's wrath if harm came to him; if he saw them he would turn them back, threatening to sell them if they followed farther. Then he would prowl the city, walking until his need drove him back to his rooms, and the dreams that always waited for him there.

Sometimes he read. The poems of Sappho, which he loved, were constantly open beside him. Now he heard the verses in Clodia's voice, in her pure and elegant Greek. Slowly, hesitantly, not entirely aware of what he was doing, he began to translate the great antique love songs.

Ille mi par esse deo videtur . . .
He seems to me equal to a god
he, if it is permitted, surpasses the gods
who, sitting opposite, over and over,
sees you and hears you

laughing, laughing. The very sight
steals all my senses, for when I see you,
Lesbia, no sound of my voice
remains in my mouth

my tongue sleeps, a subtle flame
creeps down to my joints, their own
ringing is in my ears, a double night
shrouds my eyes.

He could not address her as "Clodia," for she was married and in any case too great. He remembered that she had said that everything she did was talked about in Rome, so he called her "Lesbia," after Sappho's home on the island of Lesbos, and because it had the same scansion as her name. This last seemed to him a delicious fact, a smile from his little household god. He smiled himself, with pleasure, as he wrote it. *Lesbia. Clodia.* There were a dozen scraps of paper in his room with the names scrawled on them in his small, neat hand.

"Gods," I said, coming into his room early one morning. "You look ill." He did: his gray eyes burned out of hollows, his cheeks were dark with stubble. Though it was daylight a lamp still burned on his table; last night's supper, most of it, was on a tray pushed to one side. There were rolls of books and bits of paper everywhere; he was copying something from a wax tablet onto a fresh sheet as I came in. Looking up, he smiled at me with his twisted grin.

My clothes were full of winter wind, my fingers ached with cold though my hands had been tucked inside my toga. And it was as close to freezing in the rooms as it had been on the street. He did not appear to notice; he wore only a rumpled tunic, as if it were summer.

"Look." He thrust the poem he was working on into my hand.

"Can't we have some heat?" I said, taking it and sitting down. Still smiling, he looked around the room.

"Pretty bad, isn't it?" he admitted cheerfully. "I wouldn't let the servants in—I've been busy."

Nevertheless he made no move, and I had to call them in myself. While I read, someone came in and built up the fire in the brazier, someone took away the soup and the wine, the rock-hard bread, the lamp.

"When did you last eat?" I asked, closing the roll. He shrugged, and I was suddenly worried—he looked so thin, so indifferent, so changed.

"Do you like it?" he asked hoarsely from the doorway of the balcony where he had been watching me read.

"Yes. It's . . ." I did not quite know what to say. "It's beautiful." Even that seemed inadequate. For some reason, though I knew he loved poetry, it had not occurred to me that he might be writing it—or writing it like this. After all, everyone writes a little—it's part of a gentleman's education, and so on. But he was so serious about it, and it was so good, it unsettled me. It made him seem—I don't know—someone else, someone larger and more important than I had guessed.

He was not ill; I could see that now, though I could also see that he had changed. In the winter light he glittered; his eyes shone, and his skin was transparent. There were blue veins at his temples and the stubble on his cheeks caught the light and gleamed like a dusting of gold.

"Who is Lesbia?" I asked, watching him with an intensity I could not explain.

He smiled. "That's a secret. I can't tell you." But he did, of course; he wanted to. He made me swear a dreadful oath not to reveal it and he waited until I had repeated every word before his god in the shrine in the wall. Then he sat down opposite me at his table.

"It's Clodia," he whispered. I could see that even to repeat her name gave him pleasure. "Clodia Metelli." He said it again. "She's beautiful, Caelius." He leaned forward as if to persuade me, as if he thought that I doubted it.

"So they say."

"You've never seen her?" He was disappointed: he wanted me to tell him about her.

I shook my head. "She's old, though. I know for a fact that she's at least thirty-five. . . ."

He flushed red, the clear transparent color washing up under his skin. His eyebrows drew down and he said hoarsely, "What difference does *that* make?" He was angry, his eyes flashed in that intimidating way they had. I said, "None, I suppose."

He forgave me; he smiled and showed me drafts of his poem—his translation. He talked about her: he told me how much he wanted to see her again. "But how?" I asked several times. "How will you see her?" I believe I pitied him for the intensity of his hope.

But he was living somewhere beyond hope, in a certainty so great it made him glow. It was as if the sun of another city, warmer, stronger, clearer than ours, was shining on him. "I will," he said, and he smiled at me across the border, from far away.

He sent her the poem. I hadn't expected him to do that. And even more strangely, she thanked him in a charming note, peppered with Greek expressions and allusions, warm with wit. He showed it to me. "I never thought she'd answer," I said, handing it back. He was not even surprised. He did, however, go out and get drunk on the strength of it.

It was a troubled time in the life of the city, a period of great tension and unease. Pompey had brought his armies back from Asia, where the wars he had won had made the city rich; he was a hero in everybody's eyes. He had not yet dismissed his soldiers; in the city we heard that he was going to keep them together to parade in his triumphal procession. He knew a triumph was inevitable—we owed him our gratitude and would have to show it, though we had reason to be wary of him, too. His armies were immense, enriched by loot and loyal to their general. No one knew if they were loyal to the city as well. All over Italy people poured out of their houses to see him as he rode toward Rome; towns threw open their gates to him with feasting and festival. In Rome, excitement was intense, though it could not be denied that fear was mixed with it.

Into this tension, Clodius's exploit fell like a stone in a pool. It broke the silence that had hung over the city: people began to talk, to argue, to laugh. To many his daring announced a change in our fortunes; since Clodius was popular, there were men, especially among the poorer sort, who said it was a change for the better. The conservatives who had ruled us for so long— the loose coalition of the heads of the great families with their land, their rents, their huge houses—had received word that their day was done and young men with newer, bolder ideas would take over. Pompey was the sign—he came from a family of no real distinction—and Clodius was the proof. But to others the sacrilege meant dismay: they saw the fabric of our lives unraveling, the old pieties and glories swallowed up, the luck of our armies lost. One heard of men sending their families out of town; my next-door neighbor buried his treasure one night secretly in his garden. Fights were common, especially in the workmen's clubs, the baths, the bars—the most ordinary remarks took on a political undertone; every meeting however it began turned to this question in the end. The Senate began to feel it would have to take action; an indictment was proposed and debated; Julius Caesar divorced his wife. When they asked him if that meant he believed that Clodius had seduced her, the tall and elegant City Praetor only smiled and said that his wife had to be above suspicion—an eminently proper answer that satisfied no one. The talk grew louder, more aggressive, less restrained.

It was into this atmosphere that Catullus proposed to go that night— against my advice, for I saw that the letter from Clodia had raised him above himself, and I feared trouble. He cared little at best for politics, and now he was allied, no matter how slightly, with one of the great political families of Rome. The merest mention of their name was provocation in the city now, and Catullus intended to mention it over and over that night. He could not keep himself from talking about them—it was a way to talk about her.

He drank steadily, too, going from tavern to tavern. The last thin snow of the year was winding down out of a dark sky into the light of the torches; the air was cold, the ground already too warm for the snow to stick. The stones gleamed black and gold in the light; they were slippery with water underfoot. Inside the taverns it was noisy and warm. Catullus drank and argued, his cheeks flushed with wine and heat, his gray eyes glittering. When there was music he sang, and people shouted at him to be quiet, for his voice was terrible. He only laughed and sang louder. Once he tried to dance, and the barman, a huge fellow with a nasty scar—a veteran, no doubt, of some foreign war, though he looked a lot less respectable than that—threw him out. I could not persuade him to go home.

In another place he began a contest with a neighbor at a table, making up obscene verses about whatever came into their heads. Unfortunately, what came into his neighbor's head was Publius Clodius, and the verse he made was vulgar, pointed, and explicit.

He shouted:

"What does he need Pompeia for?

His own sisters give him that, and more."

Catullus went suddenly still. The color drained out of his face, leaving his eyes very light against the whiteness of his skin. All around us the people who had laughed at the verse were quiet. One or two, catching sight of Catullus's face, backed away. The silence spread. Then, very slowly and deliberately, Catullus picked up a jug and smashed it against the edge of the table.

"No, you'll get hurt," I shouted, trying to reach across the table to him. He was holding the broken neck of the jug, the jagged end pointing at his enemy.

I was too late. They were on each other on the floor, rolling amid the crash of crockery and the shouts of men nearby. I heard the whoosh of the stranger's breath as Catullus's knee went into his stomach. I heard the thud of blows. Once Catullus's head snapped back, and blood started out over his lip from his nose, his mouth. Though the other man was older, he was taller and heavier; his fists landed more often, and the sound of them made my stomach heave. People were laughing and shouting, egging them on; one or two poured wine or water on them as if they had been dogs, but as they turned over on the slippery floor I saw Catullus's eyes. He was trying to kill the other man. The punishment he was taking was terrible, but he was not deterred. Slowly the jagged edge of the jug was moving toward his opponent's throat, his left hand was reaching for his eyes. His own face was red now where it had been struck; there was blood on his tunic and smeared all over his face. His eyes stared out of swellings, fixed on his opponent. Each time the man hit him, they wavered, unfocused, and each time came back to glare at the man he was trying to kill.

I pulled at them and shouted. People in the crowd hissed at me, as if I were spoiling their fun. "Curse you," I cried at them, my breath beginning to sob in my throat. The other man had a long cut across his cheek; there was blood on it, mixed with the wine and water and oil on the floor. Catullus's eyes had swollen nearly closed, his breath whistled harshly as if something were broken in his chest. Still he tried, and the sharded edge swept along the man's shoulder, laying it open, white for a moment, then red with seeping blood.

At last the men in the tavern saw it was serious. Two of them pulled the fighters apart, others held them, for Catullus, shouting now, was plainly prepared to go on. He struggled in their arms, shouting unintelligibly through a mouth that was beginning to swell.

"Look," I said in an undertone to his opponent, "you look like a reasonable man. Apologize, will you? He's not sane on this subject. He'll go on until you do."

He was in bad shape himself, marked with Catullus's fists and knees, his clothes torn, his shoulder bleeding heavily. He said in a bewildered voice, "What should I apologize for?"

I had to laugh. "You don't even know?"

He shook his head, but it hurt him, and he closed his eyes. Across the dirty space Catullus was twisting in the arms of the men who held him, shouting. One of the men had a mark along his arm, the other was drawing back his fist, swearing.

"He's crazy," his opponent said, staring at him.

"He's in love with Clodia Metelli."

He gave me a blank look; he didn't even remember what he had said. I explained. "All right," he grunted. Raising his voice he shouted, "I'm sorry. Whatever I said, I didn't mean it. I apologize."

Catullus turned and looked at him. His hair was plastered against his head; his eyes blazed in his face. "You said she slept with her brother," he managed to say, very clearly and slowly.

"Oh, well, that's nonsense. It's just a thing people say. It doesn't mean anything."

Catullus stared back at him, still hard and hostile across the room.

"Look," the man said, "if I'd known she was a friend of yours, I would never have repeated the verse. All right? It was just a stupid jingle, a political joke. It doesn't have anything to do with her, really. You can see that, can't you?" He had walked across the filthy floor and now stood before Catullus, a man a little older than we, but not much, with a kind, friendly face under his bruises, and a good-natured smile.

"Just don't say it again," Catullus said, still bristling.

The other man nodded. "I've apologized," he said peaceably.

"All right."

Someone brought water; they cleaned themselves up. Catullus's face was swelling around the cuts; an angry lump was rising beside his twisted mouth. He smiled painfully.

The other man muttered something. He was exploring a broken tooth with a finger. Catullus shook his head as if to clear it. "Allius?" he repeated.

"Manlius. Manlius Torquatus."

"Gaius Valerius Catullus. From Verona." He said this with his usual hostility, but suddenly he shot his hand out to Manlius, who smiled.

The crowd had gone back to their tables, the talk and the drinking resumed. The barman was demanding money for the damages. Catullus reached for his purse.

"I'll pay half," Manlius said.

"You needn't." He was short with him—he was always touchy about money, since he had less of it than other people.

But Manlius insisted. "No, really. I shouldn't have said what I did." He smiled again.

Catullus's eyes lighted up and he gave him a smile back. In a few moments we were outside in the winter dark.

Our slaves were waiting with their torches and their staffs; the snow was gone, turned to rain. On the warming air the faint, sharp smell of the sea came to us, under the perfume and sewage of the city. From somewhere there was the scent of violets, early, but fresh and strong. '

"Clodia Metelli is your mistress?" Manlius asked. I caught my breath, fearing they were going to start again.

"Yes," Catullus said. I waited but he did not say that it was only in his mind that she was.

To my relief Manlius said only, "Well, you're lucky. They say she's very beautiful."

Catullus was happy, glowing to hear her praised. Perhaps, too, he felt closer to her now that he had defended her name. For myself, I was remembering the fight, which both of them seemed already to have forgotten. I had been astonished at how far he would have gone. I was astonished still. If he had not been stopped he would have killed this harmless man, or died. What amazed me, what left me breathless on that dark street, was that he did not care; it mattered to him not at all which it was. Whether he lived or died had been the same to him. And standing there in the winter rain, I envied him, though he was battered and crazy and already in pain from the beating Manlius had given him. There was something he knew that I did not, something that took him farther than other men would go. Farther from safety and contentment—that I already saw—but that night I suspected for the first time that it would take him somewhere I could not follow: into joy, perhaps, like the joys of the gods, which are stronger than ours, and do not end. I think then, for one moment, I wished him dead. But he turned and smiled at me and apologized for the scene, and I forgot that moment.

A memory, around that time: a winter night, ringing with cold, a clear, black sky chimed with tiny stars. The crack of ice in the pool, the steady drip of water from the bare-branched tree above. It is Cicero's garden, and he and I have gone out into it for a breath of air after dinner.

From the Forum down below a long, low noise, growing louder in the stillness. Voices. Cicero beside me turns to call a servant, and while the man goes to find out what it is, we stand in the cold, listening. It sounds like the wind, like the rising sea, like a river swollen in its banks. Words are caught up in it and tossed above the flood like branches in a winter torrent. "Pompey," we hear shouted over and over in the roar. "Pompey, Pompey. . . ."

"What does it mean?" I cry, maddened by curiosity. Cicero's eyes are serious, his massive head is tilted to catch the tossing words. He smiles a little, but I am not calmed.

The servant comes back, out of breath. "Sir, it's Pompey. He's come back. He's landed in Italy. The towns have come out to meet him."

"And his army?" Cicero asks steadily, though everything depends on his army.

"Disbanded, sir. He told them to go home and wait for his triumph."

"So," says Cicero, but he is smiling more broadly now. "I thought he might." He is looking around the garden as if its chilly bareness were a satisfaction to him. "Well," he says presently. "That leaves us a good deal of work to do, doesn't it?"

Later that night I ask him, over a letter I am copying out, why Pompey is not bringing his army with him, for as far as I can see there was virtually nothing to stop him. Cicero leans back and laces his fingers over his chest. "That's an interesting question." The lamplight shines on his humorous, intelligent mouth, his thoughtful, experienced, lawyer's eyes. "Perhaps he believes he can have it all anyway," he says, giving me a small, ironic smile.

"Can he?" I am fascinated as always to watch his mind at work.

He nods, but his eyes are still thinking, and his trained and beautiful voice says, "Perhaps. Perhaps he can."

> *Sparrow, my girl's delight*
> *whom she plays with as she holds you in her lap*
> *giving you her fingertip*
> *and teasing you to bite . . .*
> *Bright-shining, my desire and my love.*
> *I believe she feels her passion in her like a weight*
> *and solaces her pain.*
> *If I could play as she does*
> *my drooping spirit would rise in flight.*

There is a gap in the record: the leather case holds nothing to tell what happened here. Plainly he saw her again, and around that time, for afterwards the notebooks, the letters, the poems, show clearly what ensued. But of this meeting—where it was, what they said, if they were alone—there is no word. Only this poem, and its telltale "I believe." That is date enough, context, place, for afterward, he knew.

He began to be invited to her house. There were always young men there—political colleagues of her brothers', literary men, relatives, clients of the family, friends. Her husband had gone back to the province he had governed in the north, but as many great ladies in Rome were beginning to do, she continued to entertain in his absence. Perhaps the atmosphere was a little freer without his pompous presence—certainly the wine was mixed a little stronger, the young men danced more often, the poems they read spoke more frankly of love. But her brothers—wild Clodius or the sober and conservative Appius—were always there and everyone behaved perfectly correctly. Catullus enjoyed himself, though he paid little attention to the others and noticed only her. He had a recognized position: he was the official poet of her little court. He told himself it was enough, though he had grown thin on the dreams that haunted him at home; he thought of nothing but her. When he was not with her he wrote to her, when he went to her parties, he recited in his hoarse voice only to her.

> Mourn, O Venuses and Cupids
> and all who love what's beautiful
> my girl's sparrow is dead
> my girl's delight is dead
> which she loved more than her eyes.
> He was as sweet as honeycake
> and knew her as well as a girl knows her mother.
> He never left her lap
> but hopped around, now here, now there,
> chirping all the time to greet his mistress.
> Now he goes along the dark way
> from which they say no one returns.
> O curse you, you vile shades of Hell
> that devour all beautiful things—
> now you've taken a pretty little bird,
> O cruel, o poor little sparrow,

> *Because of you my girl's sweet eyes*
> *are red and burn with tears.*

For that poem she kissed him, in public, to the applause of the others. Her black eyes glanced once quickly into his, her pale mouth pressed against his startled lips. He caught her scent, as cool and fresh as the hint of the sea on a sweltering day; he heard her breath sigh once in his ear. Then she was gone, the wine went around again, someone started a dance. He stood in the circle as if he had been struck. I think he really felt that a goddess had touched him. Presently someone caught him up into the round; he laughed and drank down his wine as he joined the dance.

Around that time he called on Julius Caesar. Perhaps she asked him to—in view of his promise to her, I rather think she did. He had his own reasons: he went out of concern for her brother, because the Senate, under pressure from Clodius's political opponents, had voted to try him for sacrilege—a crime unknown heretofore in Rome. No one knew what it meant except that the old men were determined to make an example of Clodius. And in their fear of Clodius's popular support, they had gone so far as to decide that Caesar, the outraged husband, should pick the jury himself.

This piece of injustice infuriated Catullus—I think it would have even if he had not known any of the people involved. But since it was her brother, and his friend, he determined to use what little influence he had.

He called on one or two of the men he had letters to—the old ex-consul, Hortensius Hortalus, with whom he had studied when he first came to Rome, a man known for his conservative views but also for his vast eloquence and learning, a valuable ally in a law court; on Marcus Porcius Cato, the upright and acerbic leader of the old, and old-fashioned, men. He got no real satisfaction from them—they disliked Clodius's wildness and feared it. Catullus tried one or two others who would not even admit him at their gates.

At Julius Caesar's he had better luck. He went again to his house, this time, of course, openly, and gave his name at the door. There was no trouble; without surprise the servant showed him in, and he took his place between a workman in a rough woolen tunic and a leathery up-country farmer, who nevertheless wore a patrician's striped toga.

He waited a long time. It did not bother him—he had enough to think about. He remembered her comments about the house, and amused himself by examining its decoration with an eye made critical by her own taste.

At last he was shown into the library, a room even she would have approved, for it was handsome, with bookshelves to the height of a man's waist and dark gold walls above. Caesar sat at a long table, making notes on a fat roll of paper. His secretaries bustled in and out; it was some moments before he looked up.

"I know you, don't I?" he said, when at last he noticed Catullus in the visitor's chair. The pen still hovered in his hand, to show he intended to go back to work immediately.

"We've met. At my father's, in Verona," Catullus said, adding his father's name very distinctly as if he were afraid Caesar would miss it.

The City Praetor nodded. He was about forty, tall, with fair hair beginning to go thin, and deep, green-brown, intelligent eyes. His clothes were odd and rather elegant—his tunic had sleeves that reached his wrists and were embroidered in gold, the fringes had been dipped at least half a foot deep in purple. His face was strong and narrow, the cheekbones high, the mouth, long, flexible, and good-humored. He waited, no longer impatient, but plainly unwilling to spend time on courtesies.

"I came about Publius Clodius Pulcher," Catullus said, looking directly into Caesar's dark, ambiguous eyes.

It was a risk; the tall man might have been angry, for people were laughing at him behind his back over his wife's infidelity. It was certain that he knew it and that he had divorced her for that reason. But he only raised his eyebrows and waited.

"Look," Catullus said, leaning forward. "I know there's been a lot of talk, and all that. But really, you must see that Clodius meant no harm. It was a prank, just fun. He was a little drunk."

"Before the first hour of the morning?" The strong eyebrows rose farther; he was not amused. Catullus, however, found himself well launched and sailed on, unintimidated.

"You don't know him. He's very bold. He'll do anything if he gets the idea. He just thought it would be amusing to break into a women's festival—he didn't mean anything by it."

The tall man leaned his arms on the table. "The world is full of people who don't mean much of anything, young Catullus. They're dangerous, all the same."

"Dangerous?" Catullus said, growing warm with anger. "Really? What did he do that was dangerous? Saw some objects he wasn't supposed to, some women dancing?"

The tall man frowned. "The rites were profaned. The Vestals had to purify the house and perform them again. The Goddess might have been offended; harm might have come to the state, to those responsible for the state. This is serious business, young Catullus."

"Is it," Catullus said flatly.

The eyes rested on him thoughtfully again. "What are you getting at?"

"You were young once yourself," Catullus said with unconscious cruelty. "Surely you remember what it was like?"

Rome was full of stories about Caesar's youth, of course: perhaps he thought Catullus was referring to them. Perhaps he was. There was a verse they repeated in the taverns sometimes, about his military service in Bithynia when he was just beginning his career: "Every woman's husband," they sang, "and every man's wife." He was said to have slept with the wives of most of the prominent men in Rome, and with the king of Bithynia himself. Possibly it was just soldiers' talk, like the gossip about Clodius, but the tall man took it seriously. He looked once more at Catullus, a long, sharp, hard, assessing gaze. Then, slowly, he grinned.

"Bold, is he?" he said. "I'll say he is. And he's not the only one."

Catullus's thin skin flushed, but his fierce eyes did not waver.

The praetor's mood changed. "My wife was involved. I couldn't let it pass—they'd never get over it in the city if I did."

He understood that, and he understood that he was being addressed as an equal by a man much older and more experienced than himself. He said, "But you've stopped the talk, haven't you, by divorcing her? And now there's no reason to ruin Clodius's life, or his family, for that."

Caesar did not answer. He sat back in his chair and looked thoughtfully at the younger man. "His family?"

He thought he might blush, so he scowled instead. "His sisters—Clodia Luculli, Clodia Marcii. Clodia Metelli," he said in a different voice.

"I see," the praetor said, smiling. Catullus could not help smiling back. The next moment he felt foolish, as if a clever lawyer had trapped him in a damaging admission. Caesar changed the subject.

"I don't know exactly what you think I can do, young Catullus. I'd like to help—I wouldn't want a beautiful woman to suffer, if it could be avoided." The eyebrows rose again, and he smiled; Catullus wondered if he was laughing at him. "But it's out of my hands. The indictment has been handed down, the bill has passed the Senate—in spite of the friends Clodius has there, and elsewhere." His changeable eyes were remote; he was thinking behind them even as he talked.

"But if you tell them that you don't think he did it . . ." Catullus began, but the older man was already shaking his head.

"It wouldn't work. It's too late for that. The Senate's bill is what it is—I can't refuse to do what they want. If they order me to pick a jury, I suppose I must, eh? We're all servants of the Senate; we can't ignore what they say. Too many very powerful men would be offended. . . ."

Catullus listened to this with rising dismay. In desperation he cut in, "Well, but couldn't you talk to Clodius, see what could be done?"

It seemed to Catullus that Caesar had been waiting for this question, though there was nothing to show it. The tall man spoke, when he answered, with great reluctance. "It won't help." Then, apparently relenting, he added, "Since you ask it, young Catullus. For your father, and his friendship, which I value. Since you ask it."

Catullus began to thank him, in the formal way he had been taught, but Caesar was already busy with something else. He called his secretaries to him and began to hand them notes, rolls, letters.

As Catullus got up to go, however, the brilliant, preoccupied eyes came back to him, and the tall man said, "Don't expect too much, young Catullus. I'll do what I can, but feeling is running pretty high."

"Anything you can do will help."

Caesar shook it off. "Forget it. But if you want a bit of advice—from a man who, as you say, was young once—I'd keep out of it. She's a beautiful woman, but that family is very powerful. They go their own way, they do what they want. People who can't keep up with them can get badly hurt."

"What makes you think I can't keep up?" Catullus demanded, his eyes going light with anger.

Caesar did not answer. He had turned back to his secretaries and was dictating to two of them at once.

A borrowed house—Manlius Torquatus's—out by the river, in what was once a village street, before the city grew out into the suburbs around it. A narrow entrance between a fly-specked bakery and a shop selling the poorer sort of household goods: lumpy cooking pots, tin baths, ill-tied brooms. But inside, the house was filled with the greenish-tawny light of the river, and its damp sweet smell. A willow in a minute garden trailed its yellow leaves over the bank; in the distance the temples and houses on the higher hills shone softly blue against the deeper blue of the sky. She had told him she would come if the trial went in her brother's favor. "I'll be too upset if it doesn't," she said.

He had brought wine and little saffron-colored cakes, which he spent some time arranging on a plate. He carried out a couch from the dining room and set it in the sun. The river murmured through reeds; the walls of the garden caught the early-spring sunshine. He lay down on the couch and prepared to wait.

Noon came and went, the sun in the walled space grew hot, the river noises chuckled drowsily; lying on the couch, he watched the yellow leaves against the sky, thinking of her—of her beauty and courage. He knew it could only have been love that had made her agree to come. He saw that she must care for him more than for her husband, more even than for the obligations that bound her to him, more than for the traditions that sustained her formidable pride.

The long afternoon wore away; the sunshine grew paler on the grass, and the shadows crept out to cover it. Losing its tawny gilt, the river flowed umber and ultramarine under the trees. He imagined he could hear the speeches in the Forum as the lawyers argued; the words were rising, thin as the whisper of the leaves, into the pale sky. He could not eat, but he drank some of the wine as the first shadows touched him with their chilly edges. Presently they covered him. He was stiff from lying on the couch and the warmth of the wine had drained out of him, leaving him empty and cold.

He began to pace through the damp, dark rooms with their musty furniture and mottled walls, through the atrium where the stone-rimmed pool was already reflecting a golden sky, out into the narrow hallway to the door. He had brought no servants, thinking discretion required it, so the hall was empty. The porter's hut was vacant; the iron door to the street barred the entrance like a word.

He told himself he understood. Her brother had not been acquitted and she had turned to her family for consolation in that disaster. Her husband had returned unexpectedly from Gaul; her sisters had prevented her from coming; her sense of her own position had overruled her love. It must have shamed her even to contemplate adultery, for she was descended from people who upheld the state in all its ramifications. In the dark hall he smiled his twisted smile. "Well, Catullus," he whispered to himself, "you'll have to be satisfied with that." He meant that he knew she loved him, but she would never show it. It was thin comfort against the cold, dark hall, but it was something, and he held it to him.

He had no desire to leave; he felt close to her where he was, leaning against the iron door and staring at the clumsy mosaic at his feet. There was a picture of a dog worked in pebbles and the word "Beware" underneath. He thought that after all she had preferred her husband. He wondered if the people who had owned the house had kept a dog, or if they had believed the picture was enough; he wondered if they had been happy in this house, and he felt that he might come and live there himself, alone, never seeing anyone, filling the shadowy rooms with images of her.

He had discovered that the mosaic was not square: there were a hundred and fifty-two stones along the top, ninety-seven on the side. He was trying to calculate the area from this when, unbelievably, she was there. He heard her on the other side of the door, the clatter of her chair as the bearers set it down, a word of command he could not make out, even the creak of the curtains as she pushed them aside. With hands made slippery by excitement, he fumbled at the bolts and pulled back the door.

> . . . Thus did Allius help me:
> he opened a gate over a barred field,
> he gave me a house, and its mistress,
> where together we have proved our love.
> There my white goddess delicately stepped,
> setting her foot on the smooth stone
> as she pressed her shining sandal down.
> Even as Laodamia came burning with love
> to the house of Protesilaus . . .

She was already pulling the pins from her hair. "Dear heart," she whispered, smiling her clouded smile at him. "Don't look so surprised. I said I'd come." Her hair fell suddenly over his arms as he held her to him;

he could feel it, slippery as silk and slightly cool, then warm and soft. "Oh, gods," he murmured, lifted into joy. She reached up her mouth and he kissed her, suddenly aware of his body—of its size, its awkwardness, its lack of delicacy. Then he forgot it, and was aware only of hers. Her breasts were firm under the smooth material of her dress, her thighs pressed against him, strong and clinging. He kissed her again.

"Is there a bed somewhere in this house, Valerius Catullus?" she murmured.

It was too late for the garden, the last of the sunlight was already breaking on the tops of the trees, down below the river was blue with shadow and the air was cold. He carried the couch into the house, afraid all the time that he would find her gone.

But she was waiting for him by the drowned green atrium, standing beside the pool, her face hidden by her long hair, her head bent as if she were reading something at the bottom of the chilly water.

"Set it here," she said without turning around.

He feared he had offended her. Perhaps he had taken too long over the couch—on the way back he had been clumsy and the bulky thing had caught in the doorways. Perhaps she had changed her mind and was thinking of leaving. He did not know how to change it back; he did not dare to touch her, she looked so remote and self-contained as she stared thoughtfully into the clear water.

As he set the couch down she turned slowly; her hands went up to the pins on her dress. It fell in a long rustle to her bare feet and she stood in front of him, naked and beautiful, and held out her arms. The greenish light lapped over her; she seemed to step out of it, gleaming like a pearl. He saw her breasts rise as she lifted her arms; the complex double curve of her ribs and hips lengthened and grew subtle; the dark wedge of hair between her thighs shone blue against the pallor of her flanks as she walked through the shadows to the couch.

It was like his dream—the heavy black hair, the slim, taut arc of her body, the tips of her breasts like bits of coral, pink and hard. Her hips moved against him, he felt her arms pull him down as they had in his dreams. Except that in his dreams he had entered her over and over again. This time he could not: a moment of resistance—damp, hot, tight—then overwhelming darkness. Her body rose and fell under him like a wave not of the river but the sea, pulling him under until he seemed to travel to the bottom of the ocean, deeper even than the continents that float on the surface, and he cried out in wonder and joy. He was carried beyond sensation into knowledge: he felt he had penetrated not a woman but a mystery. Then a rush of light, of feeling, the long, shuddering return to the surface, the painful gasps as he filled his lungs with air. She lay under him, damp with sweat, her head turned away, her long hair tangled across her face. She looked broken, abandoned; for a moment he feared that she had ceased to breathe.

"Clodia," he whispered into the seaweed wrack of her hair. She turned her head slowly to him. Her mouth looked bruised and soft, her eyes full of complex thoughts like pains. His heart ran away with fear: he thought she regretted what she had done, that she loved her husband best. But she put her arms around him and pulled his head down on her shoulder as if to comfort him. Her hand stroked his hair, slowly, as a mother's does when she sees, sadly, further into the future than her son.

Then for a long time they lay together, perfectly still, on the couch. The light died in the room, the oblong of sky above the pool faded and grew deep. Swallows crossed it, going home on the clear sapphire air. As they do at night, the river noises grew louder, and the damp air was thick with a shivering chill. He willed himself to immobility; he was afraid that if he moved she would awaken and go.

At last, when the room was fully dark, she opened her eyes. She sighed deeply once, but when she sat up her movements were brisk. In the night-gray of the opening in the roof he saw the curve of her breast under her raised arm as she pulled her fingers through the snarls in her hair, saw her bend to reach for her sandal on the floor.

"No," he whispered hoarsely.

She turned to him, her face an oval glimmer in the dark. But she was smiling as she leaned down and kissed him; her hair fell over them and brushed his chest. He felt her hand slide down his belly to his new erection.

"Darling," she said in mock surprise, laughing at him as she slipped her thigh over him. He held her over him for a moment, grinning at her, but she was too strong for him. Her hips thrust down on him; against his will, but, finally, with his consent, he entered her again. She seemed to know how to torment him, or to please—he was prepared to believe that she knew everything. She thrust herself up and down until he thought he could endure no more. At that moment she stopped, and, holding herself with perfect stillness, lifted her body from him only to put her mouth down over his so that he cried out in pleasure and pain. He tasted salt; her hair smelled of the sea. Her fingers teased and stroked; her tongue, her lips, her very hair, seemed to crackle like summer lightning when, smiling, she brushed them across his skin. He saw that she was teaching him, rebuking his ignorance and his youth even while she used them for his pleasure, and her own. Frequently she made him groan with frustration, but she only laughed. He began to struggle to follow her, until he feared he would no longer be able to. She seemed at that moment to guess: she lifted herself onto him again; his arms went around her, crushing her to him. He felt her nipples against his chest; her mouth opened, her tongue was inside. His hands found the cleft between her buttocks and he held the two tight mounds firmly as she pushed herself onto him as deeply as she could. The shudder of his surrender he felt first through her—a torment, a pleasure, longer than the first, less haunted by mystery, more complex, fading to a softer end. She was smiling into his eyes, lazily, mockingly, but he knew that she had liked it, and that she was pleased with him.

"Well," she said. "Perhaps Verona has something to teach Rome after all."

"I love you," he said in his hoarse voice. Tears had started painfully to his eyes; he felt that he would choke. "I love you."

She kissed him for that. Even now, when sensation was so spent it was as if it had been washed out of him, he thought she was beautiful. The fine curve of her jaw, the deep-set eyes with their silvery whites and their infinite and thoughtful darknesses, the slim body—more like a girl's than the matron he knew she was—the long, delicate hands, the arched nose and curved mouth: he had an impulse to crush her against him, as if he could absorb her, as if only then could he be sure of having enough. She stretched herself warmly and kissed him again.

"Darling," she said. "I'm hungry. Did you think to bring anything to eat?"

He was hungry himself, famished, starved. He had only the saffron cakes, and the wine. They ate them lying side by side on the couch as if they were at a feast, though the cakes had lost their freshness in the river damp, and were too few and small, in any case, to satisfy. The wine, at least, was good—the best he could afford. Its long wait had not done it any harm.

"Never mind," she said when they had finished. She pulled her dress over them as a cover, though it was not nearly warm enough. He could not believe his luck, his joy. It was plain that she intended to sleep the night with him. He thought he had attained, in that one day, the highest pitch of happiness he would ever feel in his life. He did not ask for anything more, but breathed a prayer of thanks to his little god. He did not see how he could ever ask for anything again.

"Never mind," she whispered in the darkness. "Next time you'll bring more."

So began his great happiness. He lay awake beside her for a long time, watching a star in the deep gray space in the roof, thinking of what she had left behind to come to him. His happiness lifted him like a tide, buoying him above his fatigue, his exhausted senses, until it carried him out beyond the room, into sleep.

When he awoke it was out of darkness without dreams, into the cool blue dust of dawn. The first wagons were rumbling by outside, the insects had begun their fluting in the garden, the first birds called, though the river still splashed with nighttime liquidness. Beside him the pale curve of her back rose to the line of her hip and descended again along her thigh. In the hollows, night still hid, but the tiny line of vertebrae, the edge of her shoulder blade, her scrolled hipbone, gleamed faintly in the new light. She smelled warmly of something like summer air, and, more tantalizingly, of something dangerous, like the sea.

They made love again, in the early light, at his insistence; he wanted her as much as if he had never touched her before, and he was growing bolder. When they were finished he looked into her face; it was tinted with the first true sunlight and the room was filled with the netted reflections of the pool. "I love you," he whispered, kissing the faint coral of her cheek.

She sat up and began to twist her hair into a knot. She was already going away from him; her hands moved quickly, her eyes were busy with daytime thoughts.

"Stay." It was difficult to speak. His hoarse voice caught in his throat; it did not seem to reach across the distance to her. Yet he was aware of her so strongly; he felt that his skin had been flayed. Every move she made was registered on him with painful immediacy. "What happened yesterday?" he asked, to make her stay.

"With my brother?"

He nodded.

She laughed and bent down to give him a quick kiss. "Nothing. It was all right."

"But what?" he insisted.

She stood to put on her dress. It was crumpled; she smoothed it over her thighs, inspecting it critically. At his question, she looked up and shrugged. "We paid."

He did not understand. "Paid whom?" He reached for her, but she ducked away from his hand.

Her delicate nostrils pinched in annoyance, her eyes looked down at him thoughtfully. "The jury, of course," she said impatiently.

He was shocked. "The jury? You bribed the jury?"

Her sandal was eluding her; she searched busily for it. When she retrieved it she turned it over in her hands as if she suspected it of having been up to something while it was gone. "Well, not us exactly—it was very expensive. Some friends of ours."

She turned and caught sight of his face and her eyebrows rose. "Well," she demanded, "what else could we do? A man we know was going to swear that my brother had been with him at his country place that night, but someone saw him here. What else could we do?"

"Who saw him?"

She frowned. "Oh," she said as if she were going to spit. "Cicero. He'd have been believed, wouldn't he? The ex-consul, the Father of his Country." Her scorn was total, her eyes glittered with it.

"Yes. He'd have been believed."

For a moment he thought she was going to turn on him, tell him she was angry, but she put back her head and laughed. "Oh, darling. That's how things are done here. Don't look so scandalized. And we are very grateful to you for trying to help. We really are."

He knew he did not have the right to resent this, to be shocked. She was a married woman who had come to him in spite of law, custom, religion, right, because she loved him. If she also loved her brother enough to set her face against the world for his sake, how could he complain? All the same, he put his arms around her and held her sadly, as if the gulf between them were wide, as if across it she might be lost to him forever.

But she was not. "I'll write," she said softly. "I'll let you know when I'm free again." Her mouth was warm against his, her body supple and strong. She held him briefly to her, whispering. "It was wonderful, darling. I never dreamed . . ."

"I love you," he said desperately into her hair.

"Oh, my darling," she said, twisting free of him to go.

She wrote to him; he went, arms laden with parcels of food, to Manlius's house. She stayed an hour and sighed when she left, saying, "My husband is coming home from Gaul. He wants to present himself as a candidate for the consulship, so he has to be in Rome. The house will be full of people, too." Her childish mouth turned down at the corners; she looked so unhappy he was as glad as if she had stayed a week.

She wrote to him again: "Darling, it's so difficult just now. As soon as I can I'll come to your sweet little house, but as it is, my husband . . ." Catullus, reading this, found himself hating the pompous but inoffensive old man. Still, occasionally, Metellus's candidacy worked to Catullus's advantage. On the mornings when they held the public receptions for the dependents of their house—their clients—he sometimes went to see her being coolly gracious to the important men, and warmly welcoming to the insignificant. She moved around the atrium of the huge mansion on the Palatine Hill, followed by a servant with wine and nuts and cakes, asking after the health of the clients' families or to be remembered to their wives. She looked, as always, remote and self-possessed, her eyes shone with intelligent interest, her laugh rang out in the crowded room. He watched her hungrily; even Metellus's presence could not spoil his agonized pleasure in her beauty.

Once, during that time, she gave one of her small parties for writers that he had so enjoyed before, but this time it was a lugubrious affair. Even the presence of his own friends did nothing to make it better—Licinius Calvus's wit, his own lyric cheerfulness, Cinna's high spirits, all sputtered and died under the dull haze of Metellus's seriousness. And Metellus had insisted on inviting a number of his political cronies, men as conservative and old-fashioned as he was, who listened to the poetry with frozen disapproval, coughing through the laughter at the jokes and remarking that one seldom heard anything nowadays to equal the good, old-fashioned styles. "It's all this Greek stuff now," one said, pushing dates into his mouth and looking significantly at Helvius Cinna's willowy figure. Metellus nodded and smiled his dim gray smile.

The worst of it was that she appeared to agree with him. She was quite strikingly cold, even nasty, to Catullus. When he was presented to her husband at the beginning of the evening she looked up from the ivory chair that was set beside the candidate's couch, saying in a mocking voice, "Well, I hope you don't waste your time among us, Valerius Catullus. Rome has many distractions for young men." He laughed, startled and angry—he did not care if her husband understood; his face went dangerously pale and his eyes glittered. But Metellus noticed nothing; he nodded sagely in agreement with this trite advice. During dinner once or twice she addressed remarks to him—they were as painful as the others. It was not until the next day that he understood why.

> *Lesbia is always cutting me,*
> *and is never still.*
> *Yet she loves me—*
> *may I die, she does.*
> *How do I know?*
> *I always do the same, just*
> *to have her on my lips*
> *yet I love her—*
> *May I die, I do.*

In spite of her coldness, by the end of the evening she had found a moment when the outdoor clothes were being carried in to press herself against him so that he felt her body under her embroidered dress. She made it look like an accident, but he knew it was not. And when she handed him the wreath he had forgotten in the supper room there was a tiny note folded among the roses: "Tomorrow afternoon."

I saw them together around that time, when Pompey came home in glory to celebrate his triumph. The whole city had turned out for it: two days of parades, festivals, sacrifices, feasts, of a magnificence no one had seen before. The country people seeped into the city, filling up the streets, the Forum, the Circus Maximus, with their cooking pots and straw mattresses; at night the city looked like the evening after a siege. Everywhere little fires burned—they were cheerful, though, when you got close. As you passed, families would call out to you, offering a drink of wine, a bite of sausage, a place by the fire, in exchange for news or gossip, or, if you had neither, a funny tale. By day the parade route was so dense it looked like a river in spate; the noise was audible as far out as the suburbs.

My servants had found places for me and my friends near the end of the route—in front of the squat, dark, blood-red Temple of Jupiter where Catullus had prayed for my safety, and opposite the enclosure set aside for the wives and families of the dignitaries. I had invited Catullus, but he said he could not come; he did not say why. My friends and I ate our cold lobster and drank our wine in reasonable comfort as the endless parade of loot and captives lurched up the Sacred Way to be presented to our god. Pompey had conquered twelve million people and doubled the Roman treasury; the crowd screamed and cried, shouted and laughed, as the proofs went past: the gold, the marble, the bronze, the models of the captured towns, the slaves, the hostage princes and the wreathed white oxen—both destined for the sacrifice—the dancers, musicians, chanting priests. Blue clouds of incense rolled out into the sunlight, trumpets cried, jewels flashed, until the eye was weary and the head swam. We went home the first night drunk with the colors and the sounds. Pompey had not appeared.

The next day was more solemn: the army was to be presented at the temple. Rank after rank of scarlet and bronze went by under the nodding banners and garlands, rank after rank of faces, singing the traditional songs. After a while it grew uninteresting and I turned my attention to the enclosures across the way. The wreaths and bright dresses of the women, the clean whiteness of the togas, the sunshades and silk cushions, the tables of gold plates, the cups of wine: then I saw him. He was with her—her friends and family, under an awning striped in lavender and olive-green twice as big as anyone else's and fringed with bullion as thick as icicles on a barn. In the vivid shade the women's dresses glowed like coals of yellow, blue, violet, and rose; she wore a dress made of some kind of silver net that caught the lavender and green and sent it back, sparkling into the shadows. She sat alone—her brothers and husband were in the temple, of course— and I had to admit that she was beautiful. As I looked, Catullus stood up and raised his cup to her. I saw his lips move, a gust of laughter came to me across the way as she leaned forward to place her own wreath on his head. He smiled and I saw that he was lit by happiness—it shone through him as the sun shone through the silk above his head. He lifted his cup and drank to her.

I watched for a moment, then turned away. Pompey was coming in gold and crimson like a king—the noise in the Forum down below showed that he was already there. Someone was shouting in my ear that he had pardoned the captives and they would not be killed; someone was saying he was wearing a cloak that had belonged to Alexander the Great himself. I stood up to get ready to see him. And afterward there would be the public feast—I had been invited to sit with Cicero and his friends. Plainly I had more important things to do than to watch Catullus at a festival.

I invited him to dinner a few weeks later. I had met a freedwoman named Flora, and I wanted him to see her. She was much older than I was, but very handsome and much admired by men of taste in the city, the ones who could afford such admiration. To my surprise, he came, for he rarely accepted invitations now. It was only later that I discovered that Clodia was out of town.

Even so, the dinner was not a success, though Flora, skilled as she was, tried to please him. She praised his poems, which were already circulating in the city, and she teased him—I thought charmingly—to tell her who the lady was. He had given her one glance when he came in—she was really very striking with her red hair and her height and her elegant clothes—but he had looked away again immediately afterward. She wore some of her famous collection of jewelry, she sang delightfully, she told witty stories. Nothing she did seemed to make much impression on him. He was polite, but he drank a lot. We were both relieved when he left, rather early, pleading that he had work to do. Flora had the kindness not to take out her annoyance on me, and we finished the evening together very pleasantly. I had to tell her who Lesbia was; I owed her that much for his rudeness. She did not take offense.

There were other invitations he accepted with better grace, and other evenings he spent more agreeably. I guessed it then; now I see the proof.

> Yesterday, Licinius, was a holiday
> and we played a game, you and I,
> writing on my tablets, each in turn,
> verses now in one meter, now another

while we laughed and drank our wine.
I came away on fire from your wit.
Food did not quench me, nor sleep soothe,
I tossed on my bed, burning to see the dawn.
At last, half dead,
I made this poem for you.
Now, don't refuse me,
for Nemesis is on my side—she'll blast you
as your wit did me.

I'll give you dinner at my house,
Fabullus, in a few days, gods willing,
if you bring the food—good, and lots of it.
Oh, and a pretty girl, and wine, and wit,
and all kinds of laughs.
If, as I say, my friend, you'll bring it,
you'll have a good dinner:
your Catullus's purse is full of cobwebs.
In exchange, I'll give you
something better:
the essence of love—or better even than that—
I'll give you a perfume
which Venus and Cupid gave to my girl.
When you smell it, Fabullus, you'll pray the gods
to turn you into
one gigantic nose.

Well, I was busy myself—I couldn't be bothered if he wasn't interested. I had Flora, I had other friends—young men who understood a good time and didn't mind going to some expense to find one. I had my studies. I wish now I hadn't been such a fool.

He met her again in the house by the river. It was already full summer, the days were hot, the nights short and warm. They made love slowly, drowsily, to the somnolent drone of the cicadas and the quiet lapping of the pool. In the late sunshine birds called; from the willow a dove mourned. The thick golden dusk of the room seemed to breathe the heavy river air in and out; the ripples sent shooting lights into the greenish shadows on the walls. Her body gleamed under him; he felt again that the river was carrying him out to sea.

Later, near sleep, it seemed to him that he was a child again at home, in the house by the lake in Sirmio. A woman spoke to him; he answered her, confused. Beside him the woman on the couch murmured in her sleep and turned toward him. His arms went around her, he buried his face in her hair. Deep in his dreams, he was not sure for a moment who she was. He moved closer to her. Wrapped in her warm, even breathing and the perfume of her skin, he fell deeper into sleep to the soft, maternal cooing of the dove.

There were long intervals when he did not see her. Her brother was trying to get a political appointment to leave town; she was busy with her husband's campaign. He heard about this in the city sometimes. We all did: their wealth, the beauty of Clodia, the brilliance of her parties, her family's connections, were talked of everywhere. He was hungry for these comments, he stored them in his mind like a man storing gold in his chest, to take out and run his hands through when he was alone. Once he went so far as to reproach her for the infrequency of their meetings. He knew it was foolish, and unkind, for she was not free. He expected anger, but she only sighed. "Darling, if only I could."

"You love him," he accused her, unable to prevent himself. She had never said she didn't, never said she loved him best.

She turned away from the mirror where she sat, very slowly, as if something impeded her. "No," she said, her eyes wide and blank. "I don't."

Later he whispered, "Forgive me," into her scented hair. She held him at arm's length and looked deeply into his eyes, but she said only, "If you knew how unhappy I am. . . ." Her beautiful mouth twisted down at the corners, her eyes were full of pain.

He kissed her then, to make her happier, holding her against his chest, murmuring into the softness of her hair the words his Celtic nurse had said to him when he was small. It did not matter that she did not understand.

On the first day of the Apollonian Festival he took her to the games. Her brother went with them, as did several other young men—hangers-on of Clodius, friends, her shy, elderly cousin, who wrote verse. He did not mind. From time to time he saw the others eyeing him, and knew he was envied.

The crowd noticed them, too; he was astonished at how popular Clodius was. They called to him as he passed or came up to press his hand; from the poorer seats near the top a cheer went up. A woman threw a sprig of lavender to him. It fell at his feet, a small purple spot on the ground. He picked it up, smelled it ostentatiously, and put it in his tunic. The crowd laughed. On the front benches, some of the senators turned pointedly away, but otherwise his trial seemed to have had no effect on his amazing popularity.

Clodia was noticed, too, though less demonstratively. As she passed men fell silent, women stared. When she took her seat people nearby turned to look, and young men found reasons to drift up and down the aisles for a glimpse of her.

She was radiant. The chariot races excited her, her clear voice rang out over the crowd. Under her silk sunshade, her skin glowed, for the day was hot and her excitement made her flush. Her dark eyes followed everything, totally absorbed; she seemed to have forgotten him. All the same, when in the third race the leading chariot began to wobble and the second came up rapidly, she seized his hand and held it in a grip so strong he felt it for a half an hour afterward. She had wagered an enormous sum of money; when she won, her eyes shone and her mouth fell open suddenly, as it did in love. She spent the whole night with him in the little house by the river, and her wildness, her inventiveness, her tireless passion, passed every bound she had set on them before.

In the morning she was awake before him—he thought she had left him and in panic leapt from the bed. She was sitting in the garden under the willow, watching the early boatmen on the river. Her mood of the night before was gone. She did not even turn when he sat down beside her but kept her eyes on the shadows sliding like great speckled fish through the reeds on the bank.

"This is the last time we can meet like this," she said after a pause. Her voice was full of sorrow. "Oh, darling, it's been so lovely. But I must go away—I can't even stay in Rome anymore." Her great eyes gazed tragically into his. "We'll be gone at least a month, and afterward . . ." She waved her hand at the house, the garden, the chuckling river, as if she expected them all to disappear while she was gone.

"But why?" he managed to croak through a throat so dry he thought he would choke.

"It's my husband." She lowered her eyes and her hands pleated the edge of her dress; she watched them as if they belonged to someone else. "He insists. He says that we can't stay in the city while everyone else is in the country. It's too hot, and all the best . . . all the people we know are out of town. Usually we go in April—my husband takes the baths for the pains in his joints"—her lip curled delicately at the thought of this old man's complaint—"but this year we waited because of the election. That's something, isn't it, my darling? At least we've had this time together."

He felt as if he had heard the announcement of his death. He did not doubt that if she were gone for a month or more from Rome she would forget him; he did not blame her or question her love, but he knew there were other people, other interests in her life. One of them would intervene; she would mean to come back, but the time would pass and finally she never would. The day seemed to darken, the river ran by the bank busy with its own affairs, the birds went on singing, heartless as birds painted on a wall.

"Where are you going?"

"Baiae," she said, as if it were India. He scowled at the harmless river. "Surely you know it?" she asked. "It's on the Bay of Naples. We've got a place there, out on the point. Everyone goes there—it's really very nice." She turned back to him. "But I won't like it much this year. How could I, after this?"

He wanted to take her in his arms, but she seemed too far away. "Don't go," he said across the distance. "Stay with me. I love you."

She gave him her beautiful, broken smile. "Oh, darling, I can't. Think of what my husband would say."

He was punishing the river by throwing pebbles into it. The little plop and splash as they fell eased his mind. Calmer, he said, "Then leave him. You don't love him. You love me."

She said sadly, "But the scandal."

"Well, what of it?" he demanded. "I'm not afraid of what people say."

She had turned away; he thought she might be struggling to master some strong emotion, but when she spoke it was gently. "What about my family?" she asked, as if he were a child himself. "A scandal would hurt them. And my brother—he's got a career to make, he needs the support of my husband's friends. And everyone would talk, you know they would. They do already, I don't know why. . . ."

He held her in his arms, leaning her dark head against his chest as if she were the one who needed comforting.

"I wish he were dead, your husband."

She made the sign against ill luck, but she closed her eyes; against his chest he could feel the movement of her head as she nodded.

"I'll come back," she said, but he knew there was no hope.

For three days he did not go out, but sat in his room thinking of her. Rage and pain sawed back and forth in him, cutting him deeply, dividing him from himself. He began to think he might go mad. He made an effort to carry on with his life, going out to look for his friends in the accustomed places, but he could not. He tried to write, but even at night the sleepless city breathed out heat into the humid air. His hand clung to the page, making a little smack when he lifted it; his mind wandered, drifting like the swarms of insects in the lamplight. All he wrote were letters, all to her; impossible, passionate, hungry letters, full of his desire and his pain. He never sent them. He must have been afraid they would fall into her husband's hands.

Around that time, my father, waking like a sleeping lion to the noise of my life in Rome—and my requests for money to support it—wrote that he was sending me to North Africa, to our farms out there. He said it was because I needed the experience of estate management; I knew otherwise. But at least he had arranged to send me with a relative of Pompey's who was going out to a political job, a connection that could only do me good. I was to be this man Quintus Pompeius's assistant, in addition to looking after the farms. I began to pack, not entirely unwillingly; I said good-bye to my friends. I gave Flora a present, rather more lavish than I could afford, for in truth I was already growing a little tired of her. I knew she would talk about my gift to her other men; I wanted it to make the right impression on them. She seemed pleased enough with it, so my mind was at rest.

Still I lingered in the city, unwilling to leave. I told my father I was staying for the elections. He accepted that, saying they were the sort of thing I ought to study, but I spent little time listening to the speeches. I wandered around the city, going to the games when they were on and the theater rather more often, visiting the markets, looking into shops. I did not even bother to stroll down to the Forum when the election results were read, though I heard that Metellus had won, along with several others I had claimed to be interested in.

Slowly the city emptied for the summer. The great houses in the Clivus Victoriae on the Palatine Hill were closed and shuttered, the servants lazed all day in the doorways. The best shops closed or followed their custom to the resorts; the poorer ones put up their shutters as their proprietors went back to their families' farms in the country. The city was given over to emptiness, heat, the cloying river dampness, fever, sewage, and sun. Still I could not leave. The barbershops and taverns where I used to meet my friends were closed or full of strangers; the baths no longer rang with arguments and jokes; the girls had deserted the porticoes of the temples, leaving them to old men nodding in the sun, grinning with toothless malice as I passed. You could have met a ghost as easily at noon as, in the old days, you might have seen one at midnight. So at last I booked my passage and sent my cases to the port.

On the last night Catullus came to see me. I had not seen him in a month; vaguely I imagined that, like the others, he had gone—home to Sirmio, or to one of the house parties at someone's country place. I was glad to see him, in spite of the coolness that had grown up between us. I thought he regretted it, that he missed me; I was prepared, with a little coaxing, to admit that I had missed him—even that I was in part responsible for our estrangement. I should have known him better. He had missed only her. She had been gone some time already, keeping open house for her husband's political cronies in the south. Catullus, sitting in my room, swore when he thought of it.

"She's too good to him," he said, staring moodily into his wine. "She ought to think of herself. . . ."

"She's his wife," I said, annoyed.

He lifted his gray eyes to me. "I know," he answered, laughing a little. "I know."

"Oh, but look," I said, rubbing the bridge of my nose. It was a gesture I had recently acquired, thinking it gave weight to what I said. "You're not being reasonable. What do you expect? You're . . ." I could not say it—even after his rudeness, his abstraction, his lack of appreciation for a beautiful woman. I still liked him, I found; I still cared what happened to him. And perhaps I was still in awe of him as well.

Even though I did not say my thought aloud, he understood. In a month I had forgotten how quickly he could understand. "I'm nobody," he finished for me. "Her lover. Her amusement, her toy. Is that what you mean?"

"I suppose so," I admitted unhappily.

He shook his head. "No. I don't blame you for thinking that; a lot of women in her position have lovers, I suppose, and they're no more than that to them. But you don't understand her—she's different. It's more than that."

"More than what? That you write poems for her? Anyone would. That you love her? She can have a hundred men, a thousand. And some of them could offer her much more than you can."

"Not love. Not love like mine."

I did not answer. I did not need to.

"Well, but listen," he said, but instead of finishing he drank off his wine and poured another cup. "I've got to see her, Caelius."

I could see that he meant that she would forget him if he didn't, and I had to agree.

"But how?" he said once or twice looking into his cup.

I meant to shrug to let him know that I did not think it mattered what he did, that it was a waste of time and money to pursue her, but I could not. He would not have listened, and he might have been angry. Instead I sat silent, and he began to talk about me. He asked how I was; he praised Flora for me, enough to please me, though I think he meant it sincerely enough, for he was never a flatterer; he apologized for his coolness the night of my little party; he sympathized with my unhappiness over leaving Rome, but he said, acutely enough for someone so uninterested in these things, that he thought it would be a good idea to let Rome forget me for a while. "They need to see you as you are," he said. "Now you're only one of the young men who was on the fringes of a disgraced political group. But when you come back all that will be forgotten. You'll be an administrator, a man of proven competence and skill. Believe me, it will make all the difference in your career." He teased me about my attachment to the city, saying the sun of Africa would make me look distinguished, like a bronze statue of a successful general. "The women will go wild, and the men will think you're a real, old-fashioned Roman. What more can you ask?" In the end I was cheered, and faced my departure happier than I had been for some time. And, in the end, I tried to lend him money to go to Baiae. He did not ask for it, I pressed it on him, but he refused anyway, saying he had already written to his brother and arranged to borrow from him. He hadn't; he did that afterward, for I have the letter with its unambiguous date in my hands now, but perhaps I gave him the idea. I don't know why he wouldn't accept money from me—I would have been glad enough to give it to him—but I know that the offer lightened his mood. We spent the rest of the evening very pleasantly, even happily. His mind wandered from the moment only a few times, and his eyes stayed mostly on me.

Baiae was crowded; the little fishing town was thronged with holiday-makers, fingering the goods in the shops, sitting in the restaurants before plates of garlicky shellfish and jars of the local wine, strolling past the brightly painted boats in the harbor. The prices were outrageous—city prices for country goods—but the crowd spent willingly, exclaiming at the simple charm of the clumsy things they bought.

Catullus found a room over a netmaker's shop in the town; it had a balcony that faced the minute harbor—its only merit, for inside it was hot, smelly, and none too clean. He did not mind. He wrote to her, a brief note with his new address; his freedman had instructions to give it only to her. Then he waited, as he had done so often before, sitting on the balcony. This time, instead of his courtyard, he watched the pink and ochre village ripple upside down in the port, while the boats breathed slowly on the water and the crowd passed under his feet.

The very rich had houses along the point of land that embraced the bay—huge places behind high walls, where the lawns ran down to the water under tall trees: from the balcony he could see the jetties of one or two of them and the brightly-colored pleasure boats that plied the waters around them, though he never saw the people who summered in the houses or sunned on the boats. Women from these villas came frequently into the town, carried in their chairs, but Clodia never did. Catullus knew that if her husband wanted her at home she would stay out on the point, behind the wrought iron gates and the sun-warmed wall. Perhaps she would even prefer that to being with him. When he thought of this he ground his teeth and swore.

Though he did not see her, he saw nearly everyone else—it seemed to him that the whole city had migrated south and jammed into this tiny town. Her brother was not there—he had gotten an appointment as a quaestor and gone to take up his new job in Sicily—but many of his friends passed up and down the crowded streets of Baiae. Catullus recognized them from the receptions at her house on the Palatine Hill. There were others, too. At night the expensive prostitutes from the city strolled in the lamplight, to the fury of the local girls, flashing their jewelry and their half-naked breasts at the city businessmen; during the day the village might have been the Roman Forum, crowded with rich men in senators' togas, matrons in covered chairs, well-dressed servants buying in the shops. He watched them all. Once he saw old Hortensius, the lawyer, surrounded by his friends and secretaries, strolling on the quay so close under his balcony that he could have reached down and touched his head; the same day Metellus himself came out of a shop and glanced up and down the street. Catullus ducked behind the door of his room, but it was not necessary— the dazzle of the water was so bright, the shadow of the building so deep, he could not have been seen. Among the crowd outside a fashionable wine merchant's one afternoon he recognized Licinius Calvus and another of Valerius Cato's pupils, a man called Pollio. Catullus and Calvus spent a long day together—the only one on which he forgot for a time his obsession with Clodia—in a rented boat. They sailed out to Capri, that beautiful island just outside the bay that swims like a double-backed dolphin in the summer sea, and that night they got drunk and lay on a beach, splashing like children in the shallow water and telling silly jokes; it was a night like a thunderstorm that breaks, if only for a few hours, the heat and tension of a sweltering day.

Mostly he waited alone. Then, one night, not long after the day he had seen her husband in the town, she appeared without warning in his room. She came alone, though the port was not a place where respectable women went at night. She had no fear: her eyes were wide with excitement, her lips parted as if she had taken a drink. He stared at her. "Darling," she said, leaning her back against his door, "can you believe it? A man just offered me money to go to bed with him."

He was still shocked by the suddenness of her appearance where he had looked for her so long. It took him a moment to understand what she was saying. "Who?" he demanded then, grabbing his knife from the table. "Which one is he?" He went a step toward her to the door.

She laughed aloud and threw her arms against it to prevent his going out, saying, "What difference does it make? I can't tell which one." She was excited and her voice was throaty. Softly she said, "Aren't you glad to see me?" He could see the outline of her body arched backward under her dress, her breasts strained the thin Egyptian cotton. "It was difficult enough to get away." She pouted up at him while her eyes laughed.

He fell on his knees before her and rested his head against the curve of her hip. His cry was muffled against her, an inarticulate compound of desire and happiness. He could feel her hands on him, stroking his hair.

She arched her body farther; he felt the smooth slide of muscle over bone and his breath caught in his throat. His hands went under her dress to her warm skin. He moaned with longing for her. She had spread her legs a little and leaned back into his hands; the mound of dark hair between her thighs thrust forward, parting slightly. He kissed it, running his tongue over the folded, secret flesh.

He could feel her trembling, a fine shudder running through her, and joy rose in him like a tide. He thought he had found again the mystery she represented for him; he thought his little god had rewarded him for his wait. Her body pressed against his face, smelling of salt and a resinous spice like an altar where incense is burned during the sacrifice. He cried his happiness aloud into her, clasping her closer, pressing his mouth to the tiny, aromatic folds.

She was sobbing, cursing him, calling on the gods, saying she loved him over and over; she was pulling him upright so that as he stood his erection slid between her thighs and entered her as she cried out. Shuddering, she cursed him once more. Then she came as he let himself go deeper. The secret took him up like a wave and carried him out into the darkness until he heard her calling him back softly. "Oh, my love, my darling," she whispered. "Oh, I missed you. Oh, my love, my love."

She was standing before him; her dress had fallen around her feet. In the lamplight she was golden; her slender shoulders and thighs were gilded by the light; her mouth, her nipples, the marks of his hands, were as dark as wine; her hair shone like water under a summer moon. She smiled at him with glowing eyes.

"Do you love me?" he demanded proudly, for he knew now he could make her say she did.

"Oh, darling. How can you ask?"

He threatened her, bending his head as if to slide it down her belly and running the tip of his tongue over her skin. His fingers teased the damp and folded flesh between her legs until it rose again stiffly under his hand.

"Oh, yes," she breathed. "Oh, yes, I do."

"Say it," he insisted into the trembling curve of her stomach. He lifted his head to watch her mouth open. "Say it," he cried again, drunk with joy. "Say you love me better than him."

"I love you," she said, looking down at him. "Great Mother, I love you better than anything in my life." She bent her head for his kiss.

> Joyous, oh, my life, you swear our love will be,
> and it will last forever.
> Great gods, make it true, make her words
> sincere and from her soul.
> Grant it all our lives,
> this eternal pledge of sacred love . . .

> Let us live, my Lesbia, and love:
> forget the gossip of old men.
> Suns may rise and set, but rise again;
> for us, night is only one eternal sleep.
> Give me a thousand kisses
> then a hundred, then a thousand more,
> another hundred, or a thousand more;
> when we've kissed ten thousand times
> we'll destroy the sum,
> then no old man can blast us
> with his evil eye.

> Caelius, my Lesbia, that Lesbia
> that dear Lesbia whom Catullus loved
> more than himself and everything he owned . . .

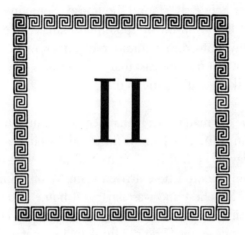

II

The long cold winter has blown itself out in fury and noise while I have been sitting in this little room, writing and remembering. The small bronze god I set on the table before me; his dark eyes have watched me solemnly all these past weeks as my pen has scratched over the endless paper. Perhaps he approves of the work, for I have done more than I expected to—it is easier than I thought it would be, and more absorbing. I feel, in fact, that I have scarcely looked up, though the first slow stirrings of spring have begun outside. When I go out now the sky is clear but harried by small puffy clouds that in turn are chased before the wind; the lake waters dance and sparkle; the low gray herbs that covered the point all winter like musty fur have put out fresh green. Away to the north the mountains rise, visible now but still cold, and to the south the road to Rome is open at last.

I could go home. The winter ruts have dried, and white dust already lies thickly on the road; I can see it hanging in the air for miles behind the carts, themselves invisible in the distance, as they cross the countryside. Letters have come, and boxes of books and clothes and furniture that I have sent for from the city: if they can get through it is proof that I could, too. Yet I make no move to go; I tell myself that nothing prevents it, but it is not true. Something does, as surely as if winter still barred the road. I feel it—at night I hear the city calling me, by the light of the oil lamps beside my bed I see the road open before me, but in the blue dusk of morning I do not go; instead I wander helplessly around the house. Sometimes I stand by the raw newness of the tomb on the point, thinking that my contacts, my career, are falling into dust without me, far away in Rome. At such moments I know that it is the past that still hampers me; memory, and its bright, tangled skein, still tie me to this place.

I expected the old man today: he has been to see me once or twice, for I have been sending him what I am writing. Today would have been his son's thirtieth birthday. If he had lived. If he had lived. The old man did not come, but around noon a note arrived from Verona. Old Catullus had taken a chill to his chest and was staying at home. He would offer the prayers and sacrifice to his household gods for his son. He added that he would sacrifice for me, too. I do not think that even if a god remembered me it would do much good, but I was touched by the old man's gesture and sat for an hour on the point thinking about it after lunch. Around me the place slept—the servants dozed in the house, the bees drowsed in the olive blossoms, the swallows called plaintively in the shadows of the eaves—only I was restless, unable to sleep. Even at night when I lay down my head, the past clamors in my mind, bright-colored, meaningless, and cruel.

The last time the old man appeared was a week ago. He sat on the atrium bench as he had before, his eyes on me, missing nothing. He took in my nervous hands playing with the edge of the rough paper roll, the muscle that twitched under my eye. I wondered what he would make of the story, and for days dreaded his disapproval, his disappointment in his younger son, but all he said was that many young men have had affairs with married women. "The fellow who used to dine here—one of the young Julians," he said stiffly, "used to tell me stories. . . ." His sharp old eyes rested on me. "He said it was the way things were done in Rome nowadays, and a woman of powerful connections was a great help to a young man."

"Yes, sir," I said. "That's true." The young Julian he meant must have been Julius Caesar. He was famous for his affairs, of course, but he was by no means the only one to use them for his advancement. The old man heard the hesitation in my voice.

"You disapprove, Marcus Caelius Rufus? I cannot bring myself to condemn such a young man very much. If a woman will disgrace herself and her family name for the sake of a passing pleasure, or a trivial sense of power, and if her husband will tolerate, not to say encourage, such behavior by helping her lover, young men will naturally take advantage of such a situation. It is wrong, but the wrong has been done in so many places that I cannot fix all the blame on the boy."

"Well, sir," I said, for I believe I am a tolerant man, "she was very beautiful. And I believe that his love for her was sincere."

"That should make no difference."

"No, sir."

He said nothing further except to remark that in what I wrote I had plainly imagined much of what I was telling him.

"Yes, sir," I agreed, thinking it rude to disagree so often. "Though perhaps not as much as you think. The notebooks are very frank, very detailed. They are like letters, strange ones, to himself . . . and there are real letters, too, to his brother, to Calvus, to her, in which he explains. He was a vivid writer: in a few words he makes you see everything. And, of course, they are places I *know*, and people. . . . I have not *invented* anything, though I have perhaps filled in from my imagination a little— you know the way one does—to make a story clear to oneself. I am telling the truth all the same."

He said, "Yes, I see. I believe you," and his black eyes were sharp with comprehension, but he said nothing further. I have sent him the last roll by the servant who came just now with the note, and am sitting again in my little room, the box open at my feet, my pens and paper spread out on the little table, and the past is pulling me back into its mystery and color once again.

He sacrificed everything for her. Like most young men in Rome he had been ambitious, and since he was a patrician his ambition had been for political office. Business and banking were both closed to him—though nowadays many patricians involve themselves secretly with such enter- prises, choosing knights like my own father to represent them on the boards of the various enterprises they direct anyway—but Catullus, with his wit and his talent for invective, had seen that his way was the traditional one, through the law courts to the magistracies and from them to the glory of the highest offices our country can bestow. It was for that glory that he had come to Rome, for it he had studied the ancient writers with such diligence—and made me study them, too—for glory he had become the pupil of Valerius Cato, the critic, as I had been the pupil of Cicero, the practical advocate. He gave them all up when Clodia loved him; he closed his books and never looked at them again, as a man packs away the clothes and furnishings he will not need on a journey he plans to take.

He kept his books of poetry, for they seemed to speak to him of the country into which he was traveling; though in the end, as all the world now knows, they did not take him far enough, and he had to go on alone. For myself, I do not know why he wanted to go on—there was neither happiness nor glory on his road. It was a journey, but a meaningless one, a march in appalling conditions, but a march to conquer only a waste, a desert, a tract of land so barren and harsh no one would want to go there. . . . It is all meaningless: his life from beginning to end makes no sense at all, though it is certainly painful enough. Depressed, I sit and puzzle about it night after night, trying to find some significance, trying to find, in fact, a pattern—any pattern—to explain why he was willing to go on. To do all that for a woman . . . I cannot understand it. I am wasting my time. If it weren't for the old man with his pitiable grief I would have left here long ago, gone back to Rome and the real and important things that await a man there.

For nearly a year he was happy. He met her often in the garden she owned across the river in the Tiburtine district. There, under huge feathery plane trees, flowering bushes which had come over the passes from India soaked the air with their foreign perfumes. Birds sang in cages or in the trees; the lawns went down to the river where she kept brightly painted boats, and musicians to play on them and young men with voices as pure as the birds' to sing as they floated down the stream.

Sometimes there were parties there in the months her husband was away. There were lights in the trees then, and silk couches among the flowers, and poetry and dancing, and games with kisses for prizes. She was generous—there were other prizes, too: his rooms in the apartment building in the Subura began to look like a shop, crowded with silver statues, painted cups, books rolled in white leather, wreaths with gold ribbons as thin as real ones. . . . I do not know what became of these objects—perhaps he sold them, later, after the music faded and the flowers died—for there is no sign of them in the box his father gave me. But they were in his rooms; I saw them myself not long afterward, each one a treasure, each as beautiful and elegant as she was, and the life they led together that summer and bursting autumn under the trees.

I did not see him during that time, of course. I was away myself, in Africa. But Licinius Calvus wrote to me, a letter that I read with a vague disquiet I did not stop to examine. He was worried, he said. Catullus had disappeared from the places he had frequented in the city; he had done no work; he scarcely wrote poetry anymore. Calvus had gone several times to Subura, but Catullus was first at her gardens in the Tiburtine, then at her house in Baiae with a house party she had there, and Calvus never saw him. I meant to answer that letter, and to write to Catullus, but I was busy with our estates and the social life, such as it was, of the colony, and I never did.

There were others who wrote uneasily, too. Catullus's brother Quintus, four years older, on his way to Asia Minor where he had an appointment in the administration of the governor of Bithynia, tried in vain to see him to say good-bye. His letter, bewildered and sincere, is among the papers the old man gave me. In view of what happened, I consider it the most painful document of all.

QUINTUS VALERIUS CATULLUS
TO GAIUS VALERIUS CATULLUS
BRINDISI, THE KALENDS OF SEPTEMBER
694 YEARS FROM THE FOUNDING OF
THE CITY
My dear brother, I came by your house to see you on my way south, as I wrote last month, to join my governor in Bithynia. Did you not receive my letter? I sent it by a most reliable man. I had hoped for one last glimpse of you. I was there at the appointed time, and I waited as long as I could. It must be that you never got my letter. Please write, my dear brother. I embrace you from Asia. Be well.

This letter is crumpled and stained, as if someone had tried at one time to destroy it but changed his mind. The thing is, of course, that the earlier note is there, too, the one that fixed the meeting. He had simply ignored it, or forgotten it.

The reason isn't far to seek. By then, by the first of September of the year Metellus was consul, Catullus had begun to believe that Clodia was unfaithful to him.

One evening, passing her house, he had seen a chair waiting in the alley. The porters had spoken some dialect or language he did not know—when he tried them in Greek and Latin they shook their heads dumbly and he could not find out whose chair it was. It was clearly a man's, for there were no cushions and the curtains were of plain, cream-colored wool. It sat unobtrusively just past the bend in the wall, hidden from the casual eye in the evening shadows; if he had not actually been in the alleyway he would not have seen it himself. As long as he could he waited, but no one came out and he did not like to stand there so long he might attract attention. He did not want anyone in the house to think he was spying on her.

On the exercise ground in the Campus Martius the next day he heard a fat senator puffing between knee bends say that she was going to divorce her husband and marry someone else—an ex-consul, he said with a wink—too important to name. In fact, he added, wiping the sweat from a face as round and red as the setting sun, she had already left for Sicily where her new lover had a house. Hearing this, Catullus threw the javelin he was practicing with so wide he barely missed a young man, and had to apologize before he could get out into the open street.

It could not have been true, for two days later he received an invitation to a party at her house across the river, and it asked him, charmingly, as usual, if there was anything he could read to them. Though he reread the note four times he could find nothing in it different from any of the hundreds of others she had sent to him over the last eighteen months. In any case it was in her own handwriting; she could not have sent it if she had not been in Rome.

Then, the night before her party, he saw the chair at her house again. This time he followed it, for it was occupied, though the porters carried no torches and the curtains were drawn. It swayed through the nighttime streets to the foot of the Caelian Hill where it stopped before a big house with bronze doors under a half-moon colonnade. He waited in the shadows expecting to see a man descend, but when the curtains were drawn back it was by a woman's hand, and a moment later a figure in a black cloak ducked under the columns into a door that stood open to receive it. It was Clodia. He was sure of it; he could not have mistaken her for anyone else in the world. In the tavern down the street they told him the house belonged to a Spaniard who had only recently moved in. They did not know his name as his servants spoke no Latin—in the shops of the quarter they indicated what they wanted by pointing to it, and they paid without even asking the price.

He stayed in the tavern until it closed, drinking silently and steadily while he watched the street through the bead-hung doorway, but the chair did not pass again.

That night he could not sleep, but lay on his bed, sweating and cursing like a man in a fever. He was so new to suffering that he did not even know why he ached, why the bed was as hot as coals, his head as stuffy and at the same time as light as a cushion. He thought he was ill—once in the night he roused his servant and sent him to buy beer in case he was.

He could not think of another reason for his uneasiness. He believed he had given her the benefit of the doubt—he was ashamed of having followed her, and he made a hundred excuses to himself, a thousand reasons why she might have gone, alone and evidently in secret, to a stranger's house. Yet he tossed and his eyes burned, his shoulders throbbed as if he had been beaten, while the sweat poured off him and soaked the sheets. At last the sun rose, thrusting the September heat down over the city with an iron hand, giving him, at last, a reason for his misery. It calmed him a little and he got up and dressed. By evening when he presented himself, bathed, shaved, and dressed again, at the summer house in the gardens, he had told himself, with fair success, that he had imagined it all. She was the same as she had always been, she loved him, there was an explanation, he must not be too quick to judge.

He found the party in the garden, lying on silk cushions under the trees where the jasmine flowered. A series of basins caught the jets of falling water with different musical notes; the river ran by humming plaintively; over the bridges the lights of the city glowed against the dusk. There was lamplight through pierced lanterns like the shadows of leaves over the bodies on the grass; when he approached she stood up in a rustle of silk and gave him her cheek for a kiss, gazing as always into his eyes with her sad, cloudy, ambiguous smile. In the moment he was allowed by custom for this kiss he felt her body against him, firm and flexible as it had always been, and smelled her warm, familiar scent. "I love you," he whispered as she stepped back. Her smile deepened and in her low voice she said, "I love you, too."

But there were others there—he had to join them: young men, some of whom he knew, and women in dresses as full of movement as liquids, with jewels at their necks and ears. She was more beautiful than any of them, and wittier, and kinder. They ate and drank as the night around them deepened and the lights of the city went out; the stars overhead blossomed as whitely as the jasmine under the trees. The man next to him turned and introduced himself. "Egnatius Rufus," he said, smiling through his thick beard. "From Spain."

The food was cleared away, the wreaths and the wine were brought. He set the circle of flowers on his head, hardly knowing what he did; he drank without mixing his wine with water, as if to put out a fire inside him. She was talking with a young man near her—a rich, rather dissolute creature named Ravidius, with an earring in one ear that flashed as he talked. She put back her smooth black head and laughed.

Someone called on him for a poem; scowling, he refused. Then there was music, and one of the women began to dance in the open space among the cushions where the dinner tables had been. Her dress clung to her breasts and thighs; her arms snaked whitely in the dappled lamplight as the music throbbed with desire. Then they were all dancing, a long swirl of color and movement over the lawn. Up ahead he could see Clodia's black hair fly as she danced between two men he did not know; he tried to move closer to her, but there were too many in his way. They laughed as he stumbled and tripped among them, and someone pulled him back into the line.

The white-armed woman had bared her equally white torso, and her bouncing breasts gleamed with sweat. All along the line men were taking off their togas to move freely in their tunics. The music was louder and faster. Catullus, still trying to get to Clodia, staggered, and a woman in the line beside him held him up. Her face leaned over him, panting and gross, as she spoke some unintelligible word. For a moment his head cleared and he knew he was very drunk. He shook his head and threw himself back into the dance.

The line was broken: a few dancers remained, circling the white-armed woman who could do strange things with her belly and hips while her bare feet did not move at all on the grass. Here and there on cushions panting men drank to cool themselves as they called out to her. He looked for Clodia, but she was gone. So were the young man with the earring, and the Spaniard, and several other men and women.

Near dawn, he went home. Trembling and sick, he stopped frequently to rest against the walls; at a public fountain he drank deeply to cool his violent thirst, but it only made him drunk and sick again, and he had to sit with his head on his knees until the street steadied and he could walk. He had not seen her again, though he had wandered in the whispering dark for hours. Now, filthy and ill, he climbed the steps to his apartment, where it waited, full of the grateful coolness of the morning breeze and the soft, wet breath of the river.

She invited him to dinner, sending a note as if nothing had happened. He ground his teeth in rage, but he went to the party.

Her husband was there—there was less drinking and no dancing at all, only some Persian musicians during dinner and a rhetor reciting Homer afterward. The talk was mostly of politics and polite rather than animated, for they were a mixed group of men from various factions and parties in the city. Cicero was there, as conservative as Metellus but much wittier; Julius Caesar reclined on a couch with another representative of the popular faction and a stiff young man from Cato's following who obviously expected to see great wickedness at Metellus's rather ordinary tables. Egnatius the Spaniard smiled at Catullus from the couch, but he turned away. One or two of the guests were interested in poetry and knew Catullus; after dinner they asked him to recite. So under Metellus's cool, uncomprehending stare he stood up, glancing once at her.

> Egnatius, who has white teeth,
> smiles eternally.
> If people come to the prisoner's dock
> when the counsel for defense has everyone in tears—
> he smiles.
> If they're weeping at the funeral of a dear son

when the distraught mother is sobbing for her boy—
he smiles.
It's a disease.
Here's a bit of advice, my good friend:
If you were a Roman, or a Sabine, or a Tiburtine,
or a pig of an Umbrian, or a fat Etruscan
or a black Lanuvian, or a Gaul like me,
or anybody, anybody at all
who washes his teeth in clean water,
it would still be a disease,
this smiling eternally.
But you're a Spaniard, and it's worse for you:
In your country, as everybody knows,
they wash their white, white teeth
in the filth they drink.

Everyone laughed, even Metellus, and, after a moment, the black-bearded Spaniard as well. Catullus saw Clodia raise her eyebrows to her husband, then heard her voice chime in with the others. "Darling," she called to Catullus. "That was very funny, but it wasn't kind. Read us something about someone else, someone who isn't here, whose feelings won't be hurt."

"Very well," he said, hearing her call him "darling" and going very white around the jaw. "A poem to my girl. Her feelings can't be hurt." He saw her eyes go blank, but Metellus nodded seriously and said, "Ah, the mysterious Lesbia. My wife's right—read us a poem to her."

He bowed to Metellus, then to Clodia.

Was it a lioness
from flinty Libya
or six-headed Scylla,
the man-eater,
barking from her belt
that bore you,
lewd, disgusting, cruel . . . ?

He saw the color wash into her face and her hands clenched once on the arms of her chair. She turned her great eyes on him; he knew she was angry, and that she feared what he might say, but her head was high and she had forced her lips into a smile. A wave of pity and admiration for her went through him and he said in a choking voice:

> How can you mock a loving man
> who only breaks himself
> upon your stony heart?

They were applauding, and Metellus was saying, "That's much more like it." Catullus caught Julius Caesar looking oddly at him out of the corner of his eye, and the Spaniard grinning uncertainly, but his attention was all on her. She stared at him, open-eyed, then, looking back at her husband, raised her chin and said, "You were right, my dear. That was much better." The rhetor came in with his roll of Homer, and Catullus took his place on his couch, but he was still shaking with emotion, and at the earliest opportunity he made his excuses and went home.

He learned the names of all the men who had been at the garden party. It took him some time for the party had been large, but one of the women, the daughter of a freed slave who earned her living at parties like that, was willing to help. It cost him a good sum of money, which he had to borrow from his brother, for the woman did not part with her secrets easily. But when it was done, he had a list. Then he began to write.

> Whorehouse tavern, and you band of friends
> at the ninth pillar from the Brothers in the Hats
> do you think you're the only ones with pricks,
> the only ones allowed to do the girls?
> That everyone else stinks like a goat?
> Line up, then, a hundred,
> two hundred, more, stupid, on your chairs—
> do you think I can't screw you all myself?
> where you sit? on one bench?
> Believe it, for I'll put the names on the tavern wall:
> my girl, gone from my arms,
> lives there with you now,
> though I loved her as no woman has been loved.

Well, you all love her too, rich men, men of rank—
even, to her shame, you little creeping lechers
and you, long-haired son of rabbity Iberia,
with such a lovely beard
and teeth you brush with Spanish piss.

I swear—may the gods love me—
it didn't matter if you smelled
Aemilius's mouth or his behind;
one is as filthy as the other.
No, I'm wrong.
at least his asshole has no teeth.
In his mouth they're two feet long
with gums like a cart frame,
gaping like the cunt of a pissing mule in summer.
He chases women, and pretends to charm:
why hasn't he been mated with the mill wheel jenny?
Any woman who'd touch him—don't you think?—
would lick the asshole
of a public executioner.

What can I say, Gellius, about why
that pink mouth is paler than snow
when you get up in the morning,
when you wake from your soft sleep
in the middle of the day?
I don't know: is the rumor true
that you dine at noon on a boy's big thing?
I do know this: poor Victor's exhausted haunches
prove your meal—
that and the snow
around your lips.

When these poems got around—and he took care that they did—there was talk. An insult is always appreciated in Rome, but these went further than anyone had gone before. And they were funny. Everyone laughed at them, even where the names were disguised; there is no keeping a thing like that secret in the city, and they knew who was meant. Vatinius, Gellius, Aemilius, and several others had to swallow a heavy dose of mockery, and they were angry. Gellius particularly suffered since he had been a friend of Catullus's. He went so far as to complain, but Catullus, eyes burning with anger, laughed at him and threw him out of his apartment.

> *Gellius is slender: why not?*
> *He has a loving lusty mother*
> *and a sister*
> *and an uncle he devours—*
> *he eats girls everywhere,*
> *why shouldn't he be thin?*
> *Even if he swallowed only what he should*
> *there'd still be reasons he'd be lean.*

Poor Gellius tried everything, for there were several other poems of this nature about him circulating in the baths and taverns, and even in the Forum. He asked Ravidius to intercede for him, since Ravidius was so far unscathed—a mistake, as another poem proved:

> *What insane infatuation, miserable Ravidius,*
> *drives you to impale yourself*
> *on the points of my verse?*
> *Did you offend some god?*
> *Do you want to hear your name in everybody's mouth?*
> *What do you want?*
> *Is it fame at any price?*
> *Well, you'll get it, since you've chosen*
> *to love my girl.*
> *But you'll pay.*

He even wrote to me, poor bewildered Gellius did, saying, "But what did I do? I thought he was my friend. Is he insane? He looked crazy enough, Caelius, really he did. You should have seen his eyes." Concerned myself, I sent off a letter to Catullus asking what was wrong. I got no answer, but Gellius did.

I hoped, Gellius, that you would be faithful
at least to me
in this miserable, this ruinous, love of mine—
not that I didn't know you
or thought that you were anything but base—
but because she whose love was burning me
was neither your mother nor your sister.
I thought she would be safe.
I was your friend,
but there's no love too sacred,
    or too vile,
for a man like you.

The poems are full of rage, but the notebooks show something else
again. He suffered agonies of pain and longing. At night it was especially
terrible, for then he was unable to prevent himself from thinking of her.
She seemed to be there with him: he felt her arms around him, her soft
warmth against him, her mouth pressed sadly on his own. He held her
gently, cradled by her, safe and sweet, he made love to her in joyful release,
and felt his heart join hers in happiness. From these dreams he awoke to an
emptiness and silence so unendurable he thrashed his head back and forth
on the couch until he cried. Then, exhausted, he dragged himself from his
bed and staggered out into the street. There he wandered, drinking heavily,
until the rage came back to fill him, and he could face his empty room
again.

I hate and I love.
You ask how this can be?
I do not know: but I feel it
and I am crucified.

This poem he did not circulate, but left in his notebook, alone on a
clean tablet as if it stood for everything he felt.

At last she had to notice. She sent her brother, for her husband was still
in the city and would not have allowed her to go out alone; Clodius,
glittering with his own anger, led him, over his objections, to her house.

It was a day of rain, the first of the autumn showers, though this was driven on the winds from North Africa. The dirt and heat of that continent had been swept up in it as it came and the rain fell with cloying warmth and stickiness now, blindingly, leaving muddy traces on the buildings everywhere it touched, like dirty tears. The drumming of its fall enveloped him; there was no chance to speak, and he followed his guide through the grayness hearing only the footsteps of the small man in front of him, the clatter of water over stones. His mind was blank and felt as dirty as the air; the shadowless drabness of the streets offered him no thought, no image, no idea.

When Clodius began his attack, he did not listen. He stood easily, looking around the atrium of her big house, but except for the two of them it was empty. Rain fell through the opening in the roof into the pool with a hiss like steam condensing in a bathhouse pool. Thick heat clung to him like a panting animal; the dullness of the day had seeped in here, wreathing the corners of the room in mist, hiding the paintings on the walls, the household altar, the curtain over the doorway to the back. He felt slow and stupid, as if he were not really there.

". . . an upstart provincial like you?" Clodius was saying when he finally heard. His rage was scalding, every curse and threat from the lowest life of the city was in it; the elegant, many-pillared atrium rang like a soldiers' training ground. ". . . think we can do nothing about this? You forget who we are . . ." and again, more fiercely than he had ever heard anyone speak before, "Listen to me, you fool." Then the small man was standing in front of him, challenging and dangerous. His hands were on his hips, so that his brilliantly white toga had fallen back and the hilt of his silver-chased knife was visible in the belt of his tunic. ". . . do not lie down under insults," he was shouting. Over his head Catullus searched the thickened air, ignoring Clodius's noise.

"Look at me," Clodius said, stepping closer. Catullus could smell the wine on his breath, see the hard glitter of his eyes, so like hers under the same white brow. His own anger kindled and burst into flame.

"I'll talk to your sister," he said through his teeth. "Not to you." His face was hot, his hands sweating. He had to force his breath out into the clogging air.

"Oh, no you won't. You'll listen to me, you stupid bastard. You'll . . ."

"No. I won't."

Clodius's face went red. "By the gods, you will," he muttered, moving so quickly he seemed to flash in the murk. The knife glinted; he crouched, holding the point upward in his crossed hands; his eyes narrowed, his mouth opened in fury.

"Hah," Catullus shouted, suddenly freed from his lethargy. He threw back his head and laughed. "Where are your friends, Clodius?" he shouted happily. "You think you can take me alone?"

"Come on, you little cocksucker."

And Catullus, caught up in the rising flame of his own anger, plunged toward him, reaching for the hand with the thin, gleaming blade.

They were shouting, lurching together over the damp stones. A pillar crashed into his back, knocking the wind from him: the pain startled him, adding fuel to his anger; he could feel Clodius writhe against him, hard and dangerous. Something like joy lifted him. He thrust his free hand, fingers stiff, toward Clodius's eyes.

"Just what is going on here?"

The cool voice cut through the heavy gray-green air like a splash of icy water. He lifted his head. Clodius gave a quick wiggle and was free, panting noisily in the heat.

She stood on the step from the back of the house, very white and still against the swampy colors of the hanging behind her. Her black eyes looked like bits of jet in her face. Catullus caught his breath and stared back at her.

"I'll take care of this," Clodius said, picking up his toga and draping it awkwardly around him. "Don't bother yourself over this madman. He's just going to apologize and get out."

She was still looking at Catullus. "No," she said without turning her head. "I know him. He won't go now that he's here."

"No," said Catullus. "I won't go."

She was more vulnerable in her icy mask than she wanted him to know; he could see the tremor of a vein in her throat, the rise and fall of her breasts. "What do you want?" she demanded coldly. "What are you after?"

"Don't give him anything," her brother said from the other side of the pool. "There are easy enough ways to shut him up." He had put away the knife, but he was still angry; it showed in his short, jerky steps as he paced. "Let me call some men. . . ."

"Do you want money?" she asked. "Is that it?"

"No," Catullus said. "Do you?"

He heard Clodius gasp on the other side of the pool, and he saw her go whiter than before, but she must have signaled to him, because he made no other sound. "No," she said coolly. "I want you to leave me and my friends alone."

"Your friends?" he demanded, raising her eyebrows. "Your lovers, you mean."

"I'll kill him here," Clodius shouted, leaping into the pool and wading through it in the rain.

Without turning around, Catullus said, "I left word where I was going." He spoke calmly, but the back of his neck was clammy with sweat.

She lifted her head and said across him to her brother, "He's going now. Leave him. There are other ways." The hanging fluttered once and hissed on its rings as she disappeared as invisibly as she had come. Catullus turned slowly and looked at her brother, who stood staring at him knee-deep in muddy water, his hair dripping dirty rain into his hot black eyes.

"I'm going," Catullus said. He was trembling, not with fear of the small man so ludicrously wet in the pool, but with his effort to suppress his pain at the sight of her. He had to hurry to reach the street before tears rose as far as his eyes and swamped him with their scalding flow.

> Miserable Catullus,
> born too soft,
> you know she's lost.
> Once the sun shone brightly on you
> you went where your lady led,
> you loved as no one ever has.
> Then there were joys, as many as wheat stalks in a field.
> Truly, the sun shone on you.
> Now no more—
> she wants you no more
> and you, poor madman,
> must want nothing, too.
> Don't follow her,
> don't cry,

learn to be a stone.
  Endure.
Farewell, my lady.
Now Catullus stands like a rock:
he will not follow you against your will.
Ah, cruel one.
But you will feel it,
when you've no one else:
what life is there for you?
Whom will you see?
Whom will say you're beautiful?
Whom will you love?
By whose name will you be called?
Whom will you kiss?
Whose lips nibble in your joy in love?
And you, Catullus.
  Learn to be a stone.

He did not expect to see her again; he had given up his only weapon against her—his poems—and thought she had forgotten him. His weeks of anger had passed, leaving him prey to a pain so intense he felt broken under it, and he sat all day, unshaven and sour, afraid to move for fear of making it worse. He had not written: if she thought it was because of her threats, he could not help it. The empty paper mocked him, but he could not force himself to write, and after a while he ceased to care.

I really think he was close to madness at that point. He had lost so much weight that people said his skin looked transparent and his bones showed through at his shoulders and his wrists. His cheeks were hollow; he had a persistent sore at the corner of his mouth; there was something unfocused in his eyes, as if he were looking at something no one else could see.

He was tormented by dreams and images so loathsome he hated them, so fascinating he could not leave them alone. Awake or asleep, he saw her all the time now, raising her face under the dappled lamplight to kiss a mouth in a thick, black beard, twisting her body whitely under the weight of anonymous men, avid-eyed, wet-mouthed, her thighs open and gleaming with their sweat. He saw the men, exhausted, fall away from her, and still she continued to demand their substance and their strength, still she fed on them, thrusting them aside when she was finished. He saw the men, white and drained, as if it had been their blood she had sucked; he saw her as she lay on the dark grass, bloated and glistening, amid a heap of bodies, demanding more. Perhaps he even called up these images, perhaps he hoped they would cure him, as a man hopes by taking poison to ease a fever, though his ears clamor and his joints shriek from the dose. . . .

She came to see him. In the soft, clear, oblique light of an October morning that edged every object in its path with gold and hazed the long black shadows with a film of blue and violet, she stood in the doorway of his room, unspeaking, alone, her smooth head bent, and her hands clasped.

"Are you ill?" she said after they had stared at each other for some time. She sounded as if she were not sure that she should speak.

"No." His voice was cracked and harsh, as if it had rusted in his throat from disuse.

A shaft of sunlight fell across her dress, sculpting the folds; it revealed her arm coming out of shadow and her finger tracing a line back and forth along the edge of the table. Her plain, old-fashioned iron wedding ring marked her knuckle with a band of black.

"What do you want?" he demanded, and his voice seemed to him to shatter as he spoke.

Out of the indigo shade she said hesitantly, "You must stop writing those poems about me. You must. I have come to ask you . . . to tell you . . . you are wrong about me."

"Am I?" A little flame of his old anger rose up in him from the ashes of his feeling for her.

She turned her head slowly toward him. The sunlight caught her earlobe, making it glow suddenly translucent red; it glanced sharply off her crystal earring, lay golden along her cheek, shone into the hollow of her eye, where the white gleamed bluely and the rim glittered with tears. The flame in him died. "Yes," she said. "You really are."

He had crossed the bright space between them and was holding her in his arms. He could feel the little sigh that shook her against him; where her tears fell there was a cold patch on his tunic. "I was never unfaithful to you," she murmured against him.

He held her tighter to him. "It doesn't matter." His own eyes stung with tears; he pulled her convulsively closer. Presently he felt her body distinguish itself into parts against him; the plane of her shoulder, the knots of bone along her spine, the soft swell of her breast. Her mouth was slippery and hot with sweat.

He lifted her and carried her to his bed. "It's true," she said, looking up at him like a frightened child.

"I believe you," he said happily. Outside, voices drifted to them from the courtyard like the cries of birds; on the last warm breath of the year the scent of the damp and fruitful earth mingled in the quiet room with their sweat and laughter.

Even as I write this, I doubt it. I cannot bring myself to believe that he was weak enough to forgive her, to ignore what she had done. Here in the arbor on the point, everything gives it the lie. The sunshine rejects it, the dancing shadows of the new spring leaves flinch away from such unhealthiness. Even the lake laughs at him, sending up sparks of derision. The grape arbor puts out its hard green berries in mockery, for he planted it. He dug the root-twisted soil himself, carrying the clay jars of water to the growing shoots, tying them to the wicker hoops with a peasant's patience and a countryman's durable hope. It was not the act of a man so tangled in love and weakness that he went back to her.

Yet there it is, the proof, the poems, the words. He disguised himself behind another name, but he is there. It doesn't take much to see "Valerius" behind "Volusius," and Clodia's pure, cold face behind "my love."

> Poems of Volusius,
> good for nothing but wiping your behind,
> pay a vow for my love:
> to Holy Venus and her sacred son,
> she swore
> if I came back to her
> and ceased to hurl my verse
> she would give Vulcan, the limping god,
> the best lines of the worst of poets
> to burn on the fire of a barren tree.
> A pretty joke she thought she was making,
> but, all the same—here they are.
> Now, Venus, Born of the Sea
> Haunter of Holy Ida and of Urii,

of Ancona, reedy Cnidos, all the places
sacred to your name,
record the debt as paid—
it was an elegant vow, and a suitable one.
Meantime, limp here to the fire
broken-footed, rustic lines,
poems of Volusius,
toilet paper.

So he burned his poems—how many? I wonder—and went back to her, and I cannot dispute the fact that he did, though I do not understand why.

"It was weakness," the old man says, sitting straight-backed as a judge on a chair I have brought out under the arbor for him. He is more fragile now in the first bright sunshine than in the winter cold: his old voice creaks like a beetle's, and his ancient flesh is as thin and scaly as a snake's. But his eyes are still the same pointed, painful instruments they were before.

"Was it, sir?" I say, depressed in the laughing sunlight.

"What else?" he demands, but I have heard, under his harsh, elderly judgment, that it is truly a question, and he wants to know.

"Well, sir," I say, looking out over the point where the wild gentians nod, as blue as what is visible of the lake amid the feathery fennel and the early green of the thyme. "I have been thinking about this for some time, and I think, I believe, that it was simply that nothing else was quite real to him by then."

He straightens his thin lips into a hard blue line. "Of course nothing was. He had abandoned everything else: career, family, friends, study. In a life so deprived, naturally she would matter. But it is not the life of a man, to tie all his hopes, his dreams, to a woman. It is . . ."

"Dangerous?"

"Childish," he snaps. But his fragile temples beat with a pulse under his neat white hair and his wrinkled eyelids have closed in pain over his sharp black eyes.

Childish . . . perhaps it was. But I cannot help thinking there was something magnificent in it, something noble. In a way he was like our ancestors, the men who founded our city—not that they would have recognized it, for they felt as little for love as he did for political life, and no more than his father would they have understood his obsession with a woman. But he was like them all the same. He had their courage, their obstinate certainty of right, their single-mindedness; absorbed entirely in his destination, like them he took no thought for himself, and threw himself away after what he wanted. It may have been childish, but it was Roman. And now it was worse; he kept nothing back: he gave himself more violently to his love than before. He was like the fields that produce more beautifully after the frost, putting out in hectic brilliance the fruit, the grain, the flowers of a waning year; for like the fields, he had felt the icy touch of the god's breath that whispers, "You see? Nothing will last forever."

> If anyone ever got
> what he wanted so desperately,
> never dared hope for—
> that's sunshine to the soul
> more treasured than gold.
> That joyous light has fallen on me also,
> Lesbia, now that you have come back to me
> who loves you without hope.
> Yes, you gave yourself back to me.
> Oh, blessed day, oh, festival,
> mark it in the annals with a whitened stone:
> nothing that lives is luckier than I am.
> Who can name fortune in life better than this?

Another day: she had sent him a message—her husband would be at an all-night political meeting; if Catullus wanted, he might come to her. She enclosed a key to the low door in the alley.

It was cold; the early-November night fell as deeply as the dead of winter, the torchlight ripped and tore in the cutting wind, illuminating now a wall, now the face of a passerby, now the stones of the street. Overhead the stars blinked brightly in the rushing air. He sent his servant home and walked quickly through the noisy dark alone, enjoying the turbulence. A maid, bundled against the cold, led him through the garden where the bare branches rattled and the dead leaves scuttled across the paths like crabs on a deserted beach.

Inside the house he followed her dark, anonymous figure over marble floors as slippery and cold as glacial ice. Wrapped in his cloak, he saw little of the rooms they passed until they stood before a heavy curtain. The maid lifted it, pushed open the door behind it, and stood aside; the curtain dropped behind him with a hiss.

He was in her room, a space like the inside of a rose. It smelled of honey from the tall candles in the corners; on the walls woven hangings showed glimpses of fat pink Cupids, rosy goddesses, saffron-colored clouds; the ceiling was carved and painted with fruit and flowers in long garlands of gilt and lavender and mauve. Over the great black-and-silver bed someone had thrown a coverlet—it was worked with scenes from mythology: he recognized the marriage of the sea nymph Thetis with the mortal Peleus and touched it once, for luck. A tiny draft, all that remained of the violent wind outside, brushed an alabaster bottle on the dressing table, making it ring with a clear note in the warm silence. When he lifted the lid the scent of oriental flowers was released into the room.

He had time to notice all these things; she kept him waiting for over an hour. He sat stiffly on a chair with a silk cushion the whole time, for there was nothing to read in the room, and he did not like to lie down on the bed.

At last there were footsteps outside, running, then slowing to a walk; a woman's voice hurled a word in passing to the servant at the door. Then she was inside; she threw herself into his arms so suddenly he was startled. A draft of chilly air swirled into the room behind her.

He kissed her: the edge of her hair where it grew from her forehead was cold to his lips; her earlobes and fingertips were as icy as marble. "Why are you so cold?" he whispered. "Have you been out?"

"Out?" she asked uncertainly. "Why should I have been out?"

"I don't know," he said, smiling. "You tell me. I thought you wanted to see me—you sent for me. . . ."

She was crying; the astonishing realization came over him, and he lifted her chin in his fingertips. Her huge eyes swam with tears. Her mouth fell open like a child's. "My dear," she said. "He hit me."

He forgot everything else and stood rigid, staring at her. "Hit you? Who?"

"My husband."

He could say nothing, he was slow to take it in. He watched as she threw herself into the ivory chair in front of the dressing table and, looking into the mirror with unconscious criticism, began to pull at the intricate braiding of her hair. "When?" he asked stupidly, coming to stand behind her chair.

"Just now, as he was going out the door. I told you he has a meeting tonight. . . ."

He was not interested in the meeting. "You must divorce him," he cried.

"Oh," she said mournfully to his face in the mirror. "If only I could."

"Why not?" he murmured, bending forward to kiss her hair as it fell from her stilled hands. "People get divorced every day, and if you told him you wanted one, asked him. . . ."

Her eyes flashed at him. "I wouldn't ask him for anything."

"No," he said, sadly. Then, brightening, "You could leave him. Surely he would divorce you if you left him."

"Not Metellus. He wouldn't stand for the scandal. You don't know him, how old-fashioned he is, how strict. He would make such a fuss, you can't imagine. My brothers' careers. He would tell everyone about you. . . ."

He said carefully, his heart pounding, "You could tell him you wanted to marry me."

Her small face opened suddenly like a flower in the sun. "Oh, darling, do you really mean it?"

He slid his hands down from her shoulders, holding her against him while he looked steadily into her eyes in the mirror. "Yes."

The chair fell over with a crash that neither of them heard, for she had stood up and pressed herself into his arms. She was murmuring, a sound like the sea in summer, meaningless and happy; he could feel the vibration running through him as he pulled her shoulders to his chest and put his mouth down on hers.

The candles had burned down, except for one, like a child's night-light, glowing softly in a small alabaster bowl of water. A draft touched it, and small reflections of ripples shook across the painted ceiling, the naked arms of the goddesses seemed to writhe on the walls. "Why did he hit you?" he whispered. "What was he angry about?"

"Let's not talk about him. Tell me about marrying you."

He ran his hand along her back exploring the strong muscles, the tiny knobs of bone, the deep hollow below her waist.

"When you are free," he began, but she said sadly, "I will never be free of him." He was going to speak again, but she went on. "My father bound me to him in the most ancient and strict of all the forms of marriage: my husband owns me like the furniture of his house, like a racehorse, like a slave. My father said the dignity of the Claudians required nothing less. He signed away my rights—even my dowry belongs to my husband, and he could keep it if he divorced me. And he would," she added, shaking her head. "If there were any hint of a scandal, Metellus and his whole family would gladly see me starve. My husband's a monster, you don't know; if he wanted to, he would do anything to hurt me. . . ."

She was crying again; he had to get up to find her something to wipe her eyes and her nose. "Your brother would take care of you, wouldn't he?"

He could see that she didn't want to talk about her brother, but he did not know why. She was pressed against him urgently in the bed again, and her hands were clammy with sweat. "Listen. I was married at thirteen. My father chose Metellus—he's my cousin, and it was suitable. The Caecilii Metelli have influence, and though my brother Publius was still very young we could see that he was going to go far. He's very brilliant. . . . Anyway, my marriage was a political alliance. A political alliance," she repeated wonderingly. "I didn't want him, you mustn't think that. Not even for Publius, I swear. It's you I love. And Metellus was old, and already . . . unpleasing." He wanted to laugh at the force she gave this odd word, for he knew that most marriages are made like hers, and did not see why she was upset, but he could see that she was serious, and he did not want her to stop. Presently she went on. "My father beat me," she said in a flat voice. "I went to my wedding with welts from the strap across my back, and tears under my veil. . . ." He was glad then that he had not stopped her. His hand caressed her smooth, unbroken flesh. "On my wedding night, when the women left me prepared in the bed, he stayed away, out in the dining room, drinking with his friends. I could hear their voices outside—all the coarse, stupid old jokes. I was alone, and frightened in the dark. I was *thirteen*. The women were all gone—my nurse, who had promised to stay with me, kissed me and brought me a piece of cake to nibble on, but she left me, too. I had never been anywhere without her before. She had taken away the light; it was dark, and the room smelt of orange blossoms—I have hated that smell ever since. When he came, he did not speak. He threw off his clothes—I could hear him, I could smell the sweat and the wine. He cursed when he stumbled against the bed." In their own bed he could feel her shuddering as if the draft had gotten under the covers. He muttered words to her in the dialect of his province; he held her tightly and kissed her to stop the tremor. Her hands and feet were cold again, reminding him of her when she came in. "In the bed," she was saying, "he did not speak. He used me from behind, anally. Do you understand what I'm saying? He was clumsy and hasty, too. . . . I was in tears before it was over."

"He hurt you," he cried, holding her tightly to him.

"He treated me like a common whore," she corrected him in a hard voice.

There was nothing he could find to say. He held her to him, feeling her tremble, knowing now it was from anger. Yet when she spoke, she sounded sad. "I endured him for three months. I never told anyone, I was too ashamed. At last I made up my mind to die."

"Ah," he said, his heart suddenly ripped with pain.

In the rosy darkness her voice went on. "I would not eat. I refused everything they gave me; at meals I sat at the end of his couch, as I was supposed to, but I would not touch anything. I prayed for death to come quickly."

"Poor, poor child."

She lifted her head. He saw her bruised eyes, her mouth twisted and slack with pain. "I'm glad you didn't die, little goddess, little girl," he said.

"I was pregnant." Her mouth trembled. "But the baby died. I cannot forget that. I know it was his fault, that he wished that baby dead." Her eyes looked into his, daring him to say anything. "It was then that I decided to take a lover," she said flatly.

He felt a chill along his back, but he kept his eyes on hers. "He deserved it," he answered, making his own voice as cool and even as hers.

Sitting up in bed, she said, "That was twenty years ago. Since then there have been many men. . . . That is what he will say. And it is true, you see. Many. Until you."

He could see the candlelight along her hair as it fell down her back; through its tangled lattice her skin gleamed, her profile glowed as rosily as it must have when she was young. The curve of her breast was as firm as an apple, and the small violet nipple stood erect in the draft.

"Many men?"

She turned her huge eyes on him. "Yes. Until you. You are the last."

He held her against him in the warm space under the covers, watching the light play on the ceiling. The candle guttered and the shadows came closer. In the silence the note of the alabaster bowl rang distant and sad. "Somehow," he whispered, vowing it to the goddesses on the walls, the small gold Venus glinting in the darkness of the mirror, "somehow we must make you free." He thought she was asleep, but she answered him from deep in her even breathing. "Free." It was a sound as soft and distant as the ringing of the bowl.

Black November rain, cold and dark, the last of the Plebeian Games, which had to be played by torchlight in sand that the rain made viscous and brown. I saw her briefly in the stands, for I was back from Africa and celebrating my return. She was sitting with her husband, who presided as consul, smiling, with her eyes on the gladiators down below, her hands clenched with excitement in her lap. All the same, she did not stay long. Metellus spoke to her, and her beautiful brows drew down in a frown. Giving him a dutiful cheek to kiss, she stood up, protected from the driving rain by her oiled silk parasol, and went quickly to the gate. She seemed to take a spot of brightness out of the day with her. I supposed her husband had asked her to do some errand, and I admired her wifely virtue, or the pretense of it, for I knew her reputation, in going so promptly from something she enjoyed. I wanted to watch her go—whatever she did, watching her was a pleasure—but my eye was distracted: behind her in the less distinguished seats there was a small flurry of complaint; I looked up and saw Catullus, pulling the edge of his toga over his head, dash for the archway to the exit. I had not seen him since I came back. The sight of him drove Clodia out of my mind, and I did not connect his going with hers, though now I know that he met her afterward. Then, I did not guess at such a possibility. I caught my breath to call to him, but he was already gone. In any case, I suppose, by that time he would not have heard.

A basin chiming with water, musical and fragile, in the pavilion of her gardens across the river. He had brought her a poem he was working on, but they had long since given up looking at it. The marble bowl of the fountain reflected their bodies, tangled together on the mosaic floor like puppies at play. They were in a room giving on the garden: palm trees, their roots deep in marble urns, arched their dry wings over them; lemon leaves as thick and glossy as leather gleamed against the walls; cyclamens showed their flames in pots of moss. The floor was warm, heated by pipes underneath, but outside the bare branches of the trees tossed against the cold blue sky. Through the open doorway the chattering of sparrows mingled with the drip of water.

They were warm in spite of the open door; as they rolled over, their backs shone with sweat. She was on top of him, clasping his hips with her narrow knees, plunging up and down on him. He held her away from his chest so that the muscles stood out on his shoulders and forearms; his head was back, his eyes closed. A cry escaped her, and he groaned; then they were lying side by side, laughing. Pulling the twigs of moss from her hair, she tickled his chest with them as he lay staring at the sky through the high window.

"Here," he said, reaching for his book. "Listen to this." He began to read.

She listened, lying on her back with her arms behind her head, for some time, but presently she stopped him by putting her hand across the roll of paper.

"I must go. He'll wonder where I am."

"You only just got here."

There was a little silence into which the basin dripped its monotonous note and the sparrows outside chirped. They were summer sounds— mingled with the smell of the damp earth and growing plants, they removed the room from time, from the quick, cold wind outside and the bare branches scraping together like dry old fingers.

He sighed. "I hoped we'd have time to talk a little." He wanted to talk to her nearly as much as he wanted to make love. He wanted to sit with her in a room where no one else might come in; he wanted to lie beside her every night in their own bed. It occurred to him that this desire had become the heart of his love, and her body was only the means.

"I know. So did I." She was putting on her sandals and the band of linen she wore to support her breasts. "Fasten me up, darling." She held out the gold pin for the shoulder of her dress.

"We'll have more time soon," she promised, pressing herself, fully dressed, against him. He could feel her thighs through the linen as they clutched him quickly, the mound between them pushed against his groin. "Soon," she whispered into his mouth, and pulled herself from him as his erection swelled. She smiled, and touched his penis, saying as if he were a child in his bath, "We can't let that sweet little bird fly away."

He grinned at her, but there was misery in it. She had not understood.

He tried to explain the next time they met. It was almost a month later, the day of the games, when I had seen them get up from the stands and go. They met at his apartment—I suppose they had arranged it beforehand. "I want to talk to you," he said. She had taken off her dress and handed it through the door to the servant to be pressed. Now she sat, naked, beside the brazier warming her hands.

"What about?"

"Just talk," he said helplessly. "Just sit together somewhere. You know."

"Don't you think I'm attractive anymore?" she asked sadly.

He had to kiss her then to show her that he did, and then, of course, they made love. She was demanding and lewd, as she had been in their earliest days, and he found himself drawn after her as he had been at first. The rain isolated them from the city noises; they lay in his narrow bed when they had finished, as solitary as if they had had the city to themselves. His body ached slightly from his exertion, and his shoulder was sore where she had bitten it in her extravagance.

"It's November," she said, smiling at him through sleepy eyes. She was sprawled against him, still gleaming with sweat, her legs parted, and her hand curled open on his chest like a child's.

"Umm," he mumbled, hardly hearing her. He was trying to work out why he had not been pleased by their lovemaking, though he had certainly been satisfied.

"At the end of next month my husband will go to govern his new province." Her fingertip played with his limp penis, letting it fall softly back on his thighs. "There's trouble there—he's likely to be gone a long time."

He woke up suddenly and sat up. "How long?"

She shrugged. "A year. Almost a year."

"It's not enough," he said seriously. "I want you forever."

She said calmly, "Pray then. Perhaps the Gauls will get him." She was laughing, but he knew she meant it, and a chill walked along his back.

"They won't look with favor on a wish like that," he said carefully.

"I don't see why not," she said, and laughed.

If she did not, he did. He prayed frequently to the god in his room. He prayed only to see her, and once in a while that her husband would die. More often he begged to be relieved of the wish for another man's death. The little god must have grown tired of his pleas, his petitions, his sacrifices. It did not seem to do much good, either, since he saw her even less than before. In December she was busy with plans for the Saturnalia, and the preparations for Metellus's departure. He met her once during the week of the festival, at a party at the house of his old friend and teacher, Hortensius Hortalus. She was with her husband and did no more than smile at him.

Then, on the first of January, the day when the crossroads are blessed and the peasants begin new work, his luck changed. He had gone down to the street to join the festival: at every corner an altar had been set up with its broken plow, its wreaths, its wheat and wine, just as if the crowded city streets were the intersections of country lanes. Vendors sold the traditional foods—the acorn bread the people in poor districts still sometimes eat, the wine from the first pressings of the fall before, the roasts of pork and mutton turning aromatically on the spits. Up on the Capitoline Hill the smoke rose from the sacrifices as the two new consuls were installed, but down in the plebeian quarters people were paying little attention, wholly occupied as they were by the music and dancing, the food stalls, the passing of the crowds in the dappled winter sunlight.

Catullus was standing on a corner watching a bearded man in trousers dancing with a bear when someone yanked his arm. Beside him stood Clodius, still in his immaculate clothes for the ceremony on the hill, a scowl on his face.

"My sister wants to see you." The line between his eyebrows deepened, as if he disliked the message.

The bear put its paws over its eyes and danced a few steps more. Laughing, the crowd threw small coins at its feet. "Where?" Catullus said at last.

Clodius said nothing. He ducked and disappeared into the moving mass of people as behind him a troop of acrobats tumbled into the space where the bear and his trainer had been.

*   *   *

The huge house on the Palatine Hill was open, the great black door stood wide to the sunny street. He supposed it was for a festival, or a reception for the consuls that would replace Metellus and his colleague. But inside the house he was not so sure. Certainly the atrium was crowded with distinguished men—the ceremony on the Capitoline Hill must have finished—and a large number of the less important clients of the family as well. These stood in clumps near the edges of the rooms while the togaed senators conversed in the middle. The conversations were subdued, a low hum interrupted at times by long silences that no one seemed to want to break. The faces of all the men were grave. Servants had put out wine and food, but no one had touched it yet, though among the poorer of the clients a few were eyeing it sadly.

Clodius was gone. Catullus, puzzled, stood near the door, watching the thin sunlight as it fell from the hole in the roof across the banded clothes of a group of senators, until a servant appeared and whispered in his ear, "Please come, sir." No one in the crowd seemed to notice his going, any more than they had noticed his coming in.

Clodia was waiting for him outside a room he had never seen before. As he approached she lifted her finger to her lips. "My husband is ill," she said, so softly he could hardly hear her.

He stared at her, shocked into forgetting that he was supposed to keep silent. "He must be very bad for a crowd like that to have collected," he said, unable to take it in. "Yes." She seemed as calm as ever. "Very bad."

"What happened? He was all right a day or two ago."

"We don't know. He collapsed suddenly just after the sacrifice this morning. He put his hands to his chest and fell down." Her face was no paler than usual, but her hands were clasped so tightly in front of her that her knuckles were stretched. It was as if she feared something might escape if she opened her fingers.

"I shouldn't be here," he said.

She smiled her sad, anxious grimace of desire. "I'd like you to be."

He was uneasy; he felt that suddenly everything in that house was wrong, though he could not tell why. "Come," she said. "You can wait in here." It was a doorway to a dark space, not, as he had feared for a moment, Metellus's bedroom itself. "I'll be next door." Holding the curtain to leave, she turned back and, for the first time, smiled. "It will make me glad to know you're here."

He had been waiting for a long time in the dark and underfurnished little room. He thought it was a dressing room: a long mirror stood propped against the wall, making his heart jolt every time his eye caught the dim movement in it as he passed. A box of folded clothes was pushed against a corner, and an object he could not identify—some sort of portable bath, perhaps—impeded his path in the confined space.

Beyond the curtain there was light; it seeped grayly around the edges of the doorway, making the room gloomy but not absolutely dark. Once he pressed his eye to a gap and looked into the room that adjoined—it was full of ashen winter light. On the bed Metellus lay, unshaven, cyanosed, and thin. The flesh had pulled away from his face; against the dark gray wall, his nose, prowlike, made a curve on which the winter light lay whitely; his chalky hands rose and fell on his chest as he breathed in hoarse, loud gasps.

His wife sat on an ebony chair with silver feet, her dress foaming motionlessly at her sandals, her dark head turned toward the figure in the bed. She leaned forward; as he watched, Catullus heard her murmur something to the sick man, saw her raise a silver cup and urge him to drink. By the head of the bed two doctors were conferring; one of them rushed forward and took the cup from her hands and held it to Metellus's chin. The man in the bed made no response, and his harsh breathing continued to fill the room.

There were others in the bedroom—men Catullus recognized. In a corner, Cicero, the old man's neighbor and political ally, sat with his toga drawn over his head so that it shadowed his intelligent eyes and his grim mouth. Several others, Metellus's brothers and friends, talked quietly in a group, breaking off from time to time to glance unhappily at the figure in the bed. Near the one small window Clodius stood, a vivid spot of black and white, like her. At the sound of her voice he lifted his head and his brilliant eyes went first to her, then to his brother-in-law. They rested on him for a moment, then he turned back to the man he had been talking to—a tall, vague figure with his back to Catullus and the others in the room. In the glare of the window, his head was oddly crinkled and furrowed, like a field of parsley. As Metellus's breathing changed to a racking cough, he turned. Catullus could see the corner of his cheek—the skin was a peculiar deadened white, unhealthy and unnatural. Then Clodius was moving forward, going to Metellus. From the old man's mouth spittle was shooting in a stream as the coughs twisted his body, jerking it off the bed. Catullus gasped. Clodia looked up quickly and gestured to him; he pulled back his head; the curtain hissed. There were voices briefly in the other room, and the heavy rasping of the dying man.

Suddenly, beyond the curtain, a new voice spoke, rising loud and strong over the murmur of the others. He thought it was calling his name, and a cold sweat broke out over his body as his heart rocked violently in his chest. "Catullus," the voice called. "Catullus." A hard thumping followed, as if someone were pounding on a door. Catullus, eyes at the gap in the curtain, saw Metellus, twisted nearly upright, hammering on the wall; his face was red, his mouth open. "Catullus," he shouted again, and the thumping rose to a tattoo.

There was a flurry of movement; the doctors were rushing to him, were easing him back in bed. "Catullus," he shouted once more, thinly and helplessly, his eyes going once around the room. Then the doctors were in the way, and Catullus could not see him. Someone was wailing, a rhythmic throb; a hand waved the doctors aside; someone reached over and closed the dead man's eyes.

It was almost an hour before she pushed back the curtain and came to him. He was sitting in the dark on the box of clothes, his hands twisted between his knees, his eyes full of the last sight of the dead man. She knelt down and put her arms around him. "It's over," she whispered.

He looked at her blankly, "My name," he muttered. "My name. . . . His hand was knocking on the wall." He knew he was hardly coherent, but he could do nothing about it, his tongue was so thick in his mouth, his mind so slow.

"Your name?" she said, stroking his hair.

He made an enormous effort. "He called me. He knew."

"It doesn't matter. He was wandering in his wits."

He was shuddering with cold. Stupidly, he thought she had not understood. "He knew," he repeated patiently. "He knew all along. He called me."

"No one paid any attention," she soothed him. "It's all right. No one understood what he was saying, and no one cares what a dying man says anyway."

Through his tears he said, "That's what's so terrible. Terrible," but she held her cheek against his temple and whispered in his ear, "I'm free. Oh, gods, I'm free at last."

There is a dry sound beside me under the arbor, a little cough like the grating of grasshopper legs in the shadow of a stone. The old man says, "Who was the curly-headed man?" At the sound of his voice a yellow lizard sunning itself on a bench opens its bright black eyes. Its throat pulses and swells as it glances hostilely at us.

"It could be anyone," I say.

"You don't know?"

"Some friend of Metellus's, I suppose." I find I am more interested in the lizard, which has opened its small avid mouth to yawn.

He nods. His attention, always so meticulous, has gone back to his son, and his piercing eyes are resting now on the papers. I watch him as they move back and forth over the lines. Slowly he says, "You have not proven this." He looks at me. "And, Marcus Caelius Rufus, I do not believe it." The lizard flicks itself off the bench, leaving only a single bobbing leaf to show where it has gone.

The sun is hot overhead, a spring sun that flattens the waves of the lake to hard, slatey blue; it glances off the sky and the tall grasses, as if they were made of green bronze and copper. I wipe my face, for the arbor offers shade but with it the stifle of trapped air. The old man, however, is dry and still, and his black eyes are as clear as ever. "You say that Metellus called my son's name." He puts his finger on the page where I have written "'Catullus,' he shouted again, and the thumping rose to a tattoo." Upside down the words look nearly meaningless. The old man says, "But you do not know. You were not there."

"All the same," I insist, not liking to argue, "it is true. Cicero will confirm it. He heard it as clearly as—"

"As?"

"As I hear you."

"He told you my son was there? Cicero told you that?"

"No," I admit. "He didn't see him, I think. But he heard old Metellus call his name."

"Old Metellus," he says under his breath. "I doubt he was much more than sixty." He sits with his hands folded in his lap, looking out over the water. "No," he says at last, looking up at me now. "You are telling me that Metellus knew of his wife's infidelity with my son? That he tolerated it, and that it killed him? If you are, I must say that I do not believe you. Nor do I believe that my son ever prayed, even in spite of himself, for a man's death, or that the gods answer such prayers. If you wish me to accept that, you will have to offer much more proof than you do."

I had not expected this, and I do not know how to answer it. In the long, peaceful regularity of my days here I have forgotten the way people argue in the city. Here no one argues. I rise in the dawn and go down to the kitchen for a sop of bread in wine among my servants; the talk there is all of the work of the day. For me, that is planting and weeding with the acrid salt of sweat on my lip, the cool humidity of the soil on my hands. My shoulders ache from bending, my legs from lifting water jars. I have probably not exchanged three words with anyone all day. In the evening I lie alone on my couch, watching the light fade as I eat my simple dinner—my lentils and vegetables, my watered wine, my scrap of meat on holidays—like any other farmer. Nothing could be further from dinners and discussions in the city than this.

I have set myself to make a garden around the tomb. I cannot bear the sight of the scarred earth, the barren dust that hangs in the golden air. It reproaches me, as if I owed him something, but what it is I cannot guess.

I have shown this project to the old man. Today, when he arrived, I led him along the pathway I have laid with gravel from the pit near the village three miles away, gravel I have loaded in sacks on the wagon with the slaves and driven out along this narrow spit of land, poured with my own hands into the trench, lined with stones and shrubs I have set with my own labor. At the end I have cleared a space where I will plant jasmine from Persia, roses, hyacinths, cypresses, vines. . . .

"Why?" the old man asked, standing before the new brick tomb.

Because I must have something to do, because I cannot be idle and endure my thoughts, because his son planted a grapevine but had no time for anything else, because I never wept for him, who was my friend, my cousin, and who died so suddenly. "Flowers are a gift to the dead," I mumbled, uneasy at the question. Here no one questions me.

He looked at me once sharply, then away.

At night, by the light of his son's beautiful oil lamps, I read, I remember, and I write. The smell of herbs is sharp and clean on the night air, the nightingales sing of betrayal and pain, the small flies rise, gilded, just beyond the flames. Overhead the stars are thick and clear; the night wind is full of the cool vastness of the heights. Toward midnight when I go to bed, I sleep, and in the morning I begin again.

I think of this now as, the old man watching, I rest my finger on the page; the words swarm, meaningless as the flies, in their black dance across it. There is earth worked into my knuckles that no amount of scrubbing will dislodge. Beside his well-groomed whiteness they look like a peasant's hands. I am no longer the urbane lawyer from the city; I have become something simpler, coarser, cruder. . . . It occurs to me that in all these three months I have not spoken to a woman, or, except for him, a free man, or a person who has been to Rome.

So when he tells me that he does not believe me, I do not know how to answer him. "No, sir," I say, looking toward the garden that is just out of sight beyond the olive grove. It seems a better place to me than this.

His fingers click impatiently. "You are a lawyer, Marcus Rufus. A man trained to make the worse case seem the better, is that not so? What can you know about my son?"

If in the long silence of my stay here I have become less able to speak, I seem to have become better able to hear. And I know that in the old man's grasshopper voice there is desperation now.

"Yes, sir," I say, looking down to the ground. A man who is unwilling to look at the facts cannot be argued with, no matter how skilled the advocate may be. If he wishes so strongly to think well of his son that he blinds himself, I will not be able to make him see.

"You are not convinced?" he asks. He, too, hears well—like, I think suddenly, his son. He wants me to be convinced, and again I am surprised: why should he wish for my opinion, this proud old man? I am, after all, only a young man of twenty-eight, from an unimportant provincial family. Why should he care? Yet his longing is plain, though he does not willingly let it show: he wants . . . I don't know what he wants. Some last glimpse of the boy he loved and did not understand, some touch that will make him live again, some proof he is not gone forever, was not gone long before he died. . . . Ah, gods, it is what I want, too.

Seeing this I see also that I have reached the center of the knot that all the threads were leading to. My wish and his are identical. I have found the reason I am here.

And I cannot give his wish to him. With a hammering heart I say, "I don't believe he didn't want Metellus to die. At least that, that he wanted it. It wouldn't be natural if he hadn't, considering what he felt for her. And he was there that afternoon, when Metellus died. He was there."

The old man's eyes rest on me, weighing me uncomfortably, and he shakes his head, but he says nothing.

"He wanted it," I insist. "I know because of what happened afterward. There cannot be another explanation for that." I am whispering, as if I do not want anyone to hear. I cannot look at him. Staring at the pebbled ground, I hear my voice go on as if it belonged to someone else; I listen to it as it convinces, without my will; I see it tie me yet more helplessly into the pattern of the past—so tightly now that even those old eyes will never cut me free.

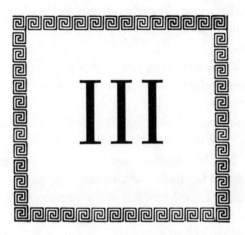

III

Metellus was dead. The trumpets blared it against the winter sky, the wax faces of his ancestors stared, heavy with the news, into the cutting wind. Up on the Rostrum the black togas whipped and snapped as the small figure of the speechmaker gestured. This was the second speech; the first had droned on for over two hours, and this was showing every sign of lasting at least as long. I sighed and shifted my weight on my icy feet. Metellus, white-faced, hands crossed over a new robe, lay at the foot of the Rostra while the wind tore the speaker's words to shreds and flung them over our heads.

A crowd had collected, as one always does when something is going on in the Forum; it stamped restlessly as the speeches went on. "Gods," Catullus muttered. "It took him less time to die than they're taking to bury him."

"He was a consul," I said between chattering teeth. "You have to expect a certain amount of ceremony." The wind seemed to have sliced my fingers like a knife, my ears stung, my eyes kept trying to water. These things distracted me, though I was trying to hear the speech. I had forgotten, in

North Africa, how cold a Roman winter could be. "He deserved it," I said now. "He earned the right to an important funeral."

He did not answer me. He was watching the women under the invisible torches by the bier. Their wailing sawed across the words, their white faces shone as dully as the masks. I caught a glimpse of black hair tangled by the wind as one of them stood unmoving among the others.

"Is that Clodia?"

He nodded, not taking his eyes from her. I was curious to see her closer, this woman Cicero called "Juno" on account of her fabulous black eyes, this woman that everyone said was the most beautiful woman in the city. She looked, that afternoon, more like Hecate than Juno with her blotched and witchlike face and her snarled mane, but mourning does not flatter the looks of women, and her behavior was certainly correct enough. She had marked her face with her nails and torn her hair, but now she stood with true Roman discipline, perfectly still in the swaying mob of women from her household. As I watched she bent down and put something into Metellus's clasped violet hands.

"Come on," Catullus said hoarsely. "I've had enough of this. There's a place near here where the wine isn't too bad." His mouth was set in a thin, sharp line painful to see.

"I know a better one," I said, suddenly warm. His brows lifted in surprise. I led him up the steps to the Palatine Hill.

"There's nothing here. There aren't any bars in a neighborhood like this." He sounded as if he resented it. His hands were busy under his toga, I couldn't see what they were doing.

In the Clivus Victoriae the sun came out. On the black-and-silver doors of the Metelli's house the mourning wreaths fluttered cheerfully. The half portico of Crassus's mansion down the street raised its marble columns out of drowned blue shadows.

At the building opposite Crassus's house, I stopped. "What's this?" Catullus said. "Aren't we going for a drink?"

"They'll give us one here." I knocked at the door. It swung open; the porter, seeing me, bowed. "It's my apartment," I said, standing aside to let Catullus see.

He gave a shout of laughter. "Yours? Africa paid off, then?"

"My father did," I said, leading him inside. "He's finally realized that if I'm going to make any kind of career I'll have to spend money. Lots of it—

do you know what it costs just to be elected aedile? Not to mention anything higher than that. And I need a place of my own, to be near the law courts, and for entertaining, and receiving clients. You can't expect people to go all the way out to the Tiburtine district. . . . I suppose I finally convinced him, because all he said was that in that case I'd better have a good address, too."

My father had lived in Rome for years, but when he got too old to go to the Forum anymore he sold our big place on the Aventine Hill and moved to the country house we had on the other side of the river. But he still knew how things were done in Rome. He insisted on a place for me in the Clivus Victoriae, since it was the best street in the city, and he had not even argued about the rent, though it was thirty thousand sesterces a year—a huge price for an apartment, even one like mine, on the ground floor. All he had said was that it wasn't worth more than ten—and indeed, except for the fact that it was on the Palatine Hill, my landlord couldn't have expected to get even that. I doubt Catullus, for instance, paid as much as three thousand, though of course he lived in the Subura, which was crowded and plebeian. And he did not have the use of a garden, as I did.

So I was well pleased and agreed for the first time with my father. Perhaps it wasn't only the address, but I already had my first case—the prosecution of a former colonial governor for extortion in his province. Cicero was defending, which guaranteed a crowd at the trial but meant I had to have an outstanding speech to win. I was working on it seriously every day. In the evenings I was beginning to give parties, dinners for the useful men everyone has to know. I thought myself well started, and I could see my satisfaction redoubled as I led Catullus through the brightly painted rooms to the walled winter garden at the back.

He looked around with genuine pleasure. "Not bad. It's a lot better than my rooms." He smiled warmly as I handed him a cup of wine the servant— my servant—had brought. The sun filled up the garden; the grass glittered like shards of green Egyptian glass. I sat back and began to tell him about Africa.

He listened, but his eyes were hidden from me and it was some time before I realized that he was thinking about something else. His reddish brows were drawn down; his high white forehead gleamed with worry. He drank his wine, too, very quickly, and helped himself to more without looking up. "What is it?" I demanded finally, annoyed.

He looked at me then. "What did she put in his hands?"

I stared at him. I was wondering if it was possible that after eighteen months it still mattered to him. I did not see how it could; in eighteen months in Africa I had loved three women, all beautiful, accomplished in their different ways, all charming, all, ultimately, unsatisfactory. One of them, the wife of a local planter, had wept when I left her, threatening even to harm herself: a disagreeable scene but one that, shamefully, still had the power to touch my vanity. I could not stay with her, of course—such scenes are dangerous to a man with ambitions. Besides, I was already keeping a little Alexandrian dancer, no more than sixteen years old and supple as a twig.

"What was it?" he demanded, his gray eyes shadowed with anxiety. "What did she put in his hands?"

"A ring. A plain iron wedding ring. I suppose it was a gesture of respect, meaning something like a sign that she was still married to him, to his memory. I must say, I wouldn't have expected it of her, with her reputation for . . ."

"No," he said, suddenly lit through like an alabaster lamp kindled in a dark room. His mouth was twisted into a smile; he looked younger, more vivid, more alive. His eyes were fixed over my shoulder as if he saw something in the sunny little garden invisible to other men. Even as I talked on, bewildered by this change and very far from guessing the reason, he nodded and smiled, and watched his vision where it hung in the brilliant air. I never dreamed that he was thinking of her, of love, and marriage and a life of respectable and domesticated passion. How could I even have guessed that he would want such a thing? It would have struck me as bizarre if I had. But all the time I talked his fingers kept turning the ring he wore on his left hand while his eyes stared over my shoulder. I should have realized that he was watching the cypresses in her garden a few houses away. Well, I had no idea, and completely in ignorance, I saw him, twenty-five years old and already battered by his pain, realize that at last his life was about to begin.

Yet at the same time I saw in him the beginning of the strange dissociation between thought and action that dominated the next few years of his life. He was like a man who moves in a dream, not knowing quite what he does or where he goes, so that in the afternoon he greets a friend he has been with all morning in the Forum as if he has not seen him for months, and he passes another in the streets without a word though he has been away with the army for a year. It was not illness; I don't know what it was. Perhaps it was the result of the death of Metellus, of the burden of shock or remorse he carried over that. He did not admit it, if it was so, even to himself. He told himself that he thought only of her, and Metellus's death was incidental and nothing to do with him; he wrote in his notebooks that in any case it did little good to think of it now. But all the same, it made him seem odd—it was as if he were no longer quite Roman and the city looked different to him from the one we knew. I would see him stop sometimes and stare at the facade of a temple with a puzzled frown, as if the building were somehow not where he had expected it to be; sometimes I found him in the Forum or walking near the river, covered with dust as if from a journey, though he always said he had been at home working on a poem or talking to a friend.

In the long nights he lay with Clodia. He was working on a new kind of poem, a miniature epic, and he would read it to her, watching her expression in the lamplight and thinking that she was more beautiful than ever. Sometimes his voice stumbled over the lines as he read, and his thought wavered like the flame of the lamp.

And, indeed, in the first month or so after Metellus died she seemed to everyone more lovely than before. Her pallor had a new tranquility and purity; her eyes and hair glowed with hints of hidden warmth. Cicero's wife, Terentia, who hated her, said she looked as if she might be pregnant; no one thought that this was so, but no one could deny that she looked different, like a woman who has heard a favorable prophecy, or taken a new lover, or gotten word of an approaching joy.

Quite soon she resumed her life as it had been when her husband was away in his province. Her door was open in the mornings to her family's vast array of clients—tenants of their buildings, managers of their factories, farmers, former slaves they had set up as shopkeepers and small craftsmen, clerks and overseers, even substantial businessmen and political figures of considerable importance to whom they had lent money or support of other kinds. Now that Metellus was dead, she saw them herself, tending the business they brought her, overseeing their accounts, hearing their complaints, their problems, their proposals, their ideas, studying the ebb and flow of the family's fortune with Metellus's large, efficient staff, now trained to answer only to her. Of course, she was not legally the owner of these things—that would not have been possible, for she was a woman—but Metellus's brother, who was now in charge of his brother's affairs, seemed content to leave the management of that huge and ramifying estate to her. He was busy with his own business and political career, and besides, she was the only one who understood Metellus's complex finances and the thousands of details involved in its administration.

In the evenings she gave parties again, serious discussions like the ones her husband had held, but now the politicians were men of the other side, the popular faction, and Metellus's old conservative cronies began to stay away. Her brother was almost always there; for a time, Caesar, the new consul, dined there nearly every night—until a public quarrel with Clodius broke up that friendship. From that evening, the evening of the argument, she came to bed late, muttering in anger. Catullus, who had been waiting for some time, nearly quarreled with her himself that night, for she was restless and distracted. When he reached for her she pushed his hand away, saying, "Can't you see this is important?" He thought of saying that his love was important, too, but she was sitting up in bed, her eyes hot with annoyance, her lips pressed together angrily. "Oh, that fool," she said, turning to him. "He'll ruin everything. He'll throw away his chance for a career no matter what I do. . . ." He saw that she was really upset, and he stroked her silky arm, whispering nonsense until, calmed, she lay down again. "What would I do without you?" she murmured to him. But she was still thinking about the argument, for in the dark she whispered, "Still, my brother was really in the right. . . ."

To amuse her he wrote a little verse about Caesar and a military architect called Vitruvius Mamurra who had served with Caesar in an insignificant little war in Spain and become his friend:

> Prettily they agree, these two prancing boys
> Mamurra the effeminate, and Caesar.
> No wonder, either—they're filthy, both.
> One is Roman filth, one filth from stinking Formiae;
> rubbed into the grain of one another,
> they can never be washed out.
> Both sick with the same sickness
> in one bed, spouting pompous poetry.

One is no less voracious in adultery
than the other—rivals, and companions,
in the girls.
Prettily they agree, these two prancing boys.

He read this poem at a party she gave of the old kind, a party for poets.
He was happy that evening in the old, simple, uncomplicated way: he saw
that she had given the party to please him and he wanted to give her back
some of the pleasure that he felt. That night she came to bed laughing over
his joke, whispering, "Wait till that gets around—'these two prancing
boys'—that will teach him to insult a Claudian. We have other friends,
don't we?"

He was disconcerted; he had not thought of his poetry as an instrument
of her family's ambitions before. He said nothing, for she was kissing him,
and her happiness was apparent. He gave in to his pleasure and to hers, and
the tiny uneasiness that he felt was swallowed up in his love.

At the same time, in other ways, Catullus's life was beginning; other
doors than hers were opening to him. The seed of his talent was growing in
him, coming to flower. He had left Valerius Cato, his teacher, though he
still saw him; his tiny epic was talked about though no one had heard it yet;
he was being asked to other great houses to read, for his poems about the
mysterious beauty he called "Lesbia" were repeated all over the city. A
number of people I met over the next few weeks—for I had begun to get
invitations myself in return for my hospitality—asked me about him.
Several men wanted to know who the woman was; one well-known
political hostess at whose house I dined hinted that it was she. Catullus put
back his head and laughed when I told him that; he stood up to look over
the wall of my garden to the row of cypresses in Clodia's.

One evening an elderly general leaned close to me over the couches and
asked, "Who is this Valerius Catullus? You know him, don't you?" I agreed
with some annoyance that I did, for even here, it seemed, he had been
before me—this old man was interested in me only because I knew him.
"Well," he said on a fruity breath, "he's got a dangerous tongue." I asked
him what he meant, but he stared at me with drunken solemnity. "Tell him
to keep away from politics," he said, giving me a look like a tipsy owl.

"What do you mean?" I demanded, my annoyance increasing because this was only, after all, a stupid old man. "I've never met anyone less interested in politics in my whole life. I don't suppose he could tell you the names of both consuls this year." I was going to say more, but the old man stared into his wine cup, muttering, "If he's your friend, you'll tell him to watch out," and turned his shoulder to talk to someone else.

I couldn't understand it—it was not for some days that I did. Then in the baths one morning I heard someone reciting an epigram, and I knew.

> Quintia is beautiful,
> many say.
> Tall, blond, straight,
> I'll give her that.
> But beautiful? Oh, no.
> She has no charm, not one
> in all that billowing white body.
> Now Lesbia is beautiful,
> more lovely than anyone,
> and with the magic of all the Venuses
> in one small shape.

The next day I heard another:

> Why wait, Catullus? Die now.
> Nonius, that tumor, sits in the magistrate's chair
> Which Vatinius is perjuring himself to buy.
> Why wait, Catullus? Die now.

Well, Vatinius was an opponent in a lawsuit that Licinius Calvus had made his speech against—I suppose Catullus thought it was a personal quarrel. But I could see that it was not being taken that way in the city; the old general's reaction was probably typical. And the poem about Quintia, that was even worse.

Catullus laughed when I told him about that one. "It's not politics. It's about a woman." But I persisted, for the old general did not seem so stupid anymore. I thought he had been far less drunk than he had pretended to be, and he had known perfectly well who Catullus was.

"You're annoying a lot of people," I said. "Do you know, for instance, whose mistress Quintia is?" I lowered my voice to whisper the name—it was the same Mamurra. It was getting to be an important one in the city. Anyone would have known that, of course, but Catullus.

It was an evening in early spring. We had found a little restaurant we liked very much where we could eat simple food and drink outdoors under a scrawny arbor, undisturbed by the noise from outside. The garden clung to the steepest side of the Palatine Hill—through the bare branches of the trees below there was a view of the river, trembling gold and black as the gleaming water went sliding past into the night.

He shrugged. On the other side of the table Lucinius Calvus said, "It's a good idea to be careful. These are touchy times."

"I haven't had any trouble." Catullus was drinking rather a lot; he mixed his wine very strong now, too, though he said it was to keep out the cold. He was from a cold country; why did it bother him? And even for early March it was not so bad—I suppose I was getting used to it myself again. Yet sitting in the dark garden that night, I shivered and put my hands under my arms to keep them warm.

The lights on the river were nearly all out. He had finished the wine, and the proprietor was standing in the doorway with his arms folded, waiting for us to go. Inside, behind his back, the benches were stacked with their feet in the air, and a slave was mopping the dirty floor.

Calvus said, "Come on. I'll walk you part of the way to your place."

Catullus's gray eyes were somber. "No. I'd rather be alone." He had turned the wine jug upside down over his cup, but it was empty. "Gods," he swore, under his breath.

Out on the street in the darkness he said, "Come on. I know where we can get a drink without being chased away."

Calvus shook his head. "We've had enough." He had brought five hefty slaves—ex-gladiators—he had bought when he won his first big lawsuit against Vatinius and his name had been mentioned as a rising young man's. "The ex-gladiators are for Vatinius," he said, laughing aloud. "The torch boy is for me." He was a man extremely fond of women, but he was very ugly—I suppose he liked good-looking people around him. You saw his short figure surrounded by these servants all the time now, even in the Forum, even in daytime.

Catullus said nothing. Perhaps he had not even heard, but he walked off willingly enough into the narrow street after the sputtering torches. The ex-gladiators fell into step behind. I went home myself in an unusual state of caution. Once or twice in the dark streets near the Temple of the Great Mother I thought I was followed. It was probably not true—it was a heavy night, moonless and misty, and the air rang with the smallest sound. It might have been thieves, of course, or ghosts, but most likely it was nothing at all. All the same I was glad for my own servants around me, and glad to think of Catullus with Calvus and his band.

Two nights later Calvus came to see me on his way home from some important function near the Campus Martius. He accepted a drink, but there was plainly something on his mind.

"Look," he said, as soon as he was sitting down. "I'm worried about this. The other night he didn't stay with me, you know. I couldn't persuade him. Not that he argued. I'd have known what to say to him if he had," he added, warming his wine over the brazier near his chair. "What's going on with him?"

"He's drinking a lot."

"He wasn't drunk."

He hadn't seemed to me to be either—at least there was nothing wrong with his speech, and he walked well.

"It's that sow, Clodia," Calvus said, looking into his wine.

"Oh, that's all over," I assured him. "He hasn't seen her for a long time." I had heard this on good authority, and I believed it. Why not? He had said nothing to me to contradict it.

Calvus gave me a look and set down the wine cup. "Don't let the wind have my words." He got up to go. "Try to keep him from wandering around at night, will you? I do my best, but I can't be everywhere."

I did try, but it was not possible. The next day I canceled an invitation and asked Catullus to dinner, thinking I could talk to him at home and he might listen, but he refused, sending a note to say he was working. I had no choice but to accept that, and if he were working he would at least be safe in his apartment. Perhaps if I had known where he really went at night I would have done more; in view of what happened, perhaps I should have tried— but really, I do not know what I could have done. He was a free man. How could I keep him from doing what he wished?

He had begun to have bad dreams. Many nights they drove him out into the streets, those hauntings of obscure terror that he could not recapture or understand. He would stand, shivering, at some small bar on a street corner far from home, gulping down spiced wine mixed with hot water until the chill of fear at the back of his neck dissolved and he could talk and laugh again. He became a familiar figure in certain parts of the city—not the best parts, I'm afraid—for when the fits had passed he would go inside and join the singing and the dicing games, staying until the bars closed and going home under the first graying of the sky. He always went alone—the girls who inhabit such places had no luck with him, though they came, I think, to know him well and to like him for his jokes and his terrible singing voice. But he never sought comfort from them; that he still found, though I did not guess it then, with Clodia.

Some nights, of course, he went to see her; there in the deep rosy quiet of her bedroom he forgot the world outside. The hissing of the charcoal in the brazier, the soft circles of candlelight on the carved and painted ceiling, the muffled warmth of the tapestry and coverlet, kept him safe, and the familiar dreams had no power to touch him. Her beauty itself was a protection to him, like a goddess's hand held out over his head; he had only to look at her to feel he was the young man so single-heartedly in love he had once been.

One evening, while he waited in her room, he was visited by the feeling that someone was watching him. It caught him without warning; he had been lying in her big bed, waiting for her to come in from a political dinner she had gone to with her brother. He was annotating a volume of Meleager's *Garland* he had recently bought, and the Greek lines, with their complex metrical technique, echoed in his mind, even as he sat bolt upright and his body broke out in an icy sweat. He put down the book and looked around, but the room remained empty and quiet, and the light burned as evenly as before. Reassured, he picked up the book, but his hands were trembling and when he tried to read he could not keep the words in his mind. They seemed to float on a sea of images, drifting out of his grasp even as he reached for them; by the time he came to the end of a line he had forgotten the beginning, and the words, as he reread them, were meaningless and dull.

He could see nothing in the room to account for his fear. He stood on the sheepskin rug beside the bed, shivering though the room was warm. The goddesses on the walls still danced blithely, the cupids still hovered, fat and frivolous, the clouds still floated smugly in their saffron prettiness.

There was no draft: the flames of the candles stood upright, the charcoal in the swan-shaped tripod burned warmly and cleanly. Even the shadows were harmless, their soft violet edges still, their amber deeps glinting with rich and reassuring tones of gold.

On the dressing table a servant had left a jug of wine and two glass and silver cups. He forced his trembling legs to carry him across to it, jumping a little as a reflection moved across the mirror and grinning in ferocious relief when he saw it was his own. A little statue of Venus on which she hung her jewelry winked at him as he passed, disquieting and lewd. Then he saw it: leaning against the wall in the shadow of the table was a mask. The wax had been tinted to a lifelike pinkness, but out of it the eyes stared—too bright, too wide, too artificial—with an odd effect of horror. It was Metellus. He had just managed to pick the grisly thing up when the curtain gave its familiar hiss and she came in.

"Oh, gods," she said, smiling at him and coming over to the table. "Where did you get that? It's supposed to be outside, in the atrium with the other ancestor masks. How did it get in here?" She smelled deliciously of flowers, and in her dark hair the white stars of narcissus were woven with pearls.

"I don't know," he said, feeling that if he smiled his face would crack.

She called the servant and had it taken away, while he stood beside the table, peculiarly exposed and nervous, as if he were standing naked in a public place. She turned back to him.

"Darling, what's the matter? You look terrible."

He poured himself a strong cup of wine and quickly drank it down. "Nothing." He managed a smile and a kiss as she slipped into the circle of his arms saying, "Sweetheart, don't think anything of it."

"All right," he said, holding her to him, and smiling into her hair.

In bed he was comfortable again, stroking her body and enjoying the smooth flow of curves from her breast to her waist, her belly, her thighs. She was excited; the coral nipples rose immediately under his hands, her mouth softened and her eyes closed, her body pressed against his and her thighs opened quickly. But he was slow to rouse; the contact with her body seemed pleasant rather than stimulating, and he lay a long time without an erection. It was some time before he noticed her urgency, and when he tried to respond to it, at first he could not. He did not enjoy their lovemaking after that—it seemed to him rushed and effortful—but he said nothing and concentrated his energy on pleasing her, which to his satisfaction he evidently did, for she lay at last looking up at him with shining eyes. Later, beside her as she slept, he studied the carving on the ceiling, thinking that as usual she had restored him to himself, for he had forgotten the discomfort of the early part of the evening and felt eased.

Yet his discomfort came back, washing over him from its hiding place as soon as she awoke. "Darling," she whispered. "You'll have to go now. It wouldn't do for you to be seen, and it's nearly dawn." She had said that before on other nights, and he had understood the necessity, but that night it caught him painfully, and he said angrily, "Why do I have to go?"

"Oh, darling, you know why."

"Yes," he said bitterly. "So you won't be compromised. Though why it should compromise you now to be seen with me I don't understand. We're getting married, after all, aren't we?" He was growing angrier as he spoke, though he tried to keep quiet so the servants would not hear.

She sighed. "Don't start that now. Of course we are. As soon as . . ."

His anger burst, a great relief of scalding rage. He stood naked in the middle of the floor, pouring it out at her. "Why not now? What are we waiting for? There hasn't been any talk, has there? No one has accused you of anything."

He had kept his voice down and she did not realize that a flood of rage carried him. "It's to protect you, too," she said, sitting up. She held the coverlet against her breasts; her hair was tangled around her face.

"Well, don't." He had pulled on his tunic and thrust his feet into his sandals. With his reddish hair and gray eyes very dark against his pallor, he looked both handsomer and younger than usual. "I'm not a child," he said between his teeth. "I can protect myself."

She smiled. "Someone has to think of these things."

His rage broke out of him, and he swore, loudly, variously, and for a long time. "I'm not a child," he shouted at her. "By the gods, I'm not. Don't treat me as if I were."

He had twisted his toga around him, and it impeded him as he tried to gesture to her. That made him swear again, and his face went red.

She said, trying not to laugh, "Oh, darling, what is this about? Really?"

Baffled and nearly speechless, he shouted at her to be quiet; her own face turned pale and her eyes narrowed. "Just a moment," she said. "You can't talk to me like that."

"Can't I?" he sneered, mocking her voice. "And why not? Is the goddess offended?"

"Get out of here. Get out or I'll have you thrown out. Immediately."

"Don't bother," he said, coming very close and hissing the words into her face. "I'm going." He threw the edge of his toga over his shoulder and turned on his heel to push through the curtain. On the other side the servant waited, impassive, to lead him to the door.

The sudden sweep of his rage had surprised him as much as it had her; he did not know where it came from, and when, later, he examined it, he knew it had been baseless. After all, she had been thinking of his reputation as much as her own. He wrote her a charming note, full of all the graces of language he could muster, all the complex little jokes and odd turns of meter—for it was in verse, of course. She wrote back to him, forgiving him and fixing a meeting for a few days later. At that meeting he exerted himself to amuse her, and they spent a happy night together under the sea-nymph coverlet, laughing and making love as they had the year before. He told himself it had all been a mistake, some passing ill wish of a god jealous of their happiness, and that their quarrel had been the sacrifice the deity required. Everything would be well now, he wrote in his notebook. Everything would be as it had been before.

Yet he continued to drink, and to suffer from dreams. He spent many nights in the taverns and eating houses of the poorer parts of the city. And there was something else that drove him out into the streets at night. His brother died. Away in Bithynia, he met an arrow in a skirmish, the wound festered, and in a week he was gone. Catullus got the news in a letter from his father, which he carefully preserved.

For ten days he fasted and prayed before his little god, never leaving his room; at night violent and terrifying dreams chased him and he woke sweating like a runaway slave that hears the pursuers behind him. This time he knew why the dreams came for him. He remembered how he had failed to meet his brother when he had come to Rome; he knew it was because he had been preoccupied with her. He swore, he wept, he raged against himself, but he never blamed Clodia. He loved her more than before; now that he had lost his brother his need for her became as insistent as a thirst.

At last it was too much for him, and he went, late at night, to the Clivus Victoriae and stood in the shadow of a wall, watching her door. Perhaps he thought of letting himself in, for he still had the key she had once given him, but he was in mourning for his brother, still polluted by the death, and he did not want her to have to share his grief. But he could not be away. He stood out in the street, feeling consoled by her closeness. It was quiet that night, though down the way across the alley, her brother's house was lit for a party. Her own was dark and silent. He went home eased a little, but the next night he went back, and for several after that.

On the night he left Calvus in the street, he went again. This time there were lights in her house and people coming and going. From his shadowed corner, he saw her brother-in-law, Metellus Nepos, arrive in a covered chair, then leave soon after; he saw Clodius, handsome as ever, swagger out in a blaze of torchlight and laughter. He thought he might have been seen, but Clodius gave no sign as he disappeared down the street to his own imposing mansion. After that there was silence, though the house continued to burn with lights, now growing paler and hazy in the gathering mist; the music flowed out as slowly as if the thickening air were suffocating it. Around him the night noises of the city drew closer; a footfall on the cobblestones in the Via Nova some distance away echoed just behind him, making him jump. It was cold; he drew the edges of his toga over his head and hid his hands inside, hugging himself to keep warm, because in the darkness he began to feel again that someone was watching him. Presently this feeling grew stronger; a tree creaking in a neighbor's garden made a sound like a shoe on stone, a fountain coughed hoarsely in the phthisic cold. He pressed his back closer against the wall. Suddenly there was a burst of noise and lights, the door opened, a flood of men in togas poured out, laughing and talking. Behind them came their servants carrying torches and staffs and favors from the party.

They filed into the street, filling it with noise and light for a few moments, and he considered attaching himself to their party to go home. If someone was watching him he had a good chance of eluding him that way.

The great house went dark again as the servants closed the heavy doors and pulled to the shutters of the upstairs windows; the house was plainly being shut up for the night. If he wanted to catch up he would have to hurry—the party of guests had already reached the steps and was going down to the Forum; yet some god in an evil mood prompted him, and he stayed where he was.

The lights in the garden went out, then the haze of reflection on the roof where the lamps of the atrium had shown through the opening. The solid mass of the house now loomed dark and vague in the mist before him. He waited, shifting his weight from time to time in the cold, listening to the night noises from the river, the first rumble of the carts arriving at the markets to unload before daylight, the creak of a branch, the sleepy cluck of a rooster in a coop as he woke himself to signal for the still-distant dawn.

A thread of sound was winding through the mist—someone was singing, a group of people, men. Their footsteps came magnified through the heavy air, a flute made a sad, low comment in a foreign cadence. Torchlight smeared the mist, and came closer, flaring and dazzling. Catullus pressed himself deeper into the recess where he stood. A crowd poured into the street—foreigners: women in bright dresses, dark men with slight, graceful bodies and extravagantly curling hair, playing tambourines and flutes. They threw flowers on the stones and danced barefoot over them. A phalanx of men passed him, Phrygians from Asia Minor. The torchlight glinted off their purple trousers and scarlet tunics, off the strips of gold coins that dangled from their ears, their necks, their wrists. They, too, were singing, and the flutes went past with them, fluttering and groaning like animals in a trap. A huge shape, distorted by the fog, followed them—a tall green pine tree, bound with red bands and decked with violets. Catullus gasped. From the middle of the trunk a figure dangled, crucified—a young man with horribly liquid skin. His too large eyes stared in agony, his broken body writhed. The flutes shrieked with pain. It was a statue: as it passed his hiding place Catullus saw that it was made of silver, and its eyes of jet. His breath jolted in his chest; wiping the sweat from his cold hands, he leaned back in his niche and closed his eyes.

The procession passed, leaving silence behind it, clean and pure; into it seeped the muddy river smell of the thickening mist. He stood for some time with his back to the wall waiting for his heart to calm. When he opened his eyes, Clodia was in the street, disappearing into the swallowing fog, half a house away.

He had already taken a step to follow her when he saw that she was not alone. A pace behind her and a little to the left a man was hurrying after her. The last haze of torchlight from the procession far down the way threw into relief the tall figure, the curled hair, the ridges of leather on his shoulder—a soldier, or someone, in any case, who wore armor in the city in spite of the fact that it was illegal. He bent to say something to the small black figure beside him; her head tilted toward him in a gesture Catullus knew well. Then the mist and the darkness took them both.

So he went home that night, that morning, down into the lower streets where the fog was thickest, in the poor and crowded quarter where he lived. He did not confide his feelings to the notebooks. He knew she had gone with the man somewhere in the city, as she had gone with him in the old days to Manlius's house by the river. As I say, he did not record how he felt. But the next time he climbed the hill, he took a knife.

That was the afternoon of the day he refused to dine with me: a raw, sullen day. The fog had not lifted, but had grown thicker all morning. In the shops the lamps were lit by noon; men groped their way on the streets by torchlight, as if it were already night. The wet smell of river mud clung to the air, the barking of a dog as Catullus passed sounded hollow and distant. In a little square invisible branches dripped cold fingers down his neck. Shapes were unrecognizable: a small house on a corner loomed as large as a temple. Twice he lost his way near the Forum—once mistaking the entrance to the House of the Vestals for a portico; once, thinking he had come to the Palatine Steps, wandering into a political meeting in the Temple of Castor, from which he was abruptly turned away. The streets were slippery with damp, the buildings smudged and vague in the dimness. Even the temples on the Capitoline Hill had pulled the darkness over themselves and retreated behind the dripping air.

On the steps to the Palatine the stones were greasy with water. He slipped once, swearing as he caught his foot and his ankle gave beneath his weight, but at the top he was rewarded by the sight of her house—dark that afternoon, though a yellow haze above it showed that the lamps in the atrium were lit. He resolved this time to knock at the door, even if there were people there—his heart lifted to see that the house was quiet. He went toward it with quicker steps.

He hurried past the door of Cicero's house and the mansion of the banker Seius with no trouble, though the street was as deep in darkness as a winter night. He could hear his steps ringing off the buildings on either side, and the ticking of the rain in the breathy fog. A portico loomed on his left, the columns a lighter darkness against the blackness under the eaves. Perhaps he heard a sound, a faint clink of metal on stone or an indrawn breath, for he stopped and pushed his icy hand under his toga and got out his knife. Far away in the Forum a speechmaker shouted unintelligibly. Catullus whirled around; a door had opened down the street, a haze of dim light flickered. He heard her voice. The light went out, but not before he had seen the vast distorted shadows of two men in the flaring mist, and caught a glimpse of white and purple and gold through the fog.

Then the crowd of men was on him. They must have been waiting under the portico, for they came at him from behind. He heard a rush of sound, he had half turned, before an upraised club caught him behind the ear. The street exploded with light and noise, roaring filled his head—it was his own voice shouting the traditional cry. "Your good faith, Romans," he bellowed. "Help me." A club slammed into his ribs, another fell hard on his shoulder. The knife in his hand flashed and came back dull as someone swore in the darkness. He thought there were seven or eight of them, but he could not be sure—in any case there were enough so that they got in each other's way. He could hear them over the roaring in his ears, panting and cursing as they slipped on the stones. He caught glimpses of them, though they had pulled their cloaks over their faces: an eye, glaring and bloodshot under a black brow, the gleam off the ridge of a heavy nose, a curl of oddly sweaty hair, a scar . . . he could not look for they were all around him. "Your good faith," he cried again. He no longer felt the blows of their clubs, though he knew he was injured, for it hurt him to breathe and his head seemed light and far away. He shouted again; he heard his voice go out of him as he thrust about him with the knife, amid the thuds of clubs.

For a time he felt no pain. His muscles worked smoothly; he plunged and darted among the bodies, stabbing and shouting as he went. The men surrounded him, a cage of sweating, grunting bodies he hacked his way through, though every time he struck, another figure, cloaked and dark in the fog, seemed to appear before him. He saw their outlines, a glimpse of grayish flesh, a shine of soaking light on wool, on bronze. He laughed and struck again, confident he would escape. His breath thundered in his ears.

It was growing hard to see; there was blood in his eyes, and he could feel it on his hands where his fingers slipped on the hilt of his knife. A dark shape loomed above him, descended with another crash of light and noise and pain; his twisted ankle gave beneath him and he fell to his knees as the knife slipped out of his fingers to fall with a splash into the gutter in the middle of the road. His mouth was full of blood, its metallic taste choked him; he could hear the grind of bones in his shoulder as the clubs came down again and again. Then the roaring took him, amid running footsteps he heard the crash of his own fall and felt the cool rush of water on his face.

There were hands under his clothes; he thought they were reaching for his purse and he tried to prevent them, but he could not. Someone bent over him saying, "He's finished." In his pain he took it for permission, and gratitude flooded through him as the welling darkness carried him away.

For a long time the tides of darkness and bright burning light washed him back and forth. There was noise, rushes of sound that rose and diminished in vast waves. Sometimes he thought there was music in it, sometimes voices calling. His mother spoke in his ear, but the light hurt his eyes so that he was distracted and could not understand what she said. The moon leaned over him; it had Caesar's face. "Young Catullus, speak to me," it said, and someone answered, but it was not he. Clodia said, "Who is it? What happened?" and he tried to turn to tell her, but she was gone and an elderly man was peering down at him instead. Someone was lifting him up, the pain shot through him, so intense it brought the sea flooding back, and he let it take him away again.

I saw the crowd in the street when I went out some time later on my way to a dinner party. It was a last-moment invitation, but from a hostess too important to refuse, and I nearly brushed past the huddled group in my hurry. I was also a little drunk—I had been celebrating the victory I had won in my lawsuit that afternoon, the first of many I was sure—and it took me some time to work out what was going on. The fuzzy flare of the torchlight, the massed and distorted shadows leaping and jerking through the deepening darkness of the afternoon, confused my eyes. At first, too, I saw only the backs of the people crouched over him—people from the neighborhood: servants, women, men who had been passing by. A face turned toward me, an oval in the mist—my own servant, Philo. He lifted his head and nodded to me, pushing someone aside so I could see.

Catullus was lying on the cobblestones. In the torchlight his face was the color of lead, and the blood that pooled under his head was scarlet and gold. His eyes were closed by a mass of already clotted gore, and his mouth was damaged again—I could not quite see how. Someone had neatened him, pulling his tunic down so that it covered him decently, but it was torn and already stiff with blood. His toga had disappeared altogether.

Several people began to tell me what had happened. My head was swimming; I felt ill. The voices rang loudly and unintelligibly in my ears. I know I shouted several times, "Get him out of the street." He looked cold and small and defenseless lying there on the glistening stones.

Someone sent for poles; someone else brought a blanket and put it over him. Philo was already knocking at Crassus's door half a block away, for Crassus was rich and kept a doctor. Four slaves appeared from Clodius's house with a stretcher; the porter from the Metelli's was moaning as he wiped Catullus's face.

The doctor appeared, a tall Hellenized-looking Jew with a dark, melancholy face. He stood over the stretcher looking down at the battered body.

"Take him to my house," I said to the stretcher bearers. "No," Clodius put in, bobbing up suddenly from the crowd. "He'll be better off at his own home. Take him there."

The doctor looked up, raising an eyebrow over a sunken and discolored eye. The small man stared back at him, hard and bright and somehow better defined in the hazy light than anyone else. "He'll be better off at home," he repeated aggressively, as if someone were arguing the point, and he barked some orders at the slaves.

"Just a moment," the doctor said, holding up his hand. The bearers glanced uncertainly at him, then at Clodius, but the doctor had already bent over Catullus, probing gently at his body. I had a moment to notice his hands, how finely shaped and sensitive they were, and how clean. Then the crowd gave a little gasp as the doctor held up a purse. "What happened here?" he asked in his rough-textured Palestinian Greek.

"What do you mean?" Clodius demanded. He looked pale, and I thought he was angry that the doctor had countermanded an order he himself had given, for the doctor, of course, was only a slave. Well, all I can say is that this one had great authority.

He ignored Clodius, looking at the crowd and patiently repeating his question. "He wasn't robbed," he added, though that was obvious, for as he lifted the purse he brushed it against his hand to make it clink. The crowd murmured and glanced uneasily at Clodius, but no one spoke.

I said in a low voice, "He was going to visit . . . a woman," for I saw that it was the only explanation. He had already passed my house, and he knew no one else in the street. I could not look at Clodius.

I felt rather than saw the doctor's eyes on me, and I felt them move away. Looking up quickly, I saw them rest thoughtfully on the small man, who had flushed red under his pallor. There was a little silence.

"Very well. Take him home." The doctor glanced once more at Catullus, nodded to the bearers, and backed away.

Slowly they carried the stretcher to the end of the street, the doctor pacing along behind. They did not go down the steps, but the other way, toward a street with a gentler slope, as Clodius had instructed them to do. I watched them out of sight in the enveloping fog, then, nodding to Clodius, I made my way down the street toward my destination.

He was a long time recovering from his injuries, whether because the journey had made them worse, or because they were already so serious to begin with, I don't know. In any case, they were grave enough. His shoulder was broken, and so was a rib, which had pierced his lung. He had taken some bad blows to the head, and for several days was conscious only intermittently, though that may have been the result of the drugs the doctor gave him. Whatever the reason, his memory was faulty for some days afterward, and he lay on his plain, uncarved bed looking at the ceiling trying to bring back the facts of his life as April passed and deepened into a flowery and abundant May. When the doctor at last allowed him to get up, he was weak, and had to sit quietly all day in the sun. Calvus and Helvius Cinna chipped in together to get him a nurse, an accomplished and knowledgeable man of about sixty from Campagna, with silver hair and a commanding nose, but Catullus refused so strongly to have him that they were forced to accept his decision, though they cannot have guessed whom he reminded him of. They sold the man again, and left Catullus to himself. Other friends took care of him, too—we all sent him presents of game or beer—and slowly, with the sun and the good food, he began to grow stronger. Quintus Cornificius, who was richer than all of us put together, lent him his secretary to read to him in Greek while he was too ill to read by himself, but presently he was able to do without even this, and the table on his balcony was heaped with scrolls and tablets in the spring sunshine. Clodia neither wrote nor went to see him, though she was frequently in the city now, even without an escort, and she could have gone. After all, he was almost a client of her house.

I don't think he minded; I'm not sure he even thought of her, though he had thought of nothing else for so long. There is not one word in his letters or notes or poems about Clodia or "Lesbia" or his love. He sat among his books in the warm sunshine, reading desultorily, making occasional notes, thinking about his friends or his home, but the events of the year before seemed to have faded from his mind. I think, myself, that his pain, and the doctor's ministrations, and the long, quiet days of tranquil weather, created a kind of distance around his feelings for her, isolating them from the surface of his mind. Neither the past nor the future troubled him—even his brother's death seemed far away and trivial—and for a time he was like a boy again, the boy he had been before he met her. He was content to have it so, and to sit in the sun, dreaming and serene.

As he grew stronger he began to write: a wedding song for Calvus, who was marrying a cousin of his called Quintilia with whom he was in love; another for his friend Manlius Torquatus, who had been married some months before, when Catullus had been too preoccupied to pay much attention. He had made a note that the little house by the river had been sold—at the time it had seemed only another sign that his love was being swept away on a flood of disaster. But he wrote now, sincerely and charmingly, about the happiness he wished for his friends. The sunlight of that exceptional spring seems to play everywhere around those lines.

When he was stronger he went to Verona, then to Sirmio, to recuperate. Here in this house, built by his brother on land that had come down to them from their mother's people, he rested, slept, ate, swam, worked in the garden, walked. He planted the grapevine, directing the slaves himself and setting the young shoots in the ground with his own hands; he sailed on the lake in a borrowed boat; he read a little. For a time he seemed to have forgotten Rome.

But Rome did not forget him. It called to him, sometimes literally. Manlius Torquatus wrote to him, thanking him for a poem of consolation when his new wife and he quarreled—the letter, which I would have prevented him from sending if I had known about it, is lost, but not Catullus's reply:

> . . . And so, when you write, "Catullus, it's a mistake

to be in Verona when all the best young men here
warm their legs in your cold bed"—that, Manlius,
is not a mistake, it's a misfortune.
Forgive me, therefore, if I don't write as I once did,
for grief has taken the strength from me, and I can't.
As for not having books at hand, that is because
Rome is my home, my place; my life is there.
When I came here only one box out of many—one small
      box—
came with me. And so, don't think me selfish if
I haven't written much. I would have offered to unasked,
if I'd had the power.

This call he refused, closing his ears, denying he had heard, but after that he could not rest peacefully in Sirmio any longer. His nights grew restless, and his days were interrupted by the constant pull of Rome.

He tried to ignore it, but he could not. As a man knows even when his eyes are shut where the sun is, he felt the city all the time. Finally he could bear his discomfort no longer. He closed his house and started back, making the journey slowly, for he was not yet entirely strong. Once he was on the road, his restlessness was stilled a little, though as he approached the suburbs of the city it grew again, until he could hardly sit still in the wagon, or stop for the night at an inn.

The first thing he did was to go and see Clodia, but the house was shut up and the servants were gone. The doorkeeper shrugged and waved his hand vaguely south—perhaps she had gone to Baiae or to stay with friends.

"Did she leave a message for me?" he asked. The heat of the stones came through the soles of his shoes and washed back at him from the wall. The old man mumbled, and clanked the chain that kept him to the door, and Catullus had to give his name, though the senile creature certainly knew who he was. "No, sir, no message," the old man said with dull eyes, and closed the door in his face.

He wandered around the city for several days, going back a few times to her house, but the answer was always the same. She was gone, and Rome was peculiarly empty without her, as if the tutelary goddess of a town had been taken away, leaving only a collection of streets and stones without meaning or connection to bake in the sun. He could not settle down to anything, and spent hours walking by the river, until his skin felt rasped by the heat and his tunic was soaked with sweat. Most of his friends were away—I was visiting in the country myself—and in any case no one expected him back from Sirmio for months. He was alone. In his restlessness, he began to prefer it, though he still went every day or two to her house. She was never there.

The city, what there was of it, was as restless as he was: the elections were about to be held, and the Apollonian Games, so that all the country people had come into town and the lower streets were jammed. Posters for the election or the sports were painted on virtually every surface, giving the names of chariot racers or urging votes for candidates. In his own street there was a large one: "The Leatherworkers' Guild supports P. Clodius Pulcher for Tribune. He will lower our taxes." Every time he passed the sign, the name seemed to leap out at him, and he jerked his head away.

He did not go to the races, but he saw the revival of Ennius's tragedy *Thysetes* that was offered the next day. There was a disturbance in the audience—hissing and booing, even jeers and shouts mixed with the stamp of heavy shoes thundering ominously on the wooden floorboards when the actor came to the line, "To our misfortune, you are Great." His voice rose and stretched out, he turned slightly to the audience as if to say, with charming helplessness, that, after all, he hadn't written it, and couldn't help if people took it to refer to Pompey, could he? The hissing and stamping increased until the whole temporary structure rocked and shook and the seats under their new linen canopies seemed in danger of giving way. Over the noise, the actor's voice rose in the next line. "The time will come when you will regret that power. . . ." People stood up on the benches, roaring and shouting. Down at the bottom in the seats reserved for the distinguished families, someone was shouting, "That's right. That's right." It was Clodius. Catullus had forgotten how much he resembled his sister. His dark eyes tilted under a brow like hers; his narrow, arched nose was carved by the same masterly hand. Even standing on a bench and shouting, he had the same air of luxury, the same aura of excitement. Catullus, watching him shout, was jolted by his memories. Standing up abruptly, he pushed his way outside. At the entrance he brushed quickly through the crowd that had gathered, hardly seeing the consul approach with his lictors. As the tall figure went in the noise diminished, but in a few moments it started again. Catullus had meant to go home, but he waited instead, drinking at a little bar from which he could watch the entrance. When Clodius came out in a crowd of his supporters, he fell into step beside him.

The small man shot him a glance but said nothing. Catullus said, "I want to see your sister, Pulcher." He was still handsome: his eyes were shaded with lashes as long as his sister's, his mouth was pale and curved like a bow, but he was, for all the delicacy of his features, entirely masculine. He crackled with it as an Egyptian cat sparks on a stormy night, and in the Forum the girls under the portico turned to watch as he went by.

"She doesn't want to see you," Clodius said; his hand was on the hilt of his sword.

"I'll believe that from her," Catullus said, ignoring the gesture. "Not from you."

Clodius stopped and turned to face him. His supporters, evidently deciding they were not needed, halted a few paces behind. "Listen," Clodius said, looking Catullus up and down, "the wind must have blown away my words. She doesn't want to see you. Is that clear?"

"Why not?" Catullus demanded, planting his feet and eyeing the sword.

Clodius said, exaggerating his patience, "My sister was very kind to you once. She didn't have to be, you were in no position to offer her anything in return, were you?" His gaze traveled insultingly over Catullus's clothes, which were in fact quite good, though not as luxurious as Clodius's own. "I mean, really," Clodius went on, drawling out the syllables. "Who are you? A boy from the provinces, with no money, no connections to speak of, and with no idea of how things are done in Rome. No wonder my sister was . . . bored."

"You were glad enough of my connections once." Catullus's face was hot and he was keeping his temper with difficulty. His own hand had begun to move under his toga to the knife in his belt.

"And she repaid you, didn't she?" Clodius sneered.

"She loved me," Catullus said, looking him in the eye.

There was a silence. Then the angry little man said, "What if she did?"

"Well, then, she ought to be my wife," Catullus said firmly.

Clodius laughed. He put back his head and opened his mouth, bending nearly double as if the exquisiteness of the joke were too much for him.

Catullus fought with a strong wish to put his knife into him. "What's so funny? That's what love means, Pulcher. That's what people do when they love each other—I wouldn't expect you to know." Only the small man's resemblance to his sister was keeping him back from his weapon, and even so his hand had closed on it under his toga.

"Perhaps in Gaul," Clodius said deliberately. "But listen, this is Rome. See? Look around you. This isn't some sleepy provincial capital with a fair twice a year and horses drinking from the public fountain. How would you hope to know the difference? But I'll tell you, free, and for nothing. A woman like my sister isn't bound by the conventions of some dust hole in the wilds—she does what she wants. She's the daughter of a Roman citizen. I can hardly expect you to know what that means, of course, but you might remember that no hairy Celt from Bologna or some such godless village will tell her what to do."

"Verona," Catullus said contemptuously. "If you're so ignorant you really can't tell one from the other."

The small man's face went white, then red. He swore several times, apparently unable to say anything more.

"You'd better remember, too, whom you owe your present . . . eminence to," Catullus said, cutting across the curses.

Clodius stopped cold. His skin returned to its normal color, his mouth shut grimly. The band of supporters moved a little closer. "All right. Now you listen to me. You have no rights over my sister. She's not your wife; she will never be your wife. She's the daughter of a Roman citizen; she has her own life, her own money, and it has nothing to do with you. Her education is as good as yours, and her breeding much better. She will do what she wants—she is above the criticism of anyone here, much less of a person like you. Is that clear? And if I ever hear that you've said a word about my political career anywhere in this city, I personally will cut your throat." His black eyes bored into Catullus, and he was sweating with anger.

"I want to see her," Catullus said calmly, unmoved by this.

"You can't." Clodius turned on his heel and gestured to his followers. They began to move off through the Forum, going toward the Temple of Castor.

"Just a moment, Pulcher," Catullus called. "I intend to see her. You just tell her that from me." Suddenly his worries burst from him and he shouted, "Is she all right?"

Down the way Clodius stopped on the hot paving stones. His small figure turned, dazzling white in the sunshine. He was smiling. "Oh, yes. She's fine. She's got a new lover—they're very happy." His laughter rang out against the buildings of the Forum as he turned back to his friends and walked away.

At first he did not believe it. His anger kept alive his hope, and he told himself that Clodius was unreliable, tricky, dishonest, drunk. All of them were true, and he went on for several days thinking that, therefore, what he had said was a lie. But he knew it wasn't. He remembered too well the dark figure that had accompanied Clodia down the foggy street: he told himself it had been a bodyguard, but he knew it was her new love. One morning in the baths he came upon a conversation that was hushed as he approached. He said nothing, but that night he did not sleep. The next day at a dinner one of the *libertini* tried to pick him up. When he turned her down she said, "I thought now that you were . . . unattached. . . ." The host caught her eye and she fell silent, but she sent him a note later by a servant inviting him to call on her. He rubbed it out, but that did not prevent the words from coming back to him a dozen times a day. He knew they were true: he was unattached. He felt like a dog that has lost its master, and the temptation to stand in the middle of his room and howl with grief and rage was nearly irresistible.

He began to think that people were talking about him, watching him out of the corners of their eyes, as if they all knew more than he did. It was not as demented as it seems, for Rome loves gossip, and they may have. Now he avoided the places where he might run into them. As Rome filled up for the elections he began to have a horror of seeing people, and he stayed away from the public places; he refused the invitations he got so frequently. He stayed away from all those people at whose parties he had been such a figure, all those influential families whose patronage was worth so much in the city, and who had done so much to make him well known.

In October, life flowed back into the upper city. People returned from country houses, from abroad. I was back myself, looking for old friends and good times. We met again in all the places we had before—the baths, the exercise ground on the Campus Martius, the law courts in the Forum, the dinner parties at the big houses on the hills. I never saw Catullus. He had disappeared into the warren of streets in the Subura or down by the river, and once he left the upper levels of the city it was as if he had sunk out of sight entirely. I knew nothing of his life: he was gone where no one could follow him now.

Not quite completely out of sight:

I beg you, my sweet Ipsethilla,
my darling, my lovely,
let me come at noon
and take a siesta with you.
And if you say yes,
don't let the servants bar your door,
don't go out.
Stay at home and
we'll do it
nine times in a row.
Really, if you agree,
I'll come right over:
I've had my lunch
and I'm lying here
poking through my clothes.

Who was Ipsethilla? I don't believe anyone knows. Some back-street party girl, no doubt, or some rich man's mistress with a taste for younger pleasures. . . . He never mentioned her again, or wrote another poem to her.

Your honeyed eyes, Juventius,
if I could kiss
I would a hundred thousand times
and never have enough.
No, not if the kisses were thicker
than ears of wheat in a summer field.

Juventius is easier. He was a boy Catullus began to go around with at that time. About sixteen and just into a grown man's toga, he came from a good family—not the Juventii, though I won't embarrass the real family by saying who they were—but even at sixteen he was already seen in some of the rougher parts of town. A certain kind of man made much of him, and he plainly felt that their interest protected him from anything. Catullus took him to Helvius Cinna's, to a party I happened to attend and one of the few Catullus went to now, where the boy lounged on the end of his couch shooting glances at everyone from under lashes that wouldn't have disgraced a girl. He was obviously spoiled, self-indulgent, and corrupt, though I had to admit he was handsome, and his eyes really were the color of honey. Catullus treated him with a mixture of amusement and contemptuous affection, as if he were a dog that could do clever tricks, and fed him bits off the dinner plates to see him open his rose-petal lips and his startling eyes. When he did, Catullus gave a grunt of laughter, but he did not address a word to the boy during the entire meal.

Cinna's party was rather wild—there were women there, and they made a lot of noise. Though I had the third place on Catullus's couch, I could not speak to him myself. Finally, when the evening had grown late and the women had mostly disappeared with one or another of the men, I said, "I haven't seen you for a long time."

The boy was asleep—drunk, I suppose—curled up like a child on the end of the couch, looking innocent and young. Catullus, reaching over, twitched his tunic down over his thighs and gently lifted the wreath of crumpled November crocuses from his head.

"No," he said, putting the wreath on the table in front of our couch among the spilled wine and little sticky cakes. His own eyes were ringed with shadows and his cheeks were hollow. He had grown a small beard, like a workman's, rather ragged and redder than his hair. There was a sort of fashion for little beards just then—before his election as tribune a short time earlier even the elegant Clodius had worn one, though the older men claimed it was because he was courting plebeian votes. In any case, as soon as the election was over he shaved it off, and now you seldom saw them except on men of the lowest classes and one or two very liberal politicians. Catullus, of course, was neither, and on him the beard looked strange. It changed him, and he looked older and a little foreign, as if he had been traveling in another country and adopted some of the customs there. When he reached out his arm I saw that his shoulder had lost the roundness of youth and had set into the hard-edged muscle of a man.

"What have you been doing with yourself?" I asked.

He gave me a look from his own dark-lashed eyes—rather a hard look, I thought, and a tired one. "Come and see."

"What do you mean?" I asked, but he had turned away as if I wearied him, and was shaking the boy awake.

"Come on," he muttered to him. "Let's go. Time for your beauty sleep." The boy, waking, remembered to open his pink mouth prettily in a yawn. As they went out I saw Catullus put his arm around his waist.

I did go. I had acquired, like Calvus, a band of servants and clients to go around with me—large men whom I kept armed. I even carried a sword myself. It was dangerous in the streets: Catullus's beating was only one of many such incidents all over the city. Everyone talked of it, and there were reports and complaints at every party now. As the administration of the city seemed helpless to deal with the problem, men were forced to take their own precautions. Cicero kept twenty men from Reate, a small town in the Sabine country from which Clodius also recruited bodyguards, and several men I knew had bought gladiators or other criminals to protect them. My own men I had gotten from Interamnia, where we Caelii are landowners and the local people are loyal to us and glad to help—the gods know we have done enough for the town: my father built the first public baths and my uncle a temple to Jupiter much admired in the region. So I tramped through the poor streets to Catullus's apartments surrounded by my men when the early-November sunset was fading in the sky. When he saw my men, he laughed.

"You won't need them where we're going," he said, pouring out what I thought was the latest of a number of cups of wine and handing one to me.

I thought he meant to take me to a party at someone's house. "Everyone has men like these now. Your friends won't mind giving them something to eat in the kitchen while we're visiting."

His servant had brought him his cloak, which to my surprise he put on directly over his tunic.

"Aren't you going to wear your toga?" I asked.

He looked me up and down. I thought I looked well myself; my own toga was bordered with crimson and gold to a depth of nearly half a foot—wider than anyone else wore them and, if I say so, more beautifully made. I am tall, and can wear that much embroidery without looking foolish. But he curled his twisted mouth at me. "You won't need that either. We're not going to call on the consul, you know."

"Well, where are we going?" I beckoned him to help me off with the toga. It infuriated me that he, as always, seemed to know so much more about the city than I did.

He said nothing, but raised his eyebrows when he saw my sword, so I took that off, too. He nodded and handed me a knife.

"Here. This will do you more good." He had one himself, a horn-handled thing that he must have used for hunting at home. He slipped it into the top of his boot, so I did the same, feeling like a child about to go on an expedition with the older boys.

Out on the street he dismissed my men and waited until they were out of sight, standing patiently in the light of an open storefront while their footsteps marched off into darkness. He looked burdened and sad standing there. I have seen a slave stand like that, or a mule, tired and indifferent, waiting for the command to resume his work though he has no interest in it and does not believe it will ever be done. I began to wonder with some urgency exactly what we were going to do that night.

As the last of the footsteps died away, Catullus lifted his head. "Come on. You'll enjoy this." His little beard concealed his mouth in shadow, but I thought he was smiling.

"All right," I said, suddenly excited and happy. "Let's go."

He led me through the street with a sort of practiced efficiency, as if he had done it many times before. He was so silent, even in his boots, that no one turned to look: groups of men who lounged in the open doorways of bars ignored us; the prostitutes on street corners paid no attention; the barbers with their chairs in front of their shops let us pass without a word. More and more the night began to take on the aspect of a hunting expedition, and we went through the streets as if we were moving over the dead leaves of a forest floor.

We were in a part of the city I had never seen before, and I was thoroughly lost. The streets were labyrinthine and dark, for the shops were beginning to close and it was getting late. I could not see the little gods in the niches on corners over our heads anymore, nor be sure if the black openings we passed were alleyways or streets. From somewhere I could smell the river, and once I heard its liquid rush magnified in the space between two buildings, but I never saw it; it might have been only the gurgling of a sewer and the smell of mud from a patch of garden in another street. In this part of town the apartment buildings were tall and jammed together—I could not get a glimpse of the upper city. It was as if the Capitoline and Palatine hills had disappeared; we might have been in another city altogether.

Outside a dark building he stopped and tapped his knuckles on a shuttered window. Across the way a ship spilled light into the street and in its glow I could see Catullus leaning against the wall of a dingy apartment house. The hollows of his nostrils and his eye sockets were deeply shadowed, and his mouth showed suddenly in carved relief in the yellow radiance. Behind his head a peeling poster from the games announced the names of the gladiators who had fought. Someone had scrawled the outcome of the combats, and added an obscene comment. The words wandered on the wall. . . . "Perished . . . perished . . . perished. . . ." In his distorted shadow the comment seemed to float out of the darkness like a disembodied laugh.

A figure appeared in the doorway, wrapped in a cloak and hurrying toward us. As it came into the light I saw the boy's eyes golden under his hood, and I saw him reach out and touch Catullus's arm.

"Come on," Catullus said, opening his eyes and standing free of the wall.

Yet it was an ordinary bar he took us to, the sort of place workmen go for their meager suppers and their acid local wine, the kind of late-night, shabby restaurant where he and I had gone in the old days after a party or when we did not feel like sleeping: a long bar made of stone, with one face open to the street, the other turned toward a few crowded tables inside; another room beyond where men sat hunched over plates of beans in fish sauce or played dice games on battered boards. A couple of women, rather handsome for such a place, waited on the tables or leaned on the arms of the dice players; a string of mottled sausages hung on a rack from the ceiling, a couple of erotic pictures were painted on the walls—not very different in color or texture from the sausages, and largely obscured by smoke; a hot water heater steamed in the corner; wine jars with their openings level with the bar were neatly ranged; a rack of cups hung behind. The floor was dirty. Behind the counter a middle-aged woman mopped the bar with a filthy rag. I could not imagine why we had come so far to this uninteresting place.

Catullus, stopping at the bar, asked a question of the woman that I did not hear. No one looked at us, but it seemed to me that the men at the tables had all seen and noted that we were there.

Carrying three cups of wine, Catullus led us to a table at the back of the second room. One of the serving girls looked up at him as we passed, smiling and nodding. He nodded briefly back once. Plainly, he was known in this place.

We sat over the wine for a long time. Slowly the rooms filled up and grew noisier, livelier. Men began to lean against the bar, to stand behind the dice players' tables, to sit on the benches along the wall. I noticed that the crowd was changing—not all the men looked like workmen now. Among them there were some dressed in the toga or in good, smoothly woven tunics, which they wore with an air, like patricians on a holiday. Perhaps they were, though I had not seen them anywhere before. There were women among them, too, pretty girls like the ones who haunt the porticoes in their bright dresses and call in soft voices to the well dressed among the passersby—surprising again in this kind of place. They sat at the tables with the men or leaned against the bar talking quietly or touching up their makeup as they glanced through the steamy air at their small bronze mirrors.

Catullus said nothing and drank his wine and water, leaning back in his chair so that his head was against the wall, looking out from under his eyebrows at the crowded room. The boy sat beside him, his eyes going liquidly under his lashes from one face to the other, his pink tongue following the curve of his lips, greedy for the drops of wine that clung to them.

There was a commotion at the entrance. A group of men had come in, packed tightly together, laughing and calling to each other over the noise of the room. They were greeted by shouts and cries; the smoky room seemed suddenly a little brighter. Catullus, too, looked indefinably more alert, though he had not moved; the boy was sitting bolt upright and smiling radiantly.

The group of men parted. In the middle stood a tall woman in a long, pleated gown bordered and sprinkled with jewels. Her hands glittered with gold and stones, her hair was dressed with more, her slender body seemed weighted by the light that flashed and winked through the steam. Before her face she held a mask, painted and beautiful, supported on a gilded stick that she grasped in one ringed hand. Behind the holes for the eyes there was only shadow. As she turned her head the blank gaze swept the room like a goddess's, leaving a path of silence where it went. Then she began to move, a progress between the shabby tables, followed by her courtiers. Men reached out to touch her or raised their hands to speak to her; she nodded and spoke a word to some of them and passed on, leaving them silent and smiling behind her, as if they had been blessed. As she approached I heard her voice over the noise of the bar. It was the loveliest voice I have ever heard: low, musical, vibrant, fresh, feminine . . . a voice like water in a stream, like a cool breeze, like spring rain.

Catullus remained with his back to the wall, his bearded face tilted upward, his eyes narrowed to peer through the steam and smoke. As the woman approached, his eyes followed her, until I saw her empty mask turn and rest first on the boy's face, then on his. His lips tightened at the corners. It was the only move he had made for over an hour.

The goddess stood before us, as graceful as a poplar and nearly as tall. She smelled of Persian roses, and her dress was deep blue silk. I could see the tiny stitches along its border, see the stones set among them wink like eyes in a dark night.

She said, "Darling, won't you introduce me to your handsome friend?" She was not young, though her voice was. I don't know how I knew. Perhaps it was her hands, or perhaps the mask let something through.

The boy looked up at her from under his long lashes and curled his lips. Catullus smiled. And suddenly I knew. She was not a woman. Behind the mask, if I could see, would be the face of a man—bearded perhaps, or bristled, heavy-jawed and narrow-eyed. I glanced, a little wildly, at Catullus, who with perfect calm and a small half smile was saying, "May I present my friend, Marcus Caelius Rufus?"

I could hear the answering smile in the voice of the tall man—he was tall even for a man, as tall as I am—and he leaned forward and said, "Delighted. And this . . . young person?"

Suddenly it occurred to me what kind of place this was. I shot a glance over my shoulder at the other women: now I could see that they were men, too. I could not imagine, in fact, why I had not known before. Everything seemed to shriek it at me—the too bright dresses, the too tightly coiled hair, the makeup, gray-white in the dim orange light of the smoking lamps. Yet they sat like women, nodding over their low conversations or their mirrors, their fingers playing with their hair, their jewelry, their cups of wine. . . . It was as if they were both at once. Even the waitresses, even the woman behind the bar, still swabbing at the spills on the stone counter. . . .

The tall man said a few words, and Catullus answered, "Yes, of course we'll come. We'd be honored." He ran his hands over his hair to smooth it and smiled.

The masked figure bowed punctiliously and gracefully, like royalty acknowledging a compliment. "The honor is all mine," he said. I saw the blank eyes go to the boy, then turn to me. For the first time in my life I regretted that I was born with looks. A burst of laughter came from another table; there was a clatter of an overturning chair. Someone had begun to play the cithara, a Greek song, one of Anacreon's, full of longing and of love. . . . The tall man lifted his masked head and swept away.

"Who was he?" I asked, it having dawned on me that he must be someone of importance in the city as well as here, to have such an air.

Catullus let his chair down from the wall and smoothed his hair again. "Xanthius," he said, raising his eyebrows to indicate that he had heard the pronoun.

"Xanthius?" I repeated stupidly. "That's a slave's name." I was right: it was Greek, and most likely that, or a freedman's, which is hardly better.

The boy said, "The comic actor. He's very famous."

He was. He was a friend of Cicero's, of old Quintus Catulus the senator, of the Metelli, of all the others. He dined at their houses, talking politics like anyone else. It was only by chance that I had never seen him there. He was rich, too: he had made huge sums of money and had the best advice for his investments. Half the bankers in the city advised him; rich men left him gifts in their wills for the pleasure he had given them on stage.

Catullus was standing up, drinking off the last of his wine and throwing a clattering coin down on the table. At the door the crowd had swallowed up the tall man and grown fatter on the diet, though the room was as busy as before. Catullus, looking toward the mass of people at the door, said, "Come on. He's invited us to a party."

"His parties are famous, too," the boy said.

Somewhere down near the harbor, I think, though I cannot be sure: I could not find the upper city to orient myself at all—the Temple of Jupiter Optimus Maximus, usually a familiar shape against the sky, never showed itself; the trees on the Palatine Hill were hidden by the roofs above us. The man in the beautiful dress strolled at ease through the narrow, twisted streets, surrounded by his friends. In the torchlight his jewels winked as many-colored as a field of flowers. Sometimes he sang, raising his clear, sweet voice in the darkness, while the others joined in like a chorus. I walked along, trying to conceal my nervousness. Catullus, beside me, smiled into his beard.

It is odd to see that moment in his notes, but there it is: "Caelius, beside me, the boy. . . . Voices in the dark, which a graceful woman wears twined in her hair like stars in the branches of a tree; where she passes the air itself is vibrating. . . ."

He stopped before a heavy gate and a porter with a lantern led us across a forecourt where a fountain played under painted columns, then through a house built in the Greek style. The rooms were white-pillared, the ceilings slate blue, the walls deep rust with borders in gilt. In the dining room there were pearwood couches, and lamps and statues of bronze. All this I saw by the porter's lantern, which he set on a stand near the door, for Xanthius did not ask for the lamps to be lit. Wine was already set out on a tray—Chian wine with a taste like pine and anise on the tongue, as austere and delicate as his house, and as Greek.

The crowd stood around him in their tunics or their bright-colored dresses. I could hear the jokes, the laughter, but did not join in. Instead I turned away, pretending to examine a small statue of Dionysus riding on a goat. The work was beautiful—to this day it remains in my mind as the most exquisite object I have ever seen—but the god under his flowered wreath seemed to leer at me. My hands were sweating.

Xanthius was standing by the wine table, half a head taller than anyone else around him. He had put one arm around a curly-headed man, the other around a fragile-looking youth in a pink dress. The mask still covered his face, but I could see him looking at Catullus's boy, Juventius. Behind him his shadow danced across the wall, huge and inhuman, like a goddess's, full of mystery and beauty, full of threat.

"Drink up, darlings," Xanthius said. "No servants tonight." It was a signal, I suppose, for someone blew out the lantern. There was a long rustling sigh that I thought might be people settling on the couches, a small hum of conversation. Catullus pressed my hand briefly in the dark. "What happens now?" I asked in a voice that came out too high and squeaky, like a bat's. A vision of the street rose before my eyes; I wondered if in the dark I could find the door and let myself out into it. "Catullus?" I whispered, but a voice entirely unfamiliar to me said, "Is this the first time you've been here?"

Beside me on the couch I could feel the warmth of another person, though I saw nothing. I could smell perfume, too, flowery and feminine, though the voice, I was sure, had been a man's.

"Yes," I said. "The first time."

In the center of the room they were whispering, and someone's dress hissed like a branch in the wind.

"Who brought you?" the voice beside me said.

"A friend," I answered. I could feel the hilt of my knife inside my boot and wondered if I was going to use it.

The voice said, "That's right. Discretion . . ." and a hand brushed mine.

Someone had opened a door or lit a lamp in the room beyond, for a faint light like the nimbus of the moon in mist flowed along the marble floor to the center of the room. A group moved in it, an arm, an eye, the shadow of a head, a curl of hair. The masked face rose above it on naked shoulders, a man's bare chest, slender and gleaming. A silk dress lay twisted on the floor.

The hand was stroking my arm. It was pleasant enough, almost impersonal, like the ministrations of a slave in the baths. Two large eyes, crowded among small features, looked up at me, tentative, young, anxious. "You are the handsomest one here," he said, smiling hopefully at me.

In the middle of the room, someone laughed—Catullus. I recognized his voice. The masked head had turned and the beautiful voice said, "Darling, hush." The tall, slender figure reached out its naked arms. I saw the dim light on Catullus's reddish hair, as he raised his bearded mouth to kiss the boy Juventius on the lips.

The boy's hand was on my skin, stroking me along my thighs. I tried to ignore it to peer into the darkness where Catullus and the boy Juventius were locked in an ambiguous embrace. On my own leg, the boy's hand moved higher. I heard Catullus laugh again; I saw the brief flash of his smile against the light. The tall man turned and through his mask his eyes and Catullus's must have met, as the boy Juventius slid his beautiful head along Catullus's belly down into shadow. I saw the tall man step forward, I saw Catullus lift his bearded mouth. The mask descended. At the last moment he must have lifted it, for the light from it glanced across the ceiling, but his face, too, was now in shadow. I saw him bend his head, I saw Catullus's mouth rise toward his. Catullus arched his back and closed his eyes.

The boy beside me had put his hand on my crotch; he was stroking me. It was exciting, a small disquieting sensation like touching the fur of an animal in the dark. I could feel my erection, as hard as it had ever been. Briefly my excitement puzzled me: the boy was not attractive. Not as attractive as a woman—the plainest woman—would have been. Puzzled and amused by this, I let him go on. His eyes looked into mine, he smiled again, then bowed his head over me. I felt his mouth, then only warmth and suffusing pleasure. I closed my eyes and gave myself to it.

Someone had shut the door, or blown out the lamp, for the room was dark. There were still rustlings and whispers in the blackness near me, but the middle of the room was empty, the crowd gone; the masked face disappeared, leaving an odd vacancy. Catullus, too, was gone, and presumably the boy Juventius with him. The boy who had made love to me lay on his back on the couch, asleep. His mouth made a dark O in his pallor. Easing myself off the couch so as not to wake him, I stood for a moment looking down. Sleep and darkness made his features vague. He might have been any boy, and I did not think that if I ever saw him again I would know him. I felt obscurely that I had passed a test and that he had been the instrument of it, but all the same, I did not want to think I would recognize him.

I wandered vaguely around the house, looking for a drink. The rooms were all like the one I had left—or as far as I could see in the nearly total darkness they were—all decorated plainly and beautifully in the Greek style, all with couches full of whispering in the dark. There was no sign of a drink, or a light anywhere, and without an atrium I found it difficult to know where I was. I thought the house was very large, but I may have passed the same room more than once. At last, thinking of waking a servant and asking to be shown home, I pushed through the door to the back of the house. A hall stretched before me—tile instead of marble, plain stucco instead of paint, dimly lit and drafty. At the end I could see the open doorway of a kitchen, and the gleam of metal pots hanging from a rack.

A man was sitting at the big pine table in the middle of the kitchen. Beyond him the beehive-shaped brick oven gave off the smell of bread. Perhaps he was waiting for the loaves to finish, for he had one on the table before him, round and brown and fresh, with a little pot of salt to sprinkle on it, and a cup of wine. A slave, then, taking a moment from his tasks.

He wore a plain wool tunic, well made, as everything in this house had been, and he turned to look at me as I came in. He was the handsomest man I had ever seen. His hair was gray and as he turned I could see that his eye was a bright dark blue. Even the stubble on them could not mar the perfection of his cheekbones or the line of his jaw. His profile was as pure as the face on a coin, and he was obviously Greek. It was odd that a man of such beauty would be a cook. But as he faced me over the back of his chair I saw that he had a defect—one eye was unfocused and wandering. It made him a little frightening, of a piece with the strangeness of the rest of the house and its austere Attic loveliness.

"My good man," I said, a little taken aback by the eye, "I wonder if you would be good enough to find someone to accompany me to my house."

The chair scraped loudly across the tile as he stood up. "Certainly, sir." He smiled at me with what I could not help feeling was a certain insolence. "Would you care for a drink?" Perhaps it was only the effect of the eye.

He gestured, beautifully and economically, to the table. My tongue seemed to swell in my mouth with thirst. "Thank you," I said. "That would be very agreeable." He found me a chair and a cup, all with his simple grace, and sitting down he poured me out some wine and a little hot water. He looked away into the kitchen, abstracted, full of his own thoughts. I thought it was obvious why he had been bought, for the owner of this house must have been overwhelmed by his looks. He had the manners of a favorite, too—the lack of humility, the self-absorption, and the calm certainty of right. But why he was kept I could not see: he was middle-aged, almost old, and his looks more intimidating than attractive now. Where I sat I could not see the eye, and I was relieved.

I sipped my wine. The fine white hands on the table before me moved toward the bread; the pure gray head turned. The wine was Falernian, deep, heavy, rich, unbelievably expensive and difficult to buy. No slave, however pampered, would drink it without permission; no master, however indulgent, would give it to him. I was looking at the owner of the house.

"Have a little bread," he said, curving his lips like an archaic Apollo. He studied me for a moment; I think he was noting that I was tall and not bad looking.

The bread was good, plain and crusty, still warm inside. The magnificent wine ennobled it; the vintage must have been all of fifty years old.

If my looks interested him, he did not show it. He paid no attention to me while I ate, only sat with his eyes on the far wall, thinking his own thoughts. At last he said, "Some people left early to go on to another party. Were your friends among them?"

"I don't know," I said, wondering why this simple excuse had not occurred to me. "I couldn't find them. I didn't look very hard. . . ."

He looked at me out of his unwandering eye. "I see. This is not your sort of party," he said after a time. His mouth curved again. A god might smile like that, from his distance.

"I've been to parties like this before," I said hotly. "After all, in Rome . . ."

"Of course," he conceded gracefully. "One meets all kinds."

I could not tell if he was laughing at me. Perhaps not. He said gently, "Whom did you come with?"

"Catullus." I wondered why I had not recognized him from his voice; it was more beautiful even than his profile or his long, narrow-knuckled hands. "Gaius Valerius Catullus. He writes poetry."

He repeated, "Gaius Valerius Catullus." His dark blue eye was remote again, thinking. "He brought the boy, Juventius," he said at last.

"That's right."

"Interesting." He shrugged. "These are not his kind of parties either."

"He seems at home here," I said sharply. "He and that boy."

"Oh," he answered me, though he did not appear to. "We don't shock him. Not much does, I imagine. But all the same, he is not really one of us. He should have been a Greek," he added, pulling off a wedge of bread and looking at it as if it, too, ought to have been a Hellene.

"What do you mean?" I demanded with some hostility. It offended me to hear a member of a race that, for all its admitted distinction, has fallen into such weakness and disorder that we Romans have had to go in and manage their affairs for them. And I was not shocked either; surely he could see that?

He made no sign that he had heard my hostility. His fine fingers picked up a pinch of salt and twisted it over the bread; it seemed to take all his attention. The small smile still curved his lips.

He tasted the bread and took a sip of wine, looking away into the middle distance, where his thoughts were. "We Greeks are not like you. We have had our empire; we have had many, really, though none was as large as yours. . . . Even Great Alexander never dreamed of conquest on the scale that you do." He turned his smile on me to show that this was a compliment. "Where you go the people put down their arms, the forests fall to the ax, the fields are cultivated, the seas calm. But you have lost something, too—something of value that you did not know you had, and you are not . . ."

"Not what?" I demanded suspiciously.

He shrugged.

"Well," I insisted. "What's wrong with that? Surely it's better for everyone if the world is an orderly place."

"Of course," he said gracefully. "No one can deny it." He was a Greek, he spoke with two meanings at once. And I saw suddenly, though I do not know how, that he hated and feared us, though he would never say so.

"But the Greeks are different?" I said. "You don't want to make the world better?"

"Oh, no. Very painfully, and at great expense, we have learned that it is not our business. Now we only want to see it as it is."

Suddenly, he looked feminine again; I could see the woman in the dark blue dress that had stood by our table in the bar. He sat for a very long time in his strange, contradictory posture. Then, all at once, his mouth twisted into a smile of pain, his eyes narrowed, his long hands went up and smoothed his hair. For a second he looked younger, shorter, less Greek, more Roman—even his eyes seemed to fade from blue to gray. He coughed and said in Catullus's hoarse voice, "You see, my dear, I only want to know."

"Know what?" I asked, laughing, for his imitation had been so skillful and accurate it was comical.

He nodded to me, acknowledging my amusement. Then, serious again, he said, "I don't know. It is too dark for me. I cannot follow him; I doubt anyone can—where he is, he is alone. No one understands what he feels, no one respects him for it. After all, a woman . . . He is the most isolated man I have ever seen. He is like a captive from a country so distant that no one he lives among has ever even heard his language. Not even we, who are, you might say, his neighbors. . . ."

"You seem to understand him well enough," I said jealously.

He shook his head. "No. It's too dark for me. What you have just seen is the only mystery a god has ever shown me." He was silent for a long time. A trace of Catullus came back into his looks and he sat with bowed shoulders at the table. "But I will tell you one thing more," he said at last. "He is looking for something."

"What kind of thing?" I asked, impressed in spite of myself. Surely his god had, in fact, shown him something.

"I don't know. He came here, so perhaps it was love he wanted to understand."

"Love?" I cried, choking on the word. Nothing I had seen suggested to me that love had anything to do with what these men did here.

The Greek, of course, heard my incredulity. "You're right," he said, nodding gracefully. "This is not love. And every day I thank the gods for that, for I am free of a great burden. Oh, for some of us it's a serious matter, though you Romans despise it, or treat it as a game, like imitating our music or the forms of our poetry. The feeling of one man for another can be . . . profound. Look at Achilles and his suffering over the death of Patroclus, at Alexander's over Hephaestion. You see what I mean."

I nodded. "But . . ."

"That is all very well; a man should be loyal to his . . . friends. But that is not what Catullus. He is trying to find in ordinary sexual love of the kind we feel for our friends—" he gave me a small smile—"or some men for women, something . . . I don't know. Something more. . . ."

"Sexual love?" I said, trying to take this in. "Do you mean that he's in love with that boy?"

He tapped his finger on the table. "That's a vicious boy. He's beautiful, all right, but he is not good. Spoiled, lazy, selfish, thoughtless . . . no, it was not that boy your friend was looking for. Though perhaps he has learned from him. . . ." He was easy, friendly in his mysterious and imposing way, and I said without thinking, "I'm glad to hear it wasn't a boy he loved. . . ."

"Oh," he said indifferently. "He tried." He turned away, not hearing me. His god was calling him again from the shadows, and his attention was all for him. "But you know," he said, more to himself than to me, "he will go on looking. He will not stop. He is like a man consumed by his desire for knowledge. . . ." His flat, sculpted shoulders shuddered faintly as if a chill had touched his skin. "It frightens me," he said.

"That he won't find it?"

He turned his fine eyes on me. "No," he snapped, harsh with obscure anger. "I'm afraid that he will."

In the early light of dawn I found Catullus at last, asleep on the couch with another man. The other man lay with his back to him, his face hidden in the crook of Catullus's elbow. I could see nothing of him except that he was dark with an Arab darkness, or a North African, and no longer young. Catullus lay on his back, his head against the curve of the couch. He looked worn and exhausted. I wondered if it was true that he was looking for something: if so it seemed that he would not have the strength to find it. He was thin, too: over his collarbones the hollows were filled with gray morning shadow, his arms showed every sinew, even his fingers curled loosely, as if they were too tired to close.

Feeling my eyes on him, he opened his own and smiled at me. I nodded and tilted my head toward the door, raising my eyebrows to tell him it was time to go. He slid out from under his companion and pulled his tunic over his head. We had some trouble locating his boots, and rather more finding our way out of the house, but at last we were on the street in the milky-blue winter dawn. We looked a little rumpled, I suppose, but to my surprise there was nothing to show where we had been or what we had been doing.

Catullus smiled when I told him that. "Well," he said, leading me through the streets with accustomed sureness, "did you enjoy yourself?"

"It was interesting," I said with reserve.

He smiled again. In the poor quarters the shops were beginning to open, slaves were already out with shopping baskets, and men were hurrying with night-closed faces toward the houses of their patrons for the morning assemblies. At a bar Catullus stopped and bought us two cups of wine. He drank his quickly in spite of the hot water it was mixed with, then another.

"Well, it's not for everyone," he said. "What did you think of Xanthius?"

I was sipping my wine and wondering whether I could get a bowl of gruel. "He's impressive. He says you're looking for something."

There was a little silence beside me, cold and withdrawn. It surprised me, and I turned to look at him, but the barman had come back and I asked him instead about the gruel. "Certainly, sir. It will be ready in a few moments."

"Looking for something?" Catullus said. "Did he say what?"

He had another cup of wine and I could hear it clink on the stone bar, but I did not turn to look. The barman had set down my steaming bowl; I was so hungry I had to force myself to wait and stir it with the clumsy spoon. "No," I said. "He said it was too dark for him. You were going too far, you were like a man from another country, and he did not speak your language . . . but he meant that it had something to do with love, or some consequence of love. I couldn't quite understand. He was afraid for you."

He laughed, a hard, bright sound in the dim street. "I wouldn't worry," he said. It sounded as if he was angry. "I'll be all right."

Though I had waited, the gruel was hot and it burned my mouth. I held the bowl in my fingers to warm them, for the dawn wind was cold. "Is it true?" I asked. "Are you looking for something?"

"No," he said, shrugging. "Of course not. Xanthius doesn't know everything."

Perhaps he had not known everything, but as the winter slowly wore on under its gray skies I began to believe that the Greek had known something. I did not go out with Catullus again, but I began to hear rumors, stories, hints, about his life. They were conveyed to me in whispers at dinner parties or in undertones in the Forum or the baths by men who looked variously disgusted, pitying, or shocked by what they said. One or two— Calvus, for example, and Helvius Cinna—looked puzzled and upset, because they were his friends, and like Xanthius, who may have been one as well, they feared for him.

Even if they were friends, he did not stay long with the actor and his circle. The boy, as Xanthius predicted, was unfaithful. I could not tell whether Catullus, too, had expected it; he did not seem much upset, though he wrote a poem about it. It is nothing like what he wrote about Clodia, though it is clever enough, and it may have been sincere. For myself, I was relieved: I thought it meant he would live more normally now. The adventure of the boy was over, like his passion for the woman; he could be like the rest of us now, and live in the way the city would approve.

Within a week or two I heard that he had taken up with a prostitute—not one of the elegant women, daughters of slaves or freedmen, who grace the best parties with their wit, their learning, and their style—but a wine-shop waitress with a few customers in the back room. I never heard her name. Indeed, there may have been more than one, for he spent all day in the company of a number of such women, drinking at a table in the bar and playing dice with the men who have nothing better to do than waste their time in those places and collect their share of the dole. Once in a while he went to parties with these rough-handed men and their coarse, ungraceful women. I could not imagine why. His verse and his jokes would have gotten him invited to far better places, even if his name and connections had not.

One night Helvius Cinna told me that Catullus had been seen in a workingman's club where some of the wine-shop women had been hired to entertain the guests. The variety, and the grossness, of the exhibition had been startling. One of the women had even performed with a dog. Catullus had been, it appeared, fascinated by this display. He leaned forward on his couch, but he was watching not the woman and the animal, but the men on the couches around. The man who had told Cinna was much struck by this fact. "He was watching their faces," he repeated several times. "What was he looking for?" Cinna, telling me of this, leaned closer so no one else would hear. "I couldn't answer him," he said. "I have no idea. What is he doing?" I couldn't answer either. I went home wondering what Xanthius would have thought.

Strange stories began to circulate about him—I heard one that claimed he had been to a witch and bought poison, though no one would say why; I heard another that hinted that he had become a dealer in magic himself, and he could kill now with a word or a glance. People looked uneasy when they mentioned his name. And I heard that dreadful things happened to the men he took up with—one of his new acquaintances was found floating in the river with his throat cut, another died of wounds received mysteriously in a fight where no one had seen a knife. "Well," said Calvus, looking at me oddly under his brows when we talked about it one day in the Forum, "they were not good men, you know. They were just petty criminals, the sort of person who picks up a living by cutting purses in the crowd at festivals or hiring himself out for a little political intimidation or the occasional murder, when he can get the job. It's no wonder they died by violence—their sort usually do—and there's no proof that Catullus had anything to do with it."

"No," I said. "No proof."

He must have seen my doubt, for he added, "Remember that he made a list of the men at Clodia's party?" I did, of course: I remembered that he had found out the name of everyone there, and then he wrote poems against them—had he made another kind of list the day he was left for dead in the street? It seemed a very, I don't know, *extreme* thing to do, and I could not convince myself that it was really likely that he would go so far.

In the Saturnalia he went to a party at the gladiators' barracks near the valley of the Circus Maximus. This everyone talked about, for it became an open scandal. A number of people had gotten in—some quite well known in the city—apparently by bribing the guards, and the festivities lasted for three days. There had been women there of the lowest kind, the sort he went around with now. The participants had spread themselves on the couches, passing the girls from one to the other. They drank a vast quantity of wine: someone told me later that the fountain in the exercise ground had run with it instead of water; I don't know if it's true. It was true enough in the idea, I suppose. There were men passed out on the floor in every room. After a while those who were still standing did not trouble to remove them, but left them where they fell. The women drank as much as the men, and when too many of them were unconscious, the survivors sent out for more.

They would have gone on, too, if someone among the guests had not had the idea, on the third day, of seeing the gladiators fight. They broke into the storerom to get at the arms, but they were too drunk to control the party anymore. A fight broke out, an ordinary fight like one in a barroom, except that these gladiators were hard and desperate criminals and did not stop at using their fists or knives. They had swords now, and spears, and other implements of war. Soon there was blood mixed with the wine in the fountain, on the sand, running, they said, down the tiled corridors. The screams of the women echoed through the building, along with the shouts of fighting men, the groans of the wounded, the cries of those still sober enough to try to get away. It was like the sack of a town. Finally the noise attracted the attention of the neighborhood; the City Praetor appeared with his lictors, and it was broken up. Catullus got away before the officials came, but everyone knew he had been there. Indeed, there was no concealing it, for he had been wounded—a long cut on his arm that healed very slowly. He was said to have killed his assailant, and another man as well. At parties people asked me if this was true: sometimes men laughed uncomfortably at the thought, sometimes women's eyes shone with pity, or something worse, and they passed their tongues over their lips as if they tasted blood. I don't know if it was true, but I almost believed it, for he looked different nowadays, and not only because of his wounded arm. His eyes were wearier, and his mouth twisted in a sneer of disgust and fatigue. But there was a kind of triumph in his tiredness, as if he were accomplishing a long and difficult task he had set for himself. He was scarcely ever sober now; never quite drunk, but never far from a cup of wine. He did not mix it either, but drank it neat. And still he went out at night, but now he went to the very lowest regions of the city, to the bars where slaves went to drink, and a woman or a boy cost four pennies a night. In such places he must have seemed rich beyond dreams and, in fact, more than once he was robbed, though he did not seem to mind. When I talked to him about it, he merely shrugged, saying, "You have to expect it—it's part of life down there," but I was worried. They were desperate people with no respect for rank, to whom a knife in the dark was nothing, and a little money worth the arena or the cross. I thought of Xanthius, and of Calvus, and began to fear that they were wrong. What Catullus sought in such places was not knowledge or revenge, but something else entirely. I began to think it might be death.

Then one night he found what he was looking for.

It was the procession again. They were bringing the pine tree from the mountains, one night in late February, when the first smell of spring was in the air. The scarlet-and-purple–robed priests, the ranks of trousered men, the tall tree with its violets and its hanging god spread out among the branches, the women dancing, the flutes, the drums, were all as they had been the year before, except that this time he went with them.

He went alone, abandoned by his wine-shop women and his plebeian friends. He had come to the end, and had seen what there was to see. His money was gone, spent on drink and the various forms of his despair. There was nowhere else to go, nothing for him to look for—he had found what he had sought. If he had wanted knowledge, he had it now; if revenge, there was no one left to care. As the procession passed into the Clivus Victoriae from the Forum, he closed his eyes. He did not want to see the street, for he had been gone from it for a year—a terrible time—and he was back to the point where he started.

The parade went on; he followed it, weaving on his feet with drunkenness, which was chronic with him now, drinking from time to time from a flask that he had stuffed inside his tunic. He trod the broken flowers the dancers had strewn in the path; he joined in the singing with his tuneless voice as he stumbled along behind. He still wore his ragged little beard, but his skin was gray and his eyes deeply sunk under his reddish brows. He was twenty-seven, he looked nearly forty, and from time to time he coughed hoarsely in the chilly spring night.

The procession wound through the dense streets at the top of the Palatine Hill, the torchlight flaring off the walls of houses and the shuttered shops, the closed windows of the apartment blocks; the shrill flutes echoed in the narrow places, the smell of the pine prickled his nose. At last they stopped. Through the branches of the tree Catullus could see the back of a tall temple cutting into the night sky, a pale shape against the stars.

A small crowd had gathered, foreigners, swarthy people with bright clothes and skin that smelled of spices that Romans do not use, mountain people, perhaps, from Asia Minor. A few tall Thracians stood among them, their blond heads pale in the starlight, and here and there an unidentifiable half-breed from the dirtiest and most degraded parts of town. He was the only Roman citizen among them, but he looked like one of them: foreign, hungry, poor. . . .

A woman beside him smiled at him; a dark, compact-bodied man offered him a bunch of violets. He nodded and passed the man his flask of wine in return. Somewhere behind him a baby cried and was quickly hushed. In front of him the crowd was denser; he was taller than they, but he was still unable to see over the rows of curled and oily heads. He waited patiently, like an exhausted animal, listening to the incomprehensible chanting, alone in the mass of people.

Presently the tree lurched forward again, as the music rose. The dancers stepped into the courtyard. Behind them the torches trembled, steadied, moved; the phalanx of singing men, their dark faces gleaming with sweat, their liquid eyes shining, followed it. They went around the open space pausing only once, directly opposite a statue on a high plinth at the edge of a grove of evergreen oaks. It was a seated goddess with a battlemented crown on her head and a sheaf of wheat in her lap. Her stone eyes stared out at the hanging god in the tree, and in the torchlight his silver skin seemed to stretch and waver toward her, his dark eyes bulge in agony. The goddess made no sign.

The chief of the tree-bearers in his long purple robe began to sing a hymn, answered by the troop behind him; he bent slowly and laid a wreath of violets at the base of the plinth. The flutes cried out, the cymbals clashed. The branches of the oaks, massed in darkness behind the goddess, quivered as if a breeze had struck them. The tree-bearers' leader bowed again, the dancers lifted up their arms, and the procession entered the wood.

There was a path. Catullus could feel it under his feet and knew he no longer walked on stone. The coppery smell of decaying oak leaves came to him, mixed with the pine, making him cough again. For a moment, walking in the starlight, he forgot where he was, and thought he trod a forest floor at home. The shadows moved under the trees, concealing the others in dappled darkness. The torches were extinguished and the starlight fell like a shower of coins onto the path.

"Where are we?" Catullus whispered to the dark woman, who still walked beside him.

"Shh," she said urgently, putting her hand on his arm, but in a moment she gave his hand a little pat and pointed ahead of her.

The grove had ended. Abruptly the ground fell away, and before him he could see the city stretched out below. At the base of the cliff the long, raked oval of the Circus Maximus lay like an eye, fringed with the shadow of its rows of seats; to his right, some distance away, the empty marketplaces gaped in the midst of a complex tangle of dark and light, and down near the river the little streets were a pattern of silver and black, like a cover twisted over a sleeping form.

It was a long time since he had been anywhere so high. He stood, lost in wonder, looking at the city below. The river curled around it like fine, dark hair, giving back small flecks of light.

Around him the crowd was moving; the procession had gone on, up the steep stairs to the temple where the doors stood open under the roof of a porch. The dancers were visible, then the phalanx of now-silent men, shapes of gray in the quiet light as they filed under the columns. The great pine tree dipped and bowed as it went up the bottom step.

The dark woman smiled; he could see the whiteness of her teeth in the starlight. "You come now," she said.

Catullus shook himself as if he had been asleep. His eyes were still full of the city below, so that he was not quite sure to whom he spoke. "This is the Temple of Attis and the Great Mother, isn't it?" he asked, looking it up and down as if he had never seen it before.

The woman nodded. "Of Cybele, the Great Mother. Come. They're almost in. Inside. They'll be starting soon." Someone on the other side spoke to her. She smiled again, motherly herself, friendly, putting off the speaker for a moment. "You come," she said to Catullus again.

The phalanx had passed into the temple, and the tree had reached the first of the tall white columns that held up the roof of the porch. A few stragglers among the dancers hurried up the steps.

"I can't," he said.

She said, not understanding him, "All people come now," and waved her hand to show him that the crowd was surging up the steps in a dark mass. It had grown.

He gave her a tired, gentle smile. "I'm a Roman citizen; we're not allowed in this temple."

She was middle-aged, but she was pretty enough, in her swarthy way, and her smile was unmistakable. "Come now," she coaxed him, and pressed her hip to his. The man on the other side tugged her arm. His Phrygian cap had fallen forward over his eyes; his skin was granular with sweat, though the night was cool. But she smiled once more at Catullus and ignored his urging.

"You come," she whispered again.

He looked down at her painted face. "No, dear, it's not for Romans. You go on." He grinned with weariness as he gently detached her hand from his arm. The man beside her was already pulling her toward the crowd.

She went reluctantly, then rapidly, scurrying up the steps in her fluttering foreign dress. Presently the man beside her put his arm around her shoulders and they disappeared into the group of stragglers that was swallowed up in the darkness of the porch. The steps gleamed white and empty in the starlight. The night silence fell.

He had been standing in the shadow of the grove, dreaming a little. The wine flask was empty now and he threw it away with a gesture that went out in a half circle over the city, as if to dismiss his life there. With a tiny clatter of pebbles it struck the hillside, then the night was quiet again. The starlight moved over him in speckles; the leaves twisted on their branches and sighed. He was thinking that the sounds of the woods and the night wind, the smell of the trees, the damp stone, the moss, had grown strange to him. When he was a boy he had hunted and fished on the hillside under oaks like these, but now he had come to them after long wandering and no longer felt at home. He remembered his childhood—the long paths the animals had made through the forest, nearly invisible to human eyes; he could see his brother's back going before him, dappled with starlight and shadow in the deep silence of the woods. "Wait," he breathed into the darkness. "I'm coming with you. Wait for me." His brother did not turn.

The leaves whispered in their unknowable language, in the undergrowth some small, hidden animal scuttled. "Wait," he said to his brother, weary beyond speech. Leaning against a tree trunk, he drew out his knife.

Out on the steps a man leaned against the plinth of a statue. A stone lion crouched above him cast an irregular shadow over his folded arms, over the leather armor he wore. The ridges of the leather crossed his one visible shoulder, metal studs gleamed liquidly from the shadow of the plinth. He was tall and his hair curled crisply over his head. Under the plinth the shadow was too deep to show his face, but Catullus, staring, knew it was turned away from him, its gaze fixed somewhere on the steps above.

He turned to see what he was looking at. On the steps a woman stood, wrapped in a cloak, black against the whiteness of the stone. The starlight touched her face, and the wind her clothes; a strand of straight black hair blew from under her hood across her oval cheek. Her dark eyes were fixed on the man below.

At the bottom of the steps the man raised his hand briefly in a wave. Then he turned and disappeared behind the plinth, going quickly away toward the city. His short cloak fluttered once, like a hand, then was gone.

The woman watched him go, her face expressionless. Only when his footsteps had entirely faded into silence did she turn away, and, pulling her cloak tighter around her, went quickly under the columns into the darkness of the porch. Catullus let out a cry and leaped after her, running up the steps in the bright starlight, panting and heavy-chested, the knife forgotten in his hand.

✳   ✳   ✳

It was dark under the roof, and the porch was empty. He glanced around quickly, but he was alone. The stars were thick in the sky, the temple steps fell away to the cliff, the city slept below twined in its river. All was as it had been in the grove, except that on the air hung a faint memory—a perfume of summer flowers, fading even as it touched him, and gone before he was sure. He turned to face the goddess in the building.

To his shock, there was nothing there. A wall of dark bronze rose before him, heavy and elaborate, crossed by a pattern of acanthus leaves gleaming dully in the dark. In all his life he had never seen such a thing, never seen a temple where the god or goddess did not look out over the city or the grove, the crossroads or stream or village it protected. Yet this one, inexplicably, did not. For a moment he had the frightening feeling that the temple was blind.

The wall was only a pair of doors, closed against the city it was true, but opening when he pushed them, their heavy weight balanced so perfectly by some mechanism that they moved with eerie ease over the stone floor. When he let go of them they closed behind him with a gasp of trapped air, but they made no other sound. The air trembled in the closed space, then it was still.

There was no light; darkness was tangible, pressing on his face. Over the floor a thin draft slithered; a vast cold smell of damp stone surrounded him. His breath caught in his throat, thickened by the chill. He coughed. The sound came back to him, echoing, ghostly and thin, from the huge space before him. He strained his ears in the dark, but there was no other noise. He was alone in the darkness; the woman, the crowd, the tree, dancers, priest—all were gone, swallowed in the emptiness.

In the silence his heart began to pound. He could hear the blood hammering in his veins. The space in front of him was huge, old, sacred, ringing with awe and age, but it was still invisible. He had put his knife back in his belt, but his hand went to touch it, to feel its rough bone hilt, as if it could explain where everyone had gone. He took a step forward on the cold stone floor.

Far up in the roof something glittered dimly—a trail of damp. He could see it in the grayish light that seeped around the bricks. Then the walls began to appear, and the edges of the paving stones around him. They stretched away the whole length of the building, in an unbroken pattern. There was no goddess in the blind temple—it was deserted, abandoned, full only of his fear. He walked forward, feeling that the floor was not quite solid beneath his feet. Even the stones had a ring of hollowness and emptiness.

Yet there was a presence there. He could feel it like a cold wind, raising the hairs along his arms, drying his mouth, chilling him under his clothes as he advanced. It was not dread of the deserted space, for it came definitely from in front of him, growing stronger with each step. The light had become brighter, or he was accustomed to it now, for the huge building was no more than dim, and he could make out the corner where the walls joined to his left, and the deeper blackness of the end wall ahead.

Then he saw it—a small, formless shape floating on a plain pedestal above the shadowy floor. He choked on a cry, staring at it: a gray stone, uncarved, unearthly, pitted with unimaginable age, scarred and battered like a face. It was set in a statue of a goddess in place of the head, and unlike the temple it was truly blind. The fear came from it like a force, and he swayed on his feet.

He took another step forward. The fear intensified. He was trembling like a horse, and his body ran with sweat. He lifted his foot for another step, feeling that he dragged it through air grown thick with panic and dismay. As he moved to set down his foot he looked. A black square in the floor opened, revealing a staircase going down. He could see the top step and nothing else. Below, it was as dark as a well. He shuddered and withdrew his foot.

"Goddess," he said, letting his breath out into the coagulated terror of the air. She had warned him—he could not tell if the warning was for the darkness or the step.

"Goddess," he whispered again, this time bowing and covering his head respectfully with his arm, since he wore no cloak. "Let me pass. I must go."

The gray stone made no answer. The breathing darkness of the building, the cold exhalations of the air, the smell of damp and incense, were as they had been before. He raised his foot and set it lightly, carefully, on the topmost step. The roof did not tremble or crack with anger, as he had half expected it to do, the floor did not heave. He set his other foot on the step below.

The stone remained as it had been. Bowing to it quickly, he went down into the darkness at his feet.

✷ ✷ ✷

A dim light flickered up ahead, warm and faintly gold. He pushed through the damp corridor into a huge chamber beneath the main part of the temple, and nearly as large. There were bodies on the floor, wrapped in cloaks or blankets and lying on straw pallets in pools of lamplight. He could see both men and women, each one lying alone. If one of them was Clodia he could not see which it was—the light was too dim and there were hundreds of the sleeping forms. The pine tree with its hanging god watched over them; its branches spread in a great circle in the middle of the room. Its clean scent floated on the cold air like a cure.

Here and there brightly dressed figures moved among the sleepers, carrying lamps or jugs, or other implements he could not see. One of them approached him, dressed in a long foreign robe—a eunuch, Catullus noted with a thrill of disgust. Putting his finger to his lips, the foreign priest led him to a pallet and handed him a blanket and a bowl, indicating he was to drink.

The bowl was stone, smooth and pleasant to the touch, filled with warm milk. There was honey in it, as there had been when he was small and ill with some childhood sickness; he drank again. His chest loosened and the pain in it, so long a part of him that he had ceased to notice it, was eased. The straw smelled fresh, the blanket was rough, comforting. He lay watching the moving figures in the golden haze as one by one they put out the lamps. The even breathing of the sleepers was the only sound, and it was gentle and reassuring, soothing as the sea.

He awoke to the sound of trumpets blaring in the room. There was light again, and all around him people were sitting up, throwing off the covers, shaking out their clothes. He could not see Clodia, but the huge vaulted space was full of people and he had a feeling she was there.

The priests were passing among the people, and two groups were forming, one at the narrow entrance to the room, one under the branches of the great dark pine. Next to him a family, mother, father, a cluster of five or six children holding their mother's brightly woven skirts—Africans as black as charcoal drawings of themselves—bowed to the priest, spoke a word to him, and, folding their blankets, began to move gracefully across the floor to the door. He thought he would join them, there did not seem any other way to choose and he liked their serene elegance, but the priest was standing in front of him holding the lamp to look at him, saying, "Do you wish to participate in the mysteries?" In the trembling lamplight his curling hair shone, his black eyes winked. Catullus, startled, drew his gaze back from the Africans and glanced at him. Like the first one, this priest was a foreigner, and a eunuch. His long robe was embroidered with threads of different colors and sewn with coins. The coins clashed gently, the threads seemed to writhe in the moving light. He said again, obviously repeating a formula, "Do you wish to participate in the mysteries?" His brown hand opened, gesturing to a mass of people under the tree. Catullus, looking over at them, glimpsed a figure for a moment—a woman in a black cloak, with a white oval face and dark eyes. "Yes," he said. "All right. I do."

"Go to the group under the tree," the priest gabbled quickly. "You will be called when your turn comes." He hurried off, and in a moment Catullus heard him repeating his question to another group.

The crowd was dense under the tree; he stood on the edge of it, scanning the faces. They were all foreigners—Phrygians from Asia Minor mostly, though among them there were others, from every corner of the empire— Celts, Arabs, mountain people from the Caucasus with fierce, hawklike faces, round Indians from the river country, Spaniards, Phoenicians, Egyptians. He was the only Roman among them. He did not see Clodia.

No one spoke, but some of the women were weeping and the sound grew louder as the group by the door fed slowly out into the tunnel that led to the stairs. Priests were sweeping the straw into bundles, folding the blankets, clearing away the night. From overhead the sound of trumpets came faintly through the roof of the room where he waited.

They were alone, the dense mass of people under the tree, watching with solemn eyes as the priests finished their tasks. Slowly the crying died away. In the room a vast silence descended.

A long time passed. The room waited, the crowd neither moved nor spoke. Catullus shifted his weight on the stones. He was hungry and his throat ached with desire for a drink. His cough had come back, too— without the huge crowd the room was no longer warm.

At last a priest stood before them, tall, imposing, silent. He wore a crown on his long hair with battlements on it like a tower—Catullus, remembering the statue of the goddess outside, stared at him. His dress was a woman's, like the statue's, and it fell in pleats to a band of gold at the hem. He held a long stone knife.

He looked at the crowd out of a silent, unreadable face. Then he nodded once and turned away, walking with measured steps across the floor. Behind him the other priests fell into line, then the crowd. Catullus waited, hoping to catch a glimpse of Clodia, but the crowd, though reduced, was still large, and even when most of it had wound itself around the tree and disappeared, he had not seen her. He took his place near the end of the line and followed it across the room.

A priest held back a curtain on the wall under the small ceiling of an alcove. A dark mouth opened below it, and one by one the people passed into it. Catullus, catching his breath, ducked his head and went in, too.

He was in a tunnel, pitch-dark, going steeply down, so narrow the sides pressed against him. Ahead of him he could hear the shuffle of many feet, the whisper of clothes on a hundred bodies, the sharp, nervous catch of breath. Sometimes he bumped against the person in front of him as he went too fast; sometimes the man behind him trod on his heels and swore in some unknown language. He could smell the sharp odor of fear in the smothering cold and damp.

The tunnel went on for a long time, winding deeper and deeper. There were no breaks in it; even in the dark he could not have gotten lost. Far ahead a vibration had begun—he could feel it on the frigid air. As it passed back to him it grew clearer: voices, singing. The people near him joined the song, a long, wailing, meaningless, foreign chant.

There was light ahead, growing stronger, showing him the shape of the heads in front of him, the bodies, the colors of clothes. They were outside; in sunlight birds were singing, leaves rustled overhead. He was dazzled by the light and for a moment did not know where he was. He could tell he was near the river somewhere—he could smell the river mud and slime, fresh and green as moss, and the air was warm.

The priests had assembled them, they were leading them down a street, through the city gate, out onto a bridge over the Tiber. Glancing back, Catullus saw the Palatine Hill rise high above the stone walls, the tall temple white upon it. A priest on the top step—a small dot of scarlet—was blowing a trumpet into the fresh spring morning. The evergreen oaks tossed their branches against white clouds in a sky of clean, deep blue.

There were people on the bridge, ordinary Romans in togas or tunics, women in their everyday cloaks with baskets on their arms, children shouting. They stood aside as the singing crowd passed through them. The river chuckled and gurgled, high in its banks with melted snow from the distant hills. Occasional clumps of leaves and branches floated down under the arches of the bridge.

Then the bridge was behind them, they were walking on the flat, gray stones of the road. More people lined it, watching them. One or two made the sign against the evil eye as they went past; others simply stared, openmouthed. He remembered how, when he first came to Rome, such sights had made him stare, too.

In the shade of poplar trees along the road farmers rested in wagons, bread and cold meat in their hands forgotten as they watched the brightly colored crowd.

At the foot of a hill overgrown with green, the procession stopped. The trumpet blew again, calling all the corners of the earth. A group of men in togas or the robes of official priests stood at the head of the line, facing it. Over the heads of the crowd Catullus could see them—the Pontifex Maximus with his thin, fair hair lifted by the breeze, the College of Augurs, the two new consuls with their red-tunicked lictors, the City Praetor standing to one side with his. They spoke a moment to the tall, crowned priest. A puff of blue smoke rose—incense, carried in a censer. A chant, this time in Latin, though too far away to hear. The consul gestured with his hand; the line began to move. Up ahead Catullus caught a glimpse of a woman in a black cloak.

The officials stood to one side while the procession filed past. Catullus ducked his head and hurried past them, hoping to move forward after the black figure.

"Just a moment," a voice said in his ear; a hand fell on his arm. He was jerked out of line to stand facing Julius Caesar in his Pontifex Maximus robes. The tall man looked down at him unsmiling, and his long mouth was grim.

"Young Catullus, just what are you doing here?"

He was angry, the cords of his neck and jaw stood out. Catullus shrugged. Around him the crowd had shuffled to a halt; he could feel their eyes on him, curious and alien.

The Pontifex Maximus said, "What are you doing with this foreign insanity? We have our own ceremonies, we don't need this . . . this foolishness. This is not for Romans. Get out of that line."

The young man said nothing, but the crowd breathed audibly and pressed a little closer.

"I order you to get out of that line," Caesar said.

Catullus shifted his feet. "I prefer to stay in it," he said. He had not meant to be rude, but in his fatigue he was blunt and the words escaped without his control.

Caesar's face flushed but he said nothing for a moment, mastering himself. The crowd shifted, and his dark greenish eyes went to them.

"Do you know what you're doing?" he said at last. His voice had a considering tone, as if he were weighing something. Perhaps it was the mood of the crowd, for his eyes remained on them.

"Oh, I think so," Catullus answered. "Sir."

The Pontifex Maximus seemed to bend, and his voice became persuasive. "Do you? Why are you doing it, then? What do you hope for?" He waited, but Catullus made no answer. "What can the goddess give you that is worth what you're doing? If you feel you owe her something—I cannot imagine why you should, but if you do—there are the public ceremonies next month, Roman ceremonies. . . ." His voice trailed away, for he could see Catullus's attention waver like a candle in the wind. "Look," he said in a low voice, urgently. "If you're in some kind of trouble, perhaps I could help. I can do something for you—get you an appointment, see to it you have some kind of advancement. In a day or two I'll be leaving for my province—perhaps I could still find you a place on my staff, or on someone else's if you prefer. It doesn't matter—just get out of that line, before it's too late."

Catullus said nothing. He did not understand the tall man's urgency, and he did not much care. His hunger and his need for wine had grown stronger, and he was already a little light-headed. He smiled vaguely, wondering where Clodia was.

"At least give me the knife," Caesar said.

The young man reached for it where he had thrust it into his belt. The crowd was moving again; the trumpet blared; the song rose in the dust the procession had stirred.

"Give it to me," Caesar demanded in a harsh voice.

There was a woman in black not more than a few yards from him, moving with the crowd up the hill. Catullus, swaying on his feet, made a gesture to go after her, but the Pontifex Maximus held him back.

"She's not worth it," he said, his eyes on the woman's back. "She's worse than you think." Catullus shook his head impatiently, and the tall man said, "Oh, gods," under the now-constant shuffling of the crowd, as if he were swearing. "You can't imagine how much worse," he added in an even lower tone.

Catullus's eyes had begun to burn as if he had a fever, but he turned back to the Pontifex. "What do you mean? Tell me what you mean." His hand still rested on the hilt of his knife, where he had forgotten it.

Caesar looked at him, a deep, ambiguous glance, full of pity and unease. He seemed to consider something, some possibility, some hope, but the crowd was surging around them now, ignoring them, jostling as they followed their priests up the hill. Catullus watched them with hungry eyes.

The Pontifex Maximus shook his head, still thinking, his eyes on Catullus where he stood alone now on the empty paving stones of the road. At last he seemed to come to a decision. He shrugged his shoulders and, looking down at the young man, said very gently, "Give me the knife, young Catullus. Just give me the knife."

He reached forward and twitched it, as he spoke, from the young man's belt. Catullus, released, ran up the road to where the last stragglers were already climbing the hill.

It was night. Along the road torches flared, throwing into relief one face of everything it touched—the bent grasses on the verge, the dust and the ruts where traffic had passed during the day, the empty yellow path across the darkness—making them look too bright, artificial, unreal. Here and there people staggered down the road from the hill, in groups, in clusters, alone, men and women indistinguishable. Their faces were dazed, their eyes stared, their clothing hung stiffly from them. Under the torchlight it was possible to see that the stiffness came from great dark blotches of blood, brown as rusted iron. The walkers were splashed with it, their hair matted, their faces smeared. Their eyes shone out of it, liquid in the light.

Presently the road was empty again, then another group appeared, following the first with the same exhausted step, going back to the bridge that led to the city. Behind them came another, then, a long way after, a fourth. In their midst Catullus stumbled, his legs trembling with fatigue, his eyes burning with exhaustion. The blood had molded his tunic to his chest and his thighs; already drying, it made a faint rasping sound as he lurched along the road. When he put his foot on the bridge, he stopped.

From the shadows a figure detached itself, tall, white, grim. It stood looking at him, silent in the harsh light of the torches. Catullus looked back, bobbing and swaying on his feet.

"They killed a bull," he said in a dull voice after a while.

"A bull?" the tall figure said.

The young man nodded. His head went on nodding for a long time as if he had ceased to pay attention to it. "I'm not allowed to say how they did it," he complained. "But the blood . . . poured down on me. Underground," he mumbled. "It was above us and it poured down. . . ."

Caesar said nothing. He seemed to be waiting. And slowly, as he swayed on the stones of the bridge, Catullus began to revive. He stood straighter, his eyes looked better, he even smiled, wearily but with genuine amusement. "It was nice of you to warn me," he said finally, running his hand over his matted hair and making a grimace of disgust.

"It wasn't about that part of it that I was speaking," Caesar said. "It was about what comes next. It's terrible—nothing that has happened so far can prepare you for it."

"Ah, well," Catullus said. "I can't help that."

"You mean to go on?" There were still groups of people coming down from the shrine on the hill, walking in silence and fatigue toward the city. Caesar waved his hand at them to show what he meant.

"Yes."

Slowly Caesar closed his eyes. His lips stretched out as if something had hurt him. "Why?"

Catullus shrugged. "It's the end. I have come so far, I might as well see it through."

The Pontifex Maximus looked away into the darkness beyond the torchlight. "Is that what you want?" he said after a long pause. "The end?"

Catullus did not answer, but wearily he lifted his shoulders again.

Caesar said in a low voice, "Is she worth it, young Catullus? Is she really worth so much?"

Beside him the young man's mouth twisted in a sudden grin. It was gone in a moment and he looked away, into the shadows on the other side of the bridge, as the tall man had. "No," he said, out of an exhaustion so deep Caesar saw that he had ceased to notice it. "It isn't only her. It was never only her."

Like Catullus, Caesar smiled but grew serious again, studying his face. "It certainly seemed to be," he said gently.

"You don't understand." There was a silence in which the young man's breathing grated heavily. At last he said, "Suppose once in your life a goddess touched you, or a god, and then let you go. In that moment, what would you see?"

"Everything, I suppose," Caesar said seriously. "Everything in the world."

In the half dark Catullus nodded.

"She is only a woman," Caesar said. "She is not a goddess."

"No," Catullus agreed. "She's not a goddess. But Love is."

There was a long silence. "I could stop you," the tall man said, with no threat in his voice. He spoke as a man making an offer. "I could have the lictors arrest you, take you to my house, escort you back to Verona. This is illegal—and you are a citizen."

Catullus shook his head. "It wouldn't do any good."

"Well, then," the tall man said, but he did not finish his sentence. He stood for a long time looking into the darkness where the river disappeared, chuckling, under the bridge. Then he stood up away from the wall. Setting his toga over his shoulders, he looked down at Catullus, silent and serious. His dark, ambiguous eyes rested for a long moment on the young man's face.

Suddenly he straightened his shoulders and, still without speaking, raised his fist in a quick salute, military and final. Then, turning, he vanished into the shadows on the bridge.

The door of the temple was open. The last groups of celebrants from the rites on the Vatican Hill staggered through it, Catullus among them, into the darkness inside. A priest was singing, a high, sad, foreign lament, a thin wail of grief. The voice led them and they followed it, covering their heads, to the goddess as they stumbled down the steps.

The voice bound them, leading them together in a group. Someone leaned against Catullus in the passageway, too tired to stand up; Catullus put his arm around him, leaning in his turn on someone else. Like wounded soldiers they stood together in the center of a vaulted room, blinking in the lamplight. Catullus tried to look around, but the glare hurt his eyes, and the blood disguised the people in the crowd. He waited.

The crowd waited, too, a long time, standing together in a dense mass, exhausted, battered, and cast down. The voice went on, incomprehensible and pure, impossibly distant. He thought hours passed listening to it, but he no longer knew.

They were in another passage, not the entrance to the cellar room or the long descending one that had taken them into the city that morning, but one so low they had to stoop, then crawl, over the rough and humid floor. The voice called them, impersonal and remote, from somewhere far ahead. Behind him someone sobbed, his own aching body shook with coughs in the weeping dark. His knees burned from the stone, and his hands were scraped.

Then someone was lifting him up, firmly, warmly. His clothes were taken from him, water touched his body. He gasped, cried out. Someone was washing the blood from him with long, soft strokes. His hands stopped stinging. Tenderly someone set a blanket over his nakedness, gave him a bowl of milk and honey, set him on the floor. The voice sang on.

He became aware that he understood the words, though he could not have told how he did. They referred to what was happening, and suddenly, something was: a curtain had opened in darkness, a beautiful young man danced in the light of a forest before a crowned goddess seated on a lion throne. The words said he was her lover, and her son.

It was winter, and the forest was white and desolate. Nothing would grow; stones creaked their cold messages, black branches their dead, wintery cries. The goddess sat unmoved, her frozen eyes gazing straight ahead. Behind her stretched a world: rivers, plains, seas, other mountains, all small in the distance and bleak in the winter light.

On the rocks in front of the throne the young man danced, pleading with the eloquence of his beauty and his youth, twisting his body in the agony of the winter wind. She ignored him, as she ignored the desolation around her.

Women were weeping, begging her to forgive him, to hear, to be moved. Catullus could feel tears on his cheeks. He meant to wipe them away, but the young man's dancing was so beautiful, and the voice was still singing.

The dance had changed. Now the young man tried to charm her; he displayed his manhood, strong and noble, before her, the long wedge of his shoulders and his ribs, the narrow hips, the straight erection rising like a tree from the growth of curling hair. Even his slender feet were beautiful for her, moving surely over the rocks and moss before her throne, holding him upright as he danced, living, graceful, proud, in the ruin of the winter. Still she scorned him with her stony eyes, and the wind cut at the trees.

He began to despair. On the rocks his feet still moved with hope and beauty, but flecks of blood had appeared on them, and on the stones. His shoulders dropped, his fine head hung on his curving neck, his flat chest curled forward in an arc of pain. Even his penis hung now, limp and insignificant, against his trembling thighs.

Women were screaming in the crowd; sobs and groans tore from the throats of the men. The noise filled the room, echoing and shattering in the dark. The goddess sat, indifferent and unmoved. Before her throne the young man stood. His ribs heaved, his chest dripped with sweat. The crowd screamed and cried; the goddess sat unblinking, frozen and cold as the snow. He reached down and, picking up a shard of stone, raised it to show her. The women shrieked, the men screamed and roared, drowning the high, pure voice of the singer. Catullus, cold with horror, felt himself lifted out of his seat. All around him men were standing in the crowd, watching the young figure in the wood. He raised the shard again and held it for the goddess to see. She did not move.

With a quick gesture the young man grasped his penis, lifting it out of the way. He danced a few more steps, exhausted as a driven animal. Then he threw back his head and let out a long, abandoned cry. The shard descended. In his upraised hand he held his scrotum. Blood poured down his leg and soaked into the ground.

The goddess did not move. Holding his grim trophy before her, he smashed the small sac over and over on the stones. With each blow the crowd drew its breath, letting it out slowly when the young man, arm shaking violently, threw it into her lap, then stood, exhausted, on the bloodstained ground. He waited a moment, eyes on the goddess, sides heaving, his trembling legs coated scarlet from the wound. She made no sign. The young man's head sank, his sides caved in, his shoulders slumped. Slowly, as if each step pained him now, he dragged himself away and leaned his mutilated body on a stone. Slowly, his eyes still on the goddess, he died.

The men in the crowd were standing up. They had thrown off their blankets; they waved their fists and cried; they shouted and wailed and sobbed. Under their voices, music began, cymbals clashing, horns sobbing their long calls, drums muttering and bellowing. A file of priests stood at the edge of the forest, their eyes on the goddess's throne. The music rose.

A change had come over the scene. The winter light was still white, harsh, cold, but it had grown stronger and the wind had fallen. The body of the young god was disappearing, changing slowly as they watched into a tall pine that stood near the throne; his white arms were hanging, and from his fingers the black needles were sprouting; from the ends of his feet, resting on the rocks, twisted roots went down into the thin ground. Violets had sprung up—a carpet of them, all around the throne, thick and beautiful, at the goddess's feet—Catullus saw that they came where his blood had fallen. The priests were dancing over them to the discordant music, naked, with stone knives in their hands. As they swirled around the tree, they cut themselves along the arms, the chest, the thighs: small gashes that splattered the tree with blood as they moved. Their faces were rapt in the noise of the horns and the drums; as they cut themselves they did not flinch. The flint blades flashed dully, and still the priests danced, throwing back their heads and twisting as they went, bowing to the goddess, who did not look at them. As they turned and leapt Catullus could see that they had given themselves permanently to her service, for they were all eunuchs.

The light was growing brighter, yellower, more full of sun. Near the violets on the ground a faint green haze was spreading—the first flush of blades of grass, of moss, of growing plants, so fine it was nearly invisible among the purple flowers and the dark gray stones.

A man leapt into the middle of the dancers, black-haired, wild-eyed, a Phrygian with a curling beard and a strong torso—a stonemason or a bricklayer, perhaps. He danced among the waving priests, offering himself to the goddess, showing his thickly muscled ribs and heavy shoulders, his knotted thighs, his sex. A priest handed him a knife, and he flicked his arms and chest with it, sending drops of blood flying toward the throne.

Others had joined him, men from the crowd, drawn by the movement, the music. Their bodies moved with the shrieking flutes, the throbbing drums. Drops of blood fell like spring rain. The light grew. On the bare branches overhead a film of brown, of purple, of rose, had appeared.

Catullus, too, was dancing—he never knew, then or later, how he had come to caper and prance on the stones. His hand held a knife, a length of chipped stone, cold and sharp and clumsy in his hand, but he did not know where it had come from either. His eyes were on the goddess, and he was praying over and over, "Let me see, let me see," though it was not clear to him what he wanted vision for. The goddess's skin was silver, shimmering with light, her eyes as dark and blind as midnight. They looked down at him, inhuman, pitying, kind. His blood was on her feet, her throne, the stone beneath it. The flint knife in his hand was red and wet, but he felt no pain.

The bearded man held up his hand. From it dangled his own genitals, bleeding down his arm. Dancing closer, he beat them against the pine tree as the young god had beaten his against the throne, his eyes still swiveling blankly over the scene. With each stroke he grunted while the crowd shrieked and the music pounded its fierce rhythm. A swirl of priests surrounded him, holding up white robes. Dancing, they threw them over him and wrapped him in them, leading him away. Another man stood in his place, waving the long knife with the same blank-eyed stare. Catullus danced on, feeling nothing, watching the silver goddess as she sat. She had changed, was changing: her lips smiled, her eyes gazed down at him, gently, going from black to gray. Her silver flesh was warm with human tints. She lifted her hands and held them out to him, opening her lips to say his name. Like a man he worshiped her, erect and proud; like a child he loved her, his blood an offering to her still, maternal eyes. He raised the knife.

The women were sobbing. Near the stones he saw a group of them, faces upturned in the spreading light. They shrieked and bent like poplars in a storm, urging him or calling him back—he could not tell which. A white-faced woman stood among them, watching him, her dark eyes open at his nakedness, her pale mouth wide. Tears had marked her cheeks, her hair was matted around her oval face, but she stood with perfect stillness among the swaying women; her fists were clenched and her small body was held rigid and panting.

He glanced back at the goddess. She sat on her throne, her stone lips smiling faintly, her obsidian eyes remote and eternal. Around him the men still danced, the music roared, the blood fell. The white-faced woman stared at him, wide-eyed and silent. Slowly he let his fingers open; the knife fell to the floor, unused.

Light had spread over the scene. He stepped down from the stones, picking his way over green grass, tender and young, among lichened boulders to where she stood, wrapped in her black cloak. It was Clodia. Roughly he bent down, and, lifting her into his arms, carried her into the darkness away from the stone goddess on the throne.

She stood in front of him in the warming light, small, rejecting, cold— a figure that might have represented winter itself. He pulled the cloak from her, so roughly the pin at her shoulder tore, and the white dress it had held fell with a hiss to the floor. Her breasts stared at him, the nipples dark as berries against the whiteness of her skin. Her belly curved like a hill of snow, the hair in the blue hollow of her thighs was tangled like a frost-burned vine. Between her ribs a pulse beat, heavy, thick, but her hands on his arms were as cold as ice.

He pushed her to the floor, pressing her under him. Her mouth opened, her eyes looked up at him, dark with apprehension in their bluish whites. He put his mouth down on her, hard, feeling her lips give toward the sharpness of her teeth behind them. He thrust his body down, forcing his hips against her, feeling the pressure of her belly as his weight spread her thighs.

She cried into his mouth. Breathing hard, he pushed himself into her against the resistance of her flesh. He felt her struggle to twist beneath him, heard her breath gasp in her throat, felt his own cutting from his lungs. Clenching his thighs, he drove harder into her as she moaned and turned her mouth away from his. Sweat broke out on his back, on hers, he could smell it on the chilly air. She was muttering into his mouth; he could not tell whether it was to urge him to go on or to stop. His hands punished her nipples, his mouth bit down on hers. He could feel the grip of her thighs, the rake of her nails along his back.

She was crying, heaving and thrashing under him, begging him to stop. He pushed his mouth over hers to silence her, but she twisted her head away, this time cursing him, spitting and short of breath. A spot of blood had appeared on her lip. It enraged him—he drove harder into her, slamming her against the floor. She cried out, a sound that died into a long, trembling moan full of anger and satisfaction. Then his own release took him and thrust him still deeper into her as if a huge hand had shoved him violently into darkness.

He lay beside her a long time, sick with pain and humiliation. The cuts
on his body throbbed vilely; he falt nauseated and ill. His skin was slippery
and cold with sweat; the sea taste of blood was in his mouth. Beside him he
could hear her even breathing, regular as waves on a shore. He could not
bring himself to look at her.

The air was warm. He could smell green plants in it—new grass and
pine resin, moss, fern, flowers. Birds sang: a thrush warbled and a cuckoo
called. Nearby someone laughed and was quickly hushed.

He became aware that his face was pressed into her long black hair where
it trailed across the floor. Her beautiful ear gleamed in it; the sculptor's
curve of her cheek cut firmly across his sight.

"I'm sorry," he said.

She turned her face toward him, so close he could see the fine hairs of
her eyebrows, the deep, pleated blackness of her eye, the crimson lining of a
nostril. "Why?" she said calmly, and her soft breath touched his cheek.

"I shouldn't have hurt you," he said, choosing between confusions,
angers, fears. She was as still as marble, she might have been a battered
statue lying beside him on the ground. Blood stained her flesh—his, her
own—smeared like the drops on the stones.

Her lips moved in a smile; at the corner a crease appeared. There was
another incised in the violet hollow under her eye. In the pure line of her
jaw a minute separation had begun, the first sign of slackness in the
muscles underneath. His eyes widened as he saw.

Raising himself on his elbow, he lifted a tress of her hair, studying it
where it spilled like black water across his palm.

She saw what he was doing; he saw her mouth go straight with pain. "My
maid pulls the gray ones out," she said wearily, as the hair, shining like silk,
ran swiftly through his hands.

"Ahh," he said fiercely, overwhelmed. He pulled her to him, his
tenderness as thick in his throat as grief. He could not speak. When he
kissed her, gently now, he tasted salt. It was a long time before he knew that
the tears were his.

They were many hours in the cave, if cave it really was, for slowly he
began to realize that they were in fact in the great room under the temple
where he had slept the first night. "What happened to the temple?" he

whispered to her once under the chanting of the priest. His knees were scraped and his palms red and raw, but there was no sign anywhere of the tunnel they had crawled through. "I don't know," she whispered, smiling at him. The goddess still sat on the throne, the pine tree still spread its branches beside her, decked with violets and strips of scarlet wool; the silver god hung among the branches. But the forest was gone, the birds, the flowers, the soft air of spring, and only the flickering of lamps illuminated the vast, vaulted space.

The huge crowd was calm after the sorrows and the joys. The new priests, dressed in white, sat among them; it was like a family party at a festival. Catullus and Clodia sat with them. When the crowd sang, they sang; sometimes they chanted, sometimes they danced. At night, when the lamps were darkened, they slept side by side in the breathing of the crowd.

On the last day the priests lifted up the statue and carried it around the room. The new priests in their white robes sang; the old ones, in purple and scarlet, followed silently. The crowd, dressed again in what they had worn before, went quietly after them out through the long descending tunnel out into the city.

It was spring. While they had been in the cave the trees had budded, then leafed. The sky was blue, the air delicate and warm. The trumpets called against the breeze, and the thousand chirps and trills of birds answered them. The river, far below, ran golden in its new green banks.

They carried the goddess into the country. A small stream rippled like honey over stones, to join the Tiber among tall reeds and overhanging bushes. Kingfishers flashed blue and gold, an otter splashed and disappeared. Catullus and Clodia sat on a bank watching the priests wash the statue in the clear water. Catullus could smell the sweet, flowery scent of her perfume, feel the warmth of her hand in his.

"I love you," she said, her dark eyes squinted slightly against the brightness of the sun. The light, warm air teased a lock of her hair across his mouth.

"I know," he said, smiling as he pulled it away.

Her eyes were on the grassy slope below them where the crowd watched the priests knee-deep in the shining little stream. Music—flutes and cymbals—floated with lazy insistence on the breeze; bright clothes fluttered. A young man, crazy with happiness, stood up and danced a moment before hands pulled him, laughing, to sit down.

Catullus beat her hand gently on the grassy bank and she turned to him. Blushing like a rose, she said, "I do, I really do. I love you more than anyone else," but her eyes had gone again to the young man down below.

He put his arm around her and looked away. "I know," he said and smiled again.

There is no one, my woman says
she'd rather marry than me.
No, not even if Jupiter himself came courting her—
she says. But what a woman says to a man who loves
       her:
write it on the wind, write it on running water.

Caelius, my Lesbia, that Lesbia
that dear Lesbia whom Catullus loved
more than himself and everything he owned . . .

I have closed the book and sent it, completed, to the old man in Verona. There is nothing more to say, nothing of interest or importance. Catullus lived only a few years longer, and he had already had the best of his life. He had done what he intended, seen what he wished to see, gone where his vision took him. There is no point in dredging up the rest.

In the little room I packed the objects in the box—the toy yacht, the embroidered ribbon (when did she give him that? I suppose no one will ever know), the letters and notebooks and poems that recorded his long search. Only the little god remains, smiling at me as it has this whole long, wasted time. For I can feel nothing for these pathetic scraps—they are as faded as last year's flowers, and as dry. I do not know why I have spent so long over them: they have offered me nothing that I wanted. I was wrong—I suppose that's, as the philosophers say, the essence of the thing. There is no pattern here, no meaning to the past. It happened, it is gone, there is nothing more to say. The rest is painful, and the old man does not need more suffering. It would tell him nothing he needs to know at all.

In any case, the last details are only like the ones he knows, and much more quickly told. His son was happy—it comes down to that. He had learned to know Clodia as she really was. It cost him a great struggle to find out, but he accepted her at last—he knew now that there would always be other men. As long as she loved him best, as long as she was discreet and tactful, he accepted that. And he had his reward. He was happy, as I say, in his love for her, his life became what he had wanted—ordinary and content, like any young man with a beautiful mistress and a growing career. After a time he even thought of the future. He traveled to Asia with a governor going to his province, as do most ambitious young patricians; he made money there; he returned and interested himself in politics and literature. He had a reputation as a poet, and he added to it; he began to think of the *cursus honorum*, the list of offices that mark the stages of a political career. It would have worked out—you could see in him the middle-aged man he was going to be: steady, respected, honored. But his health was weakened by his struggle, his terrible time among the poor and the degraded, and he did not live. In four years he was dead. That is what I wrote to the old man. I have not had an answer.

I have not had an answer. It is odd. I expected one—perhaps I even hoped he would object to my going. In the months since I have come here, living in sunlight and silence on this deserted point, I have grown close to him. It is as if the past, which ties me to this place, has bound me also to him. His thin, sharp voice, his eyes, his dignity, his pain, his age, have all meant something to me. What it might be I am not sure. I had hoped . . . I do not remember what it was I hoped. I am not sure I ever knew.

So I pack, in silence, in the house that keeps its cool secret under the hot June sun. The servants do not speak. In these months they have grown used to me; they know without my telling them what I want them to do. Only my secretary, Philo, has risked a word.

"Sir," he said to me yesterday, shifting uneasily from one foot to the other. "Are you sure?"

"Sure of what, Philo?" I asked shortly. I was busy sorting papers, deciding what to take, and the interruption annoyed me.

"Are you really ready to go home, sir?" His nervousness was palpable, though I could see no reason for it. Irritated, I snapped, "Of course I am. Or I would be if you hurried up with those boxes, you lazy ass."

He caught his breath reproachfully and shoved a leather case at me. He would not look at me, but kept his eyes on his work as he should, but I was so annoyed I had to go outside for a breath of the hot summer air. Ready, indeed. Of course I am. All around me in the house the stacked and waiting boxes are the proof.

In the late afternoon, before I was to leave, I went out to the point and stood in front of the tomb. The brick was already mellowing, the roof lichened. In the long, slanting twilight it seemed old, weathered, part of the surrounding earth. The garden was not finished—I thought as I went through it that it never would be now—but it was well begun; under the prompting of the little god, I had done a lot of work. The paths were laid, the gravel swept and neat. In the flower beds the best of the season's roses bloomed softly against the walls. There were holes ready, waiting for the trees—the rows of cypresses I had thought to put in to keep the wind from the tomb. Bushes tied in linen waited by their places. It was tidy, but in spite of that, draggled and sad in the darkening evening, as if the meaning were missing from that, too.

It seemed to me that now, at the last, standing before his tomb, I ought to be able to cry. I thought that the tears I had never shed for him might come now, when I was finished with him. Now, surely, his life is over, I told myself, and mine will begin. I ought to be able to give him that last gift.

Yet I could not. I stood a long time, looking at the tomb, while the swallows darted in their long, zigzag flights across the limpid, wine-colored sky to land on the eaves. Wild doves nested there, too, their soft calls thickening the cooling air. Presently the air grew still colder, the birds fell silent, the noisy chuckling of the lake filled the night instead. I turned to go. I could no longer make out the tomb at all, except as the darker shape against the star-strewn sky, and there was no point in remaining.

My heel had already scraped on the gravel when from the tomb a voice spoke to me. I turned back, the hair rising on my neck. It spoke again, a high, chittering giggle, very horrible to hear. The night seemed suddenly much colder, the house, with its bustle and lamplight, very far away.

"Catullus?"

There was a sound from the tomb. I waited, wishing foolishly that I had thought to wear my sword—though what use such a thing would be against a ghost I cannot imagine. The night was full of noises: the creak of a branch, the whisper of leaves, the scrape and rustle of small stones on the beach below. Each of them came to me as something else—a leather breastplate, a shoe on the gravel, the sigh of a human breath in my ear. The tomb was silent.

Suddenly I was wild with rage. Shouting at the top of my voice, "Come out. By the gods, come out," I ran to the door. Its iron bars shocked my hands by their coldness as I shook them, yelling as loudly as I could. The voice inside screamed in my face, coming closer, whistling like a kettle on the fire; a draft touched me, then a heavy object, ghostly white, soft, moving fast. A sparrow, looming as huge as a hunting hawk, flew through the bars directly at me. Its wing brushed my cheek; its black eyes stared for the space of a heartbeat directly into mine. Then it was gone, gliding off in silence toward the point, leaving me shaking and ill on the path.

Servants had appeared from the house; torchlights shone on leaves. I brushed the rust from my hands and went to join them.

That night, my last in the bed that had grown so familiar to me, in that little room where I worked and lived for so many months, I lay awake for a long time listening to the quiet noises of the night, breathing the sharp, clean scent of the wild thyme that drifted everywhere through the house. I was thinking about Rome, which in four days I would see again; the city I had left behind seemed very far away, and unimaginably strange after the silence of this place. I dreaded it. The fact came to me like the sparrow, flying out of darkness—the irritation of a million people jostling against each other seemed frightful to me now. The noise, the press, the rub, the intrigue, ambition, clamoring for place, all seemed meaningless as I lay there in the quiet room where there are only the noises of the lake and the cicadas in the trees. My face grew hot; my hands clenched under the light blanket on the bed. It was only by an effort that I was able to turn my mind from the images and fall asleep.

But when I slept they returned, though I think what I saw was a dream. Indeed, what else could it have been? Yet it was very close to real. I lay on my bed as before; the summer night had not changed. Out in the garden a nightingale began to call, then another, then a third. Far away, on the road, a wagon rumbled, passing into the silence of the night. Catullus stood at the foot of my bed. His back was to me, but I could see that on his head he wore a wreath of wilted flowers, ghostly blue gentians draggling through his reddish hair. Though I could not hear it, I knew there was music around him, and the faint, spectral sounds of merrymaking—city life: voices, the clatter of wine cups, a woman singing to a lyre. Catullus stood as if he had just gotten up from a couch at a party to answer a knock at the door. He turned his weary smile toward me; I saw it clearly for he no longer wore his beard, though his face and body were dim, as if the night were visible through them. He stood there for a long time, but I could see that he did not mind—his look was kind, forgiving, friendly. I was not afraid, and it seemed natural to see him there, as if he expected me at this party, as if I had gone to it in the hope of seeing him. His hand was still outstretched to let me in. Then I saw that the flowers of the wreath were not wilted, they were drowned. The water from them dripped into his hair, darkening it, laying it down in points around his face. His clothes clung to him, river weeds trailed muddy tracks down his shoulder and his arm. I was aware, without knowing how I knew, that he had been in the Tiber, probably for a long time, and that his body was corrupted and decayed from his immersion. His face, too—I saw now that blotched over his pallor were patches of discoloration, pale and shining in the dimness of his shape, and his smile had become a fixed and hideous grin. . . .

As I watched he opened his palm; his fingers had become transparent, as if the flesh were falling from them and the bones were showing through. On his palm a heavy key glinted black as a hole, but gleaming with silver lights. I stared at it. It grew larger as I watched, and darker, heavier, uglier. It was as big as a man's hand, his head, his arm; it throbbed and swelled on his palm. Catullus stood still, smiling in spite of the weight, which he did not seem to feel. Then he raised his hand and threw the object at me. My heart jumped violently in my chest as it struck me.

I sat up. My heart was thudding, my breath hurt my chest. In my mouth was the taste of iron; I could smell the rankness of the Tiber. The room was empty. Outside, the nightingales still called, the cart rumbled, fading away into the distance toward the south. Slowly the river smell faded and the fresh scent of herbs came floating back.

I suppose it was a dream. I got up and lit the lamps on the table where the last bits and pieces from the old man's leather case still waited to be packed. The bronze god smiled at me gently over a drift of paper scraps, a broken pen, the last liquid drops of ink.

The lamplight wavered into life and the night outside retreated a little. The colors of the room—the blue of the walls, the white, carved beams, the red tile of the floor—began to glow; the crumpled cover of the bed was as solid as a row of hills, the shadows in it deep as valleys. It was almost possible to see the little farms, where men might live among the woolly furrows in safety and in peace.

I got back into bed. The little god on the table smiled at me, but I knew the smile was twisted with weariness and pain, and the god's small gaze was cold.

They say omens come in threes; I suppose it's true. In the morning when Philo called me there was a note waiting on the table in the atrium; a servant had ridden all night from Verona to bring it. It lay, a small folded book of wood and wax, tied with black thread and sealed with the old man's crouching cat, on the marble tabletop, a black oblong on the colored space. I took it up to my room and sat with it in my hands for a long time.

The window was open on the summer morning; I could hear the servants shouting to one another as they loaded the last boxes on the wagons. The air was still cool, though under it the heat of the day had begun to move, like a current of water rising in a mountain lake. The birds fluttered busily in the dust, cheeping and crying; the deep shadows of the trees lay like pen strokes across the brightness of the day.

I did not want to open the note. I knew what it said: I knew he would not let me go. The past, which has bound me so tightly to this place, has not finished with me yet. I turned the thin strips of beechwood in my hands, imagining the words inside. He would want to know how his son died, I told myself, trying to find a way out quickly. Well, I could explain that. Or perhaps he would ask what happened to the woman. That, too, was easy enough to tell. The whole world knows the answer to it, anyway. Probably the old man knows as well as I do.

I sat for a long time, holding the letter in my hands. Slowly the wagons filled up, the doors of the house slammed with a final bang. Someone below began to wonder aloud where I was. I became aware that my hands were sweating.

Angrily I told myself that there was nothing he could ask that I could not explain quickly and easily—all the complicated questions were not really difficult at all. I took a deep breath and broke the seal.

But it was a simple question. I am sitting here now with the blood draining out of my face, the cold sweat starting on my back. I see that like a tethered dog that believes itself to be free, I have been running all these months, and now the rope, so long forgotten or ignored, has caught me, brought me abruptly to a halt. Choking and gasping, I stand at the end of it, looking back along it to the past. All the pain I have not felt, for a young man's too short life, his bitter suffering, has caught me, all the pity and the fear I have never allowed myself to feel. I was right not to, of course, for now that I have I will never be free of it again. Some of the horror of my dream comes back to me, and I glance involuntarily at my sword where I have propped it against the table to take home.

A simple question. Seven words. Not even new ones, for he has asked me this once before. Yet it is unanswerable. One line of writing incised in the wax, and it feels as if it were cut into my own flesh. Through my anger and pain I can see the little god still standing on the table, looking grave, bitter, sad. Under his feet there are still some scraps of paper; a pen still rests on the inkstand. Slowly I take it up and begin to write, the letter propped before me. "Who was the man with curly hair?" That is all it asks. It is enough.

It is enough to take me back into those last few years of strangeness and violence, enough to remember how he changed. I suppose he had to, for he still loved her. The country he was traveling in had become bitter and broken; rocks and desert were everywhere now, and shade and clear water rare. Yet he kept on. I do not know why—there are things in that scene I have had to imagine, and that is one of them. Perhaps the goddess in the temple had shown him something when he danced for her. He prayed to her, I know, to see—that wish is there in his notes, along with a description of the dance, or at least that part of it which it was not forbidden to mention. But what he wanted to understand he does not say. Perhaps the goddess had let him know that though he was not her priest he was still her possession; perhaps he had gone farther than that and seen, as he had said to Julius Caesar about Clodia, that even the goddess was not the end of everything. It may be that whatever truth the Great Mother revealed to him—for that is not in the notes either—hid still another truth, and his search, far from being over, had only just begun. I don't know. I had hoped never to find out.

I saw him, oddly enough, almost immediately after the ceremony in the temple. He had taken Julius Caesar's advice and gone to the Megalesia, the public games in honor of the Great Mother, that were held in the Circus Maximus and open to Roman citizens. Clodia was with him—she seemed to have recovered a taste for his company. I remember I was surprised. I knew nothing of the secret rites, or that he had gone to them. It would have struck me as a great joke if I had guessed.

And there was nothing at the Megalesia to suggest that he had any special devotion to the Great Mother. He sat on his bench like everyone else, throwing small coins and flowers to the eunuch priests as they danced into the arena, bowing his head respectfully when the statue of the goddess was brought in, swaying to the music of the horns and cymbals, which moved everyone, when the women danced. During the combats that followed the parade, he watched with careful attention, though he was silent and sad and did not cheer when the better blows were struck. Still, others were silent, too—people who had bet on the wrong man, or who found the technique of the combats insufficiently interesting. It was nothing unusual. The only real difference I noticed at the end. Then, when the fights were almost over and the sand was already very wet with blood, I saw him lift his head and stare at the temple on the hill. I did not know what he was thinking, but I saw him turn and look at Clodia, who did not see. She was intent on the battle, wide-eyed, and openmouthed. He looked at her for a long time, then back at the temple, and his own mouth set in a firm, sad line.

After the games he came up to me in the crowd. He had gotten together a group of young men—Calvus, Quintus Cornificius, Manlius, several others—to go to the public dinners. Did I want to go with them? I agreed, though when I saw that Clodia was to come, too, I nearly refused. I thought it might make trouble—women did not go around the city then, though now, of course, there are some who do. At least they did not go then unless they were prostitutes, and certainly they did not go to the dinners the guilds and priesthoods gave. I thought, though, a second time, and decided that if there was going to be trouble I did not want to be left out. The others were laughing and talking together; Catullus was waiting for my answer. So I went.

But there was no trouble: we must have been too numerous and too loud. No one, that year, wanted more violence than we had already had. Or it may have been, simply, that we were all together, laughing, joking, going from one temple courtyard to another through the smoke of roasting oxen and the smell of wine; we were still young, after all, and very cheerful. The old men looked at us and smiled, shrugged, turned away. A few asked Calvus or Catullus for a song, a few pressed drinks on us. Some of them, the most conservative, I suppose, frowned and ignored us. In our midst Clodia laughed and licked the grease from her fingers, nodding in time to the songs, joining in the dancing and the wit and the fun. It was a long evening, and entertaining, and when at last, near midnight, the married men or those with other engagements went home, I was sorry to see it end. Indeed, Catullus intended to go on—he took me aside, saying he and Clodia were going to a private party and did I want to come? But I imagined that they wanted to be alone together and left him to his reward, walking home myself up the Palatine Hill in the early-morning damp and chill. I found out later that they had in fact gone on to a party, and to another after that—they did not get home for two days. So I could have gone with them, and was sorry I hadn't.

There were many evenings like that, and I went along on a number of them. Catullus knew everyone in the city now, and he did not forget the people he had met in his year without her. Clodia, it seemed, liked his rough friends and the strange corners of the city he had found, and he took her to many of them in spite of the objections of her family and the gossip of the better sort of people. I was there when he introduced her, one late spring evening, to Xanthius, after a performance at the theater. The party that night was a good bit more subdued than the one I had gone to with Catullus the year before—hardly more than an ordinary dinner, really— but Xanthius wore his beautiful women's clothes and Clodia liked it well enough, I think. For his part, he watched her behind the openings in the jeweled mask as he listened to her clever talk. Afterward, when we were going home, laden with the favors he gave—mine was a small rock-crystal statue of a sea nymph on a golden throne; a hinge concealed a tiny cavity made to hold salt—I hung back. As the others found their wraps and their torchmen, I said quickly to Xanthius, "Well, is she what he was looking for?"

The jeweled mask winked at me, the shadowed eyes behind the holes were unreadable. "He has found something. He's different."

"Happier?"

He did not answer, but behind the mask, I guessed his eyebrows rose.

"What do you think of her?" I asked into the awkward silence.

Again he said nothing.

"She's beautiful," I insisted. "You have to admit that."

"Yes. She's beautiful." He leaned forward, a graceful swoop, so that the mask nearly touched my face. "But, my dear," he objected in a drawl. Then as suddenly he drew back, and, standing very straight, made himself cold, upright, pale. His very wig seemed to become smooth and black. Then he was himself again. As I went out the door he whispered, "If I ever have to play Circe, I know where to study for the role."

I laughed. "Oh, no. That's not fair. She's really not like that. She has great charm, you know, and more feeling than she shows."

The hidden eye winked at me, the mask refused a comment. "Come back soon, darling." He pressed my arm and swept away, his rustling silk trailing over the marble floor.

She had acquired an appetite for the less-tame pleasures, and she began to demand of Catullus that he provide them for her. At first, I suppose, he was willing enough: he had invitations everywhere, and there were many places where he could have taken a woman, even a woman like Clodia, but those were not the places she wanted to go. He was taken aback, and he refused to escort her to the others, but she went anyway, coming home at all hours of the night, until at last he gave in. They went out nearly every night, going down into the dark city to drink and dance at the wildest parties with the least respectable people in Rome. I suppose he thought that while she was with him she would not be insulted or injured, and indeed that seemed to be true. Yet he did not like it, and she knew it. He pleaded with her to stay home, but even when they did the huge house on the Palatine Hill was filled with these people—street entertainers replaced the philosophers' discourses and the recitations from Homer of Metellus's day, common prostitutes sat where the *libertini* who had graced the men's evenings with their wit and learning had been before. Nor did she stay away from these banquets, but presided over them like a queen, more imperious and elegant than he had ever seen her before, her beauty and delicacy thrown into relief by the sordidness of her guests. In the early years her style would have intimidated him, but now he saw the woman behind the pale smile, and he loved her. Yet he hated those parties and he objected to them; sometimes they fought, he and Clodia—bitter quarrels, full of hot words on his side and cold silences on hers. More than once he left her, only to come back when she sent for him. Her manner then was regal and domineering, but he knew that under it she was afraid to be alone. In an odd way she had come to need him as much as he needed her; her pride rebelled at this, and it made their battles fiercer. He learned to hide his knowledge of her from her furious eyes. He learned to tease her, and to make sure that it was always he who begged for a reconciliation. When he wrote now, he wrote graceful little jokes to make her laugh and forget her anger.

He spent a lot of money on her, more than he could really afford. Even the cheapest prostitutes become expensive after a while, and parties every night cost money. He gave her presents, too, valuable things he ordered from the best workshops, for he saw that she liked them. They smoothed over the rough places in their love and made their reunions easier. But as their quarrels grew more frequent, so did the gifts, and his old frugal life was gone. He began to worry about it; it haunted him sometimes, and he woke at night from dreams of his brother's reproachful face looking down at him, reminding him that they were poor men from a modest house, and the money he had left Catullus would not last forever.

Yet Catullus did not grudge it to her. She was still Clodia, and he still loved her. Late at night in the great house, when he would lie beside her, her familiar warmth curled against him, her sweet scent in his nostrils, he would know a moment of happiness as pure as any he had ever felt. It paid him for the quarrels, and he began to hope again.

In the late summer, they went to Baiae. There, in her cool, high-ceilinged villa with its wide green lawns, its jetty and brightly painted boats on the bay, its rows of statues and colonnades in the gardens, they spent a week alone together, making love. Away from the city she was softer, more remote, more beautiful. He held her in his arms at night as if she were a child, as her white face closed itself behind her lashes as if she were wandering in a dream; the delicate hollows of her cheeks seemed to be shadowed by the moonlight of a different year. His own dreams began to fill with images of the kind he had known before; often he thought of walking with her in her garden, of sailing on the lake, of sitting in the small atrium of some plain but beautiful house that belonged to both of them. He saw her then reading to him in her unaccented Greek as he watched the small movements of her face in the lamplight. He thought of meals together, journeys, books. He thought also, with a passion that astonished him, of children. He was nearly twenty-seven, and ready to settle down; he began to talk to her again of marriage. "Do you think we might?" she asked, as if it were something unimaginable, and kissed him. "Why not?" he said. She laughed at him then, but he had grown experienced in her nature and said nothing. That night she held him closer than she had before, and her body demanded his with a fierceness she did not conceal. He understood that she was afraid to lose him now, and when she fell asleep at last he lay awake beside her, trying to plan for the future, trying to think of ways to find money, knowing that, poor, he could never set their lives in order. He began, after that, to think seriously about this; he talked to me about it when he returned from Baiae; he mentioned it to all his friends. He spoke about his financial worries, and about what he was fitted to do; he began, in fact, to look for some employment.

Then, one day, it fell into his hands. I suppose such things must happen if your family is patrician enough to have the connections his did in the city. Gaius Memmius, the praetor, was going out to Bithynia as governor for a year; he was assembling a group of young men to serve as his staff there, and he offered to take Catullus with him. Memmius liked poetry and patronized poets—I suppose that helped as much as Catullus's connections. At any rate, Cinna was going, and he persuaded Catullus, though he hated to leave her for so long.

No doubt it was in his mind that in Bithynia he could also pay another kind of debt—the one to his brother that had weighed so heavily on his spirit the year before when grief and guilt together had nearly undone him, and the loss of his love had made his neglect of his brother seem futile as well as wrong. In Bithynia perhaps he would be able to set it right again and be free. The future seemed better to him, and more real the more he thought of it, and the money he would bring back from so rich a province would almost certainly be enough for them to begin.

So he said good-bye to Clodia. They spent two days together in her rose-pink bedroom at the end of February just before he left, planning for his return. She promised to marry him. In spite of everything he was surprised, and he made her swear it on her little statue of Venus, which she did, laughing all the time. Yet on the last night her lovemaking was desperate and violent, her kisses had bites in them, her small, ineloquent body followed his with a kind of hungry anxiety. On her skin he tasted tears, though she said nothing and her face was calm, but when they slept at last, exhausted and sore, her hand clutched his all night. He took it as proof that she loved him and intended to keep her promise, and though he was sorry for her unhappiness, he was pleased to think she minded his going so much. It repaid him a little for the pain he had endured for her. But in the morning, almost as if she knew this, she held her head up and would not stay to see him out of sight.

We heard from him while he was gone, of course. He wrote frequently, and his letters were amusing and sarcastic and full of fun; people often read them aloud at parties as if they had been poems. He didn't care for Memmius, the governor he was working for—he complained that he kept all the money he looted from the province for himself. Everyone laughed when they heard that, for it was probably true enough, though not one of the things you were supposed to say. I resolved to write to him more frequently myself, but seldom actually kept this promise—I'm not sure why. At least I kept in touch with him through the letters he sent back.

One night Calvus announced at a party that he had received a poem, which he wanted to read—"Something different," he said, "something he's never done before." We listened as if our ears were thirsty and the poem wine:

> *Through many countries and over many seas*
> *I have come, brother, to bring these sad gifts*
> *For the last time to your grave*
> *and to exchange, in vain, this appeal to your*
> *ashes.*
> *Oh, my brother, fate has swept you away,*
> *torn you from me, too suddenly, too soon.*
> *All that is left are our fathers' ancient rites,*
> *the offering of this empty sacrifice.*
> *Accept it, wet with a brother's helpless tears,*
> *And forever, brother,*
> *greeting, and farewell.*

Many of us had tears in our own eyes when he had finished that. I went home bemused and melancholy, and, seeing the lights in the sanctuary of the Temple of Jupiter, climbed the hill and offered a small prayer for my friend's safety, far away in Asia Minor. I hoped that now things would go well with him, for no one had deserved better of the gods than he. "He is worth more than all of us put together," I told the god. "Take care of him, for surely he belongs to you." Then, feeling vaguely silly and ashamed, but somehow eased, I went down the hill and through the echoing Forum to my house.

One day toward the end of March, almost exactly a year after Catullus left, Calvus came to see me, stepping with a short man's self-important briskness into my entry hall. "They're back," he said. "I just saw Cinna in the Forum. Catullus went directly home to Verona, but he'll be here in a day or two."

I was taking off the armor I still wore to go out—though the violence that had so plagued us the year before had abated, some of us still took precautions in the streets—and I looked up to see him eyeing me. I had become an enemy of Clodius's, but Calvus was still loyal to him and to the democratic faction he represented, so our friendship, never very warm, had grown much cooler. It annoyed me now that he was the first to know about Catullus, but I concealed it. "That's marvelous," I said, offering him some wine.

He waved it away, no doubt perfectly aware of my dislike. "I can't stay. I just thought you'd like to know."

"Of course I'd like to know."

"Cinna says Catullus has bought a yacht," he said, making an effort at friendliness.

"He must have done well, then."

He nodded and turned away. I thought his heels sounded angry as they tapped across the stones.

I was busy, of course, which was one reason for my coolness. A young man named Atratinus had brought a legal action against me, and I had to spend a lot of time preparing my defense. It was a malicious prosecution— I had won a case against his stepfather some time before, and this was his revenge—but all the same it had to be answered, and answered well, so I spent a good deal of time with Cicero, who had agreed to speak for me. I was, therefore, seldom in the public parts of the city. But I did hear of

Catullus. Apparently he was still in Verona visiting his father and recovering from the journey. Of course I was much too busy to write, but a poem of his on his homecoming preceded him down to the city, and someone kindly showed me a copy.

> *Almost-island, Sirmio, and of all islands,*
> *the brightest eye both Neptunes keep*
> *in clear water or on the salt sea—how good*
> *it is to look upon you: I can hardly*
> *believe I have left Bithynia's mountains*
> *across the unplowed waves, and see you,*
> > *safe at last.*
> *Oh, what is better than to lay down*
> *the mind's burden and the aches of voyaging*
> *at our own hearth, in our own familiar bed again?*
> *This one moment is worth every weary pain.*
> *So, greetings, lovely Sirmio:*
> *be happy, too, you blissful Lydian lake.*
> *Laugh with all the laughter sparkling at your command.*

So I knew he was happy. I began to wait nervously for his return.

He arrived in the city on the third of April, a bright day full of the shadows of clouds and the chatter of birds. The fountains sent their spray over the stones, the new leaves whispered in the squares, the crowds strolled and drifted among the pillars and shades of the porticoes. He stood in the middle of the Forum with his cases at his feet, gazing at the new construction, watching the people, glancing up from time to time to the stucco temples on the Capitoline or the green gardens that tossed behind the mansions in the Clivus Victoriae. He seemed content just to stand there, looking around, but presently he took a few steps toward the Palatine Hill. Halfway there he shook his head, and, turning in the other direction, went out of the Forum toward the Subura. His servants took up the cases and followed him.

He went slowly, taking his time, looking into the doorways of shops, stopping to watch a barber at his chair. In a bar he drank a cup of wine, and farther down the way, he ate a piece of roasted meat wrapped in bread; he gave a coin to a flute player on a corner, and another, because he felt lucky, to a ragged child begging on a sidewalk. At last he climbed the steps to his rooms and stood looking around, grinning with happiness to be home.

That night Calvus gave a party for him. All his old friends were there: Manlius, and Cinna, of course, and all the young poets he knew. Even old Valerius Cato, who had been his teacher, and one or two very young men who hoped he would talk to them about their own poetry. I could not go. My case was scheduled for the next day, and I had work to do preparing for it. And I thought that Clodia might be there, and her brother. They were both witnesses on the other side—I did not want to spoil his homecoming with an incident, or even with coolness, so I thought it would be better to stay home.

A long time later Calvus told me about that party. Catullus lay on his couch at the head table, drinking Calvus's best wine, a wreath of hyacinths on his head, a grin of happiness on his strong-featured face, while his friends talked all around him. He had grown tanned and fit: his eyes looked lighter against his sun-darkened skin, his hair a little faded and gray around his ears. He had shaved off the beard and was once again entirely Roman; he even had a few military mannerisms—a way of tapping on the table with his forefinger to emphasize what he was saying, a way of peering into the jug when it was passed to him, as if he had been drinking water that was much less clear and healthy than our own. He had a dry cough, too, as if the cold dust of the high desert of Bithynia was still in his lungs. Many returning soldiers and administrators have it, and it is nothing out of the way. In a few months it is gone.

Of course, he was chosen master of the feast. Calvus, telling me about it, confided that he had been uneasy about this decision, for he remembered how much Catullus had been drinking before he went away, but his fears turned out to be groundless—Catullus called for the wine to be mixed in the traditional four to one, and proposed only two healths: one to Calvus himself, and one to Lesbia. There are only six letters in those names, so no one was going to get very drunk on that.

Sometime that evening, after the perfumes and the flowers had come in and the big wine *krater* on its lion feet, when they were all playing dice and shouting happily across the tables, Xanthius appeared, accompanied by two extraordinary boy slaves as handsome as Cupids. He was dressed conventionally enough in a Greek *himation* as plain as a philosopher's but much more elegantly draped on his tall figure. His appearance startled everyone into silence; his beauty and austerity were like cold water after wine, and everyone was suddenly very conscious of having grown sweaty and disheveled.

The Greek bowed with dignity to the head couch and indicated to the boys that they should take off his outdoor shoes. While they knelt he rubbed a little perfume on his hair and greeted the company, who nodded back, a bit uneasily.

"Won't you recite something for us, Xanthius?" Calvus said, hoping to lighten the atmosphere again. Xanthius's deep blue eyes rested on him thoughtfully. Then, drawing himself up, he began to declaim a particularly repressive and high-minded passage from Zeno the Stoic—on virtue, or some such thing. His bare shoulder gleamed, his mouth was straight, his voice solemn, practiced, dull. It went on, too, for a long time. The guests shifted restlessly on the couches, longing for the end; poor Calvus thought his party had died and begun to smell.

The voice droned on. All at once people began to snicker, then laugh aloud. Catullus, head back, was trying not to grin. Xanthius looked around in surprise. Though his voice did not falter, his face was suddenly transformed by an expression of the most comical dismay. He glanced down at the boys, still kneeling over his shoes.

They seemed to have been subjected to a peculiar and private breeze, for their tunics were flapping in it, floating over their heads and baring their pink behinds. In addition, Xanthius's own robe was disarranged. As he recited, still reeling out the huge, slow periods, the boys' hands climbed higher along his legs until they reached his thighs. Ineffectually he slapped them down, while the supper room roared with laughter. He tried to ignore them, continuing his speech, but they had grown more insistent. He twisted, eyeing them uneasily; he staggered backward, but they crawled after him, sliding their fingers under his clothes. As he reached the climax of his speech, eyes rolling, hands waving, they pulled him down. A huge leather phallus popped out of his robe and wobbled under his nose. He ignored it, though he had to throw back his head or the thing would have hit him in the mouth. The audience roared with delight. The boys lifted him, still declaiming, and carried him to the head couch, where they set him down amid the laughter of the whole party, and handed him his wreath and a cup of wine. He sat up, bowed to the company, laughing now himself, and drank off the wine.

Of course, after that the party was a success. Xanthius was obliged to demonstrate the devices that had lifted the boys' clothes and the phallus, which he did with much good humor; Catullus and Calvus both recited epigrams; there was a lot of singing.

Toward midnight, when they had thrown off their togas and were dancing in their tunics, Clodius came in with a retinue of followers. There were shouts of welcome, and the wine went around again. The small dark-haired man and his friends stayed a while, dancing and drinking, but it was plain he had come with a purpose and the party was secondary. As soon as he politely could, he drew Catullus aside. Under the cover of the noise he said, "My sister wants to see you. Can you come?" Catullus's dark face lit up.

He saw Xanthius's grave blue eye on him, but he was nodding and agreeing already. As he made his good-byes to Calvus, the Greek turned to him, saying very seriously, "Are you sure? Is it the best thing? Why not let it be?" but Catullus only smiled; in a few moments he was gone. The party hardly missed him, and the drinking continued until dawn.

The curly-haired man . . .

It was the morning of the Megalesia. The eunuch priests were already begging in the streets, the cymbals and horns and drums already shattered the daylight. They were preparing for the parade that would take them to the Circus before the games. Though it was early, hundreds of people were out, moving slowly toward the lower parts of the city for the entertainment. The shops were closed, the streets where the priests of Cybele had passed were strewn with flowers crushed into the stones. I hurried through the crowds, head down in the early-morning chill, to the Forum. I had to talk to Cicero before the case began, for it had been called in spite of the holiday, and we had to appear that morning. Cases of violence were important enough to call anyway, and it was a measure of Atratinus's desperation that what he had dreamed up to accuse me of was the murder of a party of ambassadors—they had been murdered, in fact, but no one but a madman could imagine that I had anything to do with it. Anyway, the jury was bound to resent being kept from the games, and I wanted to be sure that Cicero planned to say something to placate them. As I passed Clodia's house I saw her getting into her chair—an unwelcome and unexpected coincidence, since the witnesses would not be needed for some time. Catullus stood beside the chair, lifting his head to the wind, talking to her. I saw her shake her head and bend her mournful smile at him; I saw him nod, and grin and go off down the alley. He was going to the games—she had not wanted his company in the Forum, I suppose. I didn't blame her. She was, after all, a witness for the other side, and I knew Cicero planned to discredit her testimony if he could. Well, it was his job to do it. But I did not think Catullus would like it, and I was glad, as I hurried past, that he was not going to be there.

He went down the narrow alley. The first light of day was in the sky, colorless and cold; the walls of the houses showed gray and muffled as sleeping animals, the trees rustled new leaves against the growing light. He knew the way: he went quickly through the warren of little streets at the top of the Palatine Hill, coming, just as the sun was rising, to the Temple of the Great Mother and ducking under the oaks. In the grove birds were singing; the sky had turned blue. Down below the first crowds dotted the stone benches of the Circus, bright in their holiday clothes; farther out the river glinted under the breeze while gulls, making their way inland from the sea, fluttered like scraps of silver over the tawny ripples. The goddess on her lion throne smiled secretly at the windy sunshine. He remembered the night two years before when he had stood under the fringe of trees watching Clodia go into the temple, but he remembered it as a man remembers a dream, and it had no power over him now, except perhaps to make his happiness more real. Much closer, so close that he could still smell her perfume, still feel wrapped in the warmth of the huge black and silver bed, was Clodia herself, whispering joyfully into his ear that she loved him, that she had missed him terribly, that they would be married as soon as possible. He felt her kisses, the smooth curves of her body, all as mysteriously familiar as if he had never left her; he felt the sense of rightness being with her always brought him, and he smiled happily back at the goddess on the throne. He had brought a bunch of violets, which he now laid at the statue's feet, for he had an idea that the goddess had given him this joy, forgiving him, perhaps, for his failure to become her priest, and turning toward him a warm, maternal face, ensuring him his most cherished wish. The goddess smiled, and for a moment he almost turned back and followed Clodia down to the Forum, but the wind, which was freshening, brought him the cries of horns and flutes from the parade, and he glanced down at the Circus. It was filling up. He bowed, saying, "Very well, if that is your wish," and went down the steps to the path.

The day had grown warm. The sun, low overhead, glanced and glinted off the stone, the sand, the silver statues at the end of the long oval, the weapons of the small figures in the arena. All around him people cheered, standing on the seats to see the fights. He cheered, too, and stood up when they did, but his mind was distracted and the noise of the crowd did not reach him. He wanted to be with her even if it was only from a distance; he was going to marry her, and he felt he had a right to spend his time in public with her. The wind had died, in addition, and his seat was in the sun; he had not remembered to bring something to shade his head. In the break between the sets of combats he got up and went out to get some wine.

Down in the street it was cool, and the breeze from the river blew, bringing with it the smell of spring which had been missing up above. The long shadow of the Circus kept the sun from the stones, the booths under the colonnade were shady and pleasantly dark after the dazzle of the light. He began to enjoy the day again. There were crowds around the booths— he was not the only man the heat had made thirsty—and he waited, letting the little breeze ruffle his clothes, listening to the talk. From time to time he glanced toward the Forum, invisible behind the buildings and the curve of the Palatine Hill. Men were drifting from the games toward it; someone said the trial was nearly over and Cicero was speaking—"That's as good as the games any day," the man beside him said, leaving his place by the stall to go after the others. "And much cooler," someone else muttered. Catullus smiled. "He's talking about Clodia Metelli," a boy reported, having run up. His father, putting down his cup beside Catullus, laughed and said, "That will be worth hearing." Catullus put down his own cup and went after him.

It had been a long morning. The prosecution had brought a number of charges in addition to the original one, there had been a parade of witnesses, the speeches had gone on for hours. I had spoken in my own defense, as had my patron and neighbor, Crassus the banker, and now Cicero had taken over. His speech had gone on for some time already, and the jury was well warmed up, laughing at the jokes, looking grave at the serious parts, nodding their heads as Cicero's beautiful voice ticked off the points he was making. He was still working hard—he had too much experience to miss the possibility that something might happen to turn them against him at the last moment—but under his high solemnity I could see his satisfaction creeping in. He must have known his case was won, he had too much experience to miss that either. There was little left for me to do. I leaned against the plinth of a statue half in the warm spring sunshine, half in the coolness of the shade, listening to the speech and watching the crowd to see how it was going.

And a crowd was collecting. The word was going around that it was something to hear—and indeed, I have heard Cicero give many speeches, but I never heard him give a better—and the Forum was filling up. Idlers from under the porticoes had stepped across to hear, disturbing a flock of seagulls that had been scavenging on the stones; near the fountain and under the sacred fig tree men had stopped playing dice or arguing to raise their heads and listen; a political debate on the steps of the Temple of Castor had lost its audience almost entirely. I was pleased: mine was going to be the most public vindication Rome had ever seen.

The first parts of the speech were finished: my character and my strict and worthy upbringing. My faults were glossed over, as was my involvement with the radicals when I was twenty, and I was shown as a serious man. The jury seemed happy with this picture, and nodded sagely at the right places. Now Cicero had passed on the people who were behind the prosecution. Atratinus's youth was made to excuse him for the foolishness of the charge, his father's guilt for the malice behind it. Now he had come to the Clodians, friends and allies of Atratinus's family. As he launched himself into this point I saw Publius Clodius move closer to his sister. Cicero was saying, somewhat sharply, that he was involved. There was a gust of laughter, and Clodia flushed angrily and drew her cloak over her head.

The seagulls called raucously, disturbed by the noise. Cicero waited patiently for it to subside. He had come to the biggest point of all, his indictment of Clodia. Her information against me had been damaging; now he had to discredit it, and he was prepared to. I could see the crowd lean forward as he drew himself up and grasped the edge of his toga with his hand.

"At this point," Cicero said, contriving to give his voice a gentle softness, though it could be heard in every corner of the Forum, "I will speak generally—I will mention no woman by name. . . ." His eyes went with a certain look of significance to Clodia where she stood with her brother and an elderly cousin who had joined them; my own eyes went out over the crowd. It had shifted to see her, and in the space suddenly left empty I saw Catullus. He stood alone, looking, like everyone else, at the small figure in the black cloak. His mouth was twisted with pity and anger, his fists were clenched. Cicero said, "If a woman opens her house to everyone's desires and lives in public the life of a courtesan; if she goes to dinner parties with men not even related to her; if she does this in the city, in her gardens across the river, among the crowds in Baiae; if not only her behavior, her dress, her companions, the boldness of her eyes and the freedom of her speech, but her embraces . . . yes . . . embraces, her beach parties, her dinners . . . yes . . . they all proclaim her not only a whore, but a shameless and provocative one at that. . . ." Well, he had always hated the Clodians.

I could see Catullus take a step forward. His face had gone red, then white, his eyes were dark against his startling pallor. I saw her turn her beautiful head toward him, her eyes opened wide then closed as she swayed against the elderly man at her side. Cicero's voice stopped. In the silence I could hear a tiny click as Catullus picked up a paving stone. His head came up, his eyes measured the distance to the speaker. He had already drawn his arm back when Cicero began again.

His voice had grown. In the fullness of its most compelling power it sailed over the crowd, angry, patient, sad, full of worldly knowledge and deep wisdom, full of pain for the helpless folly of men. It was impossible to ignore it. The crowd leaned forward; even Catullus stayed frozen where he was.

"I ask you," Cicero roared. "If there is such a woman, a woman of the kind I have just described . . ." He leaned toward her and the bite of his words would have etched a stone, ". . . one of course, quite unlike *you* . . . one with the life and behavior of a prostitute, is it any wonder, is it disgraceful or shameful, that a young man should have—over the course of a year or so, and when he was a bit younger than he is now—should have, I say, *dealings* with her?"

He turned his head to me. There could be no doubt which young man he meant. Indeed I could feel the eyes of a hundred men on me, though I was looking only at Catullus. His head had come around slowly and his eyes rested on me where I stood, half in sunlight, half in shadow, leaning against the plinth. I saw his eyes widen once, I saw his free hand move with unbearable tension to brush the straight reddish hair off his forehead. Nervously I raised my own hand and ran it through my damp, sweating curls.

The stone dropped to the ground. I heard it go, I heard it break on the cobbles beside him. Then the voice began again, the crowd moved. There was a small flurry where he had been, and Catullus disappeared. Cicero passed on to another point; Clodia, led away by her cousin, was gone. Surrounded by a hundred men, I stood alone in the Forum, while the seagulls cried overhead and the sun shone down on the empty space.

> *Caelius, my Lesbia, that Lesbia*
> *that dear Lesbia whom Catullus loved*
> *more than himself and everything he owned . . .*

He left the city that night. A passage in the notebooks suggests that he tried to see her, but either she had given instructions that he was not to be admitted, or she had left Rome herself—the notebooks aren't clear about which it was. "The house was dark," he writes, "and the black door barred. . . ." There is a passage after that which has been rubbed out of the wax. In it I can make out only one word—"key"—and the sentence "I will leave the city, which is not the place I thought it was." Did he mean a real key? I think he may have meant, instead, that she was some kind of key to the city for him. Long ago, in the beginning, she had represented something like that to him—perhaps she still did. I don't know what he hoped from her now, or why he went to see her—he did not try to see me. He just turned away from that closed door, and went down through the city to his home.

> *Caelius, my Lesbia, that Lesbia*
> *that dear Lesbia whom Catullus loved*
> *more than himself and everything he owned . . .*

Almost-island, Sirmio, and of all islands
the brightest eye both Neptunes keep
in clear water or on the salt sea—how good
it is to look on you again: I can hardly
believe I have left Bithynia's mountains
across the unplowed waves, and see you,
safe at last.
Oh, what is better than to lay down
the mind's burden and the aches of voyaging
at our own hearth, in our own familiar bed again?
This one moment is worth every weary pain.
So, greetings, lovely Sirmio:
be happy, too, you blissful Lydian lake.
Laugh with all the laughter sparkling at your command.

It was to Sirmio that he came: to this small spit of land three miles long, jutting out into the lake, where the mountains form a barrier against the sky and the rain cuts off the road four months out of the year. Here I think he intended to live, farming his little scrap of land, working in his garden, writing his poems under the arbor or in the small study of his plain, rustic house. And perhaps, if he had, he would have lived a long time, growing older amid children and grandchildren and the produce of his hands. It was not what he had planned, for like everyone else he had had ambitions, hopes, a future, but here, at the end of his long road, in this small place perched with such an air of insecurity between wind and water, happiness was what he found.

The wind bruises the herbs so that their fresh scent is everywhere. The birds sing, the sun warms my back as I stand by the wagon, ready at last to leave. One last time I look around at the house where I have lived, the garden I began, the lake sparkling in the midsummer sun. I am wishing that I could have found it here myself.

The old man has sent a message—one last time. It is unwritten: he is too ill to write. His servant says only, "Please come. Please come, sir, or it will be too late." His reserve, once as stiff and formal as his master's, is gone: in his old eyes there are tears, and his plain, good tunic is crumpled, as if he had not changed it for days. Greatly disturbed, I nod that I will go as quickly as I can. I put my foot on the wagon and lift myself into the seat.

The house in Verona is in disorder, like its emissary. Old Catullus's hand has fallen from it; the servants stand around in clusters in the doorways while the dust gathers in the corners and the floors go unswept. The pool in the atrium is cloudy with debris blown there by the wind, and a wasp no one has swatted is buzzing around the offerings on the family altar. At least they have made the offerings—perhaps it is not as bad as I feared.

It is worse. Not the disorder—for the small room I am shown into is too bare and plain for that. It is like the room of a soldier in a camp: it contains only a table, a leather chair, and a wooden bed so narrow it might belong to a child. The one window is unglazed and the wooden shutter propped open on the late-afternoon sunshine. In the bed the old man lies; his small body hardly disturbs the symmetry of the white woolen cover. Behind his back one cushion sets him upright. His thin hair is brushed but his eyes look out of hollows so deep I can hardly see their whites.

Yet the disorder is in here, too. He does not recognize me. His eyes wander vaguely, his fingers pluck at the covers, scrabbling meaninglessly like the legs of crabs in the wash back and forth of a shore, except that his fingers are transparent and white.

Beside me the servant, seeing him, gives a little choking sob.

"Is he worse?" I ask under my breath, though it is doubtful the old man can hear me at all.

"Yes, sir. Much worse."

"Oh, gods," I whisper. It is not a blasphemy.

The servant leads me out, through the house into a ragged garden, saying, "Wait here, if you will, sir. I will bring you some wine. They will have some ready, I'm sure they will, though who might have given the order I don't know. . . ." He is trying to hold the house together, and the effort has bent his shoulders and shaken his voice. He hurries away, but not before I have seen him stop to bow his head and brush his fingers hard against his eyes.

There was wine. It is sitting now on the stone table beside me in a plain clay jug, and there is another of good clear water from the river that runs down from the mountains through the town. I have drunk that, but I have not wanted any wine. All I want is to sit quietly in this garden and wait.

It is not an ornamental garden, such as you might see in Rome, or like the one I tried to make at the villa in Sirmio, but I am interested in it anyway. It is plain and made for use, like so many of the objects in this house, though it is clear that no one has used it for a long time. In the corner, a plum tree casts its skeletal and unwatered shade across a yellow wall; there are grapes—last year's—withered but still hanging in an arbor and on cords against the stones; an unswept gravel path wanders through grasses that toss their high and wheaty heads in the dry, sunny wind.

It is still a pleasant place—oh, gods, it is a pleasant place—but I wish I had never come. I wish I were still sitting in Catullus's little house and the lake was fading into purple against the dusty violet of the mountains and the clarity of the sky. I wish it were six months ago, and I had never gone to Sirmio, never seen Catullus closed into the red brick tomb, never sat opposite the old man, never, by the gods, looked into the box he brought. For I see it is too late now: if I go I take it all with me, all the bright threads of the past that lay coiled in the box as if I were condemned by one of those complex fates the gods inflict to do the work of weaving them. If I go I will never be free. I see now why I came, why I could not leave, why I am, in fact, still waiting here while the shadows grow long in this dead garden and the air of the June night is laced with chill.

I see that if the old man dies there will be no one to forgive me. He was all I had, now that his son is gone; he was all that bound me to living. I told myself that I wove the pattern for him, but his need revealed my own to me. . . .

If he dies without cutting me free, I will have no life of my own. Living still, I will be a ghost, as surely as my friend, whom I betrayed so unthinkingly. I will wander up and down the world, gibbering in a high, batlike squeak, invisible, a part of a story that is finished for others, but never for me. I will be a slave in fetters, trailing them along the road to frighten travelers with a glimpse of me on moonlit nights. . . . In the cool of the evening, thinking of this, I feel my face grow hot and my eyes ache, but still I cannot cry. Slowly, in darkness, I reach down and take my sword from the sheath where it leans against the stone. In the last light of day I look at it. It is sharp enough to cut the thread.

The servant has returned. In the leafy night he is a piebald patch of white and shadow as the light of the house falls partly on him. His face is invisible, his crumpled tunic only a blur. He says, bending forward, "My master will see you now."

It feels unreal to stand up; I have been sitting for a long time and I can still feel the pressure of the seat against the back of my thighs. Unobtrusively I slip the sword back into the sheath, thinking, there will be time for that later, after all, if I need it. It is a consolation.

The old man is sitting upright in the bed. His hair has been brushed and tied back with strips of wool, his room is tidy. The remains of a bowl of gruel sit among the invalid's clutter on the otherwise austere table. The plain clay peasant's lamp beside the bed is lit. I blink coming in from outside, but the old man, who has been farther, watches me without moving.

Silently the servant brings forward the chair. I cannot tell if he has done this on his own, or if the old man still gives commands. He seems to be sitting too still to do that, and his attention is all on me. Yet there comes a moment when I know I must sit down. The black eyes have said so, though the bluish lips have not parted and the white fingers still rest in the same position on the cover. But I see that under them someone has placed a set of wax tablets and an unrolled book, leaving them both lying open.

The leather seat creaks under my weight. "So, Marcus Caelius Rufus," the old voice whispers. "The curly-haired man was you."

The servant takes the bowl and bows himself out the door with great correctness, though he cannot resist one last look of more than servantly concern at his master. Then we are alone. In the soft breeze from the open window the flame of the lamp falters, then burns steadily.

"Yes, sir," I say, looking into the old man's eyes.

"You were her lover?"

"Yes, sir." When I was a child my father beat me if I made excuses, so I do not say, "Others were, too." It does not matter, though I once thought it did.

He has taken note of my answer. The eyelids, brown and thin as onion skin, have trembled over the sharp eyes and then withdrawn. I wait tensely for him to say, "You have killed my son, and I can never forgive you. You must leave my house immediately." I have been waiting for him to say it for months.

"No wonder you thought there was no meaning in the story," he says in a contemplative tone.

I shake my head to show I do not understand.

He raises his eyebrows in surprise. "You don't see?" he asks on a faint breath.

"No, sir."

"It is you who deprived it of meaning. You do not wish to see the meaning that is there, so you tell yourself there can be none. . . ."

I say with a great effort of courtesy, remembering his age, "What meaning is that, sir?"

He does not answer. Indeed, I think he has not heard. He says nothing at all. It is so silent in the room I can hear the hiss of the tiny flame along the wick as the lamp burns quietly on the table.

It occurs to me that he might be too ill to say anything more. Perhaps, indeed, he will never speak again. Well, I tell myself, my sword is still outside.

A little sigh, no more than a breath, breaks the silence. "You are sorry that you were her lover?"

"Oh, yes. Yes, I truly am." I answer quickly, bowing my head, but already feeling lighter and freer.

But instead of anger or forgiveness he says, "That is not the reason you have stayed here all these months."

He is so old, so fragile, so sharp-eyed. My protest dies in my mouth. I sit looking at him in consternation.

"Do you think I'm not telling the truth? I don't really believe I am to blame. But I am. I do," I insist, wondering as I do why I am so anxious to condemn myself. But he seems to be taking away the only meaning I can bring to his son's life, as a fire sucks the air out of a closed room. I even glance uneasily at the little flame of the lamp, as if it might be responsible for the difficulty I am having with my breath. "I was her lover, I was the curly-haired man. And when he found out . . . Of course, I am to blame. . . ."

At last I see the old lips bend, I see the cords under his hollow cheeks pull them, while the feeble muscles move. "Oh, yes. You are telling the truth up to a point. No young man would stay five months in a little place like Sirmio, not when he could be in Rome, if there were not a reason. . . ."

It is a long speech for him, and he has to wait to add, "But it is not because you were her lover that you have."

"Yes, sir, it was." I look down at the plain square stones of the floor.

"You do not really think so," he says, smiling at me more broadly now. "Do you, Marcus Caelius Rufus? After all, she was rich, she was beautiful, she could help you in your career; she was meat for an ambitious man, and you are ambitious, are you not?"

"Yes."

"Well, then. I am right: that was not the reason. There was another instead, wasn't there? You were jealous of my son."

"Jealous?" I say, lifting my head. My voice is loud, for a flood of indignation has washed through me. "That is absurd." I am on my feet. In my anger I forget that he is old and ill, and I shout, "Why should I have been jealous of him? He was a weak person, a man who never became a man: a boy all his life. He threw away his life for a woman, can you imagine? For a woman. Like some lazy and luxurious easterner with nothing else to do, like a lovesick schoolboy, or a foreigner. No wonder she treated him with contempt: he deserved it. He kept going back to her, didn't he? He never had the strength to break free. He wasted his life on her. He had gifts but he never used them. He could have been someone in Rome, but he never tried. You, of all people, ought to know that. Weren't you disappointed in him? You should have been. Why not? He had every-thing—birth, education, a fine natural eloquence. There was no limit to how far he could have gone. Memmius would have sponsored him, at least before he wrote those poems about his greediness in Bithynia. That's just typical, isn't it, of how he threw things away? And Caesar or Cicero, or any one of half a dozen men—they all respected his ability. He could have been a praetor or a consul, if he had not been too weak. . . ."

The servant has come to the door. Horrified, I stare back at him; the room seems to echo with my voice. I turn to the old man in the bed; he is looking at me with steady eyes, but his powdery cheeks are pale. "I'm sorry, sir," I say, sitting down. "I didn't mean to shout."

Another invisible signal passes between them, and the servant withdraws.

"He could have been someone important?" the old man whispers.

"Oh, yes." I am surprised that he does not know that about his son. "He could have gone as far as any man in Rome."

"Didn't he?" His eyes go to the book still open under his hand, then turn to the corner of the room where a box I have not noticed sits gleaming darkly in the corner. It is the box of papers I have sent back to him. "He went very far," he breathes.

"It was a useless journey, then."

"Was it?" his old voice grates. "Consider this: because he made it, no one else will ever have to travel there alone. Surely that is quite enough meaning for one man's life, Marcus Caelius Rufus." His eyes have gone to the papers and notebooks under his hands, and there is a moment of silence while he thinks of this.

"No, but, sir," I protest again. "He could have done something *important*."

"Didn't he?"

"All right," I concede, hardly able to keep my voice from rising. "But a lot of men are poets and still have real careers as well."

The old man's eyes stare into mine. "Why didn't he, then, Marcus Caelius Rufus?"

I am held by the stare. "Because of the woman," I say slowly.

He will not let me go. "Wasn't it really because of you? Wasn't it really your jealousy that prevented him?"

"What do you mean?"

"I don't know," he snaps. "I'm waiting for you to tell me."

"What do you want me to say?"

He raises his eyebrows. "The truth, of course, Marcus Caelius Rufus. The truth." His hands close on the book, his mouth is a thin, hard line. "In effect, didn't you kill my son? Didn't your envy extend even to that?"

"No." I am trying not to shout, but I have to force out my words through a throat that has suddenly closed. "It wasn't me. It was the woman." But tears are running down my face. I can hardly see the old man through them. They burn my cheeks, they cut my throat like acid; if I had known how they would scald me, I would never have wished to shed them. And they do not do me any good, though there are so many of them.

It is a long time before I can speak. "It was not my fault," I mumble at last. "It was just something that happened, and I am not responsible for the result. . . ."

He says nothing, but watches me. The silence this time is longer than before. Into it the noises of the night come drifting; I can hear, far away, a wagon rumbling over cobblestones, heading south, the chirp of a bird wakened in the dead garden, a thread of music from a party somewhere in the town.

"Yes," I say, looking down at the floor. "It was my fault."

"You were jealous, Marcus Caelius Rufus?"

My head feels heavy on my neck, too heavy to lift. "I suppose I was. He had everything, you see. Talent, position, the right friends. . . ."

"He had the woman, too."

"So did I," I answer quickly. Too quickly, for he says, "Not the way he did," and I have to agree.

"But you said his love was childish," I protest.

"I was wrong," he says, musing. "I see now. . . . It doesn't matter what a man loves—a woman, a country, a profession, anything—as long as he loves it enough. Then it will take him everywhere a man needs to go."

There are tears again on my face, while he waits.

"Do you want me to tell you what happened?" I ask when I can speak.

"Yes."

I have managed to stop the tears. "All right. I'll write the rest of it, if you like." As briskly as I can I straighten my tunic and prepare to rise.

His muscles move in a tiny, ghostly grin. "I don't have time for that."

I ache as if I had been beaten—I did not know crying for the dead was so much work. Or perhaps it is admitting something that is like work, I don't know. In addition I am embarrassed to have shown so much emotion—it is un-Roman, and undignified, though the old man does not seem to mind. But mostly I am now suddenly washed through with fear—fear for him, so fragile and exhausted in the bed, and fear for myself, nearly as worn out as he is. He has no time for the rest? Do I want, then, for him to know it? I suppose I must, for otherwise my fear would be only for him, wouldn't it? I believe so. "What should I do, then?" I ask, cold with my new terror.

"Tell me," he says, leaning his head back on his pillow.

"Now?" I say stupidly. "Here?"

He smiles. So, sitting straight in my backless chair, I begin.

Everyone missed him while he was in Sirmio—I must have been asked a dozen times in a few days where he was and when he was coming back. I could not answer them, of course: I didn't know. None of his close friends would talk to me just then and naturally he did not write me any letters. He wrote to other people, since they wrote to him. Manlius told him of the birth of his first son, and received a poem in return, which he seems to have sent around to Calvus and Cinna and the rest. Cinna sent some books, I think at Catullus's request; Calvus sent him literary gossip and new poems:

If I didn't love you more than my own eyes,
delightful Calvus, for this gift
I would hate you as Vatinius does.
What did I do, what have I said
for you to let me have so many rotten, cursed poets?
The gods send down the plagues on the client
who sent you this collection of sinners.
For if, as I suspect, this new and elegant
offering is the gift of Sulla, that pedant,
at least I can be pleased that you were paid for your
      labors.
Great gods, what a horrible, damnable book.
And you, of course, sent it to your Catullus
immediately, to kill him with boredom
on the Saturnalia, the best of days.
No, no, you joker, you won't get away with this:
tomorrow, as soon as it is light, I'll run
to the booksellers for a box of Casios, Aquinos,
Suffenius, all that college of poisoners
and pay you back humbly for your thoughtfulness.
Meanwhile, you worst of poets, get away from here,
let your limping feet carry you out of my sight,
you scales on the face of our generation, you burdens
of our time.

Even Cicero sent him a note. In the end he could not resist them, and late in January, through the slanting winter rains, he drove down the long, straight road to Rome.

There he visited his friends, and stayed some time with Calvus, recently widowed and glad to have company.

If any gracious thing
can reduce our sorrow, Calvus, and make
the mute grave give up to life
our old loves, the abandoned friends we weep for,

surely it's this: Quintila does not mourn her early death
half as much as she rejoices in your tears.

Calvus needed him, so he stayed for some time; he had long since given up the apartment in the Subura. But one spring day he hired a wagon and drove out to the hills, where he bought a farm. He loved that place, but he joked about it, saying that his friends would say it was among the elegant villas of the Sabine district, but his enemies claimed it was in rural and unfashionable Tibertine—he didn't know himself which it was, he would smile to whoever asked; all he knew was that it was expensive. At the same time he took a lease on a large, pleasant apartment on the ground floor of a house on the Aventine Hill. He had given up the depths of the city; he lived, like everyone else, now, as far above the noise and odors of the tangled streets as he could. He was often in the Forum, listening to the speeches with all his old intensity and concentration. Once in a while I saw him there, head bent over a tablet, taking notes or watching the speaker, seeming to absorb ideas, as he always did anything expressed in words, more through his eyes than his ears. I saw him, of course, only from a distance; I did not like to speak to him without some sign that it would be acceptable, but he ignored me so completely the sign never came. If he caught sight of me, he turned away. He was unavoidable: his epigrams and poems were all over the city and you could not go out to dinner without hearing one recited, or to a bookstore without seeing a roll of them prominently displayed:

> *Varus grabbed me in the Forum,*
> *where I was hanging around; he wanted me*
> *to meet his girlfriend—a young tart,*
> *I saw at first glance, but at the second,*
> *not without a bit of charm.*
> *So we talked of a few things:*
> *what was happening in Bithynia these days;*
> *how its affairs were going; whether*
> *I had brought back any loot from my stay there.*
> *I answered—truthfully, as it happened—that neither*
> *the natives, nor the governors, nor any of their aides*
> *can buy a flask of perfume for a festival,*

especially if your governor's a cocksucker himself,
and wouldn't lift a finger for his staff.
"But surely, you bought the local specialty—
porters for your chair?" So, trying to look
important to this girl, I said,
"Oh, I managed a bit better than most.
In spite of the lousy province that I had,
I got eight upstanding, stalwart slaves."
Now, I hadn't one, either in Bithynia or here in Rome,
strong enough to lift a broken bed leg to his shoulder,
but the pretty creature, wheedling with her eyes,
said, "Oh, Catullus, I implore you, please,
lend them to me, just for a little while.
I want to be carried to the Temple of Serapis,
that's not far." "Not so fast," I said to the girl.
"When I said I had those porters—well, I exaggerate, a
*   bit.*
My friend Gaius Cinna—the slaves belong to him.
Anyway, what difference does it make?
Mine or his, I use them just the same.
But you're a nuisance and a pain, little girl.
A man's not allowed a single slip with you."

People were beginning to imitate him, too—there was a fashion among the younger poets for Greek-style love poems like the Lesbia ones, and even boys in school scribbled epigrams like his on their tablets when the teacher's back was turned. The word he had used in his first famous poems, *basio,* meaning "kiss," was now part of our language, though he had invented it, or brought it to Rome from his Celtic ancestors. Poets used it, and people at dinner parties—even the whores who hang around the statue of Marsyus would lisp it to you in the dark. In addition many of the public figures of our day began to appear in the poems—often showered with Catullus's witty abuse. Caesar and his friend Mamurra were the subjects of several that went around the city like a dusty wind, and others were treated no better. He spent a lot of time with his former governor, Gaius Memmius, too, and with his old teacher, the influential critic, Valerius Cato; I began to wonder if Catullus was planning a political career.

"You were worried about that possibility, Marcus Rufus?" the old man says, sitting up in the bed and stabbing me with his eyes.

"Worried?" I say, looking at the floor. I have probably memorized the arrangement of the stones in it by now. "No, I don't think so. I was glad he was back, even though he wouldn't talk to me. Why should I have been worried?"

"You didn't think he might have become a rival of yours there, too? That he might, even there, surpass you?"

I raise my head and look into his eyes. "I don't know," I say at last. "It's possible, I suppose."

It seems to me that I have been lying for a long time now. Now, admitting this, I feel cleaner, lighter, freer.

"Oh, yes. You do know. You are the only one who knows the answer to that."

"I suppose I do."

Well, other people wanted him to go back to his old life, too. I was not the one who called him back to Rome, nor was I the one who kept him there. All his friends saw to that—Manlius with his new baby, Calvus with his sorrow over his dead wife, the patrons with his poems, everyone. If it had been up to me, I would have let him stay in Sirmio, let him live happily and safely, let the city forget him. I know I would have. But it was impossible; he came back and it seemed to me that the whole city conspired. . . .

"Conspired, Marcus Rufus? Conspired to do what?"

I see now what my honesty has bought me: I will have to tell him. I have gone too far, and he has a right to know. And for myself, I think perhaps it is worth the risk, for no matter what I say he may still find it in him to forgive. If not, well, my sword still waits outside. . . .

He is not interested in my thoughts. "Conspired?" he demands again. His fingers move impatiently over the hard surface of the book he holds, his voice, though thin as a winter grasshopper's, still commands. He has not much time.

"To kill him," I whisper, through a closed throat.

All the time he had been living in the city he had been looking for Clodia. No one knew, and he did not talk about it, nor did he write any poems—at least not that I heard then, or that have survived in the leather case—about his search. He seemed to live a normal life and all his friends believed that he had finished with her. All of them but me, if I was still his friend. I knew better.

I knew because, long before, when he was still in his little villa in Sirmio, I had written to him—just a few lines telling him that the house on the Palatine Hill was shut up and Clodia had disappeared. That was all I said, I did not apologize or explain. I told myself that I was telling him this as a way of doing both, as a way of letting him know that I still kept my old friendly feelings for him and I thought he would write to me in return so that we could make up our quarrel. He was my closest friend, my distant cousin, after all. He could not go on for long being angry over something as trivial as the favors of a woman like Clodia Metelli.

It was some time before I realized that he was not going to forgive me. He was back in the city and living down the street from me at Calvus's before I did. I had seen him several times in the Forum on the days when there were trials, or over the heads of the crowds at festivals. He had ignored me, but I had managed to believe that it was accidental. Now I had to face the fact that it was not. Yet I could not believe that the bond that had always united us was broken. We were too similar for that, we always had been. Once I saw him standing in front of Clodia's shuttered house. The sun was shining on his reddish hair, his face was turned toward the roof where the outline of the cypresses in the garden speared the sky above it. I was too far away to read his expression, but I knew he was thinking of the soft spring nights when light and music had drifted out into the street from the atrium. . . . How did I know? I knew him, that's all. Near midsummer I saw him in the city in the blue light of dawn, drinking in a carter's tavern and talking to the girls. I was on my way home from a party, wreathed and perfumed and a little drunk, but he seemed stone cold sober. I knew he was looking for her.

I don't think anyone else realized that she was gone for good. Most people simply imagined, if they thought of it at all, that she had gone to live a life of dignified seclusion at one of the dozen or so country houses a family like hers owns. It would certainly have been natural enough for her to do that, after the immense scandal of the trial. In fact, I happened to know, through Cicero who had a house near them, that she was indeed in the country, but living with her husband's brother's family. If I knew that, then so did Catullus. He was very friendly now with Cicero, and he did not seem to blame him for the part he played in her ruin. On the contrary, he was grateful to him—I don't know for what, but I think it must have been for information. There is a graceful little note of thanks among his political poems—I'm sure that's what it's for:

> Most eloquent of all the sons of Rome
> who ever lived, or live, or will come after us,
> Marcus Tullius—to you Catullus gives
> his deepest thanks, though he is as much
> the worst of poets as you are the best of orators.

Then, one day, as I was coming home from a visit to an estate of ours, by accident, I saw her. My men and I had taken a side street to avoid some flooding on the road, and there in a little suburban market just outside the city walls, she stood in the freezing wind, dressed in black, with a basket over her arm. Her hood whipped across her face, but I could not miss her pallor, her black eyes. She was arguing with a stallkeeper, and from the basket a bunch of turnips protruded. I checked my horse. Away in the distance the city shone on its hills like chalk against the tumbling gray clouds. The air was white with approaching snow. The shopkeeper raised his voice, and I heard her answer: it was all ordinary, plebeian, real. On the river I could hear the shouts of poor men fishing for driftwood. It was already very cold.

She did not see me, and for my part I could not bring myself to speak to her. Making a sign to my men, I turned out of the square to the main road back to town. But when I got back, though it was late, I went at once to Catullus.

I found him in his large apartment, sitting alone in the library. A brazier glowed warmly beside him, a hanging lamp on a chain cast a circle of light over his desk, his papers, his strong, short-fingered hands. I could not, at first, see his face, for it was in shadow.

He stood up when I came in. "Hello, Caelius," he said with reserve.

He looked different—older, more solid. Well, he was nearly thirty, it was natural that he should change. His clothes were better, though he wore them with indifference—he had thrown an old outdoor cloak over his tunic for warmth, regardless of the fact that it was shabby, though it was well cut. His face was different, too: the strong shadows under his cheekbones were the hollows of a grown man's face; his eyes were steady, thoughtful, and cool. As I came forward he raised his hand and brushed it through his reddish hair.

It made me smile. He raised his eyebrows as if wondering why, then glanced at his palms. Slowly he lowered them to his sides. He did not smile back.

"What are you doing?" I asked, unaccountably nervous.

He glanced down at the tablets. "Writing to Julius Caesar. I saw him when I went home to Verona. He complained about a couple of poems. . . ." He caught himself and in a hard voice said, "I've just returned. I'm sorry I can't offer you a drink, but the house is in disorder." He swept his hand in a half circle to show me. "I'm sure you'll understand."

"Yes," I said. "I understand."

There was silence. The brazier ticked and hissed. Somewhere outside the wind rattled a shutter, a voice said something sleepily from the back of the house. He fingered the papers on his desk as if he were anxious to get back to them.

"I've seen Clodia."

"Really?" He raised an eyebrow indifferently. "How nice for you."

He was looking at me, but I could not read his eyes. Behind him the dark red walls of the room glowed like the shadow at the heart of a fire, the covers of the books gleamed softly in their niches. He said coolly, "Why did you think I might be interested?"

"Surely you must be joking," I said, not at all sure that he was. "If you're not interested, no one is."

"Perhaps no one is," he said in a reasonable tone.

"Perhaps." I was still standing, and so was he; we were facing each other across the desk. Out of the corner of my eye I could see the letter he was writing—a poem, actually. "Or travel across high Alps," it said, "to gaze on Caesar's magnificent monuments." "Are you going away?" I asked.

He shrugged. He would give away nothing, admit nothing. The desk between us was as high as the wall of a city under siege, and an enemy peered over it. "She's not with her relatives. She's alone, and she's poor," I shouted, raising my voice to carry over the wall. "I saw her standing in the square of a little suburban town with a basket of turnips—*turnips*—on her arm."

Slowly he sat down. The lamplight fell on his hollow face. He bowed his head. For a moment a thread of gray shone in his tawny hair. He raised his hand and rubbed it hard across his eyes.

"Where?" he said at last.

Still standing, I told him.

He looked up. Remote and polite, his gray eyes rested on me. "Thank you, Caelius," he said, as if to a servant who has brought him his sword but cannot expect to share his plans for its use. I hesitated a little longer, but he said nothing more. Turning on my heel, I went out. I did not say good-bye.

So he, too, disappeared. Into the whirling snow that whipped through the city that year his figure seemed to fade, going down into the shivering streets along the hard-packed icy roads, out into the little suburban town. No one noticed. That year—last year—the cold was so great it preoccupied us all. It began in the autumn with drenching rains that flooded the fields around and closed the roads. The river rose, and the grain in the warehouses on the Tiber were destroyed, so that people began to go hungry; the unbaked brick of the tenements was washed away. When winter came, the rain was mixed with snow, and we did not see the sky for days. Even the river froze; no one could remember when that had happened before, and at parties—when people still gave them—it was all we talked about. Old men began to say that it was the coldest winter in seventy years. Business had to be suspended sometimes in the Forum, since no one wanted to risk the slicing winds. In the big houses people sat huddled all day in front of their braziers; the servants could hardly be made to leave the kitchens or the laundries, where they congregated for warmth. The poor behaved with great irresponsibility. In their crowded apartment houses they burned everything they could find, starting with their furniture and going on to the doors and stair rails, even their looms and tools. From these unregulated fires the buildings sometimes caught, and there were blazes all over the city. You could see the smoke and flames from the Palatine Hill, even through the snow. People lost a lot of money in those fires—though Crassus was said to have found a way to turn them to profit; I never found out how. No one paid much attention to anything outside the cold and their losses, and Catullus slipped away.

Outside the main parts of the city the cold was even worse; in little towns like the one where I had seen her, places barely woven into the fabric of Rome, the wind blew stronger and the ice lay thicker in the streets. Food was scarce there, too, since the roads were poorer and the farmers had trouble getting to the markets. Catullus, living in the one miserable inn the town provided, went three days on nothing but thin gruel. At least there was wine and hot water, and a table by the oven where he could write.

In the cold and isolation his thoughts had gone back to her, gone back over the history of their love. He was just short of his thirtieth birthday, and he had loved her for the last eight years; she had ruled, he saw, most of his adult life. Now, he thought about it. He saw again the glimpse of happiness with which it began, the bitter education in pain that followed. He thought of himself and what he had given, and he tried to describe what he had found out about his love:

> You said once that you loved only me,
> Lesbia: you would refuse even Jove himself for
> Catullus. I loved you then,
> not as ordinary men love women
> but as fathers love their children and their heirs.
> I have learned better: though I am scorched far worse
> by my love, I hold you now cheaper, and easier.
> Why? you ask. In love an affront like this
> fans passion, but makes goodwill die.

Sometimes he relieved his concentration with his old jokes and games:

> Nothing about you interests me, Caesar,
> and I have no wish to please.
> I wouldn't even send to know
> on which side of you your face is.

Sometimes he simply sat by the oven, staring out into the street where the wind hurled the snow so thickly down the narrow space that even the closest houses across the way were invisible.

In the last days of December, there was a break in the weather—not a thaw, for there was none during the deepest months of that winter—but a day or two when the wind blew less violently and the snow swirled in the streets with a diminished malevolence. Those who were able went out; a rudimentary market established itself in the little square; a few of the hardier or more desperate even managed to go into the countryside for wood. Catullus, driven by a need as great as theirs, wrapped himself in woolen cloaks and went into the street, looking for Clodia.

The afternoon had closed down, gray twilight like an iron shutter rolling across the sky, snow drawn like a curtain over the faces of the houses. He had gone as far as the edge of the town, and it was difficult to get back. In an alley between high walls he stood for a moment under the shelter of a stable roof, to rest and get out of the wind. Across the rutted track a wooden door stood open. He could see a frozen garden, shabby and disgraced. A man and a woman wrapped in black like ragged, fluttering crows stood together under the remnants of an arbor; at their feet a bundle of firewood made a twisted scrap of shadow on the graying snow. As he watched, peering in the fading light, the woman leaned back in the man's arms. For a moment he saw her clearly, the white face, the black eyes, the black hair pulling free suddenly in the wind. Her hands went under the man's cloak, her head bent to his shoulder. A swirl of snow intervened. Cursing under his breath, he struggled out from his shelter into the force of the wind. It tore at his face, clawing tears into his eyes; his cloak filled up with air, impeding him; his boots slipped on the ruts. When he could see again, the man was gone; the woman stood alone in the desolate garden, the firewood at her feet. Slowly, like an old peasant, she bent to pick it up. He pushed his way through the doorway. When she straightened up, her eyes looked into his. "Hello, Clodia," he said.

She did not answer. Her eyes stared into his, neither pleased nor hostile. He reached for the bundle of wood, and, taking it from her arms, carried it for her into the house.

The house was hardly more than a hovel—merely an atrium and a bedroom, with a kitchen tacked on in a shed to the rear. The walls were peeling, the wind whistled through cracks. He set down the firewood, and, finding rags in the kitchen, stuffed them into the gaps under the doors and in the walls. There was practically no furniture: a bed, a couch to dine from, a rickety table. He wondered if she had burned the rest. There was one servant, a toothless old slave whom he sent with a silver coin to bring back what she could from the town. There was no oil for the lamps—at night she must have eaten by rushlight if she ate at all; he suspected that she did not very often. Her body was blue with cold, her ribs showed like the shadows of furrows on the snowy ground, the cradle of her hipbones enclosed in a hollow. Even her breasts hung like an old woman's from the corrugations of her chest. She would not speak. When he kissed her, he had to hold her face in his hands: otherwise she would have turned away. He held her to him, murmuring into her silence words of consolation and of shame. She did not respond. When he carried her back to bed she spread her legs in silence; in silence she permitted him to enter her. He could not even tell if he had satisfied her when his own satisfaction had been achieved. She lay passively in his arms in the early-winter darkness. When he got up to rebuild the fire he could see her eyes staring steadily into the shadows on the ceiling.

He stayed with her for three days: he did not like to leave, even for a short time. The wind enclosed them, the cold kept them isolated in the little bedroom, where the light from the fire gave at least the illusion of warmth. She lay on the bed, hardly speaking, while the storm outside blew itself out in noise and confusion.

On the fourth day he prepared to go out. He did not like to do it—the cough he had had in Bithynia had come back and he felt light-headed and ill. But they needed food and fuel, more than the old slave could manage, if they were to live—and he wanted her to live; he wanted to live with her, now that she needed him, now that he was the only one.

She turned her head to watch him as he put on his tunic and cloak. It was the first sign of acknowledgment of his presence she had made, except to allow him to make love to her.

"I'll be back," he said to her, smiling to reassure her unmoving eyes. "We need some food, things like that. Don't worry." Her lips tightened scornfully, and she turned her head away. He was surprised when he returned, coughing from the cold, that she was still where he left her.

Slowly she began to accept his presence. She ate what he set in front of her; she drank the wine he poured; she got up and did her hair, dressed herself. She spoke to him sometimes, but she made no concessions: she treated his presence indifferently and never mentioned the food or the wine he gave her or the fires he built. At night in bed she let him take her silently, contemptuous of him or herself; he accepted what she gave. He had hoped for more, but he told himself that there were reasons for her coldness. She had been near to starvation, and alone. Her pride was damaged; he knew now that she lived by pride, and the public humiliation she had endured had wounded her deeply.

At least she grew physically stronger. Her body lost its too thin blueness, her hair began to shine, her cheeks had color in them. One day she stopped him as he was going out, taking the basket from his arm and saying, "I will go." He smiled at her, pleased that she felt well enough to go out in the cold and wind. He thought perhaps that she had noticed that he was not well himself and cared enough now to repay his devotion. He gave her money and watched her plod through the snow to the gate.

Without her the house seemed empty. He could not settle to work, but wandered here and there, worrying. The certainty grew in him that she would not return; she was still too weak, too ill—she would lie under a snowdrift and he would not find her for days . . . but she came back, gleaming, polished by the icy wind, with a reddened nose and shining eyes, and spoke to him very pleasantly about the food she had managed to buy. He had to admit that she had done better than he did—with the money he had given her she had brought back three times as much. He complimented her on her cleverness, and she smiled at him. He could not believe the pleasure that shot through him at the sight.

After that she went out nearly every day, often for several hours at a time. While she was gone the shabby house was intolerable to him. At first he forced himself to stay; he thought if he were gone when she returned, her despair might come back and she might leave him forever. But presently his restlessness grew too strong, and throwing on his cloak, he would stagger through the wind and snow to the inn to sit in front of the oven there, drinking wine and hot water and working on a poem for an hour or two.

In truth those hours at the inn meant a lot to him. The hiss of steam in the oven, the smell of cooking food, the rattle of dice and conversation, were life and health after the coldness of her behavior and the silence and bareness of the house. At the inn at least people liked him: they laughed at his jokes, they bought him drinks, they pressed remedies on him for his now-chronic cough. The barmaids mothered him, giving him milk with bread and honey in it when such things were available, and making sure his chair was in the warmest part of the room. And he worked: to feel the stylus in the wax, the reed pen on the paper—they restored him better than the jokes, they warmed him more than the wine. He would sit at the scarred and battered table, coughing heavily, thinking of Clodia while he wrote and the barmaid swished a rag over the counter and joked with him when he looked up. When he left they kept his table for him, respecting his work, and it was always there untouched when he came back.

He had tried to write in the little house—he would have tried to write in an open boat or the back of an elephant if that was where he found himself—but Clodia had objected. Not in words, for she still said very little, but in restless pacing and hard, scornful looks. He had abandoned the attempt. She did not seem to mind his going out, and sometimes when he came back and found her already there she was almost pleasant to him, though she did not show it by much directly. He thought she missed him, though he guessed she liked her independence now and was glad she felt strong enough to want it. He could not be sure, for she was still uncommunicative. She would sit for hours in her hard, backless chair, her hands in her lap, her eyes remote, getting up only to speak to the servant or to look out at the gray and turbulent air. Her mind did not wander—if he spoke she would answer, curtly but to the point. He wondered what she thought about, locked in her silence, but could not get her to say. He wondered if she was unhappy, or ashamed, or grateful. He tried to amuse her, and sometimes she allowed herself to join him, playing long, intent games of dice or listening to stories of his service in Bithynia or his childhood in Gaul. He did not talk of Rome and she never mentioned it. At night she still gave herself to him with silent contempt, looking away when he entered her, and making no sign of pleasure.

All the same he began to hope they were establishing some sort of life in their isolation. She seemed to depend on him; her eyes went first to him when they opened in the morning; she seemed glad to see him when he came in from the outdoors; she slept curled against him as if she needed the warmth at night. Under his care, she had grown beautiful again, and he saw her sometimes looking at her creamy skin and slender curves with a kind of satisfaction. If she saw him then, she would stop, slanting a look of trapped and impotent rage like a caged lion's at him, but she continued to care for herself. Once he even saw her sitting by the door into the garden, carefully pulling the gray threads from her long black hair with a tiny grimace of pleasure for every one she plucked.

He could not be sure if she was getting better, much less if she would ever take pleasure in his company again. He was sure of only one thing— that he would go on taking care of her. He had come very far: his long journey through love and pain had hardened him. In his soul he was like a soldier now, a soldier who has marched a thousand miles through every discomfort, every danger, so that his mind was toughened and his heart cool and farsighted. He knew she was not, as he had once thought, a goddess; nor was she an emblem, a symbol of all the world had to give of beauty, wisdom, joy. He saw that she was a woman, troubled, humiliated, suffering. He even saw that in her pain she was incapable of loving him.

It did not matter. In the cold gray days he saw that, too. He had come so far, alone and sometimes afraid, he had left behind his hopes, his dreams, his ambitions, his youth, as an army, marching through difficult terrain, strews its path with its extra cloaks, its winter boots, its trinkets picked up in a previous town, so as to march more quickly over the rough ground.

And he had won. He saw that now, too. It did not matter if she loved him—he believed she would when she was well, but that was immaterial. It did not matter even if he loved her. His long obsession with her had bound him to her just as she was bound to him by poverty, disgrace, and need. She was his now, his woman, as much as if she had been his wife, and to him that meant something very serious. He saw that the victory he had won was over himself, not her, and she was part of him forever.

He tried to make her understand his devotion, for he knew that she did not. At night in bed, when she lay passive in his arms, he tried to rouse her with kisses, jokes, little murmured words of love. She did not respond. Her black eyes were full of the shadows she stared at; her pale mouth stayed closed and set. He was not even sure she heard.

Then one night, she answered him. He had been asleep, or nearly, drowsing in the last light of the brazier. He had made love to her; the taste of her body was still in his mouth, the pressure of her ribs, her hips, her thighs, still warm against his flesh. He heard her voice in the rosy darkness and woke out of his sleep to see her pure profile beside him against the light. Her eyes were open, liquid in the dark, her lips were moving. He heard her mutter in the silence, a thin stream of words in the howl of the wind outside.

At first he thought she was saying a prayer, for the name of a deity was in it. She was calling on Venus, the ancestor of her house. Then he heard the rest. She was cursing him, saying his name over and over. It was detailed, specific, cold: she was asking the goddess to wither his heart, his mind, his flesh; she wished him tormented, impotent, dead. He reached out his hand and laid it over her lips.

"What are you saying?" he whispered in horror.

Her eyes turned toward him. Under his hand her lips curled as she spat a word into his palm. He felt her sharp teeth and drew back. Before he could stop her, she was out of bed. The light shone briefly on her slenderness; then she snatched up her cloak and ran.

He went after her, still shocked and numb from the hatred in her glance. The cold floor struck his bare feet, the drafts he had not been able to stop whistled thinly, whipping at his flesh. He hardly felt them; he was looking in the dark for her, afraid of what she might have done.

He found her by the door to the garden, looking out through a small watery pane of glass into the trampled dirty snow, the barred shadow of a tree. Against the thin light that leaked through the pane her hair was a mass of darkness, her skin a pale, luminous gray. On her cheekbone a small spot of silver winked.

He stopped a little distance from her in the dark kitchen, his feet cringing from the floor. A square of pale light lay between them on the tiles. "What is it?" he whispered, sending the sound across the cold, still air.

He was afraid she had gone back into the distance she had kept at first, and wrapped herself for good in the winter. He saw her oval face turn toward him; her eyes were shadowed, her features indistinguishable. She said, "You have ruined me."

The words fell on him like icy drops from the well of her contempt.

"I have?" he choked, in pain. "I am the only one who hasn't. I have done nothing—I have only loved you."

She was shouting at him; she had stepped across the space of light and her fists were striking him. She was sobbing, screaming; her hair flew, hard and stinging, into his eyes. "Who asked you to?" she shrieked. "Whoever asked you to?"

Her fists hurt him; his nose cracked sharply and warm blood ran down into his mouth; his eyes ran with sudden tears. He put his arms out blindly in the dark to stop her. Her voice deafened him, her incoherent shouts of rage, of pain, of hate. "I love you," he said, feeling his arms close over her writhing body.

She screamed and struggled against him as if his words had scalded her. Shocked, he let her go. She had lost her cloak. In the freezing air she stood back, staring at him, naked and wild. Her hair had twisted over her shoulders like a mass of snakes, her eyes glittered, her pale body seemed to stare at him, cold and rejecting. He could see the dark circles of her nipples, like embossing on a shield, her thighs were pressed together, her knees shone slightly, her narrow feet clutched the floor as if she meant to run.

"What do you mean?" he whispered. His breath was harsh in his chest and he panted as if he had been running a long way. He hoped he would not cough, for he thought it would take his attention from her, and she would retreat again behind her silence and what he now knew was her frozen, wordless hate.

"Why did you ever fall in love with me?" she said at last. "Why did you?"

He tried to answer her but found that he could not. He did not know why he had once loved her. "Does it matter?" he asked gently. "I love you now."

She jerked her head away as if he had struck her. "Curse you," she said weakly. "Curse you." There were tears on her cheeks; he could see them winking silver in the little square of light. She looked helpless, defenseless, sad: her thin shoulders shook, her hollow flanks, slender as a child's, shivered in the cold. He bent down and picked up her cloak. Then, stepping forward, he wrapped it around her, holding her body to him, feeling the chilly flesh grow slowly warm under his hands. He carried her through the cold, dark house, and set her on the bed. Her lips, when he kissed them, were as cold and salty as the sea.

For some days after this he said nothing about it to her. She remained withdrawn, passive, cold, sitting in her backless chair without moving and staring all the time into space. When he spoke to her, her eyes would come to his face very slowly, as if she were reluctant to look at him, and they would glance away quickly.

The weather was worse; the wind blew without ceasing, a constant, wearing noise all around the house. Bits of ice and hardened snow were in it, so that it struck against his face like a dozen tiny whips when he went out into the garden for firewood. It was so unpleasant that he gave up his visits to the inn and left the house only for necessities. All the same, she continued to go out and to stay away for a long time. He protested that they did not need the food she brought back now, for he had found a man at the inn who agreed to supply them, but she shook her head with silent hostility as if his words were flies that irritated her, and, taking up her cloak, she went out into the storm, her black figure upright and still elegant in the howling mass of white.

One night when he sat over his wax tablets beside the brazier he said, "Are you angry with me, then?"

She glanced up from her open hands that lay loose and empty in her lap. Her eyes rested on his face, unreadable and dark, but she said nothing.

He felt his lips tighten. With an effort he mastered the anger that rose in him, for he knew that patience was what he needed. He said gently, "Why? I was faithful to you, you know."

She looked at him directly then, a look dark and violent with hatred. Her hands were clenched in her lap as if they were strangling a helpless thing that lay there.

"We could have been happy," he said, thinking of Metellus and of his own hopes, mocked by their life together now.

She said nothing, but bent her head. He saw its smooth crown with its neat white part, the heavy coil of hair on her neck, like black water. She seemed to agree, to say mutely that they could have been. She murmured, "All I wanted was to be free."

"I know," he agreed. "And I wanted to help you to your freedom, don't you see?"

She made no sign that she had heard. After a pause he said, "I'm sorry if I hurt you. I never wanted to." He knew as he said this that it was not true, that in the first agony of her unfaithfulness he had been willing to wound. Honestly he added, "Was it the poems? I'm sorry about them if it was. I was young, you know, and it hurt me that there were others. . . ." It still hurt him, and he said sadly, "All those men. . . ."

Her head flew up and she rose from her chair to stand before him. "All those men?" she cried. "They were so I could get away from *you*." The venom in her voice shocked him; the words struck him like a slap, and tears started to his eyes. He stood up to reach out to her, but she had turned on her heel and gone. He heard the hiss of her dress over the cold stone floor, and the slam of the door into the garden.

All the same their life went on much as before. She went out, and he spent the time while she was gone working in the inn, going back in the early dusk to a meal they ate together in silence, and the long evening they spent without speaking in the one warm room of their house. She said little and ate quietly, thinking of things she plainly did not intend to mention. In bed, too, she remained uncommunicative, passively allowing his caresses, but giving no sign of either pleasure or dislike. He held her, kissed her, entered her, hoping always to arouse some spark of response, but he never succeeded. She lay there under him, her eyes open and unfocused, waiting until he had finished. If she felt anything, she gave no hint. When he withdrew from her, frustrated and unhappy, she closed her eyes and turned her back. He would hear her regular breathing, but he was never sure she was actually asleep. Her back rose beside him like a wall in the darkness, her shoulders were a fortification against his love.

Some nights, after these unsatisfactory encounters, he lay awake, as anxious and irritated as if he had not achieved physical release. He asked himself then if he ought not to let her be, allow her time before making love to her again. He wondered if, left to herself, she might come to him, her desire grown in her with her health and strength to what it had once been. In the long nights he ground his teeth for the insult of her passivity, the rejection implicit in her allowing him to use her as he did. But he knew that he was not using her—his own unhappiness told him that. There was no pleasure to him in her cold, unwelcoming body, her hard, unloving eyes. He made love to her because he thought she needed this proof of his continuing desire for her, his tribute to her power and beauty. She never denied it, and he went on, patiently adding every day to the store of his love for her, telling himself that someday she would have to acknowledge it and love him in return. Yet he knew in his heart that this last was not true. He went on because he had given his life to her, and to going on, but he knew she would never love him now. All he could hope for was that she would see—those great dark eyes would open once more, would recognize his love for what it was, that in her need she would turn at last to him. He was all that was left to her now; he would always be all that was left to her. He thought that she might someday understand.

Then, one day, going home from the inn through the densely swirling snow, he saw her leaning against a wall with her arms around a man in a farmer's rough black cloak. Their bodies moved together; over the thick shoulder her eyes stared into his, wide and blind. As he watched, as invisible to her as if he had not been there at all, her eyes closed and her small mouth opened. Over the groaning of the wind he heard her long, deep moan of satisfaction and the man's pleased grunts. He was gone before she opened her eyes again.

I had a letter from him. Early in February a brief thaw opened the roads and messages could get through. A note was brought to my door by a workman none of my servants recognized. I read it over my lunch, while the man who had brought it ate noisily on the farthest couch.

There was very little in it—just that he had found her and was living with her in the little town out on the plain beyond the gate. It was curtly phrased, too, so that my first thought was that it was written in anger. But it lay face up where I had thrust it, and presently I began to see that it was, in fact, an appeal. The conviction grew on me as I sat drinking my warmed and sweetened wine. When the workman had finished his food, I called for my cloak and my outdoor shoes, and told him to take me to my friend.

It was a long and difficult journey. In the city the thaw had flooded the low-lying streets, so that we had to go around by complicated detours, made worse by the now-heavy traffic, for everyone was trying to buy or sell what little food or wood they could find, and to see the people they had been shut away from for so long. Out in the country the roads were still blocked by drifted snow, and long lines of wagons waited patiently to get through. By late afternoon, when the short day was almost gone, the wind came up again, throwing chips of ice into our faces and cutting through our clothes. Where the snow had melted, it froze again, and the dark made the road dangerous. The wagon wheels groaned on the icy patches, the trees, invisible, screamed in the wind. It was fully night by the time I stood in the little inn, warming my fingers on a cup of wine and asking for Catullus.

They were country people, sullen and suspicious behind their politeness. He would be back soon, they said; he was staying there. They offered to show me his room in the courtyard near the stables—for proof, I suppose. I went to look, but there was nothing in it: a box of clothes, neatly folded, a bed on which the cover had not been disturbed. I asked for a room of my own, which they gave me, and food, which I ate in the dining room alone under the eye of the serving girl, as if she feared that I might steal the plate when I was finished. Afterward I sat in the bar watching the snow beyond the lamplight in the open doorway, drinking the local wine and listening to the rumble of the country voices, growing more impatient as it grew later and the wind rose to a fierce, thin howl in the narrow street. At last, certain by now that he would not appear, I did what I should have done as soon as I came in. Raising my voice, I began to insist that they tell me where he was. They shook their heads and slid their eyes away, repeating that they did not know, but I was determined, and people like that always recognize determination. They showed me his table in the corner of the room, hidden by the end of the bar, which until then I had not seen.

I stood looking down at it for a long time, the wine growing cold in my hand. There was nothing unusual about it, except that it was in a bar—it looked like his desk at home, like anyone's desk: a small jar of reed pens and wooden styli, a stack of boards ready to be waxed, a roll of good paper, blank, and another with a long poem half copied out in his neat handwriting. A shorter roll was held open by a couple of spoons, obviously borrowed from the bar. He must have been working on it. I read the first poem:

> To this degraded place my mind has been led,
>   by your faults, Lesbia,
> and so destroyed itself by its devotion
> that now I could not wish you well if you shone
>   as bright as heaven,
> nor cease to love you if you were
>   as black as hell.

I knew what it meant, though I had to read it twice. Even the first time, I already knew. I knew how far he had come, and that he had reached the end. There was something so final in it, something so much the last word. For a moment I wondered why I had come: he didn't need me, he had achieved in himself the end of his road. He knew what he was, and it had made him free. So strong was this impression that I was already turning to go away—I believe I called for my bill to go back to the city—when my eye was caught by my name.

> Caelius, my Lesbia, that Lesbia
> that dear Lesbia whom Catullus loved
> more than himself and everything he owned,
> now at crossroads, and in alleyways,
> gluts her cunt on the generous sons of Rome.

For a second I was confused, as if a man I had been talking to had suddenly reached forward and slapped me in the face. There were even tears in my eyes. Then I saw that they were there because of what the poem said. So much bitterness was in it, so much rage—I saw that nothing had been solved, nothing ended. He loved her still. Grabbing my cloak from the back of the chair, I threw it around me and shouted for a torch.

I found him a long time later, a small figure lying at the bottom of a wall. In the flaring torchlight his face was gray and shiny like potter's clay, his burning hair was quenched in melted snow. He was thin and worn, and his breath whistled in his throat. He looked up at me and grinned, but he did not speak. He was beyond speech, beyond, perhaps, even hearing, though I called over and over.

He died in the wagon I hired to take him back to Rome. When we passed under the gate of the city, he recognized it and smiled once again, but he was dead before I got him to my house, his eyes set in his head, his smile faded into the darkness over the city like the gesture of a hand that sweeps an arc, unfinished, through the torchlight and out into the night beyond. I waited only until morning, sitting beside him in the atrium of my house. Then, sending my servants to pack his belongings and follow, I started on our journey north.

An edge of daylight has appeared under the shutter, paling the lamplight in the old man's room. His eyes are closed; his old, sinewy face is quiet on the pillow. For a long time he has not spoken, and I wonder if, while I have been talking, he, too, has died. I get up, shaking out my clothes and stretching my stiff legs as unobtrusively as I can, to open the window.

The sun has not yet risen. The dead garden is full of gray shadows; the heads of uncut grass are silver with dew. I cannot see my sword in the darkness under the stone table, but I know it is still there.

Behind me the old man whispers my name, like the faint stridulation of a cricket in the predawn silence. His eyes are open, though his head still rests on the pillow, a sign—the only sign—of his immense fatigue. The white hands are as quiet as bones as they rest on the book.

"Sir," I say softly, coming to the edge of the bed and kneeling down. "Sir, will you forgive me?" I mean to say more, but I cannot think of another word.

He puts his hand on my head, a touch as light as a ghost's. I look up into his sharp old eyes.

"No." The cords around his blue lips pull into a harsh grin. I cannot speak, though now my mind is teeming with thoughts. I want to tell him I did not mean it to end as it did; I never thought his son would die. I did not send him willingly to his death; I never guessed that would be the outcome. If anything, I thought it would free him to see what she had become.

"No," he says again, like the creak of a closing door.

His hard, bony finger points to the book. In the growing light I can see the letters, the small black traces of a life, like tiny footsteps across the white desert of the page.

> Caelius, my Lesbia, that Lesbia
> that dear Lesbia whom Catullus loved
> more than himself and everything he owned,
> now at crossroads, and in alleyways,
> gluts her cunt on the generous sons of Rome.

The bony finger moves along the lines, stopping at a word, going back to the beginning, stopping again. His old eyes have seen something my younger ones have missed. A word is crossed out, and another has been written over it in Catullus's small neat hand. As I stare at it I see that I understood it once, but somehow have forgotten it, misread it, lost the meaning.

> Caelius, our Lesbia, that Lesbia . . .

"No," the old man whispers to my bowed head. "I do not forgive you, my son. He already has."

His old eyes close, his hand slides from my head to rest, open, on the bed. His face relaxes, the hollows smooth, the strong sinews soften their hold.

Slowly I roll up the book and set it beside him on the cover. The lamp is out; the little body lies drowned in shadow; the old face sleeps in peace in the quiet room, but outside in the garden the rising sun touches the year to life at last.

APPENDIX

POEM 63

Over deep seas Attis came sailing
and set his foot lightly to the Phrygian groves;
he turned to the dark woods, to the haunt of the
     Goddess.
There, deep in frenzy and joy,
with a sharp stone he cut himself free,
lightened himself of the burden of manhood.
     Now, so soon after that the earth is still stained
with his blood,
with a woman's white fingers he takes up the drum—
your sacred drum, Cybele, Goddess and Mother—
and holding the bullhide with trembling hands,
cries aloud to his frenzied companions:
"To the heights of the forest, Gallae, together,
together, homeless herd of Phrygia's Lady—
who, longing for liberty, exiles like me,
have come with me here to this place of the Goddess
over the bullying sea to this shore,

and gelded ourselves out of hatred of Love.
Bring joy to the Goddess by your wandering dance.
Be quick, follow closely to her home in the mountains
where the cymbals clash, where the drumbeat re-echoes,
the curved horn bellows deeply, the Maenads toss back
their wind-strewn hair, wailing the ancient rites
while the Goddess waits in the shadows for the
       swaggering herd."
When Attis, the now-woman, chanted this to the
       crowd,
they shrieked, their tongues rattled,
the drum thundered, the hollow cymbals crashed,
up Mount Ida went the spiraling line.
Raging, panting, gasping, they rushed
and Attis led them through the dark forest
as wild as the beast that runs from the yoke.
As wild as he the Gallae danced after.
Now, faint, drooping, weary, in Cybele's groves
hungry and worn, Sleep seized them,
deep Sleep quenched the flame of their frenzy,
and tenderly they rested from the raging of their minds.
But when Sol rose, golden, His radiant eye
surveyed the white ether, the hard ground, tumbling
       sea;
He scattered Night's shadows under thundering hooves
There Sleep left Attis, leaving him tossing,
Sleep fled the day to His nymph-wife at home.
So, rested and freed from his ravening madness
Attis recalled to heart all he had done:
with a mind clear as water he saw and was pierced.
His soul burned him: he went down to the shore
where the vast sea trembled through his tears
and spoke to his distant homeland aloud:
"Oh, my country, my fatherland, my country, my
       creator,
which I ran from like a sullen slave his master
to hide in Mount Ida's somber groves

to lurk in frozen winter among the wild aniamls
and shelter my frenzy with them in the snow—
where are you now, my country, my home?
Now I look toward you, all pain and regret,
while, for a brief moment, my reeling soul rests.
Am I to wander in this wilderness alone,
stripped of possessions, homeland, kinsmen, friends?
Forsake the Forum, stadium, palaestra, school?
Oh, my miserable soul, you have reason to complain.
Into what form is my life poured now—
I a woman, who was a youth, a boy, a soldier soon to
     be,
I, the flower of the stadium, the oiled wrestler,
I, whose doorway was always crowded, whose doorstep
     always thronged?
The columns of my house were wreathed with laurel
when I rose from my bed at dawn:
Am I now, forever, Cybele's slave?
Am I now a Maenad, a part of myself, a sterile man?
On cold green Ida am I now to do a woman's work?
I to live under Phrygia's high peaks,
with the woodland boar, the forest-roving stag?
Now I feel it, who felt nothing before."
The words went out from his tender, young mouth
carried straight to the Goddess, to Cybele's ears.
She unfastened the lions yoked to her chariot,
she lashed the left one, saying:
"Go, fierce one, in frenzy and madness,
go, murderous one—drive him to the forest.
I have given him freedom, yet he tries to escape.
Flay your sides open with the claw in your tail,
make the mountain resound with your roaring,
shake the red mane on your terrible neck."
So, menacing, Cybele untied the yoked team.
The huge beast roused himself into fury
he howled, he roared, broke the bushes beneath him.
Over wet, shining sands he thundered like surf

to Attis, who stood by the white marble sea.
Now the lion is on him—Attis runs on the mountain
to live all his life as the Goddess's slave.

Far from me, oh, Goddess, far from me and from my
      home
keep all your fury; let it be for other men.
Oh, Cybele, Goddess, Great Goddess, Mistress and
      Mother.

NOTES

ROMAN NAMES

Roman names are indicators primarily of family allegiance and rank. A woman or a slave had only one name, while a free man like Caelius usually had three. A great aristocrat might have four in this period; later, under the Emperors, we find people with many more. We know of one man who had forty. Caelius's full name is Marcus Caelius Rufus; Catullus's is Gaius Valerius Catullus.

The first element of these names is given at birth just as it is with us, except that these names appear to have been much less important among the Romans. Women didn't have them at all, and for men there were only about a dozen first names in use. Most of the time they are abbreviated, since there are so few of them. The really important name is the second one, for example, Caelius, or Valerius. This identified the owner's family, and was inherited from his father. Many names that we think of as first names are really family names like Gaius Julius Caesar's Julius.

Since families in Rome were usually great clans, and since first names had little significance, some other means of distinguishing one member from another had to be found. This was the third name, a kind of inherited nickname. These seem to have originated in some physical characteristic or some exploit of an ancestor. Caelius's name, Rufus, for example, probably indicates that he had a red-haired forebear, though his own hair may have been any color at all. Catullus seems to be derived from a word meaning "an animal cub"; Cicero means "chick pea." Some of these names reflect a rather robust view of things: dignified and important men went through life addressed as "nose," or "belly," or "drunk," and no one seems to have thought any the worse of them for that.

Some of these names come from incidents in an ancestor's life, or they may have been awarded, almost like medals, by the Senate. Pompey's name—Gnaeus Pompeius Magnus—is one of these: he was given the name "Magnus," "the Great," by the dictator Sulla, at the behest of the Senate, in honor of the victories of his youth.

For women and slaves the situation was different. In the first place they had only one name. Women's names were derived from the family name of their father. Thus, Gaius Julius Caesar's daughter was called Julia, Marcus Tullius Cicero's Tullia, and so on. Clodia is the daughter of Appius Claudius Pulcher, and should have been called Claudia, but she and her sisters changed the spelling of their name when their brother did to conform to the plebeian rather than the aristocratic use. Women did not change their names when they married, or pass them on to their children. Slaves, too, had only one name. In the very earliest days it, too, came from the name of the head of the family, but in later times they were given a name. If they were freed, as were both Caelius's servant Philo and Cicero's famous secretary Tiro, they combined their names with those of their former owners: Philo became Marcus Caelius Philo, and Tiro, Marcus Tullius Tiro. This reflected a continuing relationship of mutual obligation between a freedman and his former owner.

A NOTE ON THE CULT OF CYBELE, THE GREAT MOTHER

The cult of Cybele, whom the Romans called Magna Mater, the Great Mother, appears to have originated in Asia Minor, in part of what is now Turkey. The legend it celebrates, of the mother-goddess and her youthful mortal consort (called Attis), is related to the myth of Adonis and of Demeter. Cybele was a fertility goddess as well as a giver of oracles and cures, a goddess of nature, especially mountains, and, as the battlemented crown she sometimes wears indicates, a protector of her people in war.

Her rites were ecstatic, involving animal sacrifice and self-mutilation (including castration) on the part of her worshipers. Probably because of this, in Rome citizens were strictly forbidden to participate in her rites, and a much more Roman celebration, with theatrical performances, horse races, and rather restrained dinner parties was added to the orgiastic and bloody Asian ceremonies for their benefit. (I have contributed some gladiatorial contests, which really belong to other festivals.) These were open to Roman citizens. Her festival, which began on April 4 and lasted for seven days, was very popular.

The cult was brought to Rome during the wars against Hannibal, in 204 B.C. when a prophecy told the Romans she would help them against their enemy. It is doubtful that they realized the full extent and character of her worship at the time. In 191 B.C. a temple was built on the Palatine Hill to house the black stone that was associated with the goddess; remains of this temple still stand. As far as I know, by the way, there is neither cave nor cellar under it.

Probably the cult was very old even then—it is worth noting, as one commentator points out, that the knife her worshippers used in the ritual slaughters and mutilations was made of stone.

Several ancient authors mention the goddess and her worship, including the poet Lucretius, who describes her procession through the city, and Catullus, who combines elements of the rites and the legend in Poem 63. He is considered one of the principal authorities on this cult.

HISTORY IN THIS BOOK

The few facts we have about Catullus's life come mainly from three sources: his own poems, a single mention by the historian Suetonius, and a remark by St. Jerome that is almost certainly wrong. Jerome says that Catullus was born in Verona in 87 B.C. and died in his thirtieth year in Rome in 57 B.C. Since the last datable poems we have mention events in 55 B.C., we know this cannot be right, and since a man's age was often recorded on his gravestone, it is most likely that Catullus was born in 84 and died in 54.

Ovid tells us that the name of the woman in Catullus's love poems was a pseudonym, and Apuleius that her real name was Clodia. From the poems we know that Lesbia was a married woman with a high social position in Rome; if Apuleius is right, and if, as no one seriously doubts nowadays, the Clodia he means is Clodia Metelli, then we also know a good deal more than that. Cicero's speech at the trial of Caelius still exists: it is a detailed condemnation of her life and morals and tells us something of her history. In addition, her brother, Publius Clodius Pulcher, is well known. The incident of the break-in to the women's festivals is in Plutarch and other historians, and it is discussed extensively (along with the trial that followed) in Cicero's letters, as is Clodius's subsequent career, and his early death.

Suetonius tells us that Catullus's father was a friend of Julius Caesar, and that Catullus wrote poems that displeased Caesar. He says that Caesar complained about them, that Catullus apologized, and Caesar forgave him. The trip to Bithynia with Gaius Memmius comes from the poems, but Memmius's praetorship is mentioned by Dio Cassius, giving us the date of his governorship the next year (probably 57–56). Caelius's affair with Clodia, besides being the subject of Cicero's speech (the *Pro Caelio*), is mentioned by Catullus himself (if the Caelius and Rufus of several of the poems do refer to Marcus Caelius Rufus, which is likely). Caelius's subsequent career appears in the histories of Dio Cassius, Asconius, Plutarch, and Julius Caesar; several letters he wrote to Cicero, and Cicero's replies, still exist.

THE POEMS

We have one book of about 116 poems by Catullus. Most of them are very short, hardly more than epigrams, though there are several long, elaborate ones, and a couple of translations from Greek sources. Something like twenty-five of the poems deal with his affair with the woman called "Lesbia," whom we think of as Clodia Metelli. They seem to show the progress of his emotions, from ecstatic happiness at first, through pain and bewilderment to a final rage and despair. The affair must have begun before 59 when Clodia's husband died, and one of Catullus's last datable poems (Poem 11, which mentions the conquest of Britain by Julius Caesar) must come from 55. It is about Lesbia, and still full of bitterness and pain, showing that his feeling for her was still alive so near the end of his own life.

Catullus is a difficult poet to read, and an almost impossible one to translate. His poems are extraordinarily dense and compact, and full of puns and allusions. Their moods cover an immense range, and the technique is different for each of them. His work is based firmly in the tradition of Alexandrian Greek poetry and his technical ability and complexity are so great that he was called *doctus* ("learned") by the poets who came after him. It is Ovid who called him that, but Horace who also admired him, Virgil borrowed from him, as did Martial and other later poets, even including writers in our own language, such as Shakespeare and Byron.

A WORD ABOUT A WORD

The poem that figures so heavily in this book is Poem 58:

Caeli, Lesbia nostra, Lesbia illa,
illa Lesbia, quam Catullus unam
plus quam se atque suos amauit omnes,
nunc in quadriuiis et angiportis
glubit magnanimi Remi nepotes.

Caelius, our Lesbia, that Lesbia
that dear Lesbia whom Catullus loved
more than himself and everything he owned,
now at crossroads, and in alleyways,
gluts her cunt on the generous sons of Rome.

It is unbelievably difficult to translate, first because the meaning of the first word of the last line, *glubit* (though it is obviously sexual in connotation), is not known with any certainty. It appears to be related to a verb meaning "to peel" or "to shuck," but it is plain that its use here is coarse and vulgar in the extreme. Gilbert Highet calls it "a sexual sneer." Even the sound is ugly, and the rest of the line is bitterly sarcastic. Many translators have tried imaginative and intelligent ways to render this in English; I am indebted to all of them. To my mind, Celia and Louis Zukofsky, among modern translators, get closest to it, but their translation (London, 1966) is entirely and intentionally unliteral. Nevertheless, I have borrowed a word; if my translation is successful at all, it is because of them.

As for the word *nostra* in line one: there are many difficulties with it as with *glubit*, though the cause is different. *Nostra* is a form of the ordinary word for "our," but in the Latin of this period it frequently meant "my." The modern commentator, C. J. Fordyce, gives several examples of this use from other writers in addition to Catullus, as does the Oxford Latin Dictionary. Sometimes the substitution of "our" for "my" seems to have the character of an endearment, like the delightful North of England "our Matthew," which indicates emotional closeness, or the American (or French) "That's our Max," which has much the same feeling. Still, it's not always an endearment in Latin poetry, and its use poses so many problems most translators simply use "my," which is what most commentators recommend as well. It seemed to me, however, that no poet as skilled as Catullus, as fond of puns and word games, as aware of subtleties of feeling, would use an ambiguous expression without deliberate intent. The more I thought of it, the more sure I felt. Indeed, that ambiguity became the basis of my book.

My grateful thanks to Kurt Reichenbach for the maps.

8/20/90